MW00612870

OPENING DANGER

DANGEROUS TIES BOOK ONE

E.A. SHANNIAK

Opening Danger: Dangerous Ties Book One by E.A. Shanniak

Copyright © 2020 E.A. Shanniak

All rights reserved.

Cover Design: Harvest Moon Cover Designs

Developmental Editing: Brittany G.

Line/Copy Editing: Tiffany P.

Proofreading: Michelle F.

Formatting: Keyminor Publishing

Published by Eagle Creek Books LLC of Coldwater, Kansas

www.eashanniak.eaglecreekbooks.com

To Michelle F.

Thank you for your friendship, kindness, and encouragement. I adore your thoughtfulness and how compassionate you are to everyone; how you give back with a pure golden heart and a smile. I'm forever grateful for knowing such a wonderful person as you, and I'm so happy we're friends. Thank you for helping me make this book great, and taking the time to read it and give me feedback. You're an incredible person and I'm lucky to call you my friend.

Much love,
Ericka

(P.S. Signe from CBH, HEYYY!!! It's always so nice talking with you.)

AUTHOR'S NOTE

<u>WARNING</u>: This book contains scenes and foul language that some readers may find disturbing and/or triggering. Read at your own personal risk and don't blame me. You were warned in the blurb and now here.

This is an enemy to lover's slow burn romance. There is no bedroom fun in THIS book; that will be book two. So don't be pissed because, again, I warned you.

Have fun inside the pages of this adventurous, snarky, crazy ride. Don't hate me too much!

MORE BY - E.A. SHANNIAK

Fantasy Romance – A Castre World Novel Standalones
   Piercing Jordie
   Mitering Avalee
   Forging Calida
   Uplifting Irie
   Braving Evan
   Warring Devan
   Hunting Megan
   Shifting Aramoren – A Castre World Short Story
   Anchoring Nola – A Castre World Short Story

Storming Area 51— A Bayonet Books Anthology
   Stalking Death - short story

Clean & Sweet Western Romance – Whitman Series
Romances
   To Find A Whitman

To Love A Thief
To Save A Life
To Lift A Darkness
To Veil A Fondness
To Bind A Heart
To Hide A Treasure
To Want A Change
To Form A Romance — *coming soon*

Paranormal Romance - Dangerous Ties Series
Opening Danger
Hunting Danger - *coming soon*

CONTENTS

CHAPTER ONE

ZURI

Clicking the blinker on, I turned right, heading further into the epicenter of East OKimma, down the manicured street with precisely cropped hedges. This side of the city district, East OKimma, was occupied mainly by werewolves. The stark contrast between the districts was mind blowing. The east side was new, modern buildings, skyscrapers, everything fancy and pristine.

The werewolves kept to themselves, organizing their side of the district into neat subdivisions with perfectly paved roads and not a bush out of place. Humans, like myself, and other beings, could venture into the east district and the subdivisions, as long as we didn't cause trouble.

I made another turn, *and to your left another asshole wolf pack*, I paused at my own musings, *assholes who bare their teeth like mutts at a pound when you drive by. Please don't be*

alarmed, this is a three-thousand-pound vehicle, the dog will lose.
I snorted, feeling slightly better even though it was crude.

Overall, OKimma was overwhelmingly large. The city's divisions never ceased to amaze me. It was divided amongst the supernatural races, with humans sprinkled throughout the divisions. Each division was completely different: different styles of buildings, building materials and colors. Each district even had different plant life; the east side preferred cropped evergreen hedges and the west side preferred climbing plants like ivy and clematises.

I sighed, my skin crawling with nerves. I was ready to be back on the west side of OKimma already; the side I preferred with beautiful historic brick buildings and old wooden stores, where I could easily lose myself inside a musty bookstore or aromatic candle shop, and ultimately where I felt safest.

The district of West OKimma - Dragon District - where *actual* dragons resided had old, historic buildings of stone, small square wood paned glass windows, and hand-milled wood beams. I love the historic area of the west side. Especially when the dragons played nice and weren't complaining about a centuries-long feud with the were-wolves that no one remembered the cause of. Their memories were long but damn, holding a grudge for *that* long baffled me. It's not like their disputes weren't ever settled either. Hell, the werewolf one may have been settled ages ago. It's just that dragons never forgot.

West OKimma was the safest for beings like me: human - because *no one* desired to piss off a dragon and crime was nearly non-existent. The east side, where I was granny-careful-driving at the moment, occupied mainly by wolves, witches, and ogres was the most troublesome. They fought amongst themselves. And fights, from what I had seen on the news, could break out anywhere and at any time. I had no desire to be in or around it. Not because I was a peace-loving gal, but because everyone was allowed to carry weapons and use magic. Getting struck by an ogre's ax, witch's spell, or chomped by werewolf teeth wasn't top of my list for fun.

I flicked my blinker on to take a right turn and I scanned the houses on my left. Not there yet. But I did catch a political sign. I scoffed. The city of OKimma as a whole was ruled by a human woman gifted with dragon magic. I blew my lips. *Gifted, more like political brokering.* Queen Ariella stayed locked up in her castle home, called Kadia Castle, on the outskirts of OKimma, where spells, and every high-tech security gadget ensured her safety. She made an appearance once a year, demonstrating her power on the first Saturday in July to celebrate the god Elohi's rise to power and Diomedes's fall back to the underworld. Her display usually consisted of fancy magic works and her various paranormal minions surrounding her. Then she would go back inside for another year; passing laws and making deals from the comfort and safety of her home.

Checking the rearview mirror, West OKimma continued to fade from sight. I lived on the west side in the dragon community where I was left alone, in my little gated apartment complex with my cat, Luell. Despite my crabby, cat hoarding, old bitty of a neighbor, I loved how protected I felt inside the complex.

Glancing over to the passenger's seat, a little black box stared at me. I hated the box, and I hated what I would have to put inside. Grimacing, I pulled over to the side of the road.

This gated community, much like every other pack's, faced me with black iron bars and a matching fence that looked like vicious teeth. The gate yawned shut, clanging in place like a death toll bell after a car ahead of me drove through. Taking a deep breath, I tried to dispel the dread I felt, but only managed to feel the hairs begin to stand on my arms. I took another look, making sure to overlook the ferociously grinning teeth of the gate. In a postage stamp sized box-building, Arno watched the entrance and exit of the gated werewolf community.

I groaned. Arno and I weren't exactly buddies. He tolerated me because I knew some mutual werewolves from work and back when I was in high school, and I tolerated him as I liked not being chomped to pieces.

Merging back onto the road, I rolled down my window manually, wishing again for those fancy electric windows on the newer vehicles. I carefully zoomed across the street, pulling up to the gatehouse window and pasting a bright, fake smile for the prickly wolf.

Arno's scowl deepened across his olive toned face while he rolled his emerald eyes at me. "You're *not* welcome back," he growled, raking his fingers through a mop of ebony hair.

I shrugged, pretending nonchalance, "I have something that needs to get back to the Sandalio Holding."

Arno perked a brow. "And that is?"

"None of your business," I said, my throat constricting.

"Ah," Arno replied, a smug smirk creasing his hardened face.

I wanted to wipe it clean. If Arno knew what happened, I wondered how many others in the Sandalio pack did too.

Arno grinned viciously, exposing his fangs just to taunt me. "I will allow you entrance one last time, Zuri; then don't come back. Your ties here are done."

I dipped my head in thanks as Arno didn't have to allow me in. And I knew his silent threat was serious. "I understand."

Arno hit the button allowing the double iron gates to open inward. The thick metal silently opened into a nicely landscaped subdivision. Each house was manicured to perfection, each varying slightly in color. Beautiful maples lined in between the paved road and sidewalk.

Lifting my foot off the brake, I drove inside. I knew where I was going by heart and like my heart, it hurt painfully that all I had envisioned for myself was a lie. I swallowed back all the tears threatening to fall. Already I had spent too much time wallowing.

Arriving at the house where I needed to be, I made a u-turn in the middle of the silent road and parked. The rumble of the engine tried to drown out all the scattered messy thoughts in my head.

I glanced down at the engagement ring on my finger. I had yet to take it off, hoping maybe I was wrong. Yet me being here proved otherwise. The ring made my heart wrench and my stomach swirled with bitterness that I was duped; and wearing it, even now, reminded me not to be so careless again, or at least not so easily duped. Even now, the pain of what I must do, broke me. His last words, *I would marry you today if I could; you know that Zuri*. It was all bullshit; and it hurt deeply.

Being cheated on and abandoned was something I'd not dealt with in my life and I wasn't sure how to place the twisting emotions. Right now, I'm angry, hurt, and a little bitter. Earlier today, I felt ugly. The breakup between us was more a reflection of him than me, but it still hurt and caused me to question myself. Two years of memories, pictures, fun, all thrown away in a matter of minutes, yet it felt like hours.

Sighing, I rested the back of my head against the head-rest of the Bronco evaluating where I was physically and emotionally for a brief moment. I was inside the gated community of the Sandalio pack, waiting to gather up some courage to step out of my rig and face the jerk who'd broken my heart. Emotionally, I was a mess.

Staring at the ring, I pulled it off my finger, something I should have done two weeks ago, snorting derisively as I shoved it back in the small black box to die. Lazaro was mate bonding next week to a werewolf in another pack. They made an adorable couple. Even I had to admit it. Still, the sting of the breakup after being engaged for a year, along with the fake promise of forever love, burned my heart more than I would ever dare to admit out loud.

I checked my long blonde hair in the rearview mirror. My long, curling iron ringlets were a mess, but I didn't care. My black blouse had a small hole in the left side bottom hem, but it would be covered by my dark brown leather jacket. My dark wash jeans and hiking boots fit comfortably. I slid the handgun I carried for protection from my side holster and stuck it in the glovebox out of respect to the Sandalio pack.

A werewolf couple passed my rig, walking hand in hand; their narrowed green eyes fixed on me, before turning away. A human wouldn't be a threat to them. Shifters and magic abounded in the whole of Quivleren, let alone OKimma. Dragons stayed on their side of town while were-packs stayed on theirs, and other forms of paranormal lined the outskirts and anywhere else. Humans, like myself, were outnumbered, scattered throughout Quivleren, but we were left alone for the most part since most races found us nothing more than a mild annoyance at worst and less than important at best.

I glanced out the window to Lazaro's parents' gated picturesque mansion. Lazaro's car pulled out of the pristine concrete driveway, taking off south toward the downtown area of the west side. I sighed, opening the Bronco door. His father spotted me before I made it across the street. His gray-brown brows furrowed, and green eyes held annoyance. Like Lazaro, his father was well over six feet, broad and muscular.

"Zuri," he announced.

I swallowed. "Hello, Mr. Sandalio," tucking my long sunshine blonde hair behind my ear, I continued, "I need to give something back to Lazaro."

Arthur rolled his eyes, striding to meet me. "What is it?" he demanded.

"You'll know when you see it," I replied despondently. "I can't keep this."

Arthur opened the black box, scowling further; his bushy eyebrows scrunching tightly together, becoming one. "How did you get this? Is this some kind of joke, *human?*" Arthur practically growled the last word, sending shivers up my back. I refused to let him see.

"No, sir. Ask him yourself." I straightened my back, forcing my hands not to crawl into my jean pockets. "I know you never liked me, but you also know damn well, I don't lie."

"You're right," He conceded and spat out in disgust, "I can smell lies on you... *humans.* Whatever he did, he shouldn't have. I will take care of this."

I nodded, turning to leave. I strode across the street back to my Bronco. The car door creaked open.

"Zuri!" Arthur called.

I turned around, the wind whipping hair in my face. "Yes, sir?" I tucked my blonde tresses inside the back of my jacket.

His tone softened a fraction and I saw a hint of compassion in his eyes, "You're a good one, just not for my son or pack."

Two other males came outside from the Sandalio Mansion, glaring at me. I swallowed hard, forcing back tears.

"Thank you," I choked out before my voice cracked.

Sitting in the seat of my rig, all breath left my body in a rush. I closed my eyes and leaned my head against the headrest. My hands naturally gripped the steering wheel.

Tears tracked down my face and I wiped them away bitterly.

"At least it's over," I whispered.

The keys fumbled in my hands before I was able to insert them into the ignition. My old Bronco turned over, the engine humming with power. Today was hard. Tomorrow would be harder as I said goodbye to this beast of a vehicle. Lazaro got me the Bronco stating I needed metal to protect me, keep me safe. He found me my favorite rig and had it converted to a diesel. It had been sweet and I loved the beast of a vehicle, but it was a reminder of him and what I was to never have.

"So much bullshit in one handsome body," I mumbled.

The motor hummed. I checked my mirrors before pulling away for good. There would never be a need to come to this part of town again. I pulled up to the guard-house, handing over the guest pass.

"Don't come back," Arno said, shredding the temporary passcode.

"No need," I replied. "I returned what I needed to."

"Good. Stay on *your* side," he sneered.

I took my foot off the brake and peeled out. One thing I loved about this rig is its ability to roll coal. Black smoke plumed out the exhaust, filling his little cubicle. I grinned, hoping he choked on it for a few minutes as I took off down the road.

Even with my heart feeling heavy, returning the ring to Lazaro's pack was the right thing to do. I could not morally keep his family's heirloom.

I rolled down my window, taking in the September

breeze. I loved this time of year when the hot stench of summer faded out into the crispness of trees changing. How the colors slowly started to turn, then all of a sudden, as if overnight, trees burst alive with the last remnant of color. Fall was my favorite time of year and soon, all the coffee shops would be humming with ads of pumpkin spice lattes and peppermint mochas.

Mmm... that sounds amazing right now. Glancing at the time on the stereo, it was late afternoon. If I had coffee now, I would be awake half the night.

I grumbled. "Fuck it."

Pulling into the local coffee shop, I ordered my usual – a spiced chai tea latte – and added the drink to my tab. Taking off down the road, I took a right onto Maple Ave, heading to my little gated apartment complex. It's not the ritziest, but still one of the better ones I could afford thanks to my well-paying job. I sipped on my latte, savoring the spiciness of the chai while I pushed the button on my remote to open the apartment gates. The metal ground on its hinges, sending a shiver down my spine.

The motor in my Bronco rumbled through the complex, announcing my arrival to everyone. I pulled into my spot, turning the engine off. Hopping out, I locked and slammed the door to piss off the one person I knew would be watching the parking lot. The old bitty loved to gripe. She always had her window open and stared outside all day.

Right on cue, I thought, catching her sudden appearance on her porch balcony out of the corner of my eye.

"When are you getting rid of that beast of a car, Zuri!"

my neighbor, Ms. Thompson, screeched from her balcony. Her brown hair, streaked with silver, was wound up in bright pink curlers. As always, her oversized, mumu-style, lime green, paisley dress hung to her shins. Wiry hairs poked out of her upper lip making her scowl more comical than it already was. She had no teeth and would constantly run her tongue under her lips. "It bothers my cats. It bothers the neighbors. It's bad for the environment with all the pollution! Your car is ridiculous!" she blathered over the yowling of cats in the background.

Beginning the ascent to my apartment, I called over my shoulder, "As soon as you get rid of your fourteen cats, Ms. Thompson. Which is against the apartment contract, but you don't see me bitching."

Cats pooled like oil at her feet. So. Many. Cats. One was good and troublesome enough. Fourteen was disgusting with all the litter and food. My lip twitched and curled upward, inhaling a waft of the pungent odor coming from her apartment.

Ms. Thompson fish-jawed a few times, her face scrunched up, comically resembling three of her animals sitting at her feet. "Cats don't make troublesome noises!" she retorted.

"Cats fight, males spray, females scream to mate, one of them is meowing all day long - and those are just the *noise* problems. The *environmental problems,* just to name a couple: unvaccinated, uncontrolled population due to cats not getting fixed," I said, ticking off each issue on my fingers as I opened the door to my apartment.

I slammed the door, bolting the deadlock, and the chain

lock above it. Ms. Thompson got under my skin quicker than normal today. The nasty old hag sits outside on her balcony scrutinizing every little move anyone does and usually her acerbic remarks roll off my back. But today... today had already been rough and her acid was just another pain in my ass I didn't need. I navigated the darkened apartment to the fridge, pulling out one of the seltzer beers I loved. I cracked it open, drinking the entirety before turning back to my latte.

Meowing came from down the hallway. I smiled, bending down to pet my own cat. My only cat. Luell purred, arching her back as my fingers snaked down to her 'sweet spot'. Her soft multicolored fur brought a smile to my face. Luell was the prettiest long-haired calico I'd ever seen.

I sat down on the cool kitchen floor, leaning my head against the white cabinets. My right hand mindlessly stroked Luell. Inhaling deeply, the scent of my wax warmer I left on to cover the stench of the neighbor greeted my nose with a spicy grapefruit aroma. I sat for just a moment, enjoying Luell and the comforting grapefruit scent before I moved, groaning as I forced myself off the floor.

Luell twirled in between my legs. I smiled wanly at the cat. My heart ached and somehow Luell sensed it. Luell was a particular cat. She liked certain people and she eventually warmed up to Lazaro. I kicked my foot and sighed. Lazaro led me to believe he was a great man; a nice man with a giving heart. Stupidly, or well naively, I thought maybe I could be a part of his life, more than just a girlfriend. I was liked by his pack before the breakup; even his mother loved me. He'd even proposed, for crying out loud! Then all of a sudden, the rug was ripped out from under me. I got dumped via email two weeks ago. Two days later, after the email, he showed up at my door with roses while his liar's tongue promised me a forever.

The cherry on this mountain of craptastic sundae, his father, by an email, informs me Lazaro's getting married to Zemila from another pack and I need to cut all contact or they would end me as I was a threat to their peace treaty with the other pack. I stared at those words for an eternity, choking on my emotions. I couldn't breathe for what felt like minutes, my body refusing to inhale. For hours, tears tracked down my cheeks. After what felt like what might be the final torrent of salty waterworks, I emailed back the same day stating I had a personal item of Lazaro's I needed to return.

I tossed the empty seltzer beer can in the sink. "It's over," I told Luell.

My laptop screen lit, dinging a bothersome sound warning work was emailing me. I scowled. I had clocked out from my shift of doing medical billing hours ago. My work, for today and part of tomorrow, was completed. Skeptically, I opened the message.

URGENT: Call me. Sorry it's late. – Gretchen M., HR

What weird ass stuff is it now, I scowled further. Dragging my phone out of my denim jean pocket, I pressed with one hand the six for the human resources speed dial I had programmed while with the other, took a quick sip of my coffee.

"Zuri," Gretchen said in a chipper tone.

"Hey there, pretty lady," I said, trying to keep myself polite and not break down over the stress of the day. I took a seat at my desk chair, not knowing how long this conversation could go.

"How are you, my dear?"

I smiled. Gretchen was a kind woman, always taking the time to make certain everyone was all right and talking with them if they weren't.

"I'm doing great. Thanks for asking. Yourself?"

"Head deep in papers," she giggled. "I have some good news and bad news."

"Bad news first," I said, my stomach tightening.

I never liked bad news. Bad news with medical billing could mean cease and desist letters, fraud, government involvement, more than I cared to deal with. I stilled my racing heart waiting for the ruffling on the other end to stop.

Gretchen's perky demeanor was lost. She exhaled, "Bad news – we got bought out by a bigger billing company. You no longer work for Inner Connections. I'm sending you your final check tomorrow along with all your accumulated paid time off and sick pay."

I let out the breath I was holding, and inhaled a new one. I set my coffee down as my hand shook, and my mind raced with how I was going to make ends meet now. "Well, this is an end of summer bummer."

I made good money doing medical billing. I was the top biller, handling multiple facilities, and so much on a day-to-day basis. I would easily be able to find another job in another town, but I didn't want to pack and move again.

All the jobs here were taken. And I'd be damned if I was going to be a secretary for mediocre pay after what I made here.

"Tell me about it," Gretchen sighed. "Inner Connections was easier to maintain with the few people we had. Good news is the people who bought Inner Connections desired to keep us; you because you are one of our top people and me because I'm an amazing HR badass," she paused and giggled. "Now, you'll be the only biller. Your track record indicated not only are you efficient, you have next to none for mistakes. Your work load will increase, but so will the pay. You still get to work from home."

"How much?"

A grin split my face from ear to ear. I already handled a lot for certain, but a little more won't be much of a problem. Working for Inner Connections gave me the freedom to be home and do things I wanted to do when my work was done. But now, to still be able to be home was truly a blessing. If the pay increased, I might be able to move out of this apartment complex and into the house I had been eyeing for the last few months. I turned the cooling latte in my hands, taking a sip.

"Salary is seventy-five thousand a year."

I choked. "Come again."

"Seventy-five thousand."

"That's ridiculous. It's thirty thousand more than my current position."

"As I mentioned earlier, your work load will increase – *a lot* – according to what I was informed."

"What does it entail?"

Gretchen hummed, riffling through something. The fussing on her end of the phone went on for several seconds before a delighted chirp escaped her.

"Here it is... Only, it doesn't have any other added facilities on it nor what else beyond what you already do... How peculiar. I will message the corporate office directly."

"Thank you. When do I report for this new job?"

"October first. They want to give everyone around two weeks to get settled and adjusted while they fine tune everything and do goodness knows what. You will receive your new salary during this time, as well. I'm faxing you papers you need to sign and send back, accepting this new job, payment, and workload. I want it back in the morning. I'm sorry to ask you to call me and handle this so late."

"No worries. Thanks for the heads up and the promotion."

"Have a good night, Sweetie."

Gretchen, in her typical fashion, hung up before I could reply. I smiled. Today's travesties were made better by the promotion. I set the phone down at my desk and polished off the latte. Bending to the right, I tossed the empty container in the desk trash can, raising my hands in a victory cheer when the cup made it in. Luell meowed at my feet. I picked her up, cuddling her soft calico fur. Luell purred in my arms, nuzzling herself against my neck.

I pulled up the listing I'd been ogling for some time. *Still available.* I smiled. Ten acres of timbered land, a small two-bedroom cottage and gated entry. It was a steal of a price even though the listing said it needed a few undescribed repairs, I hoped it wouldn't be too terribly bad. The house sat vacant for well over a year with no interested people.

The wall clock chimed eight in the evening. I picked up my phone and called the agent. No one answered, so I left a message.

"Luell, how do you feel about moving?"

Luell mewled, stretching out and flopping on her back.

"Ok then, we're moving. First thing in the morning, I'm going to see about how to get that house." I gave her one last belly scratch before heading to my own bed where I looked forward to ending my incredibly confusing and emotional day.

CHAPTER TWO

ZURI

I couldn't get to my new house fast enough. It took a few days to get financing in place from the Bank of West OKimma and all the necessary details handled. But waiting a few days was nothing to finally have the key to my dream home in my hand as I drove my rig to the house. I was so excited to finally have something truly mine, where I was able to start over and fresh after the horrible break up with Lazaro.

I sighed, wriggling my bottom in the seat. I turned on the road the house was on, leaning forward into the steering wheel. I couldn't get there fast enough. Luell purred from inside her cat carrier in the Bronco. I smiled at the happy sound. The weird cat loved riding in the rig; but with long rides, it was easier to keep her in the crate than her being on my lap, or crawling around my feet. The gate to the house was open. I frowned, wondering why I hadn't had to use the remote the real estate agent gave me.

First thing I need to fix is the gate, I thought, making a mental note of what to repair. Pulling into the driveway, I left the Bronco engine running with a light air-conditioned breeze for Luell as I got out. I gently shut the door, keeping the cool air inside for my fur-baby.

I screamed happily, dancing from foot to foot and twirling in place. I whipped out my phone and sent a text to my Uncle Syrus that I got the house. He messaged back giving a thumbs up and stating he was proud of me. I smiled at the phone. My uncle was someone I could always count on to be there for me since I had no real parents. Brushing off the small dismal reflection, I stood in the driveway grinning from ear to ear as I took in the newness of my home.

I glanced over my shoulder to the Bronco holding all my belongings inside, besides the big furniture that would be delivered tomorrow afternoon. I never sold the rig Lazaro got me. And seeing it gave me a bit of a twinge. But I quickly pushed it aside, opting for logic over emotion. It came in handy for moving and it was already paid off. Why cause another payment if I didn't have to?

Turning around, I stared at the gate five hundred or so feet behind me and pushed the button for the gate to close. I cringed at the grinding on the hinges as the gates clanked shut. *One repair I apparently don't have to do now*, I thought happily. I grinned, breathing in deeply the scent of earth and fir trees. Bright sunshine warmed my back. My heart felt full. Owning my own home that couldn't be taken from me, unless I defaulted on payments, marked a big checkpoint in my life.

"My own place!" I squealed. "No neighbors, no drama, no Ms. Thompson with her damn cats!"

The house was picturesque, like a small cottage belonging to an old woman in a fairytale book. The cedar shake roof would be getting replaced next week with metal to make it sturdier against storms. And I had a guy coming out tomorrow to install central heating and cooling. The cedar shake siding was weathered gray, but intact and kept well. A black front door greeted my gaze with an ornate crow silver door knocker. White framed windows with flower beds underneath lined the front of the two-bedroom cottage. A single concrete pathway led from the gravel driveway to the front of the house.

Unable to contain myself, I ran to the front door, sticking the old key inside the rusted lock. It turned over, the door groaning on its unused hinges. My feet left footprints as I wandered through, opening up windows. White sheets, covered with dust hid forgotten furniture, so lonely and left behind. If they were in decent shape, I might not even need my own. I carefully peeled back a sheet revealing a rocking chair with a red velvet cushioned seat. My fingers traipsed down the polished wood.

The chair squeaked when I sat in it, the cushion giving off a small cloud of dust despite the sheet. I rocked two times before it collapsed. I laughed until tears came out my eyes, thankful nothing on *me* was broken.

"No fire side crocheting then," I said, getting to my feet and dusting off.

The walls were covered in a beautiful old black and teal damask wallpaper. The wall was divided by a wood chair rail running from the floor to three feet up the wall, in a polished cherry.

"All of that stays." I muttered to myself as I admired the way the colors compliment each other.

I glanced down at my watch and sighed, already tired at the thought of all the work needed to be done still. I walked out the door toward my rig to grab a load and continued my one-woman dialogue, "Time to get moving."

Two steps out and I paused, shielding my hand against the glare of the sun for a moment. Luell meowed loudly and my senses went on high alert. My Bronco door creaked open.

"Hey!" I shouted at the unknown intruder. "What the fuck do you think you're doing?"

I ran to the Bronco seeing the guy standing there with my door open. I got in front of him, my arms out protecting Luell and my belongings inside. He towered over me. Dark blue jeans and a black t-shirt, with some sort of obscure band on it, formed snugly to his well-developed muscles. I swallowed, already nervous and not even seeing his face yet. Glancing up, I squinted one eye against the sun, closing the other and refusing to let my arms down. Bright green eyes under a skater boy mop of brown hair stared back. A slight touch of a beard growing lined his jaw and tempted me to find out whether it was rough or soft. At least it did until he opened his mouth.

"Why did you leave your cat in the car?" he began, his hard tone gruff, but full of concern for my animal, "it's hot out."

"I left my rig running with the air conditioning on," I

replied defensively. "The better question is, what are *you* doing trespassing on *my* private property?"

My hand subtly snaked inside the door of my rig to the pepper spray and long hunting knife I always carried, while my eyes remained fixed on his. My hand enclosed around the cold steel handle, instinctively flicking the safety snap open with my thumb. I was ready to use it. I didn't want to, though. My phone was in my purse on the floorboard of the passenger side. I licked my lips. It'd take at least thirty minutes for the police to get here, driving time only. That didn't include the dispatch and routing time. Anything could happen in thirty minutes and my brain was conjuring all kinds of bad stuff.

The man glared down his nose at me. He was absolutely breathtaking even with the scowl. If we were meeting under better circumstances, like at a bar, I would have let him take me home. I rolled my shoulders, refusing to let my brain go there and taking a staggered stance not squared to his.

The man stepped closer to me, within arm's reach or less, and rolled his shoulders back, "Whatever you're planning to do with whatever is in that cubby," he leaned in closer, his voice growly and rough, werewolf hairs on his arms coming out, ready to shift, "I suggest you don't." His eyes shimmered. The hair on his body bristled at my subtle, or apparently not so subtle, attempt to grab a weapon. I left my hand where it was, enclosed around my knife. I wasn't going to balk at his threat and leave myself vulnerable.

Werewolf.

I rose up on my toes, meeting him almost nose to nose. "Then I suggest *you* leave, you're trespassing."

"This is *my* family's property!" He boomed, the were-wolf hairs on his arms receding. "You're on *my* land!"

"According to the Bank of West OKimma, it's mine."

The man backed down as he growled. "Since when?"

He obviously hadn't a clue. I felt bad for him. The dragon shifters at the bank more than likely foreclosed on the house after two months of non-payment. Dragons went by the books, knew the law like the back of their hand, rarely gave warnings, and they never messed around with money either. Since this house was on the market for some time, this man was super behind in mortgage payments.

The vein in this guy's neck pulsed. His face mottled over, turning red. His eyes flashed between anger at me buying his house and pain at losing something sentimental to him. He glanced at the black front door to the house, running a hand through his mop of brown hair.

I sighed, softening my tone. "I've seen this place for sale for months. I recently got promoted in my job and decided to buy a house. I signed paperwork and got the keys this morning." I released my grip on the knife, pulling my arm out and putting a friendly hand on his bicep.

Oh, that is delicious!

"I'm sorry. I didn't know," I said, smiling softly.

"Those thieving dragons!" he growled, the hair on his arms bristling again and eyes changing to gold.

Aaaaand no more wolves for me. I withdrew my hand. *I'm so good.* I made myself a promise after Lazaro's father dumped me for Lazaro, that I would not date another wolf. Despite my resolve, I was drawn to wolves. Some women liked the bad boy persona. Others liked the suave preppy guys. Me? Apparently I liked big, burly, powerful, and protective werewolves. I wasn't alone in 'my type' though. Humans who weren't terrified, like myself, often swooned after wolves. Yet, I didn't want another Lazaro. I didn't want to be left after falling for someone, for the good of the pack. Although, I guess no reason is a good reason after falling in love. But the good of the pack just felt like a terrible excuse.

Hard no, with a side of definitely not, followed up by, yeah, you're not as hot now.

I turned my back on him, reached into my rig and turned the engine off. The rumble came to an abrupt halt and I set the e-brake with my hand. The man shook his upper body like a shiver ran down his spine, pacing in short strides. Slowly his eyes went back to their gorgeous emerald and the hairs on his arm receded.

"Take it up with the bank," I said.

He stopped pacing at my remark. "What's your name?" he asked, his voice calm.

"Zuri Barsotti."

"Thank you," he said, taking off toward the gate as if this had been a neighborly visit.

"And your name?" I called out to his disappearing backside while taking Luell out of the Bronco.

"Evander Akselsen," he yelled, pausing by the gate with a side glance over his shoulder. Without another thought, he jumped, clearing the seven-foot gate easily.

I rolled my eyes, knowing he probably had a remote or something to make the gate open. Luell mewled irritability, the hair on her nape stiffening. I smiled. Luell, like most domestic animals, in my opinion, was great at judging someone's character. If Luell didn't like a person, I didn't go around them if I could help it. I should have paid closer attention to her. Luell liked Lazaro for a while, then started avoiding him later in our relationship. I was in love with the back-stabbing, lying werewolf by that time and ignored her signs. And now, clearly, she didn't like Evander. I wasn't certain about him either. Aside from seeming grumpy and incredibly misinformed, he didn't seem too bad. But if nothing else, Lazaro taught me that handsome looks could hide a whole lot of heartache. It didn't matter. This Evander guy wasn't getting in my home, bed, or heart.

"No more wolves," I reminded myself.

Luell mewled happily at me.

———

APPARENTLY I DIDN'T HAVE MUCH, BECAUSE MOVING TOOK me less time than I had anticipated. A few hours and all my clothes were in the closet. My loveseat and chair sat in the little living room on my light beige shag rug protecting the hardwood floors. A small round dining table in the kitchen sat three people. Everything I owned fit perfectly in my small cottage home.

I put the dishes away and set the coffee timer to brew at six thirty in the morning. My eyes scanned and mentally checked off where I had hidden stashes of guns and knives throughout the house. One thing my Uncle Syrus taught me was to be prepared and know where things were in case of emergency.

Internet people were out earlier, so I was all set up and ready for work in the morning. Even though I didn't start for another few days, I wanted to reorganize my work files and get a jump on the new billing system. My new desk would arrive sometime this week and I will be putting it in the spare bedroom. I broke down all the boxes, leaving them neatly stacked by the back door to put into the recycling whenever the bins got here.

I stood in the middle of the house and smiled, looking at my content cat sleeping in her favorite chair. The tv softly played an episode of something I'd left on for Luell and for the noise. I still wasn't used to the quiet of the forest and the tv noise was going to help me transition. At least that's what I'd read online. I was unpacked and settled in. Peeking outside, the sun's last rays shone bright before the gray-blue took over the sky. My skin prickled. The trees outside moved in the light breeze.

I loved this time of year - the spookiness of branches without leaves, carved jack-o-lanterns, and the overall sharp scents of fall. Being here on my own, in a new, unfamiliar place, made my senses heightened. I wasn't yet used to the trees and their movements or how the lighting played tricks on the walls.

Night had come faster than I realized. The first night in a new place always bothered me. Growing up, I bounced from house to house, guardian to guardian, from my aunts and uncles, to cousins, grandparents, everywhere but my actual mother's house. I never knew my father. My mother, from what I was told, was in and out of mental health wards and drug rehabs. One cousin mentioned she was actually the Queen of Kadia to the northeast but I doubted it. No one as screwed up as my mother or as normal as my family, could be royalty. My mother would pop in, say hello, stay a day or two, and then leave; she came and went faster than bunnies repopulated.

Eventually, I was picked up by foster care. The system discovered I was being passed around too much and wanted to give me a 'secure' place. I was passed around then too. I was in the system for a year with three different families, until it was decided I would live with my Uncle Syrus and Aunt Espe, which is where I wanted to be.

With all of that happening, I never had many worldly possessions, as I always planned on up and leaving at the drop of a hat. But now everything was different. I had a home, and *no one* was ever going to rip me from it.

I sighed, walking into the bathroom that was larger than I had in the apartment. I left the door open and cracked the window to let out all the steam. My phone played a music mix I loved as I started the shower. Stripping down to nothing, I stepped into the hot water and closed my eyes, sighing in relief as the hot water hit my sore, move-tired muscles.

My voice sang out in harmony with my favorite song – Fire Meet Gasoline. The song summed up how I felt about Lazaro. He was gasoline, quick at igniting when a spark lit around him, but his love fizzled out just as quickly. Upon reflecting, it felt like he was in relationships for the quick, enigmatic rush, the fiery passion. I just hoped he treated his new wife better. I was fire, loving, enduring, hot embers that kept the fire burning long after the fuel had disappeared. I had tried to keep it going, not knowing the fuel was gone, and now, all I was left with was smoke.

I let the water wipe my tears away. "Am I so unlovable?" I asked myself.

Maybe I was. I had baggage, more than most women. At twenty-four, I was self-sufficient. I didn't *need* a man, yet wanted to share my life with one. I didn't like being alone. My family, after I turned eighteen, mostly walked away from me. They'd done their duty. I was alive, not starved and minimally educated. All the basics taken care of. The only person I still spoke with was my Uncle Syrus. He was the father I wished I had. Syrus treated me well, not like a burden or an outcast because of who sired me. Syrus taught me to play baseball in the yard, how to swim and fish. He did all the 'dad' like things actors in movies do with kids. And I loved him wholeheartedly.

My phone buzzed on the bathroom counter as the blaring ringtone trumpeted. I stepped out of the shower, quickly wrapping my hair and body up in a towel.

"Hi Uncle Sy," I said chipperly.

"Hey there kiddo! How is the new place? Text me your address again, and I will come bug ya this week."

I grinned. "That sounds great. I love the place. It's beautiful, quiet and my entire property is fenced in. I'm away from the busy city life, which I love. I feel at home and free here."

"Good. You needed to leave that apartment and the weird cat lady. How big is it?"

"The house is around a thousand square feet and the property is ten acres." I did a little happy dance no one could see, holding my towel up even though no one was there to flash.

"I'm so proud of you. Do you want or need anything from the little gift shop you love down here?"

My heart warmed more at his thoughtfulness, "No, thank you Uncle Sy. Your visit is a treat enough."

We spoke on the phone for a few more minutes. Syrus was not a big phone talker, but, and I chuckled as I thought about this, he was a texter. I was the same. Living with him and Aunt Espe were the best years of my life. Syrus was former military, and he was tough as nails, but sweet as a marshmallow. He insisted I learn things most thought improper for a woman so I knew how to survive in the wild, shoot guns, ride motorcycles, and more thanks to my uncle. Syrus took me in as his own. Aunt Espe was kindly and distant; because me looking like my mother was hard on her. Espe was younger than my mother and watched her older sister make all kinds of trouble. My aunt and uncle never had kids, terrified they would have a kid similar to my mother. I didn't blame them. I, too, didn't want kids for the same reason.

I stepped into my pajamas, loving the clean feeling of the shower and jammies, and looked forward to then getting into cold sheets. I brushed and braided my long sunshine blonde hair in the mirror. Come morning, I would have pretty waves for a few days.

I stared at myself for a moment, wondering how I looked to others. My brows arched nicely over my honey brown eyes. I loved getting my brows waxed because plucking took too long. My nose, small and narrow, made my oval face appear symmetrical instead of off center. My rose gold nose ring sat in the middle of the left nostril. I thought it was a nice touch.

Sighing, I leaned closer to the mirror and stared. My lips were full, a light blush pink and my chin was dainty on my oval face with a small cleft in the middle. My Uncle Syrus always called it a butt chin. I brushed my teeth and stepped out of the bathroom.

The tv in the background replayed an episode of some show I didn't particularly care for. It was enough to drown out my nerves though, so I let it play. Luell jumped on the bed and hissed toward the closet. My skin prickled. Luell's back arched as she growled.

"Stop it," I chided, feigning disinterest, leaning toward the bed as if to climb in.

My hand slid underneath the other pillow where I had stashed yet another knife and my handgun.

"It's not there," a masculine voice said.

CHAPTER THREE

ZURI

As nonchalantly as I could, I strode out to the kitchen. Bootsteps sounded behind me, thundering aggressively in my small home. The hair on the back of my neck prickled at the creature shadowing behind me. I thanked the God Elohi that the one lesson my uncle had drilled into me time and time again was to have a backup plan in case of emergencies. Any emergency. In this case, a defending-myself-emergency. His training allowed me to remain calm, despite my brain racing to the various weapons hiding in my house. I'd already begun to map which ones were easiest to get to and how I'd get to them.

My body had a mind of its own. My heart thundered in my chest. My throat constricted, wanting to panic and cry out. I mentally shook my head. Uncle Syrus taught me better. With a deep breath, I navigated my way to the kitchen, willing myself to keep calm.

My bare feet hit the cold kitchen tile. I clicked on the coffee pot, getting out two mugs. My hand snaked over the ledge of the cabinet, grabbing the Taurus 9mm I had in there and slid it beside the coffee pot so it was out of sight, flicking the safety off as I did so. Booted feet marched into the kitchen, planting themselves across the room from me and blocking an exit. The hair on the back of my neck prickled. Out of my peripheral, I saw another man, a blond one, enter my kitchen and stood, blocking the back door.

"Coffee?" I asked casually, getting another mug down.

I kept my eyes focused on my task and not on the firearm. It was right there if needed and the safety was off. From what I was able to discern, there were only two people here. I was grateful there weren't more men, but the odds were not in my favor.

The brown-haired man in the doorway came closer, stopping just out of arm's reach. "Where is it?"

"Creamer is in the fridge, second shelf on the door."

"Where is the *key*?" he snarled.

"What key?" I asked, setting the mug on the counter. "I have my Bronco, house, and mailbox keys hanging up over there." I jerked my head toward the man at the back door. My keys clearly on a key hanger next to the door.

The brown-haired man who followed me first into the kitchen strode into the faded moonlight. He looked familiar - olive skin, black hair peppered with a touch of silver on the sides and dark emerald eyes. Was he part of Lazaro's pack? I wasn't sure. He looked it. Everyone in his pack was tall, dark-skinned, green eyed, breathtaking, and unbelievably cruel when it came to those outside the protection of their pack. Now that Lazaro and I were over, I didn't know where I stood. They had their own set of rules outside the ones of the general cities law. With a flick, he turned his wrist over unnaturally fast, gun out and pointed sideways like a thug. My lips twitched. He was going to shoot out my window with that poor aim. Better the window than me.

I fixed myself a cup of coffee, my back to them. I drew my pistol closer to me, feeling the hairs on my neck rise higher if it were possible. Inhaling the warm aromatic scent of coffee did little to quell my nerves.

"We know you have it," the brown-haired man stated.

"Her fear turns me on," the younger blond werewolf said from behind me growling hungrily after sniffing the air loudly. "She *is* all alone."

Setting down my coffee mug, I drew my pistol off the counter, spun on my heel while pulling the slide back. "I have six rounds and three of them are cased in silver. Wanna see which one of you is gonna cry first?"

The blond-haired man behind me shifted into his wolf form. The shift was instantaneous. His torn clothing lay shredded on my kitchen floor. His black werewolf frame took up the majority of my kitchen. His claws dug into my tile floor, leaving deep gouges in it. His back arched, head and front paws lowered like he was about to stalk and bite me. This wolf was the dang size of a small pony. Standard size to most, but to me, this wolf was a tank. My small table screeched across the floor to make room for his bulk. My laptop slid off the tabletop and clattered to the seat of the chair.

The brown-haired man by the front of my kitchen also shifted. His werewolf frame, slightly smaller and gray. I swallowed. They snarled, advancing toward me. I let out a slow breath, firing a shot at the gray one who was closest. The bullet pierced his shoulder, but did not drop him nor did he flinch.

The black werewolf bit my leg, dragging me down to the floor. I screamed, hitting the tile with a thud. I had a death grip on the 9mm, I brought it up, firing a shot into his abdomen. The werewolf growled, shifting into his human form, the blood and bullet not stopping his advances. His body rejected the bullet, pushing it back out of his olive-colored skin. My eyes widened, not knowing they could do that so easily. His skin sealed over like goo oozing over the side of a countertop.

The blond man ripped off my pajama pants with one hand while the other held me by my throat. His green eyes glowing bright swirled with hunger and lust. I beat onto his chest to get him off of me. Sucking in a lungful of air burned my throat. Bringing my legs to my chest, I tried to lift him off. With one hand, he silenced the motion by tightening his grip on my throat while his other hand pressed hard on my left thigh. His grip tightened around my neck. I could hardly breathe. I felt my eyes roll into the back of my head. I gasped but no air rushed inside my lungs. The brown-haired man yanked the pistol out of my hand. Hands on his chest, I tried to push him again off but couldn't. He was like steel.

"You smell delicious," the blond on top of me whispered in my ear, dropping lower on my body threatening to suffocate me with his weight.

His hard arousal pressed the inside of my thigh. My

black cotton thong underwear was the only clothing blocking him from taking me and I was grateful for the little bit that was there. I tried to move my legs and kick again, but failed, unable to move. My hands on his chest kept pushing back with everything I had.

The first man stood over me with the 9mm pointed at my head. "Don't scream. He'll be done soon."

Before my muddled brain could process what the brute had said, air rushed into my lungs burning with crispness. A weight was yanked off my body. My neck craned back and I looked up, my hazy vision taking in two sets of feet. The blond was off of me. I rolled to my side, scooting my back close against the base of the cabinets, coughing and thinking of nothing aside from my next breath and not letting the man on top of me again. I curled myself into a ball, my now clear eyes glancing around the kitchen for my pistol. Spotting the gun by the fridge, I crawled to it.

A shot rang out through my kitchen. One of the men dropped to the floor, eyes open and staring at me, but not seeing me, never seeing anything again. Pure silver gushed from the open wound in his head. I reached my pistol, coughing still from the roughness in my throat. Hand on the slide, I slid it back, forcing a bullet in the chamber. Even with the gun being automatic, this was habitual. I aimed at the other man's back, firing a shot at his kidneys. The bullet hit true, dropping the man to his knees.

The person who'd shot the first man, my rescuer, put a final bullet in the second man's head. I closed my eyes at the sound, flinching slightly. Silver gushed from the now dead man's head. The bitter iron smell made me gag. The perky aroma of coffee didn't help.

Tears formed along the edges of my eyes and I sucked the tears, the fear and the rushing adrenaline all inside trying to calm my shaking body. My enemies were dead. I was saved and safe. I pulled my knees to my chest and allowed myself a moment to cry. I could feel my rescuer standing there, waiting for me patiently. I hadn't even looked at them properly yet. I had no clue if they were male or female. I was just glad I was alive. This night could have turned out far worse. I let out a shuddering breath, calming myself.

"You all right?" my rescuer asked.

"Evander?"

"Yeah," he said coolly.

"I got bit and it burns," I said. "But I'm all right."

Evander knelt down beside me, taking my right thigh in his hands. I twitched at his touch and the pain from my leg. He looked it over and grimaced. Getting up, he turned the kitchen light on and I got my first look at my wound. The area was red and inflamed. Blood coagulated and bubbled together. I put a hand on my mouth, swallowing down bile.

"You won't change," Evander commented dryly, as he wetted a kitchen towel. "A werewolf's bite is more painful than anything."

I gasped as he pressed the hot towel to my leg. "Blood to blood by the full moon or you're born that way."

Evander smirked. "Yep."

He pressed my wound together, getting the bubbling blood to ooze out of my leg. I stuck my hand into my mouth to keep from crying out. I couldn't look, so I focused on the shattered chair and laptop trying to decide from here if the laptop survived.

Evander worked, going back and forth from the kitchen sink to me. He didn't say a word. I was immensely relieved it wasn't a full moon nor was the guy bleeding on me, so I wouldn't turn into a *were*. Not that I had any qualms against being a *were* in principle, but being turned by a rogue brought on a whole slew of issues. Finding a pack would be difficult. Werewolves were extremely particular on how someone originated. They wanted to know details, down to every miniscule word and interaction. Getting medical insurance benefits were less particular than joining a pack. And no one wanted to be a lone wolf. Not only because the animal instinct would drive you mad without a community, but lone wolves often had a target on their back. It was always safest in numbers for wolves.

I was distracted from my thoughts by movement out of the corner of my eye. Luell sauntered into the kitchen, sitting next to Evander and purred.

"Oh, *now* you like me," he said to Luell, patting her on the back before standing up. "Let me help you to bed. You're going to be sore."

I shook my head. "I can't sleep. Not after that."

"Couch?"

"Please," I smiled. "Can you grab my phone, please?"

I went to stand, but he scooped me up in his arms. My cheeks flamed from being held in my half-naked state. I wanted my pajama pants back on. However, the bite on my thigh needed open air, and pajama pants would stick to the open wound. My athletic shorts would be nice to have right about now.

At least I still have my shirt on. I glanced at Evander and blushed deeper. His upper lip quirked without looking directly at me.

I felt his muscles flex as he lifted me. I wasn't overweight by any means, but I wasn't a toothpick either. Somewhere between lithe, muscularly firm, and a lover of cheeseburgers. Being a touch over five foot four and wearing size six jeans, I would put myself on the medium spectrum. Evander didn't balk at my physique though. If he thought something, it never registered.

He set me gently down on my loveseat, pulling the throw down over me. Scooting the coffee table closer, he popped my right leg on top with pillows underneath.

"Keep it propped so it doesn't swell," he instructed.

Evander grabbed my phone from where I told him I'd seen it last and brought it back to me. He went back to the kitchen, grabbing each man under the arms and lifted them with ease, dragging them out the back door. I watched him. There wasn't blood, which I found interesting, but pools of silver from where they each had been struck. I found it a tad unsettling. Blood pooling meant death; it meant the decision to kill was final. No blood was concerning. Would they be able to come back and get me? Were they truly dead? Did werewolves die from a silver bullet to the head? I had no idea. Even Lazaro never confirmed my questions to it all.

I called the cops and informed them of what happened, down to every word and detail I could remember. And the event was etched in great detail at the moment. It would take them thirty minutes to get here to investigate. *Good thing I ain't dying,* I thought.

I sighed. How would those men know I would be here? I told no one but my uncle. Unless I was seen coming out to this property. I wasn't exactly discreet about moving. Didn't think I needed to be.

And I had no idea what it was about the key they wanted. The only key I had besides my main ones was one my grandmother gave me before she passed on. It was old and an heirloom. It opened absolutely nothing, but it was pretty, and I liked to look at it when I got particularly sentimental.

Evander came back inside, shutting the door behind him and locking it. He strode into my living room, standing in front of me, blocking the tv I was mindlessly staring at.

"Who are you?" He demanded, scowling.

"Zuri Barsotti."

Evander crossed his arms. "Quit lying."

I laughed. "I'm not lying. My name is Zuri Ariella Barsotti."

"Prove it."

My jaw tightened. "My purse is in my bedroom hanging over the end of the bedframe. Rummage through since you broke into my house," I hissed.

"My breaking in saved your ass," he quipped back.

"Well thanks for saving me," I grumbled. "But do you really have to be a jerk faced butt nugget?"

Evander harrumphed, turning on his heel, and taking

long, powerful strides into my bedroom. He rifled through my purse, opening my wallet. His scowl deepened, pulling out my driver's license and inspecting it. I grinned.

His head snapped over to me, his left brow perking up while his deep voice rumbled, "Explain to me what the hell the Moon Walkers are doing here!"

I shook my head. "I didn't know what pack they came from. I don't know who they are. I thought they were here because of Lazaro Sandalio."

"What?" Evander scrunched his face. "How in the world did you get messed in with him?"

My face heated. The blood throughout my body boiled. I closed my mouth. I wasn't going to tell this man another iota about myself. I owed him nothing... except my life. My jaw worked back and forth. *Dammit to hell.*

My eyes couldn't meet his angered gaze for a moment. "We were an item... for a while," I admitted.

Evander's lip curled. "You dated the heir to the Sandalio Mob! What the hell kind of woman are you?"

I brushed the tears back into my hair. "A woman who was in love, who was dumped, who at the time didn't know who he was until later, and who won't make the same mistake, *ever again.*"

My eyes focused on the neatly stitched lines of my throw blanket. The purples and grays swirled together to paint a picture of a faerie in the woods, sitting on a stump, distracting me for a moment. How nice it must be to have wings to fly away with the change of wind; to leave when the world started to crush in or start over wherever her wings could take her when needed.

Evander sat on the love seat to my right with a sigh of exasperation. Luell jumped in his lap, purring contentedly. I glared at my fluffy two-timing calico. Evander gently stroked her fur, scratching her behind the ears. He stared at my leg for a moment before his expression softened.

"You ok?" He finally asked.

I nodded. "Nothing some aspirin won't cure. You're obsessed with this house, why?"

Evander scowled, his fists clenching as his jaw set. "This house was in my family for generations. Greedy dragons at the Bank of West OKimma raised the property taxes until my grandmother couldn't afford it. I was about to buy it back when they accepted your cash offer and the 'as is' addendum," he finished with a glare as if I had stolen it from his grandmother myself.

"Did your obsession lead you to come to my rescue?"

Evander smirked, the disbelief of who I was involved with in our conversation still lingering in his eyes. He was distant, trying to be casual and friendly but struggling to find the happy medium between his anger at the situation and being polite to someone he just met. "I was driving to the bar, Lonesome Lenny's, when I saw two men hop the fence."

I shrugged. It was a possibility. There was a bar called Lonesome Lenny's, about a half mile up the road on the right. There was only one road leading past my house. He could have very well been on his way there. However, something niggled in the back of my mind warning me that his story was fake. If he saw men hop the fence, why not come to my aid sooner?

Come morning, I'm ordering a security system, buying dead-bolts and a spell from the coven of witches in town.

The silence in the house, besides Evander and myself breathing, settled me down. His presence, even though I didn't care to have it at the moment, was comforting, especially after the encounter almost a half hour ago; Evander being here took some of the spook out of being alone. I slumped down in the cushions, curling myself over the arm of the loveseat. My body ached, my heart hurt and I felt so displaced.

Never in my wildest days had I experienced something so vulgar and threatening. The attempt on my body scared me, but nothing near as terrifying as the afterwards did. What if they tortured me? Removed my limbs? Or hacked me into pieces while I was alive to still watch? What if they took me someplace, or removed my eyes, or drowned me? I shuddered. Drowning was my biggest fear - not being able to see the bottom of a lake and not knowing what was underneath was terrifying.

Knocking came from the door and Evander answered it stepping outside to talk to one of the officers. The lights from their cars flashed blue and red inside, reflecting off the windows and the tv. A human officer dressed in dark blue with lime green reflectors sewn on his uniform, came inside the doorway.

"Ma'am, you all right?" He asked.

I nodded. "Yeah. Bitten and a little shaken, but I'm all right."

"Care to tell me the details?"

I relayed to him what happened, down to every word

and detail as I did the dispatch earlier. He took my statement. At the same time, I recorded the conversation on my phone in case something backfired. With my statement completed, he left. I watched out the window as an ambulance came to get the bodies. I sighed, leaning my head back against the couch. Evander took a seat beside me.

"Are you alright?" He asked.

I nodded. "Yeah… Thank you for being here."

"I'll stay until you fall asleep."

I could only nod again. With the adrenaline wearing off, it made my body crash hard.

CHAPTER FOUR

ZURI

Come morning Evander was gone. It was how I liked it. I didn't want to be forced to make awkward conversation or answer a slew of questions about myself or what those men wanted with me and this key.

I sighed, alone in my quiet home. It gave me goosebumps and I found myself constantly staring out the living room window. The kitchen floor was spotless like last night never happened. Groaning, I rose off the loveseat. My leg was sore and stiff. The wound had begun to scab over. Evander had put some ointment on it last night after the police left, stating it would help with the healing. Whatever it was, it did make it feel better. Other than that, I felt fine.

After relieving myself, I walked into the kitchen to start a fresh pot of coffee. A note propped itself against the coffee pot.

. . .

IF YOU NEED ME, CALL OR TEXT
459-0034

• *Evander*

I PUT THE NOTE IN THE JUNK DRAWER. "WHY CALL WHEN you'll just show up?" I grumbled.

I made coffee and distracted myself to begin work early. The new bosses didn't expect me to clock in for a few days, but I wanted to impress them by knowing what I was doing with this new system. Plus, they were paying me an exorbitant amount. I might as well get to know what I was doing before I started talking to facilities and coordinating patient's care. I wanted work to clear my mind of last night, of those men breaking into my house.

Shuddering, I thanked whoever was looking out for me. Opening my laptop, I clicked the search engine and typed in Moon Walkers. Dozens of articles came up of deaths, murders, suicides, and of the police trying to locate the main ringleader, but all leads proved fruitless. Hundreds of articles detailed the ruthlessness of the werewolf pack.

"Joy," I mumbled, sighing heavily and resting my head in my hands. "I'm on their fuckin' radar for some reason."

At least the Sandalio Mob was quiet about their inner workings. I had no idea Lazaro was a mobster until he slipped one day stating he needed to handle some mob business; and because he slipped and told me, I was taken to the 'mob business' directly. The pack swore me to secrecy after Lazaro came clean about telling me. Pain of death sounded pretty serious. They didn't have to threaten me twice. My lips pursed to the side as I found yet another article detailing the ruthlessness of the Moon Walkers destroying a witch's coven.

I deleted the search history. I was looking for something deeper. I wanted to know what the Moon Walkers wanted with a key. I found nothing. I even tried to find information about old keys, like *my* key from my grandma. Nothing.

I typed in Evander Akselsen. Nothing. No social media, no newspaper articles, no awards, no anything. I even searched in my medical databases. Nothing. It was like he didn't even exist. I frowned. Even when I typed in my name, *something* showed up.

Something is wrong with all I'm finding, I thought. My body tensed from the internal warning in my gut. My chair screeched back as I went to grab another gun I had stashed away. Someone was after me for some reason. Evander was as much a suspect as the Moon Walkers.

I lifted the mattress at the end of the bed. I pulled out the .357, rolling the barrel over to see if it was still loaded and ready. It was a tough gun for me to shoot because the grip was bigger than my hand so it wanted to kick out, but one I managed quite well. I needed to get my other 9mm from my Bronco. I changed my clothes, getting out of my pajamas. Staring at the shirt and pants on the floor, made me shudder. I felt violated. I kicked the pants toward the laundry hamper. I shoved the .357 into the holster I attached to my hip. My cream-colored loose blouse came down to help conceal my gun. I undid the braid in my hair, piling it on top of my head in a giant wavy ponytail.

Walking back into the kitchen, I stared out the window. I watched the heating and cooling men arrive in a work van at the gate. I walked around to the kitchen to where my keys hung and clicked a button for the gate to open. The work van drove in. I frowned, striding to the back door. Peeking out the window, I was relieved to see the bodies from last night hauled away by ambulance and the messy silver from their heads long gone. I needed to thank Evander for cleaning up the mess.

Two men walked toward my front door. I opened the door before they could knock.

"Good morning... Ms. Barsotti," he paused looking at the clip board. "We are here to install your heating and cooling."

"Sounds great," I replied, trying to sound polite like nothing from last night bothered me.

"Sign here and we will get started."

I signed my name. They took the papers and went back to their rig. I needed to start work. Pouring myself another cup of coffee, I began a long day of spreadsheets, logs, emails, scanning and faxing. I skipped lunch and around that time, the repair men left with a job completed. In the late afternoon, I stopped with my work completed for the day. I felt off the entire day - jumpy and paranoid. Going to my room, I opened the closet to where I had a small wooden box of trinkets from my childhood. I pulled out the key my grandmother had given me along with her scribbled note, I'd read thousands of times.

SOME KEYS UNLOCK TREASURE, SOME SECRETS. MOST OFTEN IT'S *the truth. Be careful what you unlock, Zuri, for door nor chest can be re-sealed. Also, hide this key from your mother, but more so from your father. I'm so sorry to put you in the middle of this.*

LOVE, GRAMMA KAETHE

I TURNED THE KEY OVER IN MY HAND. IT WAS SMALL AND silver with three pointed teeth. One side had a tree while the other had a goat or sheep. I scowled at it, wondering if it opened an old antique hutch or ornate vintage door. Along the side of it there was something scribbled, but I couldn't make it out. I clutched the key in my hand, focusing my attention back on the note.

I frowned, wondering what she meant. How would I even know what this unlocked? How did Gramma Kaethe even come by such an item? And is this the key those men were after? I frowned, racking my brain for any other memory of Gramma Kaethe telling me anything important, but all I could recall was her recipe for a pie crust. Hiding it from my mother made sense. Whether or not my mother was a queen or a druggie made little difference to me; she would never get it. I shoved the key into my pocket as a precaution. My gut told me to keep this safe. My Uncle always mentioned following a gut instinct. Whatever this key was, it needed to be kept safe. And it was safest on my person.

I checked the back door, making certain it was locked. I went out the front door, staring at my lonely green Bronco in the driveway. I grabbed the mace by the front door, shoving it in my other pocket and also the long hunting knife I hid under the couch, strapping it to my belt on the hip opposite my gun.

You need to be prepared, Zuri, for anything. Nothing is more dangerous than a woman who is unprepared. That is when others strike and you will lose. My uncles' words rang in my ears. He was right, of course.

If I had lost my head last night, I would have been dead. If it weren't for Evander, I very well could have been. Thanks to Uncle Syrus, I was prepared. Keeping my head allowed me to pull off a few shots and keep my assailants busy enough for help to arrive. Most would call me insane, or overly prepared. But living the life I had, I was terrified of people taking me from my home.

With a deep breath, I opened my front door. My plan was to walk the property, see how people were getting in; like if the fence was down and where I could strategically place cameras.

No one was going to break into my home again or put me in danger. I stepped off the front porch, looking both ways and listening. The skin on the back of my neck didn't prickle so I continued my path; taking a turn to the right of the house, toward the better part of the ten acres of woods, I noted several places that would be good for cameras to watch the backdoor and the woodlands. My hand rested on the grip of my gun. My finger flicked for the safety, forgetting it didn't have one.

"Fuck it," I said, drawing it out of the holster, I took a path into the woods. I felt the need to patrol my grounds and felt secure with a gun in my hand.

I pulled the hammer back, even though I didn't have to, it was reflexive. I was ready for whatever was out there that wanted me. Part of me didn't understand it. I kept to myself, I hardly went out and partied at clubs. For that matter I had two friends: Gretchen from work and my childhood friend, Adiva, who lived over an hour away. I smiled, missing Adiva. Her name fit her perfectly as she was the most exuberant out of anyone I ever met. She was always well dressed and flashy.

I need to text her later, I reminded myself.

The trail I was on led deep into the forest. Moss hung down from the trees. It was overly condensed. Old rotting branches barely hung onto the trees. Overgrowth of ivy and other vegetation over the forest floor surrounded the scraggly and unkept trees. It looked like something out of a horror film. I don't care for horror movies.

I licked my lips, plugging along the trail. I would need an arborist to come in and clean some of this up, or do it myself to save money. However, ten acres was a tad overwhelming to do alone. By the time I got one area pruned and moved onto the next, the first one would need to be done again. Calling an arborist would be better, even if I paid thousands more. However, I wanted this place to be fully mine without a mortgage hanging over my head.

I pursed my lips to the side, *I'm going to work hard and do it myself.*

Howls came from inside the forest. I paused, waiting to hear if they were wolves or *were*. The werewolves in OKimma didn't howl very often. When they did, the hairs on my arms stood up and the need to run and hide took over. It wasn't a lonesome howl a typical wolf emitted, but something along the lines of anger, greed and the lust to kill. I don't know how I could tell the difference. I just knew.

I bit my bottom lip, shaking my body free of its nerves. "Cool it, Zuri," I soothed. "Level head, deep breaths."

I took another deep breath to focus my mind. My eyes scanned back and forth for any minute detail. Something I might have missed like a secret door in a tree, or a bunker in the ground, or cubby. A rune even. I wanted to find something, a secret way to get to me on my land that those men might have used. I saw nothing. I walked along the forest path to the other side of the property. When the tall black fence greeted my jumpy eyesight, I turned around and went back the way I came. My nerves were too worked up to catch anything important, like a tree house Evander might have had or a tire swing. Evander mentioned those men hopped the fence and they very well could have.

My lips pursed to the side. I put the gun in the holster, while my other hand tapped the side of the pocket where the key was. I asked Uncle Syrus about it once. He didn't know. Neither did Aunt Espe. Gramma Kaethe died when I was a child and that was when I inherited the box with the key, though I had no idea what to do with it at six years old.

I need clues. I need to understand why this key is so important to the werewolves. It's just a key.

Daylight sparkled in front me. The cedar shakes of my home brought me instant relief; my stomach fluttered. However, it was short lived. Mr. Arthur Sandalio, along with five men, stared me down from the gravel driveway. Two more came out of my house from the front and back doors. Eight men and only six bullets in my chamber. I straightened my back, keeping my gun out at my side while plastering an even look on my face.

"Afternoon, Mr. Sandalio," I called, stepping into the clearing and toward him.

Mr. Sandalio's gray pompadour hairstyle held tight in the wind due to all the gel. A tailored deep hunter green suit hugged his frame, accentuating his imposing figure and olive complexion. I swallowed nervously. I had only seen him wear that suit when it meant crucial business like me getting sworn to pack secrecy when Lazaro slipped up. His henchmen crossed their arms, exposing their own shiny Ruger's on their hips.

"Zuri," he began in a businesslike fashion. "I was informed you had visitors late last night. What was it about?"

I shrugged, attempting to be nonchalant. "I don't know, Mr. Sandalio. They mentioned a key. Since you had men in my home, did you find one, other than the ones I have for everyday use?"

Arthur scowled. "Don't get smart with me girl! Where is the key?"

My face hardened. "I don't *know* what you're talking about, *sir*."

"I *know* you do. It's a small key, silver, with three pointed teeth on the bit, a tree of life on one side of the bow and an hourglass and goat on the other. Around the shaft and collar, it has writing *'For those that shall seek, will find and those that shall protect, will endure'.*"

I refrained from touching my pocket where the key he just described lay hidden. Instead, I shook my head. "Never seen it or heard of it."

Arthur clapped his hands. "Well then, we will leave you alone. By the way, Lazaro wants the Bronco back."

I swore the blood boiling under my skin made my skin match my hair. I wasn't about to cow down to his intimidation. "The title of the Bronco is in my name. If he wants it, he can pay me for it."

"Stupid twit!" Mr. Sandalio fumed, pulling at the crease of his suit. "I told him not to date *humans*! We shall be watching you closely, Zuri."

"As you please." I said, striding past him to my Bronco.

Since people kept getting into my house, I left it unlocked. I had the one thing they were looking for and everything else was replaceable. Luell would hide in the bathroom cabinet. She always hid there when someone she didn't like came over, like those men from last night, only to come out once Evander was there.

The car door creaked open, and I checked the back seat. When no one was there, I clambered in, slammed the door shut and locked it. Taking the extra set of keys out of my cup holder, I stuck it in the ignition. My rig turned over, the low rumble soothing me. I put the Bronco in drive and I took off to the one place even wolves wouldn't go.

CHAPTER FIVE

ZURI

Holdur's 'Mythical' Shoppe sign crackled with blue neon lighting slowly burning out. The man who owned it was as eccentric as the items he carried. I had been in Holdur's shop as a young kid with my uncle and here I was again. Holdur, an old and grumbly dragon shifter, remembered everyone who came in his shop. He never forgot a transaction nor a transgression like what happened with my uncle's friend who pissed him off. And I wasn't about to cross him; I liked breathing.

I took a deep breath, getting out of my rig. "Here I go."

The gun was still on my side. No one cared whether humans openly carried weapons. We were the weaker race compared to the prowess of everyone else. The violent crime rate in OKimma was nearly non-existent since most kept to themselves.

I jogged across the street, glancing everywhere as I did. I opened the shop door and slipped inside, breathing a sigh of relief upon not seeing wolves. The place had a musty smell like wet leaves in the fall. Holdur glanced at me over his red rimmed spectacles as I navigated my way to him through shelves upon racks of items packed together like an organized hoarder home.

"Zuri Barsotti, what brings you here without your Uncle Syrus… Faulkner isn't it?" Holdur finished with a sweet, old man grin.

I smiled back. "Yes, that's correct. I need information on an item left to me by my Grandma Kaethe. It's old with an interesting inscription."

I fumbled with the key in my pocket. Part of me was nervous about showing Holdur the key. The other part of me needed answers to understand what I had. Hairs on my arms raised. Dragons tended not to involve themselves with any werewolf dealings and I was indirectly involved.

Holdur slammed his work book shut. The twinkling gleam appeared in his vermilion eyes. Holdur fancied old writing be it in a book, on a clay stone or a key. Vermilion lizard-like scales appeared on his hands then faded. *Definitely interested.* I withdrew the key from my pocket, holding it in my hands. Holdur bent down, taking in the scent first. A deep scowl creased his brow. He gently turned the key over in my hand.

"Is this a joke, Zuri?" Holdur demanded, his face pocking with red blotches. Scales quickly appeared and faded on his face.

I took my key back, shoved it in my pocket, and swallowed. "I have no idea what it is! As far as I'm concerned it's an old weird key."

Holdur deflated. Scales appeared across his nose as he

took in a deep breath. He leaned over the counter and sniffed me again. "Honesty. A good quality about you."

Holdur walked around the counter coming to my side. The man towered over me, smelling of smoky maple, applewood, and ashes. He put a hand on my shoulder, leaning down to meet my gaze. Something about this key sent shivers down my spine. It was one of the reasons why I put it in a box and never opened the damn thing. There was something ominous about it.

"Remember the war between wolf packs?"

I nodded slightly, despite not having a clue what he was talking about. I smirked inside. So much for my honesty. On second thought, I shrugged after I had nodded like a fool lost for words. Werewolves were always fighting over territory so it was difficult to pinpoint which war Holdur was referring to. I never paid attention.

The dragon's eyes narrowed. "The war I'm referring to is the war between the Moon Walkers and the Vilkas."

I shook my head. "Never heard of that war."

Holdur sighed. "You were too young to remember it anyways. The leader of the Moon Walkers wanted complete control of all wolfpacks. He wanted to be the sole dominant alpha instead of each clan having their own and getting along peaceably. The other wolf packs formed the Vilkas, and made a stand. However, the Moon Walkers planned to eradicate the Vilkas with a key that opened the portal to the underworld. A key that would bring destruction to everyone."

I swallowed. *Oh shit.* I stared down at my boots. That was not what I was expecting. Although, I wasn't sure what

I really was expecting. What in the gods was I going to do now? Moon Walkers were after me, now the Sandalio Mob and who knows who else?

"And you have *that* key." Holdur said, breaking me from my thoughts.

I blinked. *Oh shit*, was the only phrase repeating itself through my head. *Oh Gramma, what have you done and now passed to me?* So many questions and answers I would never receive. I glanced back up at Holdur waiting to hear more with possible instructions of what to do.

The dragon continued, going back around behind the counter, "The packs separated, each claiming territory, but remained at odds. Silent battles have been happening over the years. The Vilkas asked us Dragons for aid, but we refused. As the saying goes 'not my monkeys, not my circus.'"

I nodded. "Who is the leader of the Vilkas and the Moon Walkers."

"Vorath Luciani, a werewolf created by blood to blood, runs the Moon Walkers. Royan Pright, a werewolf born, runs the Vilkas."

"Who made the key?" I pressed.

I wanted all the information I could get my hands on. Dragons were a plethora of it. It was easier to ask than spend hours reading a book that gave limited or no answers.

Holdur sighed, leaning against the counter. "There are two Gods – Elohi the God of light and heaven, and Diomedes, the god of darkness and the underworld. Diomedes tried to overthrow his brother and plunge the world in darkness. Elohi caught wind of his plans and had a silversmith create the key to lock up his brother for eternity. Long story short, Elohi won, Diomedes is down below," Holdur pointed to the ground. "Somehow, no one knows how, Elohi lost the key. The god searched, but never found it. Now it is in your possession."

"So, how do I find Elohi? A temple or shrine?"

Holdur laughed. "You don't. Elohi hasn't been around in a thousand years or so. No one knows where he is. Keep it safe for not only the werewolves' fates rest in your hands. Our conversation is safe," Holdur promised. "Now, buy something in case you're being followed to make it appear you came here on purpose."

"Thank you."

I left the shop with a giant paper bag of books and a vase, feeling more hopeless than I cared to think about. Opening the back of my rig, I carefully set my purchases in. I got in my Bronco, leaning my head against the seat with a sigh. At least in this part of town I was relatively safe. Werewolves pissed off the dragons so badly, they were enemies. I remember some wolfpacks amended ties, but mostly wolves were not welcome in West OKimma.

I checked the backseat again to be certain no one was there. Wolves showing up randomly had me on edge. I had nowhere to run or turn to. My family would not help me or save me. My mother was in an insane asylum last I heard. I had no idea who my father was. I had Uncle Syrus, but Aunt Espe did not like me at the house. For some reason, I was left with werewolf items by my grandmother. Nothing about my family made sense to me; everything was swept under the rug like it didn't matter.

Sighing, I ran my fingers through my hair, grabbing and pulling slightly. I locked the doors to the Bronco and turned it over. I sat there, listening to the engine rumble, hands on the steering wheel. I curled down in the seat, resting a foot on the side and bringing my right leg up to my chest, resting my chin on my knee. My fingers tapped the wheel.

"My mother supposedly went insane after I was born. No one knows why," I spoke out loud.

I scowled, pursed my lips and scrunched my nose. I needed answers to my bloodline and lineage. Answers started with me, and it was in my blood. *I'm gonna get my blood checked*, I decided. There had to be a reason no one in this crazy family talked. I had to be part-paranormal, something that kept everyone quiet. I had to find out what it was.

In fact, most creatures in Quivleren were not human. I was lucky to run into a human twice in one week unless I deliberately sought one out. Made sense since Quivleren politics favored the magical. Humans lost the genetic lottery centuries ago as we started interbreeding. It was true that most supernaturals had human in their genetic background somewhere too, but it was often ignored because magic meant power.

We had two castles ruling over all Quivleren. Kadia and Toan were ruled by the overtly rich and incredibly power-ful. From there each major city had a governor. There were only six of those, but they operated like mini countries with their own rules and laws despite still answering to the castles. And some cities were nightmares. Chay was a city of faeries no one dared set foot in since, as a species, they were known for their nastiness and trickery. Just down the road from the damn faeries was the biggest and most diverse city in Quivleren. Aiolos was a hub for major trade and most species were found there. I'd even heard of a clan of Cyclops running an incredibly successful eyewear company there, as odd as it sounded.

I shook my head, refocusing my train of thought. *If I know what I am, it may answer why my Gramma left this to me,* I reasoned. *What did Gramma see in me? Why did she think I could handle this when one of my uncles or aunts would have been stronger, more credible choices?*

Straightening up, I checked the mirrors and pulled out into the street. I went further into downtown, making certain to stay on the dragon side. At a stop light, I found what I needed on the left-hand side of the street. I quickly put my blinker on and pulled a u-ey making sure not to cut anyone off. Then I pulled up and shut the engine off.

I walked up to the medical counter. The woman behind smiled, opening the glass window. "Hello Miss," the mousey petite woman said. "What will we be seeing you for?"

"I would like to get my blood drawn-"

"Are you pregnant?" she asked, chipperly interrupting me.

I shook my head. "Oh no. I want to get my DNA tested-"

"For STD's?" she interrupted again, eyebrows raised.

I glowered, reading her name tag. "Obviously, *Felicia*, you believe I'm some kind of whore. Unlike most you may see, I prefer my legs closed. I want my DNA tested to find out my lineage. Also, I want to order my birth certificate. Is this acceptable?"

Her face turned bright red. "I'm so sorry. I didn't mean to imply anything."

"Yeah, try listening," I replied evenly. "Can these two things be done today?"

Felicia clicked on her computer screen. "Yes, it can. Please have a seat and fill these out. Someone will be with you shortly."

I took the clipboard she handed me and sat down on the other end of the waiting room, back to the wall and facing the door. I filled out the required information, reading the fine print that DNA testing could take up to four weeks to process. The paperwork asked if I wanted to know who and what genealogy wise; who my father and mother were if they were found in the database. I checked yes.

I glanced up, noticing Evander stare at my Bronco from across the street. I glared. He was stalking me. I watched him walk farther down the sidewalk and out of sight.

After this, I'm going to buy security cameras.

Something was happening, involving me. I wasn't taking any chances.

CHAPTER SIX

ZURI

I drove home, feeling slightly better and I wondered about Evander; why was he following me? A cotton ball and tape covered my left arm. I had to use my credit card, but I didn't care. The security system in that crinkly bag gave me a peace of mind and the elite system was worth every penny in interest I would end up paying.

I drove to the sketchy side of town, where a prominent Witches Coven was, parking at the end of a long-shaded road and turning the engine off. A wooden sign staked in the ground read *Black Ash Coven*.

Slowly I made my way down the driveway. I refrained from putting my hands on my gun or in my jean pockets. The moment I stepped onto their property, I was being watched. I didn't want to attract attention to myself.

The witches of this coven, all dressed in black and red, looked more like high school goths. Witches emerged around me in smoking wisps, cautiously watching me as I made my way to the front of their home. They all carried on their right hip a wand, made out of what I assumed was ash wood since it was in their name. The area they lived in wasn't what I would think it would be based on the part of town they lived in. But as I walked, I saw nothing of the neighborhood I had just driven through. Their grounds were clean and immaculate. Their mansion home, large and boxy like a hospital, had beautiful gray cedar shake siding and open white framed windows.

A witch approached me, looking to be about my age. Dark eggplant eyes gazed at me, locking me in place. Her features were striking with the contoured make-up she wore, highlighting her high cheekbones and beautiful caramel skin; she completed her look with eggplant lipstick to match.

"Zuri Barsotti," a witch greeted. "What spell do you seek?"

I licked my lips. "A spell to protect my house and what's inside."

The woman grinned. "No need to be fearful. You mean Feenat no harm, so Feenat won't harm you. Follow Feenat."

I nodded, assuming her name was Feenat. The area I was allowed to enter to wait for my spell held a glass bauble and was in a sunroom with numerous plants writhing under the sunlight and misting water coming from the ceiling. I perked a brow at the plants, finding it interesting to watch.

Feenat worked, putting large pieces of plant, rock and bits of creatures into a small bottle neck shaped clear vase. Feenat's eyes narrowed as she worked, adding in one last flower to the vase before she capped it with a cork stopper and shook it.

"Here is your spell. Directions are in the bag. You pay Feenat," the witch said, holding out her hand.

I dug into my pocket and took out a pair of earrings Lazaro had gotten me for our first-year anniversary, setting it in Feenat's hand. I also pulled out a hundred dollars in cash, adding it to her extended hand.

"Done," Feenat stated, grinning at the satisfactory payment. "Feenat walks you out."

The witch led me silently to the end of the driveway where my Bronco waited unhindered. Feenat spun on her heel and marched back toward the house without a word. I walked calmly to my Bronco and got inside, setting my newly acquired spell on the passenger's side seat nestled against my new electronic security system. I took out the directions, reading them over quickly, paying attention to the caution part written in bold purple ink - *Do Spell Outside!*

Setting it all to the side for later, I turned the engine over. Putting my loyal rig in gear, I headed home relieved about the security. A scowl crept over my face, seeping doubt into my head about the newly acquired spell. Witches were fickle and the validity of their spell depended upon how well they liked a person. However, I would trust one over a faerie any day. Still, it made me wonder how effective the spell would be. All I had to do was set it on the doorstep and say, 'protect me and mine,' and supposedly it would work.

Either way, I would set up the alarms and the spell

tonight, so I could actually sleep - hopefully without nightmares. If anything happened, the security system would alert my phone, so I could get prepared at a moment's notice and face whomever it happened to be.

The clock in my bronco flashed nine-thirty. With a hand on my gun, I carefully got out of my rig, listening to the area around me and expecting anything to jump out. Nothing, fortunately, happened. The hair on the back of my neck didn't prickle nor did my stomach clench. With a deep breath, I knelt down on the porch stoop. Taking the witch's spell out of the bag, I set the small purple glowing glass orb on the left side of the porch.

"Protect me and mine," I said quietly.

A neon green outline of a shield appeared on my left wrist on the inside, close to my palm. It burned bright green before fading. The spell billowed purple smoke from the orb. The shimmering glass orb blossomed into the sky, floating on an invisible air stream above me. The orb burst in a glittering purple mist and covered the house. It dissipated into nothing. I scowled.

Well, hopefully this works. Good thing I got a backup. Shrugging, I went inside my quaint little home. Luell greeted me with angry mews. Navigating in the darkness, I strode past her and set the security system down on the countertop and fed the cat. Luell purred while she ate.

"I was wondering when you would get back."

Startled, I drew my pistol and spun on my heel, finger resting beside the trigger. His face was shadowed by the darkness and the light of the moon streaming through the window. The man came forward. I pulled the hammer back. The man raised his hands.

"It's me, Evander," he said, flicking on the light.

I released the breath I was holding. "You need to quit that."

Grumbling under my breath, I reached into the junk drawer and pulled out a white wooden square that fit into the palm of my hand. I ran it over his body while Evander glowered at me. I grinned inside, keeping my face passive. I was gifted this magical piece of goodness from my Uncle Syrus.

"What are you doing?" His deep voice grumbled.

"Releasing any illusion spell you might have on you."

Evander's smirk reached his green eyes. "Don't trust me?"

Part of me *did* trust him. He saved me from those men. He killed them for me and disposed of the bodies. He was always secretly watching out for me. Yet, he *was* watching me. Now I protected my house and all that was mine with a spell and he had been in the house. The spell could very well assume he was mine and protect him instead of protecting me against him inside of it as mine...

Too late to undo it now. Shrugging, I took a step back, sliding the tool back into the drawer.

"You didn't answer my question," Evander said, taking a step toward me.

My eyes narrowed, "I *slightly* trust you."

"I know they're after you."

Evander leaned casually against the counter. His surfer mop of brown hair was mussed and hid his alluring green eyes. His thick dark brows scrunched, pinching his emerald eyes together. I couldn't decipher if he was concerned whether the Moon Walkers or the Vilkas were after me, or if he was trying to decide if I was attractive.

I crossed my arms. "Get out."

Evander scowled. "No."

I shook my head. I couldn't take him on. Evander being a *were* gave him superior strength and sensory abilities to my dismal human ones. There was no way to make him leave. It was a moot point and I didn't care to die yet.

Evander smirked casually at me like he knew what I wanted to do and reasoned against it. I blew out my lips, walking to the fridge. I pulled out chicken I had marinated along with a vegetable medley.

"Dinner?" I asked.

"Is this your way of asking me to stay?"

"This is my way of asking if you want to eat or starve. I know your kind likes proteins and fatty foods. You wanna eat or not since you're *not* leaving?"

Evander's sparkle left his eyes. "I don't want to put you out."

I shook my head, smirking at his teasing tone while setting the meal ingredients on the counter. Preheating the oven to 350 degrees, hoping when it beeped ready, it bothered the dog's ears. As I waited for the oven to preheat, my mind wandered to the key and all the information the dragon had given me. Setting the rice cooker up and adjusting the settings distracted me for a second, but my mind kept going over the details and I wondered if I should fill Evander in. I did slightly trust him and I needed to talk this through as I digested the information.

Evander sat at the table, watching me. His green eyes focused, taking in every movement I made. I'm sure any other person would have had an anxiety attack or be super uncomfortable under such intense scrutiny. I was used to it. Between Lazaro and my other previous relationships, mainly with werewolves although there was a werelion in there too, I was used to the feeling of being watched. It didn't bother me as long as I knew who was watching me. It was the unknown watchers that creeped me out. I shrugged mentally, *weres* were all the same – watchful; no matter if they were wolf or lion. Werelions were too reclusive for me though. Boyfriend number two had been a lion and while I like a good night in, I also like to eat out. He did not. Ever.

I put the chicken on a baking sheet and seasoned it to how I liked – rosemary, salt and pepper. The oven beeped. I stuck the chicken in and set the timer. Lazaro hated the way I made chicken, often telling me to copy his mother; only his mother refused to tell me her cooking secrets. That's ok though. If Lazaro wanted, he could marry his mother. Or a mother-like clone. I snorted and tried to cover it with a cough, trying to blame the pepper.

Glancing over my shoulder, Evander's green eyes were still on me. *He's not too terrible. He did save me, creepy how he arrived on time – like he knew – but I'm not dead or raped. I've been an ass to him. I don't mean to be so... hard? Is that a good word for me – hard?* I sighed; *I need to apologize.*

Taking a deep breath and humbling myself, I turned

around and leaned on the counter. Evander perked a brow, waiting.

"I'm sorry I come off as rough. I'm not. Or at least I don't mean to be. My heart is hurting and I don't want to talk about it."

"Sandalio?" He asked, crossing his arms over his barrel sized muscular chest.

I shrugged, walking through the kitchen to take a seat at the table across from him. "Doesn't matter." With a sigh, I closed my eyes. "Doesn't matter anymore. I got burned and I won't let myself get scorched again," I opened my eyes, staring right into his brilliant green. "I can't take it. Love shouldn't be so hurtful."

Evander nodded, remaining quiet. I was thankful he let the topic drop. I didn't want to talk about Lazaro. I didn't want to bring up the memories I spent hours, and days repressing. But now, it bubbled to the surface and tears desired to form on my lashes. Mechanically, I rose from my chair. Cleaning products were under the kitchen sink and I figured cleaning the kitchen while I waited was a good time to process the last few days.

Glancing behind me, Evander swept and mopped the living room; turning on the tv to play something in the background. I had no idea why he was cleaning. It was a bit weird to me. No one else ever pitched in with my chores, even Adiva, but I wasn't about to open my mouth and complain.

In between cleaning the floor and emptying the dish drainer, the rice cooker popped, announcing it was done. I started sautéing veggies while wiping counters and cabinets. The oven beeped with the chicken. I got our meals dished, beers tucked under my arm, and brought it out to Evander in the living room. We ate in silence watching a movie.

I tilted my head to the side. "What movie is this?"

Evander grinned. *"Gangs of New OKimma."*

I rolled my eyes.

He grunted in response and stood, grabbing my empty plate and fork, taking them to the kitchen with his own dirty dishes. He stood in the doorframe, watching me as I leaned back against the loveseat, curled up with my beer resting on my thigh.

"Something wrong?" I asked, glancing at him.

Evander shook his head. "Why did he leave you?"

I turned back to the show. "Thought we were going to let this drop?"

He shook his head and shrugged, motions I caught from the corner of my eye. "You would like me to, but I won't."

I swallowed the lump in my throat. Werewolves being the constantly inquisitive assholes they were, wouldn't stop until they had the entire truth. They would sniff it out until satisfied; so, hiding a piece of information was pointless, like bringing a rubber duck to a gunfight.

I stood, squaring my body to his to show respect. My fingers clasped the neck of the beer bottle in my right hand, my knuckles white. "We were together for a couple years. He cheated on me with an alpha female of a different wolf pack. And now they're married. Lazaro and I were engaged, before the alpha tramp, he said he would marry me and just had to convince his dad. I believed he was working on his dad too. Until his dad emailed me about Lazaro and his lady... I loved him, but now... I think I loved the idea of being with someone and receiving a modicum of affection in return... Anything... so I wasn't alone," I wiped my eyes with the back of my left hand. I drew in a deep breath, letting it out slowly. "Your turn."

Evander went to the fridge, grabbing another beer; cracking it open and chugging it down before turning to meet my expectant gaze. The kitchen was darkened now that dinner was over, leaving only moonlight and the light on the fridge's ice maker. "I was married before. She left me saying the harshness of my job was creating a rift in our marriage. Truth was, I don't think she loved me anymore and was looking for an out."

I stood in the door frame between the kitchen and the living room. "I'm sorry," I said, softening.

"I get where you're coming from. Don't let what happened make you bitter. I had to learn it."

"How old are you?"

"Thirty."

"That is a lot to deal with for thirty."

Evander grinned, taking a sip. "You're uptight and para-noid for being twenty-four."

"Wouldn't you be, if you were in my shoes?"

He lifted his bottle, "Touché."

The silence between us felt awkward. I finished my beer, setting the bottle on the counter. Going back to the loveseat, I plopped down with a sigh and twiddled my thumbs, thinking of something to say. Instead, I stared at

Evander. His green eyes, a dark emerald, glistened in the tv light. From what I could see by the tv glow, he had a scar running from his left ear down along his jawline and curled up by his lip. It was a faint scar, hardly noticeable from his hair and the stubble on his jaw. At the right angle, it was visible and added, in my opinion, to his alluring ruggedness. His v-neck black shirt was snug against his bulging muscular arms and chest, traipsing down to an athletic stomach. I bit my upper lip, pinching my legs together.

Evander smirked. "Like what you see?"

My face heated so hot I thought I was sweating. "I believe you can smell how much." I swallowed.

He turned, facing me; he leaned in close. His handsome face, a few inches from mine. The stubble lining his jaw added to his attractiveness. His lips pulled back in a genuine smile. The smile was fleeting as his eyes grew distant and he backed off.

"I can't... I want to. I do... But no..." He got off the loveseat, striding to the front door with barely a glance back as he threw over his shoulder. "Thanks for dinner."

I swallowed, watching him leave. The torrent of emotions inside battled worse than the war years ago between the dragons and the werewolves. I hurt. His answer stung. I shrugged it off, reminding myself I had worse rejections - and super recently.

I watched through my big picture window as he left. His eyes caught mine. My heart leapt hoping he would turn around. He didn't. I turned, facing the tv. The swirling green of his eyes bore into my brain. I tried to process his final look. Evander was torn like me, if I had to guess. For me, there was attraction yet caution and it seemed to me, Evander struggled with it too.

The door shut quietly behind Evander. I stared at it for a long moment before getting off the couch. Turning the tv off, my body felt like an icicle – numbed.

Luell mewed, twirling around my legs.

My phone buzzed with a text.

Uncle Sy: See you tomorrow, kiddo!

I grinned, the numbness instantly disappearing.

Me: I can't wait! Can you bring your ladder too please?

Uncle Sy: Sure thing!

Me: What time will you be here? Planning so I can make a fresh pot of coffee.

Uncle Sy: 10:30 and make scones. Gotta make sure your oven works. Ladder for?

I snorted, a wide smile on my face.

Me: What flavor? Ladder to install security cameras.

Uncle Sy: I don't care. Gotcha. Have a good night. Love ya kiddo.

Me: Haha! Thank you. I love you too. See you tomorrow.

I went to the kitchen and opened the paper bag for the security system. With Evander out of my house, I could finally set it up, since the witches spell protected him too. My eyes narrowed and rolled at myself. Shaking off my mistake, I put the door alarms on first, then the windows. The cameras would have to wait until tomorrow when I had sufficient light and my Uncle's help. I installed the security app on my phone, syncing it with the house. I hit the armed button with a smile.

No werewolf would sneak in on me tonight. If an intruder came, a shield on my left wrist would glow from the witch's spell and my phone would ring with a horrible country song, alerting me so I have an opportunity to defend myself.

I sighed. I only wanted to feel safe. A home was supposed to feel safe. Since being here, I felt more on edge than ever. I loved this house and I wasn't getting out of it. With at least window and door alarms on, I hoped I could sleep like a baby. I chuckled to myself, maybe a rock.

Plodding to the bathroom, I brushed my teeth and braided my hair. My thoughts turned to the most recent rejections: Lazaro and Evander. I stared at myself in the mirror as I prepared myself for bed, wondering what about my appearance was so unappealing. My face was oval shaped; I'd always considered my freckles kind of cute - just a smattering to enhance my eyes and pert nose. My hair was light blonde like the yellowstone hyacinthe flower, making my chestnut brown eyes glimmer.

I pouted. *I don't think I'm ugly.* I glanced at the front door, scowling further. *But he does. And so, did Lazaro.* I unhooked my bra, and slid it out from under my shirt. I stayed in my jeans, preferring to sleep in them since I'd left the key in my pocket.

Yawning, I went into my cozy bedroom. Luell meowed, jumping on the bed. I turned down the sheets. The clock on my nightstand chimed one in the morning. Installing those alarms took longer than I thought since Evander left at eleven.

Booming shook the walls of my cottage home. The

chaos of the raging noise made my skin crawl. I checked my wrist to see no glowing light and no country song blared. Shit, had everything I just done, failed? Luell hissed and hid underneath the loose covers hanging down one side of the bed.

I dashed to my bedside table, getting a 9mm handgun from a hidden compartment inside. I loaded the gun with a fresh mag and stuck another mag of silver bullets in my pocket.

My heart pounded in my chest, and I swallowed tasting the bile on my tongue. I swallowed, stepping out of the room and wondering what I would find.

CHAPTER SEVEN

ZURI

I tiptoed to the window and glanced outside my slightly open bedroom curtains into darkness. I snatched my bra off the top of my dresser, scrambling to put it on. The racer-back workout bra would keep the girls from bouncing in my face if I had to run. I strapped the 9mm to my side.

"Open the door!" a woman screamed.

That scream. That voice sounded familiar. I tilted my head, thinking, trying to pinpoint why it sounded so familiar, but couldn't place it. I tip-toed to the front door. The security alarm finally blared. However, the shield on my wrist did not appear.

"Open the DOOR!" she screamed, leaning against the door and beating her fists.

I clicked back the hammer on the gun, and had the barrel resting over my left forearm. I peeked through the living room window at the woman. She looked old and bedraggled. Finger resting above the trigger, I cautiously opened the door. A woman with a rat's nest of brown hair and a face covered in pock marks fell forward on my entryway floor. The lady sighed heavily, laying where she was. I stepped in front of her, blocking her further entry into my home. She slithered around me, sliding up against the wall on her belly.

What a weird ass lady... And the witch's spell was a waste, I thought irritated. The shield on my left wrist didn't glow. Not even a slight tingle or faint shimmer indicated this intruder. My brows pinched together wondering how this even happened.

The lady moved like she was swimming on my hardwood floors. I perked a brow. *Is she high as a kite on Dragon Snot?* It was the only drug in OKimma I could think of that made a person hallucinate.

"Who are you?" I asked not trying to hide the annoyance from my voice.

The woman didn't answer. She continued swim-crawling like a demented worm on her stomach all the way into the kitchen. I closed the front door, following her with a pissed and perturbed expression while keeping my pistol on her.

"Can I help you?" I demanded. "Answer me quickly or I *will* shoot you in the head."

The woman glanced around quickly, whipping spittle and hair from her face. She flopped on her back, rising at her waist. It was creepy like an old horror movie.

She grinned, revealing missing teeth. "Zuri?"

Scowling, I raised my pistol level with her face. "As I said before, I will shoot you in the head. Now, *how can I help you?*" I pulled the hammer back to emphasize my point.

The woman appeared more lucid now, her eyes not wild and no stupid grin on her face. She held out her hand, revealing a hair tie. Rising to her feet, she took a seat at the kitchen table, one leg daintily perked over the other. She wrapped her hair up in a messy ponytail and smiled at me again. This smile, a bit less creepy.

"It's me, Lyvia."

My body chilled. "Mom?"

"The one and only," she winked at me.

My teeth clenched together as I ground out. "What do you want?"

She smiled sweetly. "Can't a mother come visit her daughter?"

I growled. "You abandoned me for twenty-four years. You don't get to waltz back like nothing happened."

"You forgot to begin the sentence with – 'I'm sorry, but'."

I snorted derisively. "I didn't *forget*. Get out!"

She patted her thighs, sighing dramatically, but didn't move from her seat. "I see. Well, how is life?"

I pulled the trigger, aiming at the space between her feet. The bullet went through the wood floor. Lyvia glared at me.

"Warning shot... I will not give you money, so get out."

Lyvia's face contorted to a moue. "How considerate. You believe I am a druggie? A mental mess?" she sighed rolling her eyes as if this all greatly pained her. "Whatever it is Espe and Syrus told you?"

She looked so smug that I felt unnerved. I grew up hearing the stories my uncle and aunt told about her being in and out of mental wards or she was a druggie my entire childhood. That explanation made sense as to why she couldn't, or I guess wouldn't, raise me. However, I'd been an adult for six years and she never came around. Or maybe my uncle never told her where I was to protect me?

Scowling, I backed up further against the counter to put some distance in between us. There was no way I would turn my back to her. Not even for a second. I lowered my pistol and set the hammer back gently. I slid the gun into the holster, but my right hand remained near the holster. Like hell I would click the safety on.

"Why are you here?" I pressed. "The *real* reason."

"I came for the key," Lyvia said sweetly like a kitten.

I scowled. "Don't have it."

"You don't understand what the item means."

Lyvia got out of her chair. My hand went straight to the side arm. She sat back down, diamond-like blue eyes narrowed at me. Luell sat in the doorway and growled with her hackles rising along her back. I kept my eyes on Lyvia but smirked. *I love this cat.*

Lyvia's hand glowed silver, strains of magic crawling over her entire body as she fixed her appearance. I scowled, watching her. No wand was in her hand like a witch would use and there was no bauble containing a spell. Make up adorned her face. Her brown hair now neatly coiffed back at the nape of her neck. A beautiful dark navy-blue velvet dress hugged her frame. Of all the things I expected, Lyvia having magic was not one of them.

I refrained from dropping my jaw, shocked, and instead opted for a leery scowl. This entire event made me feel better I got a DNA test done.

"I need the key, Zuri, you don't understand," she pleaded.

"Nope," I replied, with a quick shake of my head. "I don't what the fuck all that crap was prior to you opting to change your appearance but my answer is the same. Fuck nope."

Lyvia stuck out her lower lip. "How dare you treat me this way! I'm your mother!"

I shrugged. "Not my problem. Get out!"

Lyvia rolled her eyes, sighing dramatically as she tilted her head. "You don't understand what this all means."

"I don't have what you want, so let's get that straight. Why you should be here is to get to know me, your daughter." I cried angrily. I was too furious to let tears fall. Lyvia stared at me and for the first time I realized how much I looked like her. She was a beautiful woman. Lines like cracked pavement creased the sides of her eyes. Her hair was a light shade of brown. Her eyes though, were a bright summer blue, so I must've gotten my brown eyes from my dad.

I bit my lower lip. "I jumped from house to house, foster care to distant relatives, never wanted, never loved, merely tolerated because I have your blood! What I want to know is why you didn't want me. Then you can get out!"

Lyvia softened, her bright azure eyes glistening. "I've always wanted you. It was never safe for me to be around you, which is why I came here in disguise as I did. I had to leave you, to keep you safe."

"Safe from what?"

Her face morphed to a blank stare. I perked a confused brow, as she looked out the window, rising swiftly to her feet. My hand went to my side arm, drawing my pistol. She glanced at me, heading to the back door, she deftly unlocked. "Your father," she said, altering her appearance as before and leaving just as quickly as she came.

I looked outside, trying to catch a glimpse of what Lyvia might have seen. I saw nothing. The shield on my left wrist glowed though. Luell still hissed from her perched spot in the entryway to the kitchen, staring at the back door. Gun drawn, I went over and locked it.

"At least whatever bullshit followed her around waited that long to get to me," I grumbled starting the coffee pot.

The clock on the wall flashed two in the morning. There was no way I was sleeping now. Running a hand over my face, I yawned. This was not what I wanted to deal with this evening, or any evening. I wanted a simple life, waking up when my body felt like it, drinking coffee outside under the covered porch, listening to nature - crickets, frogs, actually enjoying myself.

Luell mewled, jumping on the arm of the loveseat and watched the front door. I opened the front door with a jerk, gun ready, glowering as I stepped outside. A breeze through the firs whispered in my ears, making the hairs on my arm prickle. My hair remained in the braid, tickling the back of my neck. I walked around to the back door, wondering where Lyvia slinked off to. No trace of her footsteps could be found.

My face hardened on its own. I trudged back inside, going straight to the kitchen for coffee and decided against it. I went back out in the living room, trying to rest and push my weird ass mother's visit from my head. I dozed on the couch, staring at the tv replaying reruns of kid's movies. It was mindless and easy.

The alarm in my room blared at seven in the morning and I jumped up, heading to the kitchen to work. All I had to do so far were voicemail phone reviews of a patient's care and wait to hear back from the nurse with the insurance to see if the patient could continue care. With only having to do this today, the work was light. The new work I was promised trickled in slowly which irritated me, but it got done.

I stopped for a break around ten to make raspberry scones for my uncle. Between work, making scones, and popping the treats in and out of the oven, time ticked by quickly. I quirked a brow at the clock when it read ten thirty and Syrus had not arrived. I ignored it, assuming he'd taken a wrong turn or was stopping for another coffee. Syrus loved coffee. He only drank three pots a day. I laughed to myself, *pretty sure his blood is coffee.*

I looked at my computer and the work I knew I could do, but decided against it. I was caught up and I knew my uncle would be walking through the door any minute now. So, I tidied the house a little more and started unpacking the second bedroom with all my office supplies. My left wrist began to glow. I scowled. *It does work... Then how did my mother get in?* My brow pulled down low over my eyes as I contemplated it. *Could the 'me and mine' be interpreted as my blood? If so, then I need another spell to exclude her.* I heard the faint rumbling of a car engine turn off and two doors slam shut. Looking at my phone it glowed an hour late.

I closed my eyes and breathed out a sigh of relief, wondering what happened, but knew Syrus would tell me soon as he stepped through the door. I walked stealthily to the front door. I heard two men's voices through the thick oak door.

"Thanks for helping me," Syrus said to someone.

"Pleasure is mine," another male responded.

I groaned. "Evander," opening the door with a scowl.

"Hey kiddo!" Syrus said chipperly. "Hope that glower isn't for me."

I shook my head. "Definitely not," I replied, my eyes locking with Evander's.

Evander smiled at me, extending his hand to Syrus and shaking it. "Pleasure to meet you, Syrus."

Syrus shook his hand warmly. "Thanks for the help. You know Zuri is..."

Realizing where my uncle was headed, I hurriedly changed the subject. "Help? Help with what?"

Evander smirked.

Syrus came inside the doorway. "Engine trouble. Alternator gave out. Evander, I could use your help installing some cameras," Syrus winked at me.

I sighed. Moving out of the way. There would be no dissuading my uncle. I learned as a kid, the more I protested, the more he dug in and made it worse. "Evander, would you like to stay for coffee and scones?"

He brightened, a teasing light twinkling in his eyes as he flashed me a genuine debonair smile. "I would love to."

I opened the door wider. The green shield on my left wrist disappeared into my skin. Luell mewled from the arm of the loveseat, hopping down and sauntered over to Evander. Syrus strode in last, ducking as per usual as he came inside the house. He was a large man, three inches shy of seven feet tall and pushing four hundred pounds. The man was a tank with nothing paranormal about him.

Syrus snooped around with a smile, commenting about things he liked about my home. I pushed the start button on the coffee pot, the steaming crackle of the machine indicating it was beginning to brew. Evander took a seat on the arm of my loveseat, grinning broadly at me. The mischievousness in his emerald eyes made me snort.

"Lyvia came to see me early this morning," I said as Syrus came out of the bathroom.

The big man's knuckles cracked. The happiness in his face disappeared leaving a darkened 'hell hath no fury' gleam in his eyes. I'd seen the look growing up whenever my mother tried to come around. Syrus's military instinct and training kicked into high gear starting when I was 10, and now, I can sweep my house like a champ. Hard to see a man as large as my uncle become an electrician after the military. I'm not sure how he fit into smaller spaces he had to get into for work.

"And?" he growled, the deep rumble in his voice sending a chill down my spine.

"She showed up, looking for something, then left stating she is protecting me from my father."

His face creased so deeply I could hardly see his eyes. "She showed up at our place yesterday looking for Espe," he stormed into the kitchen. His foot falls, heavy like an ogre, shook the picture frames on my wall. "Where are those security cameras you needed installed?"

"Dining table."

Evander came up on my left. My brows creased like it always seemed to do when he was around. He was my stalker. Also, my savior. I didn't know in which category he belonged. It bothered me that I couldn't figure him out. Since Lazaro, I had been dissecting my previous boyfriends, all the disagreements and more. I was as much to blame at pushing people away as they were for cheating on me.

Sighing, I took a camera, heading outside to the right of the house. Evander grabbed the ladder for me and followed. I ignored him as I told myself I would not push the next person away. My heart sank a little as I heard the lie in that thought. I would try to, but inevitably my fear of people leaving or using me would have me hold them at a distance. I knew from experience when I did try, people didn't stick around. Hard to make a relationship last when I could count on people always leaving.

Evander set up the ladder against the house, holding it while I climbed up and put the camera at the spot I wanted. Syrus waved me off, going up with his drill to install the hard wiring and turn it on.

Much to my great embarrassment, Uncle Syrus began

rattling off all the mischievous and humorous things I had done as a child. Evander and Syrus laughed while I turned beet red as my uncle relayed a story of a time where I had tried to reach something in the bathroom, slipped and ended up hanging by the back of my shirt on the towel holder over the door.

Syrus smiled at me, his eyes shining with mirth and love. I glanced at Evander, watching him smirk and the shimmer in his eyes grow slightly warm. It was a nice change from his usual hard or mischievous looks.

"How old were you when that happened, Zuri?" Uncle Syrus asked.

"Eleven," I replied.

It was one of the few times in my life where I got to stay with them for a while before something happened to pull me away from my aunt and uncle. I never knew what and they never told me; only reiterating that I would be back soon. After I left their house at eleven and was put back into a care home, I wasn't with them again until fifteen when I got to tell the courts where I wanted to be.

"What were you trying to reach again?" Syrus prodded, chuckling intermittently.

"The cubbies behind the door where Aunt Espe hid the fudge cookies."

Evander and my uncle chortled, continuing to work while Syrus continued with more stories of my food related casualties - hand stuck in jars, caught trying to open a bag of chips, or my uncle asking me if I was thirsty then promptly squirting me with the hose while asking if my thirst was better. I smiled at the fond, and more than often comical, memories. Living with my aunt and uncle were the best years of my life.

We repeated the process around the house - laughing at fond memories while hard-wiring cameras. We finished in around two hours and were left with three cameras to spare. I handed them to Evander.

"What?"

"You know this land better than me, put them up at weak points."

Evander's face tensed; lips pursed. "You're trusting me?"

I nodded, firmly stating, "Yes, I am."

Syrus raised his brows and whistled low. "That's huge coming from her."

Evander's face went blank, nearly unreadable though I wasn't entirely sure why. I figured it was just him since our first meetings and those thereafter were interesting to say the least. He took the cameras and the drill, going off into the property where I eventually lost sight of him due to the overgrown bramble. Syrus came up beside me, clapping me on the shoulder so hard I was pitched forward.

"He is a good guy," Syrus commented. "I like him more than Lazaro."

I blew my lips. "I should have listened to you about Lazaro."

Syrus grinned. "Why'd you listen to this old man? Not like I got 20 years on you or anything," He winked at me. "'Sides, you needed to discover for yourself what he was like. That's what I love about you. You don't let opinions of others cloud your own judgment."

I grinned. Hopefully my opinion of Evander was right,

whenever I came to a true conclusive decision. Right now, all I really thought of him was brave and kind for saving me, but he was also a grump, hard faced, and to the point. There was also an attraction there on my side. I folded my arms over my chest and popped one balled fist under my chin, thinking as I watched the wooded tree line for Evander. Whatever I finally decided, I needed to be firm about it. My heart couldn't afford another slip-up like Lazaro.

CHAPTER EIGHT

ZURI

Syrus left around eight at night after we had dinner at Lonesome Lenny's up the road from my house. Bar food was my favorite. It came in decent portions and was typically cheaper than an actual meal. Evander stayed behind for a bit, chatting lightly with me. I wasn't sure if the alcohol loosened his tongue, but the amiability in the general small talk we had was nice.

Evander walked me to my Bronco, opened the door for me so I could climb inside. He shut the door, tapped the side of it twice and he too left with his head down and hands in his pockets. I drove home, my mind thinking about why the spell on my wrist glowed at various times when people showed up. I couldn't figure it out and decided to go see the *Black Ash* witches coven again.

The gate was open like I'd left it. The symbol on my left wrist was dormant. Not even my phone alerted me while I was out. My body felt relaxed now that I was adequately protected. Uncle Syrus even bought me a new 9mm handgun, as he always does when he comes and visits, and I stashed the weapon in the house, in the kitchen.

I got out of my Bronco, and the hairs on my arm prickled. The front porch light flickered. I glanced down the length of the house. My cameras were missing. Silently, I pulled my .357 from the middle console. The icy cold grip soothing my sweating hands.

Taking a deep breath, I slowly tip-toed to the front door. The latch was busted in; wood was missing and the handle was crooked. I swallowed, darting to the far side of the door so no one could see me. I hesitated, breathed in deep then pivoted and kicked the already open-door in. Whoever was here or might be here, heard my diesel converted rig.

Biting the inside of my lip, I skulked down, taking slow, sure strides around the side of the house to my bedroom feeling foolish creeping like a thief in my own house. Pounding of heavy, booted strides on the other side of the wall made my blood turn cold. Pausing, I listened. More booted feet wandered farther back inside the house. Deep voices belonging to males ransacking my home filtered through the wall and I cringed as I heard crashes and imagined my tv and computer breaking on the floor. It bothered me. I didn't have materialistic things like knick knacks or anything special as I didn't care. But the items I did have, I put a lot of thought into having.

Rising up on my toes, I carefully peeked in the window. The bedroom light was off. Flashlights zooming in different directions made it difficult to focus on what was happening. Putting my hands on the glass, I slid the window open an inch.

"She's here," one man said. "I heard her rig," he paused. "I can also smell her."

"Where is she then if she's here?" A deeper voiced, agitated male asked.

"I don't know," the first one said. "But she's dangerous. She killed the last two wolves to come in here."

"Don't be stupid, Lutz," the deep voiced male spat. "She's a *human* woman"

"Mitch," a third male called, "take a look at this box."

I dared to take another peek through the window. The men found my Gramma Kaethe's box. The key that had been hidden there for years, the key they were looking for, was tucked safely into my bra, inside the removable pad part.

Dropping down to a squat, I went around to the back door. I slinked, darting toward boulders to conceal me until I was at the tree line, where I finally stood and sprinted inside their leafy safety. The wind rustled through the treetops, delicately kissing at my skin. I climbed the nearest tree, getting about twenty feet up when the intruders emerged from the house.

Three of them spoke in hushed tones, leaving one of the men behind. Scowling, I watched as two men went to the road, getting picked up by a tan SUV. The third man hung back, whipping out a long pipe he stuffed with tobacco. In the moonlight, the wisps of smoke rose into the air as the man sauntered casually to my Bronco.

My mind reeled with ways to get down and kill the

man, but my options were limited. Only the purest of pure silver could kill a wolf; not even a stab to the heart would do the trick. It had to be silver and I didn't have it. Anything else I tried, without silver, would just piss him off and do more harm to me.

Branches broke behind me. My neck cracked as I turned around sharply to the noise. I half expected Evander to be below me in the forest. He wasn't. Another man, dressed in all black, strode out of the forest. His suit was interesting like he was a maestro in an orchestra with the tuxedo tails hanging down to mid-thigh. His dark brown hair, peppered with gray, slicked back against his head. Hands in his pockets, he approached the werewolf.

The house invader startled, whipping around quickly and drew his pistol. Tobacco-man fired off three shots at tuxedo-guy. I wondered why they didn't 'wolf-out' on each other or if there was some sort of pack protocol prohibiting them from doing so. Tuxedo-guy laughed at the failed shots fired at his person as they appeared to not have penetrated. Tobacco-man, near the Bronco, morphed into a wolf. His white coat glistened in the moonlight; hairs bristled along his back. His white fangs pulled back snarling as he growled ominously at the man. I blanched, heart pounding as I waited in tense silence for the outcome.

Tuxedo-guy did the same, only he tripled in size. His gray coat mottled with flecks of white and black. He shook out his coat like it pained him to be so large. Tuxedo-guy stalked the lesser wolf. Tobacco-man growled, lunging at the larger wolf, only to have tuxedo-guy pin him against my Bronco like he was swatting a fly. The gray wolf was so large, he came up to the middle of the Bronco door.

If my eyes could bulge larger than they already were, I would turn into an owl. "Holy shit," I whispered, immediately putting a hand over my mouth and praying they didn't hear me.

The lesser wolf cowered, whimpering. Tuxedo-guy howled, and snapped his jaws, releasing the lesser wolf. Tobacco-man scrambled to his paws, scampering out of the gate. The gray wolf watched the wolf run away and howled for his easy victory.

I swallowed. Getting bit by that giant wolf would suck. *I would run away too*, I lipped.

Tuxedo-wolf laughed maniacally, changing back into his human self. I couldn't make out his hair or eye color, but if I had to guess, it was ebony black to match the darkness his presence made me feel. He had this strong prominent jaw line that stuck out a bit and elongated his face, reminding me of a box. The man reached under the Bronco, ripping the front axle off like it was nothing but a flower. My jaw dropped open. He walked around to the driver's side, ripping the door off its hinges as he popped the hood. Lifting it open, he ripped out the battery, alternator and other parts I hadn't a clue about, tossing them all on the ground. I cried silently. I loved that rig. I wiped my eyes, and willed myself not to sniff. It would be a long walk to the nearest town – if I ever got there.

I wiped my eyes again, this time allowing myself a quiet sniff. *What in the actual fuck is going on?! Why these wolf packs? Why any of this over a damn key that has been lost and a God who hasn't been seen in years?*

He slammed the hood of the Bronco down. Pausing, he glanced at the house and laughed. Tuxedo-man strode out the front gate. I waited in the tree for an additional fifteen minutes before I felt safe enough to descend. Crickets began chirping. The nighttime screeching of bats made my skin prickle but it was also soothing.

Good Gods I'm gonna die. I'm gonna be on the news as the local girl who died in a ditch and the coffee shop is gonna release a statement saying: something was wrong as she never came for her spiced chai tea latte.

I clambered down, leaning my back against the tree. Part of me wanted to go home, to go inside, and sleep like nothing was wrong. But it was. Everything was wrong. I was being hunted for a key. If this key could open the underworld, then I needed to protect it. And I couldn't do it here. All my security measures had failed me - again.

With a deep breath, I went to my house. I shoved the front door open since using the handle was pointless.

"Luell?" I called.

Her soft mewling didn't answer back.

My throat constricted. "Luell?"

I went to my bedroom where she was known to hide as well besides the bathroom. I checked under my bed. Luell wasn't there. My eyes teared. I tore apart my room, scouring for her. I checked the bathroom, the spare room and the living room, frantically searching for Luell in all her hiding places. I couldn't find her.

"Luell," I cried, tears running down my cheeks.

My heart thundered, wondering where my sweet kitty was. Icy tickles crept up and down my arms. My gut twisted, I knew something was wrong. I had to find her.

"Luell!"

Walking into the kitchen I found her. A small pool of blood exiting her body from the head. Tears filled my eyes. My knees crashed to the hardwood floor. Bending down, I shakily picked her up and cradled her against me.

Burying my face in her fur, tears like a waterfall wetted her too stiff neck. "Oh Luell," I cried.

I sat in the kitchen holding her. I didn't want to take her outside and bury her. Not yet. I hadn't had enough time with her. I hadn't been here to protect her like I should have been. Luell was the only companion I had since I was 18. And now. Now she is gone.

I went to the loveseat, pulling off her favorite blanket. Gently, I wrapped her in it, carrying her outside. I didn't have a shovel. I didn't even have a small gardening spade. On my hands and knees, I dug in the soft dirt as tears tracked down my face. I could only pray she didn't suffer long.

My hands ached, but I continued to dig deep enough to bury her. It was a shallow grave, but the best I could do with not having anything but my hands.

"This is why I left you," Lyvia's voice said from behind me. "I had to protect you."

My eyes blearing, I turned around. My mother's softened gaze stared at the hole I put Luell in. She knelt beside me.

"I'm sorry about your kitty," she offered.

My eyes narrowed in on her.

She rose up, dusting off the hem of her navy-blue dress. "Time for you to come with me."

I dusted off my hands, rising to stand toe-to-toe with her. I wasn't going with her. Whether I had men after me or not, I'd go to hell first before I went with her.

"You're going to have to trust someone at some point, Zuri," Lyvia's face hardened.

I crossed my arms. "I may have to trust at some point, but like hell it'll be you."

Lyvia stormed off to my house. "We leave in the morning."

I reached into my pocket, whipping out my phone. I considered calling Evander. He might come and help, but at the same time, I didn't want to involve him, especially when I was still unsure about him. Not to mention with him being a wolf and wolves were after me, it didn't sit well in my gut. Evander was a sexy heap of paranormal power I did not want to involve myself with - been there and done that. It also didn't sit right with me in involving him in my mess with whatever was happening.

I then thought about my best friend Adiva, but she would come and leave in fanfare as was her style and I needed to lay low. And even though I was close with Uncle Syrus, his wife made it clear I cannot come back.

My lips pursed, hands flexing. I wasn't certain about going with her but I didn't have much of a choice. I couldn't live on the dragon side of the city with wolves after me – I would get kicked out even if I begged for sanctuary. And me heading to the dragon side would put a sour taste in their mouths as they literally do not involve themselves with anything but their own dilemmas. I couldn't go to my uncle – Espe wouldn't allow it. I asked Uncle Syrus once about what to do in deep trouble and in his fantastic explanation replied - figure it out. I grumbled to myself.

I went inside. I couldn't stay here with different wolf packs after me, only two of which I identified. I grabbed my backpack out of the hall closet and walked to my room. It was a disaster. Clothes littered the floor. My dresser was ripped apart. I looked around and laughed, my morbid sense of humor surfacing. The invaders were decent enough to stack the drawers. My guns were in a pile on the bed - still loaded and untouched.

I packed them all into the backpack, dividing them into compartments. Lyvia watched me from the doorway, scowling as her lip slightly curled.

"Problem?" I growled.

"You have too many weapons. Two is more than plenty."

"Tools," I corrected. "It is only a weapon when used in anger with intent to inflict harm."

Lyvia blew her lips, shaking her head. "Syrus ruined you... You weren't supposed to be raised how you were," she paused, giving a disgusted snort. "You weren't supposed to be *this* way."

I dropped the last pack of bullets into the side pouch, spinning on my heel. "And how, *exactly*, was I supposed to be raised? How, exactly, *Mother*, was I supposed to be?"

"Not an angry, gun-toting, young woman!"

I laughed. "I'm not angry."

My mother grinned wickedly. "Then explain your tone."

"My tone is – not thrilled. I have men after me, and my cat is dead. Now, you show up and want an instant loving relationship. That doesn't just happen for me. You have to get to know me. You have to earn my respect, my love and my trust. And frankly, *you* have a lot of work to do before we get there."

Lyvia sighed, deflating. "You're right... I'm sorry."

"Thank you."

She went to the loveseat and turned on the tv, leaving me to pack what I wanted. I shoved in my jeans, under-wear, a sweatshirt, and t-shirts. Going to the kitchen I packed my laptop for work. Lyvia didn't bat an eyelash as I moved about the house. It felt empty now that Luell was gone. What made my house a home was gone and now it seemed like a shell of what it was supposed to be. And the constant intruders, my mother and Evander included, made it feel unsafe. This place definitely was no longer my home.

It irritated me too. I bought this place to fulfil a dream, to have something that was indefinitely mine. Maybe this was a mistake and I was safer in town with Ms. Thompson as my neighbor.

I went to the kitchen, pulling Evander's number out of the drawer and onto the counter. He would be back at some point. I left him a note along with my phone number as I plugged his number into my phone. I was ready to leave in the morning. What made this town, this area my home, was destroyed. It was time to leave, but not with Lyvia.

CHAPTER NINE

ZURI

Lyvia pleaded and begged with me for hours for me to come with her. Finally, I caved. She was right. At some point I would have to trust someone else to help me. The desire to get to know her clawed at me too. Never having a real mother made me curious to what an actual one would be like. The fact Lyvia promised I could leave at any point and go my own way made the decision to go with her a little better.

Lyvia drove her small silver sportscar down a long single lane paved road. She didn't tell me where we were going. I didn't ask. I would find out when we got there. And honestly, at this point, anywhere was better than my house.

The silence between us afforded me the chance to reflect and stare out the rolled down window. The fall air was warmer and brighter today than the last several. Beautiful waterfalls, fixed between large boulders and whispering pines, passed us by. Each time a waterfall came upon us, I took a picture. Even if I wasn't thrilled by life at the moment, I could still enjoy myself.

A large herd of elk crossed the road behind us. I turned around in my seat to take a photo. A bull elk stopped in the middle of crossing, his large brown eyes meeting my own. He pawed the ground, letting out a long bugle. My face split in a wide beam at the most amazing yet eerily haunting sound I ever witnessed.

I turned back around in my seat, focusing on the scenery. My phone had not sounded with a text or call from Evander since I left. I grimaced at myself. He wouldn't come around. He was only there for his house I happened to purchase and occupy. Yet, even though he confused me, part of me liked him. He was calm. He was direct, something I really liked in a man. I liked knowing where I stood, that way there was never any disappointment.

I got on my phone and clocked into work as Lyvia continued to drive down some back roads. I was able to do the majority of tasks from it. I sent a message to my boss detailing I would handle leftover work tomorrow bright and early. With work managed, and not nearly noon, I sunk into the comfortable leather seat to simply enjoy the rest of the ride.

The bright and sunny sky beating down on my head brought a grin to my face along with a light breeze tousling my hair. It wasn't overly hot or humid, nor too bright. It was perfect. My mother kept glancing over at me, smiling, occasionally biting her lip as she stared. I tried not to notice her nervousness.

Off to the left, a lumbering bear emerged from the woods and roared. I whipped out my phone, snapping a quick picture. Its dark honey colored fur moved in waves like the sea as it roared once more. I was in awe of the creature; so large and powerful. It started off after us at a lumbering pace, soon keeping up with the car. My heart leapt in my throat. Lyvia slowed down. I stared at her wide eyed as she grinned.

"What are you doing?" I demanded.

Lyvia smiled demurely. "It's someone I know. He is a werebear named Barend."

I sat down in my seat, my hand resting on my side arm. I wasn't going to take any chances - my mother's friend or not. I could only hope the six rounds in the handgun were enough to stop the bear should it come to that.

The thundering in my heart slowly mellowed out to a cautious and on edge beat. The bear approached the car. Lyvia stuck out her hand as the bear sniffed and licked it. I scrutinized the sign of affection. He immediately changed into a tall man with olive skin. His honey hair cut short against his scalp, but styled nicely like a wafted over pompadour. Silver eyes darted to the ground.

"My Queen," the man dipped his head.

I raised a brow, but said nothing.

"Barend," Lyvia dipped her head politely. "Unmask the fortress. Announce my daughter has come home. Oh, and tell Cara to make her famous shrimp things."

The scowl on my brow deepened. Barend dipped his head, backing away from the car. I looked ahead of us and saw nothing special. The road continued on for miles, way into the backcountry of Quivleren. My hand continued to stay near the side arm on my hip, resting on the cold steel I loved. Lyvia tried to get me to leave my 9mm and other guns at home earlier. After Syrus's training and all the bad luck recently, there was no way that was going to happen.

Barend took several paces back from the car. His right hand raised out to the open countryside. I tried to see if his lips moved and couldn't. As far as I could tell, this magic pooled out of hands. Silver wisps of magic poured from his hand out into the air, floating like steam. I pulled back the hammer on the pistol, ready to draw it from the holster.

Lyvia glared at me. "Don't you dare draw that weapon."

"Tool," I corrected.

Lyvia's pretty face scrunched further. I smiled, watching as the veil to protect whatever it was Lyvia had, dropped. My mouth fell open. Barend shifted soundlessly into a bear, slinking off to the edge of the woods.

"A castle?"

Lyvia grinned smugly, "Yes Daughter. I'm Queen of Kadia Castle in Quivleren. I go by my middle name Ariella which I passed on to you."

I laughed out loud, astounded by the absurdity of it all. Lyvia glowered at me and said nothing. My eyes narrowed as I took in the castle. The north and eastern sides of it backed up to a giant cliff, with a mountainous range in the backdrop. The cliff dropped straight off. There were no rocks gently cascading down the hillside. It was a complete drop off. Men of various heights walked the walls. The western side was shaded with trees while the southern side was open to the road.

The castle itself was large, dark stone gray with spires that reached into the heavens. Why anyone would want to live in one of those spires was beyond me. All those stairs would suck to walk up. Large shining silver gates opened in front of us. The gate in front of the castle was bright, polished brushed nickel metal, opening wide as we passed through and pulled up toward the double doors of the castle. The gate behind me, hissed closed.

"Got to keep your father out," Lyvia sighed. "I should have brought you here years ago."

"Why didn't you?"

Lyvia's delicate hands gripped the steering wheel until her knuckles went white and the wheel indented. "Your father still had access to these grounds at the time. For years I'd hoped to change him, thinking my love would turn his vengeful heart away from the mission he said he must complete. It didn't. And we divorced. However, he never forgave me for giving you up to keep you safe from him," she sighed as if it was a long distant memory, lessening her grip on the steering wheel. "It wasn't until ten years later after the divorce and losing you, I had this place spelled to keep him out. With me being Queen, divorces and litigation are a mess. And by the time everything was legally done, you grew up and heard I was mentally ill. If I tried to take you away, you would have fought. So, I watched you grow up with Syrus and Espe." She turned in her seat to face me, turning off the purring of the engine. "At least there is now. I would like to build a relationship with you. If you don't want that, I understand. I merely ask you to stay here where you are protected."

Something in my gut twisted and I couldn't place if it was from nerves or a warning. "So," I began, not truly knowing where I was headed. "Why didn't you come around during the process of your divorce? Why leave me?"

Lyvia's face softened. "It wasn't safe for you."

I refrained from rolling my eyes. In my mind, nothing would've kept me from my child if I had one. "So why now? You could have come around when I was eighteen."

Lyvia nodded. "I agree. I should have, but I didn't, not knowing if you wanted to see me yet or not."

"You could have tried."

"It's not so easy."

I nodded, not really buying the answer. I took quick glances out of my peripheral. "I'm leaving in a few days. I don't want anything of you or from you."

Lyvia gave a faint smirk that I might have missed if I'd blinked. It only confirmed to my gut that something was different. I tried to brush it off as maybe caution in getting to know my mother. And in listening to my body, I would definitely proceed with caution.

"Come, I will show you to your room," she said. "Keep in mind, I decorated it for a child."

I got out of the sportscar, taking my bag out of the backseat. I grabbed my one bag and my computer; thankful I had thought to bring it. I may not have a house anymore but I still needed to earn my keep and my computer ensured I could. I needed to get to work tomorrow and finish what I didn't get done. I hefted the pack over my shoulder and checked the gun on my hip. Lyvia frowned at me, but I shrugged her displeasure off. I would carry them and not leave myself unprotected. I also had more in my bag.

The large castle door opened by means of a servant with a soft groan like a child waking from slumber. I walked in hesitantly, hand on the grip of my 9mm. People bustled from place to place, bowing at the waist then rising with a warm smile for my mother while their curious scrunching eyes glimpsed sideways to me, wondering who I happened to be. Their warm regards for my mother irked me. This woman was practically a stranger to me yet they garnered her affections. I felt slighted in a way, so I pretended I didn't notice, instead focusing my attention to the castle around me.

Wrought iron chandeliers with traditional lit wax candles hung from the ceiling every twenty feet. Sparkling little crystals dangled from the chandeliers to help reflect light. Dark cherry floors with a matching staircase went up either side of this wide room leading up to double doors. The spindles on the balustrade were gorgeous with sharp angles and ridges.

Lyvia went up the stairs to the right. I followed, still a few paces behind. I kept my back to places that were solid. I didn't want anyone jumping out at me.

"Will you stop?!" Lyvia demanded without turning around. "You act like someone is here to kill you."

"Between the Moon Walkers, the Sandalio mob and perhaps even the Vilkas all trying to, and you showing up, I take *no* chances."

Lyvia stopped, turning to face me with an ashen face. "Moon Walkers?" Her blue colored eyes widened.

"Yes."

"You need to remain here, Zuri," my mother insisted.

My phone buzzed in my pocket. Ignoring it, I landed on the same step as Lyvia. "I'll be fine."

"Yes, because you're never leaving here."

I rolled my eyes. Lyvia's frown creased into motherly concern.

"I'll be fine, Mother. And I'm *not* staying here. I'm leaving in a few days whether you approve or not. You forfeited your right to care years ago, so while I appreciate this, it will take more than your five minutes of concern to convince me to stay."

Her eyes narrowed, lips pursing together. "Come," she said, straightening. "I hope you like your room."

There was a despondency in her voice which I contributed to making her feel guilty. I wouldn't balk though. She hurt me by leaving me and only coming back for the damn key.

I sighed, hefting the pack over my shoulder once more. I didn't know if I would be fine, but hiding behind a wall forever wasn't a part of my plan either. I needed to destroy this key.

A good night's sleep, and some food, and tomorrow I leave. This key needs to be destroyed at all costs. Then, perhaps, if my mother is serious, we can have that relationship she keeps mentioning, I decided.

She took me down a long hallway with bright open

windows on my right and rooms on my left. All the doors were pitch black, an interesting contrast to all the polished wood. Going through another set of double doors, she turned left and opened the door to the immediate right. I walked into a corner room. Little trinkets and stuffed animals were piled on a small child-like desk. The bed was twin size with bright pink and purple unicorns and star bedding.

I walked all the way in, looking around at it while my heart pinched. All this time she kept the room she made me, yet she never came back to get me. My emotions were like a tornado, each battling the other wanting to at least attempt a relationship and wanting to walk away.

"Like I said, it was meant for a child," Lyvia began at the doorway. "I'm sorry, but I need to protect you," Lyvia said hurriedly, slamming the door shut.

I was far enough in the room to not make it back before it slammed shut. My open palm beat against the door while the other hand tried the handle. "What the fuck!" I yelled. The silver mist of my mother's magic seeped in through the keyhole.

"Son of a bitch!" I cursed.

The door was locked and spelled shut. I walked over to the bed, tossing my pack on it. I strolled about my room, checking all the windows. None had locks to open and close but were one solid piece. Above the window were vents to allow in fresh air.

"Shit," I groaned.

This was not how I wanted to begin our relationship. As a kid, all I had wanted was for my mother to want me, to want to be around me. For the longest time, I thought there must have been something wrong with me for neither of my parents to want anything to do with me. As I got older I began to realize that some people were not meant to be parents and I was even more grateful to Uncle Syrus and Aunt Espe for taking me in. However, this relationship was going to end, the beginning certainly was rough and it only served to drive the divide further between us.

I whipped my backpack on the bed, and began filtering through it. I had two loaded guns and an extra loaded mag upon my person, but I had more in my backpack. Sitting on the cushy bed, I began loading every magazine I had with me with ammo. Whatever was to come next, I was ready.

My phone buzzed again with an all-caps message from Evander. I made an 'oops' face, forgetting my phone had previously rang.

Evander: WHERE THE HELL ARE YOU? PICK UP YOUR PHONE!

Me: I'm at my mother's castle... Kadia, near the Espowyes Mountains.

Evander: Get out of there now!

Me: Can't. I'm locked inside a spelled room.

Evander: I'm coming.

Me: You know where I am?

Evander: Yes. Don't ask me how. I will tell you when I see you.

My body deflated releasing the stress I hadn't realized I'd been holding there. I let out a large breath, a smile creasing my face. He was coming for me. And while not a romantic gesture, a part of me couldn't resist thinking about the sweetness of it.

Me: Thank you.

Evander: You owe me a date.

Me: Done. Just not somewhere with curry. I'm allergic.

Evander: Deal. Hang tight, I'm on my way.

I glanced around my room, searching for any kind of opening. There was nothing. Even the air ducts were too small for me to slide through. I whipped my 357 from the holster on my right side. I grinned. Taking aim at the biggest window in the room, I opened fire. I stopped at two shots not wanting to waste my ammo when nothing happened to the window. Spinning on my heel I wasted another two bullets on the door handle and another two on the wood of the door. Not even a splinter out of place.

I groaned and cursed, "Damn magic!"

I reloaded my pistol before reholstering it. As I walked around the room, I found no traces of any hidden doors or secret openings. I pressed my body against the wood, pushed my hands along all the wooden walls and doors. Nothing. My eyes roamed the ceiling. A small bubble, like the ceiling had a previous leak and had been patched but the patch failed, came from it. It was almost too small to miss had it not been for the angle and the shimmer on the ceiling looking like soap. Curious, I went to it. A small, silver, faint flash like from a smoke detector emitted faintly from the bubble.

I held up my hand and gave the damn thing my middle finger. A roguish smile creased my face and drew the pistol out of the holster. I fired a single shot at the camera, dropping from the ceiling. I smashed the heel of my boot against it, smiling at the plastic cracking reaching my ears.

Getting out my phone, I wriggled myself out of my shirt slightly, tucking my head and arms inside like I was a turtle. Since my room was bugged with surveillance and not knowing if it also had audio, there was no way of knowing if the camera picked up the messages between Evander and I.

Me: This room is rigged. I don't know if anyone saw our messages.

Evander: Don't worry about it. Be there soon.

Me: Thank you! <3

I popped back out of my shirt, taking a deep breath. "Welcome home!" I said sarcastically.

CHAPTER TEN

EVANDER

I couldn't seem to get her out of my mind. She was always there, lurking in the quiet recesses, surfacing whenever I had a spare moment. Her defiant nature appealed to me and the wolf inside. For a human, she was strong, dominant, something I did not think humans could possess, yet Zuri did so with ease.

I strode up the concrete steps toward my apartment on the west side of town. My single bedroom apartment was issued to me by the department I worked for. Opening the unlocked door, I stared at papers I had meticulously laid out, now scattered all along the floor. I grimaced at the open window I forgot to close. I didn't care to pick them up and reorganize them just yet. Tossing my keys on the counter, I took a beer from the fridge. The crack of the can and hoppy aroma coaxed a smile to my lips.

Chugging the beer down, I grabbed another. My eyes stared at the mess in my apartment. I needed a maid. I also needed to organize these papers so Zuri would never see them. She could never see what these were if I were to allow her to come around.

Scowling, I began cleaning up the piles I knew to be completed. I stuck them in neatly labeled folders, wrapping a large rubber band around them to send back to my commander at the department of paranormal justice.

My phone buzzed again. A smile played on my lips as I both secretly hoped, yet didn't, it was Zuri.

It was.

Zuri: This room is rigged. I don't know if anyone saw our messages.

Me: Don't mention it. Be there soon.

Zuri: Thank you! <3

My lips curved downward on their own. I forced myself to come up with a 'phase one' plan to get her out of Kadia Castle, but my damn head interrupted it with thought of her and the date. Why I asked her on a date was beyond me. I shouldn't entangle myself with a human. I wasn't hateful of them. My own experiences taught me to never date one; and not involve myself if it could be helped. Though, I would step in where it was needed.

But I was a sucker for pretty faces and distressing situations. I almost choked on a chuckle. That is how my former wife had snared me. Damn tires and cold weather. I'd been a goner the moment she'd batted her eyelashes at me and turned that pretty pout my way. Comparing Catronia to Zuri was unfair to Zuri. They were nothing alike. The only thing they had in common was the female gene and having a knack for distressing situations. Catronia was a cheating, lying bitch who tried to take me for all I was worth. Thank the gods I wised up before anything actually happened. But the whole experience made me leery.

So why couldn't I shake Zuri? My mind wandered to what I knew of her character and shook my head. Because she was different. She was loyal to a fault. Anyone with eyes or a nose could tell. Especially males. It was a trait most males desired in their females. Her beauty and fierceness were something I wished some female members of my pack had, along with her honesty. Not that I was in the market. But if more had qualities like hers we'd be better off as a race and maybe my marriage would have worked.

I came to a pile of papers about her, reading over the transcripts. The company she'd worked for was bought out by a larger company linked to the Moon Walkers. I was pretty sure Zuri had no clue about her new company. Especially since her working for them led them straight to her. How she found my family home, I believed, was merely coincidental as the damn dragons took it on and off the market as they pleased.

Zuri Ariella Luciani. I frowned, reading her name as the heading on the page with the picture copy of the driver's license I snapped. Her last name, *Barsotti,* in bold letters in the middle of the plastic rectangle stood out and niggled at my memory. My forehead scrunched further as I tried to figure out the difference in her last name for the sake of my mission. I dug through the additional stack of papers. All her other information matched yet her last names did not. Her last names never matched. And Luciani was the last name of the Moon Walker's leader.

Was she hiding something or was someone keeping something from her?

I leaned my head against the back of the couch, holding the papers in my hands. Much of her information made sense - where she worked, lived, went to high school and everything else I dug up. This name thing though was lost on me; there was absolutely no record of it changing, only that it suddenly had. I couldn't figure out why and that bothered me. I needed everything in a neat row. All the boxes checked and Zuri did not fit into any of my neat categories, boxes, or lists. I sighed again and rubbed my eyes with my forefinger and thumb. There was one person I could go to for a plethora of information though. He might know something not in all these papers. It was the same dragon Zuri went to. I cringed, my mind taking me back to the dragon I needed to see today. I could still smell the stench of burnt hair and fire. The origin of her last name needed to be answered - why did her last name change, what does it mean and does Zuri even know about it? Yet, I was terrified of the answer. If Zuri was able to decode the puzzle I longed to solve, if she was the missing piece, I wasn't sure I could refrain from killing her.

I stared at my phone. I should go get her; however, I had other issues needing to be attended to first. Starting with answers about Zuri and while she did need to get away from the evil witch of a queen and her seriously spooky castle, for the moment she was safe enough. I had to wrap up the report on her so a decision by my department could be made. The department of paranormal justice took cases very seriously. And it was my job to take them even more so as it pertained to the being in question, life or death. The report was expected this morning and I needed the final pieces to the puzzle. Even though Zuri was at the bitch of Kadia's Castle, she was ironically safe and locked inside until I could get to her. I doubted her mother would do more than irritate her at least for now.

"I need to know," I growled to myself.

I quickly rose to my feet. I restacked the papers regarding Zuri neatly, laying them inside my briefcase to mail later today. Grabbing my keys, I headed out to the one place that truly scared me. Not really the place itself, but the owner of said place. He had a reputation for hating wolves and had on more than one occasion sent one of us running with our tails tucked and fur singed and frankly he scared the piss out of me. But my need to know and put Zuri in one of my neat boxes surpassed the fear.

I mechanically drove to - Holdur's 'Mythical' Shoppe. And while I drove, every thought and encounter with Zuri replayed itself through my mind. I poured through what I knew of her and tried my hardest to shove her into one of my neat little boxes. I still couldn't. I tried to recall anything that would put Zuri in a bad light, show her weakness or disfavor. I couldn't think of anything, and that part irked me.

Holdur knew a lot more than any file inside a computer or top-secret organization ever would. He had more connections than the God Elohi himself. And it made him incredibly dangerous and unpredictable. Forget a grudge. If I said one thing that offended Holdur or sneezed wrong, I would be a mewling pup. Holdur would make life hell.

Which was why my organization used him as only an absolute last resort. He could bring the whole place down around my ears with just a whisper. Yet it was this same power I was hoping to use in order to get more info on Zuri. I sucked in a deep breath and prepared myself for the biggest suck-up session of my life.

My hands clenched the steering wheel, as I pulled up alongside the curb. The clock on my dashboard read two o'clock. I had a few hours to wrap up my report on Zuri and send it back to my department. Taking a deep breath, I let the engine idle for a few moments. I rested my head against the seat, making a plan on when to head to get Zuri. After Holdur, I had a few more errands to run in order to fit her into my little box. Satisfied with a mental list of where to go after Holdur, I turned the car off. The neon lights of Holdur's shop across the street glitched. Only half the sign was legible. I got out of the car, taking my briefcase and locked the door. Cars blared their horns as I jogged across the street.

Not wanting to hesitate, I went straight to the door. The bell to the shop jingled as I entered.

A deep voice rumbled from behind the jumbled stacks of crap, "Get out of here *wolf*, or I will eat you!"

"Your kind doesn't eat wolves. My kind doesn't eat dragons, so your threat is moot," I replied levelly.

The older man chuckled darkly. "Well, well, well, Evander Akselsen, what brings you here, now?"

I forced a smile, hoping the apprehension didn't show as I rounded the last corner to see Holdur. His face held a friendly grin, but his stance was apprehensive. I was the only werewolf allowed in his building on account I saved his cat three years ago from getting hit by a car. The interactions between wolves and dragons were coarse and to the point. Even though I had Holdur on friendly terms, I wasn't sure how long my good deed toward his cat would last.

Holdur patiently stared at me over his red-rimmed spectacles. His slanted vermillion eyes narrowed, intensely watching as I pulled Zuri's file from my briefcase. I casually tossed it and it landed on the counter, scattering dust into the stagnant air.

Holdur leaned over, reading the file. His lips thinned, "Zuri?"

I nodded.

"You haven't figured it out? I swear lad, it is right in front of your face."

I refrained from growling at the veiled insult since it would do me no good. "No, I haven't. If it was in front of my face, I would not be here. I need to know about her last names. Why are they different?"

Holdur grinned, though his body still held tension. "Smitten... She is a sweet girl, despite her origins... Her last names are different because obviously someone changed them, whether she was adopted or not, to hide her origin to keep her safe. Or as safe as one could be."

I scowled; *I'm not smitten... Not possible. I barely know her and this mystery surrounding her drives me nuts. That's all it is.* Zuri was the epicenter to the problem, so close to being solved and dealt with. The matter of her last name was merely so I could have all my ducks in a neat little row, and all the boxes checked for my commander back at my department.

My fingers thrummed through the papers. Her mother gave her the last name of Luciani, but it was changed with her adoption to Barsotti by people not her aunt and uncle. I pilfered through the papers, noting her adopted parents were now dead and their cause of death related in a feud between covens. Did Zuri truly not know her origins? I found it unlikely since most kids when they are adopted as older kids, like Zuri was, realize what's happening. Yet, she seemed confused when I asked her about her last name and pressed for more information regarding her.

Holdur leaned forward on the counter, a smile matching the gleam in his vermillion eyes. "Smitten..." He murmured under his breath while chuckling and shaking his head. "I cannot help you."

"Why?"

Holdur held up his hands in a placating fashion. "It is not because you are a wolf. It is because of Zuri," he sighed. "I wish I could, but I cannot."

"Please," I asked, hoping it would help.

The dragon smirked, vermillion scales flashing across his face before they disappeared. "I cannot help you."

I snatched the files off the counter and shoved them into the briefcase. *Dragons – riddle speaking, shifting, bastards, the lot of them*, I cursed. Being close to wrapping this report up had me longing for the closure, to where I could leave this city, this job I had for years, and return to my pack. I wanted it to be done and over with. I wanted justice done. I navigated my way through the cluster-fuck dragon hoard of items no one, human nor dragon, cared to purchase.

"Keep her safe from the ones who seek her," Holdur said as I reached the front door.

Turning on my heel, I barked, "What is that supposed to mean?" Dragons and their cryptic messages irked me.

Holdur rolled his eyes. "Obviously, she is being sought after for what she has."

"*I'm* seeking her."

Holdur came to the front of the store, flicking a few switches on a wall. The lights inside and the crappy neon flashing from outside, ceased. "You are seeking answers, ones I cannot give. But you are not seeking her. Not really. You do not want to outright kill her. Zuri is of powerful people, possessing a powerful item. She doesn't know this. Keep her safe."

I ran a hand over my face. I had no need or want to keep her safe, but I also had to in order for justice to prevail. I needed her alive and breathing. And since she was now stuck with a bat-shit crazy queen, then I had to come up with a plan to get her out after I filed my report on her.

I nodded. "Thank you, Holdur," I replied, stepping out of the shop.

My lips pursed at his words of keeping her safe. Zuri wasn't of my blood, or of my pack. Zuri was human. She wasn't in my plans in taking her home, and adding her into the wolf pack or anything. She didn't fit in *my* life puzzle. Little did Holdur know, I was going to kill her, maybe not by my hand directly, but she would die once she fit into the last piece of the puzzle. Despite his belief in me to protect her, justice took precedence.

I jogged back across the empty street and snapped the door to my car open. I clambered inside with an irritated grumble. My phone buzzed in the cup holder. I threw my head back, rolled my eyes and groaned. Glancing down did not bring me any joy. Mechanically I answered the incoming call.

"Evander, did you close the case?" My commander, Iorgas, asked, his voice hard.

"Not yet."

Iorgas grumbled. "Close the case. You were given three months to solve this case. Your three months are up. We need a verdict."

I ran a hand over my face. "I closed the other separate cases. I will be mailing them to you tonight."

"Excellent work. Why haven't you closed Barsotti?"

"I'm seeking a final answer," I grouched back. This man already knew my reasons why I took this particular case.

Iorgas breathed heavily through the phone. "If you haven't found it now, then you won't. I want the file, Akselsen."

A pleading note escaped my voice as I asked, "Commander, give me two more days."

Again, Iorgas blew his lips into the phone. "No Evander. I want the files to make *our* verdict. Send over what you have. I'm sure it is more than sufficient given your thoroughness."

My hands clenched the steering wheel tightly. I held my breath for a moment, slowly releasing it away from the speaker in the phone so Iorgas couldn't hear my frustra-tion. All this time, I searched so hard, fought for answers, came close to beating the shit out of others for them as well, yet the final one eluded me.

"Evander," Iorgas began, "I understand. However, Zuri might not be the way to the conclusion you are after."

I grabbed the steering wheel so hard, part of the bottom snapped off. "She is."

"Send me the case files," Iorgas's voice softened slightly. "I want to see what you have found. Maybe I can reward you a few more days."

I deflated, feeling a touch relieved and defeated. "Thank you, Commander."

The end of the other line went silent. The man never said good-bye, simply hung up when he was done conversing.

I drove to the overnight postal office, shipping the files as requested. Part of me felt like Zuri's file was concluded. The other battled that whatever she was linked to in my case, wasn't over, far from it. She wasn't the sweet, inno-cent by-stander she made herself seem. There was a dark-ness in her. I just had to find it.

CHAPTER ELEVEN

ZURI

My brown eyes scoured every inch of the room, yet found no means to escape. I was a lobster in a tank, or as I heard my Uncle Syrus used once, a sardine in a tin can. Lyvia was right, I was never going to leave. Whatever her reasons - to protect me or just being a psycho - it irritated me.

After losing my house, my cat, and now my freedom, being trapped here tore through my emotions. I wasn't sure if I wanted to cry my eyes out or be pissed, maybe both. I was irritated at myself for trusting my mother. I shouldn't have; deep down I knew I shouldn't have.

Uncle Syrus told me multiple times to trust myself. I often had trouble, giving people the benefit of the doubt and it led to more trust issues like Lazaro. As a kid, I had prayed for my mom to come and get me and then the prayer changed to having a relationship with her. That prayer stopped when I became an adult. By that time, I didn't need her and while my inner little girl still wondered what having her around would be like, even desired a relationship, grown up me needed proof of her trustworthiness. I looked around at my luxurious prison cell and scoffed at myself. What I used to pray for, bit me in the ass.

"I gave in to the thought of spending time with her, and look where it got me," I grumbled. "I should have never come." I tugged at the braided ends of my blonde hair. "I am such an idiot!"

Sitting on the window seat, I stared down to the activity below me. Workers bustled about the castle grounds, smiles on their oblivious faces as they decorated outside with paper hanging lanterns and ribbons. The area was small, a semicircle off the back of the castle overhanging the cliff. Stone, the color of wet sand, lined the ground and came up to form a railing, blocking idiots who got too close from falling. Potted plants lined the perimeter with intricately shaped foliage. I smirked at the squirrel tree. *Why trim a damn squirrel shape?* Bright flowers, rich in orange and pinks, covered the archways onto the balcony.

A long train of servants carrying black tables with glass tops came out from under the beautiful archway to my right. I leaned my head against the wall, intently watching each worker, dressed in a dark gray suit jacket and white button-down shirt underneath, adorn the table tops with silverware and drinking glasses.

I glanced at my phone again, wondering when Evander was coming, if he was at all since it had been about an hour or so since his message. I wouldn't blame him if he didn't. I wasn't exactly the nicest person. Getting passed around as a kid and then left by Lazaro weeks ago hardened my heart a bit. I closed myself off to protect me, yet all I wanted, deep down, was to be held, loved. I was terrified of being left, yet I planned on people leaving before they left me. The only constants were my uncle Syrus when Aunt Espe said he could come around me as an adult, still ever fearful of my mother; and the other was Lazaro for two years, until he eventually left as well. Everyone always left. The fear of being left alone and behind, kept me leery of people.

I caught my reflection in the glass and looked past it. My hand mindlessly went to the only companion who never left. The first gun I got myself was a 357. I carried pistols for protection since being a human in a world of paranormal, where everything is stronger, faster, harsher than myself, I needed something. Even the small faeries residing in Chay, to the southeast, had magic and ferocious bites paralyzing a being for hours. Even if my guns didn't completely stop a paranormal being, it would slow them down enough for me to get away.

I fiddled mindlessly with the ends of my hair as I stared at the phone in my lap. I prayed he followed through with his text and came to get me. No one else would come. I would rescue myself if I had the ability, but this room was spelled and locked down tight. If it came down to me rescuing myself, it could be a long time coming as I scoped out my mother's weaknesses.

Footsteps sounded outside my door. I stayed where I was, unbuttoning the claps on the holster for a quick draw and flicking the hammer back before the door completely opened. My lips tightened upon my mother entering. Her vivacious smile matched her frilly, ruffled chartreuse dress she changed into and curled brown hair. A maid came behind her with a large package. The poor woman appeared encumbered by the box. I carefully set the hammer back. As much as I wanted to shoot my mother right now, I didn't want to hurt her maid, nor did I *really* want to hurt my mother. I just wanted to run away.

I rose, walking to the middle of the room while my mother came to me with open arms. I didn't move.

"Zuri, my darling," Lyvia began, "This gorgeous dress will bring out your beautiful eyes. Happy birthday!"

I raised a brow, not saying a word. It also wasn't my birthday. I took the large, awkward package from the maid who smiled with relief. I didn't get a chance to set the package on the bed. Lyvia came toward me, opening it while I held it and pulled back the lavender tissue paper. A dark Prussian blue dress with a paisley overlay of diamond sparkles came flowing out of the box as Lyvia pulled it out. Lyvia held it up to me, making approving sounds of motherly delight.

I didn't care. I wasn't going to wear it. My eyes darted to the door. The maid cautiously walked through the door, shutting it behind her with a click. The spell shimmered, setting in place. I grimaced.

"It's going to look ravishing on you," Lyvia prattled, ignoring the maid's departure.

"What's the occasion?" I cautiously questioned.

It was a gorgeous gown. One I would wear to a wedding or something requiring me to dress amazingly, however, I did not see myself wearing it for any occasion. Lyvia's gaze locked on mine with maternal affection, something I longed to see. Yet, while my heart saw the love I ached to receive, my head cautioned me, reminding me even though Lyvia is here now, she still left me back when I was a kid and again now, when she locked me in this room for my supposed benefit. My stomach rumbled with caution, forcing the hairs on my arm to stand on end.

Lyvia sat herself on the end of my bed. The door opened again, admitting the same maid. The maid stood by the door, her head down. My right hand stayed on the grip of the gun.

"Try it on," she stated, waiting eagerly for my approval.

"Hard pass."

Lyvia's eyes narrowed at me, creating more cracks on the edges of her eyes. "Now."

"Not a chance. Let me out."

My mother crossed her arms. "Put on the dress and I will let you out."

My gut churned. I didn't trust her after locking me away like this. And now coming at me with a gift and no apologies just twisted the knife a bit for me. Love didn't lock people away, control and manipulation did. No one was ever going to force me into complacency. This was a mere mishap in judgement on myself. I could've gone to Adiva's for the night or even called Evander.

I wanted so badly the affection her candy-coated actions offered, but when I looked at her, when she didn't realize I'm looking, I saw the calculation and vicious intelligence and my heart hung heavy. I just can't trust her. And even though I wanted what every human girl wanted, the girly manicures and boy talk, after this whole situation, I couldn't trust my mother and wasn't sure I ever would. She'd shattered pretty much any chance when she'd warded my room so I couldn't leave.

"I give you my word as Queen," Lyvia stated, holding out the dress.

I met her narrowed expression with my own, "If it gets me out of here," I grumbled.

I forced a smile to my lips. Turning around, I strode to the other end of the room where the bathroom was. Slamming the door shut, I stripped out of my clothes. I took the key out of my bra, sticking it inside the padded breast area of the dress. It was so tight around my chest, the key wouldn't fall out. I still had on my spandex shorts and I would keep them on.

The dress opened in the back, and flowed out around my hips. It was revealing, leaving me feeling open and bare to the world. No sleeves to stick in a knife. Nothing. I grabbed the long ribbon from the back, pulling the zipper up on the dress. The diamonds cascaded across my body from right to left, wrapping around me in shining perfection. I took my hair from the braids, letting the curls release around me.

Glancing at my reflection in the mirror, I looked beautiful. I almost didn't recognize myself. My heart lurched, wondering how I would have looked on my wedding day, the blushing bride to Lazaro's handsome groom, I would never know.

I checked the dress over, my hands searching for pockets. With a triumphant smile, I found them on either side. Grabbing my pants, I whipped the 357 from the holster, and tucked it into the pocket of the dress. Grabbing the other gun, I stuck the small 9mm down in between my boobs, with the key hidden in the inside fold of the padded bra area. I stuck the extra mags from my jean pockets inside my left dress pocket. I looked at myself, spinning around to ensure the guns could not be seen so easily. I beamed. Feeling secure, I strode out of the room.

Lyvia smiled brightly, then frowned. "Remove your *tool*, please."

My hands gently clenched at the sides.

"Zuri, I swear, nothing will harm you."

I remained fixated to my spot in the middle of the room. I wouldn't remove the guns. They were the only thing I had now. Everything else was far behind me – my home, my cat, and my security – all stripped from me in a matter of days.

Lyvia sighed, rising from her spot. "Fine," she caved, handing me a pair of silver flats that matched the dress. "Follow me, please, and be pleasant."

She turned around quickly, silver magic wisping from her hands. It came to my face, fog clouding my eyes. I tried to keep my eyes open, but felt them being forced shut. My hands flew to my dress pocket; fingers clamping around the cold metal of the grip. I exhaled in relief when the 357 greeted my sweating palms.

Lyvia snorted, shaking her head. "Honestly, Zuri, you're being ridiculous. I just did your hair."

The silver mist cleared. My eyes opened. "I'm being cautious. Besides, doing my hair shouldn't have had anything to do with my eyes."

"Ridiculous."

"As the saying goes: be ever vigilant, but never suspicious."

Lyvia harrumphed, hands on her hips, "You *are* suspicious of me."

I shook my head. "I'm cautious. There's a difference. If I was suspicious, I would avoid you all together. I'm cautious because you left me as a kid, and just now locked me in a room for my own good," I said a touch angrily. "You say you want a relationship, but your words don't match your actions like - I'm locking you in a room for your own good, but here is a party dress."

Conceding the point, she strode out of the room in front of me. I looked at my hair in the mirror by the door. It was curled in large ringlets, falling down my back. A jeweled comb, pulled the hair back off the right side of my face. Little gems adorned the rest of my hair falling over my left shoulder.

"You look beautiful," Lyvia complimented, over her shoulder as she strode out the door.

I didn't reply. The silver shimmering spell to my room dropped like a kid tossing a blanket to the floor. Lyvia turned around to me, a sorrowful look plastered on her features. I studied her briefly and she was beautiful. Not in a 45-year-old beauty, but in a timeless beauty of the fae of legends. She hardly looked above 29. I saw myself in her too. Although I didn't think I was quite as beautiful. I didn't have that otherworldly quality she received when she was gifted the dragon magic. But we did share the same lithe, petite body, oval face and soft facial features.

We were also stubborn and determined. My eyes were larger than hers, more light brown in color like a cinnamon roll while hers were a robin's egg blue. My light blonde hair and eye color must come from my father.

"Be nice," she said softly.

The maid held open the door and my mother walked out. I heard the maid mumble something about the queen being damned crazy and I smirked, thankful that not all of those who served her were loyal. I followed my mother, leading me back down the hallway and the stairs slightly curving to the right. As we walked underneath the gorgeous chandeliers, voices echoed in the high vaulted ceilings.

I paid particular attention to several servants lining the wall where the refreshments were being served. I intently watched their faces change from bright and cheerful as my mother came within their sight, but as soon as she passed, their gazes hardened.

I followed farther into the open room where beings of all kinds mingled. Werewolves, lions and bears, centaurs, vampires, and witches, nymphs and creatures I had never seen before, walked outside on the bright sunlit balcony where servants laid out tables and silverware. My insides jittered.

A centaur dipped his head in my direction, his black coat shining like the inside of a chip bag. A scantily clad nymph danced past me, giggling and waving. The nymph smiled at Lyvia, throwing her arms around my mother's neck before skipping off to the centaur.

"I did not invite her," my mother leaned in and whispered tersely.

The corner of my mouth twitched.

"She is from Scirwode, as is the bare-chested centaur. The beings in the forest have no modesty."

I sucked in my cheeks to keep myself from snorting. Most of the beings in Quivleren had no modesty, humans included. The beings with the most were dragons, not even daring to show any more skin than a crew neck long sleeved shirt would allow, followed closely by werewolves and finally *some* humans. Everything else practically ran around naked.

Lyvia dipped her head to a dragon woman. I glanced out the corner of my eye in time to catch the dragon's vermillion gleam meet mine. From what Holdur had told me years ago, all dragon's had vermillion eyes. The dragon woman's rich ebony hair was done in the elegance of the retro glam waves. A beautiful diamond band went across her forehead while a plum dress hung off her shoulders. I was surprised at how much skin this dragon was showing given the modesty of others I had seen passing on the streets. Hell, the only dragon I knew well was Holdur. Other dragons did not interact much with the rest of the races as they felt themselves superior. Elves, with their seven-foot-tall forms and amethyst eyes, held the same arrogance. They came to OKimma for business and left promptly after. Elves hid themselves away in the caves around Zilar Lake bordering the Espowyes Mountains.

I dipped my head to the dragon.

"Who is this charming human, Lyvia?" The dragon

greeted. "She reeks of cautious determination and soul-fire."

I glowered at the insult. The dragon beamed.

My mother smiled fondly at me. "This is my daughter, Zuri. She appreciates your vivid comment. Why, Jadiza, I love your dress."

"Thank you, my dear. I'm happy to attend this little soiree of yours. Tell me, are we celebrating Zuri?"

My mother looped her arm with Jadiza. "Yes, doll, we are celebrating her homecoming," Lyvia explained, giving me a wink, and taking a walk with Jadiza.

My wide eyes glanced around the room. Tiny Sprites, a grouping of maybe ten, fluttered in, their wings ringing like little bells. I watched them perch themselves on a padded petite octagonal shelf, complete with their own dining area and refreshments.

A minotaur passed behind me. The creature dipped her head to me while her hoof linked itself to another larger minotaur who did not glance in my direction. I offered a small smile, glancing away to take in the other creatures here.

Werewolves prowled inside, their green eyes flashing around and darting to me. My heart thundered in my chest, secretly hoping one wolf happened to be Evander. Since all wolves had green eyes, it was hard to differentiate who was who in wolf form unless I knew what I was looking for. Evander wasn't here. Servants flitted around me, serving drinks in tall champagne glasses or finger foods on paper doilies. The servants were the only other humans in the room. Humans were easy enough to spot.

We were all under six feet tall, with either blue or brown eyes. I swallowed, wondering how my mother had been gifted dragon magic. What had she done to obtain such a feat; since no dragon, from what Holdur had told me, would easily part with it.

My eyes narrowed as I looked around the room. Nothing about my mother made sense to me. She was rich, a queen, a person of power yet... My lips pursed to the side, thinking... *Maybe my Uncle Syrus told me she was a mental case to save me the sadness,* I surmised. *It's the only plausible reason for all of this. The reason why I was told she was a nutjob since I was a kid.*

I scanned every entry and exit point around me, ready to make my escape. Sometime tonight I was leaving. This key my mother and others so desperately desired needed to be returned to the God Elohi or destroyed.

My feet pulled me through the doors leading to the opened balcony. The fresh, crisp evening air brought me sweet relief. I wandered past the potted plants to the far left, avoiding the main throngs of creatures looking in my direction. Unnerved by their eyes, I navigated my way to the edge of the balcony.

Leaning against the balustrade, my eyes scoured the land below me. Jagged rocks and crevices lined the descent to where I could not even see the bottom of the mountainous range. Misty fog clung to the base of the mountain where the treetops might have poked through slightly. A wind swirled through the fog. I spotted a tree top and my heart sunk to the bottom.

There is no escape, my mind reeled.

My fists clenched hard against the stone railing, turning white. There was at least a half mile drop from where I was to the treetops. Then if I didn't die from hitting a tree or branch, there was at least another two-hundred-foot drop from the top of the fir tree to the potential ground, if there was even a ground. I chuckled grimly at my own pessimism. Of course, there was a ground. But knowing how far down it was in this fog was impossible.

I stared at the tree. It was so far away. Yet I dared to touch the top. If it meant getting away, I would jump. I couldn't trust my mother. I couldn't rely on Evander to come save me, even if he had saved me before. There was no other choice but to save myself.

"Long drop," a male commented.

My eyes darted to the right. Barend, the great grizzly bear shifter from this morning stood by my side, his honey brown hair slicked back, bright silver eyes roamed over me. I turned toward him slightly. He smiled at me, warmth reaching his eyes and in the lines of his smile. He was a handsome man with a kind, honest face. I smiled back at him before turning back to the rocky crags below me.

He leaned against the balcony with me, gazing below at the sand and gray colored rocks and vegetation growing between. I looked behind me to all the creatures milling about and chatting. No one glanced in my direction. I could not even find Lyvia.

Thank goodness for that too.

Turning back around, I studied Barend. His silver eyes were almost crystalline. His face was soft, open, not a scar or hard line marring his body. He was a lithe man, not built like a bear, ironically.

"It is a long drop," I replied.

Barend grinned, dipping his head to me. "This was a strategic place for the castle," Barend began. "Espowyes Mountains harbor gogmagogs, fourteen-foot-tall trolls covered in blistering, poisonous warts. Gogmagogs eat other creatures like you and myself. If they don't eat you, and you're unlucky enough that one of their blisters oozes on you, your flesh will rot and fall off in a matter of hours without an antidote. Kludde, bat-wolf creatures spawned by the darkness of Diomedes himself, also reside some-where in the Espowyes."

"Is it all that's in the Mountain Range east of here?" I ventured.

I was brave but hardly *that* brave, or stupid. However, if something did happen to me while being here, knowing what was in the Espowyes was vital informa-tion. I bit the bottom of my lip, gazing to the right where the tallest of the mountains shimmered in the orange flaming glow of evening light. My mouth tight-ened in a thin line. I was trapped by the natural elements here, but also by magic. I could not go home, or Maluhia where the name meaning peaceful was anything but with carnivorous mermaids. Aiolos was promising as it harbored the same paranormal beings OKimma did.

Barend grinned at me. "Beyond the Espowyes is the Xylia forest, where the minotaurs and other shifters, like myself, are from. Scirwode is my home though. Seeing as how you offended Nadja, the minotaur queen, inside earlier, good luck getting past their colonies alive."

I scowled. "How did I offend her?"

"Your smile wasn't genuine. You averted your eyes before she did. Shows you as weak."

My back straightened, eyes glaring at him. Barend held up his hands. "I know you're not. Nadja doesn't though."

"Can I make it right?" I asked.

Barend shrugged. "No one has tried." He coughed low in his throat.

Turning back around, I watched the hanging paper lanterns begin to glow. My mother came out of the glass double doors. She strode gracefully to the middle of the little party she put on, getting help from a tall blue haired elf to stand on a chair.

How my mother knew I would come with her, how the dress fit perfectly, and how she did this all, I haven't a clue. It bothered me immensely. I didn't like being the center of attention. Little hints as to who Lyvia truly was, weren't adding up in my head.

How did she know where I lived? How did she get past the spell on my house? I didn't understand it. She would say one thing while her actions said another. I couldn't place my emotions, but trepidation filled me.

"My friends, thank you all for coming. I'm celebrating the return of my long lost and only daughter, Zuri who grew up outside of this home."

Inside I cringed. But I was also grateful. My eyes somehow found Nadja. The minotaur queen locked her sharp gray orbs on me. Her lip curled menacingly, turning her upper body around fully toward me. I dipped my head, but kept my gaze firm to hers. Nadja's upper lip quivered, eyes closed, she looked away.

"Good job," Barend whispered.

I smiled wanly.

Queen Lyvia's eyes locked on mine; hands clasped together with elbows out to the sides. "She will someday take my place, but for now, I must keep her safe as she learns all she needs to," she ended, snapping her fingers.

My brows crease together. I glanced at Barend whose befuddled look matched my own. I gathered all the fabric of my dress in front of me. I pulled it backward through my legs and took a handful of the dress in each hand. I wrapped the fabric around my front and made a knot. My legs were exposed, but now I could run and fight.

Lyvia stared at me despondently; her chin raising slightly at me, as if waiting for me to challenge her. I stared at her, wondering what she was going to do next. A silver wisp of magic formed in her left hand. "A mother's love is boundless," she stated teary eyed.

My heart raced as fifteen werewolf shifters came prowling out toward me from the crowd. Some morphed into their other half, teeth gnashing together. My back pressed against the stone coldness of the balustrade. I glanced at where I last saw Barend, not seeing him anywhere.

Lyvia unleashed magic from her hands at me. I tucked and rolled to the right, where I had some free space to maneuver. A werewolf made a grab for my upper right arm. Turning, I grabbed his arm firmly with my left hand

and with my right hand curled into a fist, I punched his elbow. The werewolf screamed as it broke.

Dashing for the balustrade, I looked over my shoulder briefly, catching the scathing look of my mother. Liquid magic pooled in her hands. She launched another magic orb at me. I hopped up to the top of the three-foot railing and jumped as the orb struck where I just was.

CHAPTER TWELVE

ZURI

W ind beat against my face, forcing tears to sprinkle out of my eyes. The whistling of the air passing my ears with such force made my head hurt. The first top of a fir tree tip came into view. My body shuddered, bracing for a possible bone breaking impact. I spread my fingers wide, reaching out for anything to grab.

My body rushed past the fir tree, my hands completely missing the branches. My body however, found one and it struck me in the stomach. I flipped over the branch and began tumbling head over feet to the ground. All the breath left my body. I couldn't scream or breathe. My muscles spasmed, wanting my legs and arms to draw in close to my body and prepare for death. I forced my arms away from my body. Hands still out, I reached for anything I could grab to slow my momentum. I didn't care if I happened to break my hands or arms; I didn't care to die from having my head smashed in. That wasn't the way I wanted death to greet me.

Closing my eyes, I did not want to witness my impending demise. My face scrunched tight; muscles clenching, waiting for the painful, and hopefully quick, smack of impact. I sucked in a quick breath, holding it in and savored the crisp forest scented bite that would be my last breath.

For a mere moment, I was surprised my impromptu plan worked. With my mother spelling me inside her castle, I was utterly delighted and terrified something this stupid, worked.

God Elohi, I thought licking my lips, *if I am to die this day, please take me to your gilded heaven.*

If I didn't die from this stupid stunt, I would be surprised for certain. I nervously opened my eyes. Death was in a hundred feet. Branches whipped by my body and face, slowing me down, but not enough to not get severely hurt when I landed.

My ass found a branch, sliding forward onto another. I cringed at the unwanted pokes. The gun in my dress pocket clanked against my side.

"At least I'm slowing down," I squeaked, spying the solid slate rock ground. "Ohhh damn," I choked out, when my crotch found a branch, slinging me forward.

The padding from my dress, bunched between my legs and around me, softened the impact slightly. My hands reached out in front of me, enclosing around a branch. My arm muscles tightened, holding me firm and still. My legs mechanically pulled up to my chest.

I dared to open my eyes. I found myself on the thinning end of the branch. It crackled like sap on a fire. My eyes snapped up at the tree branch breaking slowly at the base of the tree. Swallowing bile, I dared a glance below my feet.

Boulders and sharp slate stone cascaded down the side of a large hill that this final tree I dangled from overlooked. If I would have been a few degrees off to the right, I would be dead from hitting all the stone. Below the stone, a waterfall deafeningly roared from somewhere. I was still roughly thirty feet from the stone ground. No other branches were below me I could swing and catch onto.

"Holy shit," I squeaked.

Hand over fist, I tried to pull myself toward the base of the branch. It wasn't going well. The branch cracked more, swinging me toward the trunk. Like a drunk raccoon, my arms moved and clasped around the bark of the tree. My fingernails dug in for purchase.

"Don't fall, don't fall, don't fall," I repeated to myself.

Sap stuck to me like barbeque sauce on pork ribs, sticky and unwanted. My legs barely wrapped around some part of the tree. Licking my lips, I dared another glance below. I made a painstakingly slow descent down. Currently, I was still over twenty feet up.

Arms shaking, I moved down the trunk. I leapt away when I was still eight feet up. I landed on my butt.

"Zuri!" my mother's voice shrieked above my head.

Scrambling to my feet, I ripped off the dress. I tore the clothing off my body. I did not want any reminders of my mother nor anyone being able to trace my scent. Granted they could still smell me, but clothing would not make my smell as strong. I took the gun out of the dress pocket and the mags from the other pocket. Somehow, by the grace of Elohi, I still had my 357, 9mm and the key.

Cold, biting wind whipped past my bare skin. My upper half, completely exposed to the elements while my bottom half still had spandex shorts with the tight elastic around the thighs.

"Crap on a stick," I mutter, shoving the key in my shorts and tucking it on the inside of my left thigh.

I shoved the 9mm down my shorts on the right side of my hip. The gun was small enough to be held in place while I walked. If I dared to run, I wasn't certain the gun would remain.

I shoved the two extra 9mm mags into my spandex shorts on the left side. I didn't have other munitions for the 357, so taking it was more of a sentimental choice at this point.

My stomach roiled with indecision. The hair on my arms prickled. My heart thundered madly in my chest with the anxiousness of being discovered niggling at the back of my mind. Lyvia was coming for me. I was certain of it.

"Zuri!" Lyvia called again, her voice sounding closer than her previous shout.

I crossed my arms over my chest. The Espowyes Mountains were to the east of me, on my right, and the rest of the Xylia forest wrapped around and went to the west. Cautiously I went to the edge of the cliff. Below me a waterfall roared from the middle of the cliffside, coming right out from underground. The waterfall crashed out into a deep pool of dark indigo water, blazing a liquid path away from the castle in a jagged line which appeared, from my dismal view, to lead west.

Gazing at the 357 in my right hand, my thumb automatically pulled the hammer back. My eyes frantically scanned the surrounding area for any mound of dirt. Spying what I desired to the left of me, I fired a shot and dropped the gun. My hope was they would assume I shot myself and fell into the water. Sprinting, I leapt off the edge of the cliffside, bringing my knees to my chest.

My eyes scrunched closed. I didn't want to see how far down the dark water below happened to be, or if I could potentially smash myself against anything sticking out of the cliff wall. That was one thing I never actually wanted to know. Time seemed to slow down. And funny thing, my life didn't flash before my eyes. Just the hope that this wasn't going to be the last breath I would take. On instinct I sucked in a deep breath and then felt my body plunge into the concrete-like water.

The cold water enclosed around me, forcing me down to the riverbed under the tumbling fall. Forcing my eyes open, I saw a minimal fleck of light from the surface and I clawed my way to it, striving to reach the promise of air and light.

Sharp cold air entered my lungs as the swift current swept me downstream. I was grateful for it. I swam with the current, urging the water and my body to carry me away faster from Kadia Castle and my insane mother.

A mother's love is boundless, Lyvia said. *Then why'd you abandon me,* Mom? *Where was this boundless love 20 years ago? 10 years ago?* Being a mother, in my imagination, since

I'd never actually had a real one, meant staying, it meant wanting. It meant a love so endless, so boundless and profound, that literally nothing would be able to tear mother from child, yet Lyvia gave me up so freely.

I guess there was a slight chance she was telling the truth. That she loved me so much, she had been doing everything she could to keep me safe. But my gut told me otherwise. And I had learned to trust my gut over the years of neglect and the more recent attacks. I'd had a brief moment of ignoring the churning in my gut and the anxiety and trepidation her presence brought, but after magically locking me in a room, dressing me up and parading me around and then threatening further lock-down and who knows what, I couldn't ignore it any longer.

I pushed the dilemma of my mother out of my head. My main focus from here on out was survival. Lyvia wasn't the only one wanting me or what I had. I couldn't go home. I had to figure out where I could go so that no one would look for me.

*Yeah where the fuck to no*w, I wondered, pushing wet hair off my face.

It scared me. I had security in my home, my belongings, and my pet. It was all taken from me. It got me attacked by different wolf packs and stalked by a handsome, yet creepy, Evander.

Would Evander be able to track me? Would I even want him to, I wondered? The thought was pushed from my mind as my body collided with a boulder hidden in the choppy, steady flowing stream. I exhaled sharply. The sting of the rock on my bare skin burned under the churning depths.

The water pushed me farther down the river. I kept my knees up to my chest, floating and maneuvering with my arms to stay above water. The last thing I needed to add to this horrible adventure was a broken ankle.

My sense of direction was completely baffled since jumping into the water and spinning under and with the current. I could no longer tell if I was heading east or west. I prayed it was west. Ending up in Chay with asshole faeries wasn't something I needed. Once the river slowed down, I'd have to climb out and figure out where the fuck I was. No need to get to civilization to do that. Especially if I was headed for Chay. The shiver zipping down my body had nothing to do with the frigid river and everything to do with tiny winged creatures with giant chips on their shoulders.

The current sucked me under, forcing my body to tumble under the depths and become stuck in the motion. This had been the first time it happened to me and sheer panic ripped through my mind. My lungs burned brutally. My fingers raked through the cold water, desperately striving to get to the surface so I could force air back into my aching lungs.

The surface of the water came into view. The chilled air struck my face like a slap. I inhaled a lungful so loud, I sounded like a mating monkey. I kept inhaling, sputtering water. My head whipped around, regaining my bearings.

I fought the current, swimming toward the shoreline. My arms ached with each pull of the water. Trees and brush lined the shore of a small muddied riverbank. I clawed my way toward it. The water sifted through my fingers as I repeatedly thanked the God Elohi that I was breathing.

A smile crept across my face as my feet hit the bottom without being immediately swept out from beneath me. Muddied dirt squelched between my toes. My upper half of my body rose out of the water, immediately goose-bumping as the chilliness of the air hit my bare skin. My legs wobbled on their own.

I urged my body forward to the edge. My legs gave out and I sank to my knees. My stomach ached where a bruise was forming below my left rib cage. I felt beat to hell, but I was breathing. And that was lucky in and of itself for all the stupid shit I've done in the past several hours to ensure my freedom.

Gazing at the sky, it was nearly nightfall. I had no idea what manner of creatures to expect to encounter besides the ones Barend mentioned. If there were gogmagogs, and kludde, then I needed to get far and away and fast.

"Damn it all," I sighed, collapsing to the ground.

The forest before me was eerily silent. No birds squawked with their annoying repetitive songs. No bugs chirped or chimed. It was like death itself wouldn't wake the forest. Hairs on my arms prickled on end and I wasn't sure if it was from the chill in the air or from panic. With my gun waterlogged, I would need to clean it and allow it to dry thoroughly before it would fire - if it would at all, leaving me completely defenseless.

I checked myself over, pulling out the two mags out of my left spanx leg and my pistol out of the right. I sighed in relief as my hand touched the key. I also needed to get dry.

In the forest there was plenty of firewood. I could fashion myself a bow-drill and have a fire in minutes. However, being out in the open left me vulnerable. I may be able to see what snuck up on me, but they could see me too - especially with the fire I desperately needed.

I could float the rest of the river down to wherever it happened to go, but at nighttime and not knowing where I happened to be, I would get hypothermia before I got anywhere. If this river was part of the Zilar River, it would lead to the ocean, which I didn't have a problem with, if I could stay on the main path and not the off chute that went to Chay.

Damn it all, I hoped this was the Zilar River. The river split into two main tributaries one of which ended in a human city that used the ocean as their livelihood bringing in a ton of income through fishing and canneries. The other main tributary ended abruptly and no humans or creatures lived there because of the five hundred foot drop off into the ocean.

"Well shit," I grumbled. "This is bad. Float the river or risk it on foot?"

Part of me dared to enter the forest to find solace in its leafy foliage and coverage. The other part of me desired to be in the open with the water surrounding me, I could see who and what would be coming for me. There were problems with both though. In the forest, I could easily hide, but I could also be easily snuck up on. With being in the open, I was exposed to all the elements. I ran a hand over my face, wiping away the remnants of the river.

"Fuck," I cursed. "Where do I go?" I asked myself, my voice cracking.

Legend said, the God Elohi resided somewhere in the Harrell Mountains. They were a vast range in the middle of Quivleren bordering the Riodhr Forest. But if I was a god as powerful as Elohi, I would not be where the legends would say I would be. I would be elsewhere, hiding. If the other packs were after me for this key, they would also head to the Harrell Mountains.

"Where do I go?" I asked myself again, wondering if the answer would all the sudden come upon me.

I closed my eyes and tried to envision a map of Quivleren I learned from school. In my mind's eye, it brought me to a place to the south of Quivleren to a forest and a river to the west. My stomach roiled and I wasn't sure if it was from a decision being made of where to go or hunger.

"Zuri!"

My eyes snapped open. There was nowhere to run.

CHAPTER THIRTEEN

EVANDER

I sent my commander Zuri's files with a note attached, detailing to clear her name. Even though Zuri was linked to the killing of werewolves, like my parents, it was my deepest belief she was not guilty. However, my belief in her innocence didn't get her off the hook completely. She definitely had connections to the murderers, whether she knew it or not, and the only way I'd know how was to keep an eye on her.

After dropping off the files at the overnight post office, I went to Zuri's house to search for anything she left behind. Her house was absolutely trashed. Clothes were strewn everywhere. The loveseat was tossed to one side of the house. Cabinets were turned inside out. It looked like a tornado happened inside.

Three distinct male werewolf scents assaulted my nose. Even though I could tell them apart, I couldn't place what pack they happened to be in. Whatever their involvement with Zuri, I wasn't sure. She knew the Sandalio mob, but they wouldn't trash her house. Instead, they would take her back to theirs and do unspeakable acts. What she had done, set me on edge just as much as whomever these lingering scents belonged to.

Hairs of my inner wolf came out onto my skin, mottling my arms in their gray, white, and black tinted color. Inhaling sharply, I growled, searching her house. The second bedroom remained unfinished, boxes everywhere piled to one side, and a halfway put together desk on the other. My heart clenched, remembering spending many nights with my grandparents in this room. I exited the room and closed the door, heading to the kitchen where I knew she worked. Papers were strewn all over the ground and her laptop was gone.

What in the fuck happened, I grumbled.

Heading back out of the kitchen, I walked to her room. The tornado of a mess was most prominent here. Clothes lay littered everywhere. Her belongings, what little of them there happened to be, were smashed and tossed carelessly at walls and about the place. An ornate antique wood box laid on her bed. Opening the lid, a scrap piece of paper laid on the inside bottom.

Some keys unlock treasure, some secrets. Most often it's the truth. Be careful what you unlock, Zuri, for door nor chest, can be re-sealed. Also, hide this key from your mother, but more so from your father. I'm so sorry to put you in the middle of this.

. . .

LOVE, GRAMMA KAETHE

"FUCK IT ALL," I HISSED UNDER MY BREATH, RUNNING A HAND over my face.

Hairs on my body came out and sunk quickly beneath my skin again. The note confirmed why Zuri was being sought after - Elohi's Key. Werewolf packs have been destroying themselves trying to locate this item - this same item Zuri happened to have. The same key is said to open the underworld to let Diomedes loose. It confirmed in my mind that she was involved in the horrible werewolf war that had been waging for years, a war that killed my parents and ultimately decimated werewolves like myself. My previous notion of her being absolved from a crime or at least having little involvement, now changed. She was going to pay with her life.

This note was part of the confirmation I needed. My parents and pack were brutally killed over having Elohi's key in their possession. Our pack and its members were the only ones who knew about Elohi's key. We were the guardians of it, keeping it hidden and protected from those who desired to bring the God of Death to power. Those wolves who happened to survive were taken and forced into servitude. And Zuri was linked to it all.

There was something else I needed of Zuri; to completely, one hundred percent affirm her to the destruction of my kin. I had to know her sire, the man who helped create her. The same man I suspected helped destroy and enslave all those dear to me. The answer was vital to my tranquility.

If I can discover her sire, it will help unlock her involvement by lineage, I thought, putting the pieces together. *When that is completed, justice, with her death, will be had for my family and pack.*

I ran a hand over my face. I was frustrated yet relieved at the same time. This new information altered my perspective of her completely. If I hadn't stumbled upon the note, I might have entertained the idea of getting to know her. Now, there was no damn way in hell. My family is gone because of her and her kin. Everything was coming to a head and Zuri would see justice. The law of wolves would come to fruition. Even though Quivleren had its own set of rules, the main one being no killing, each group of paranormal had their own set of rules aside from the Quivleren laws.

Werewolves had strict laws compared to most. The rule I happened to appreciate most was if a being killed another, and the killer could not be found, the next of kin to the killer would be held accountable for the deed. Other beings, including our own wolves, did not deem it fair, but justice was justice, however it came. It was my absolute belief, Zuri would be held accountable.

Not long now... I just gotta bring her happy ass back, I mused, searching through her things. My hatred for her grew. I despised her. I despised how I felt for her before I found the note. Made me sick to my stomach. I was almost considering kissing her!

I shuddered. *Damn it, man.* I was livid. Hurt and livid.

This bitch's family killed mine and she needed to suffer, as I had, for it. First, I needed to get to her to bring her back and that task was one I would relish and accomplish quickly.

Stuffing the paper in my pocket for evidence, I began searching for Zuri's beloved cat, Luell, but I couldn't find her. Luell's scent was gone like she hadn't been there in hours. Figuring Zuri took her cat, I went outside, searching for more clues since I didn't believe Zuri would have gone with the queen willingly. If Zuri did, she was more stupid than I believed.

Knowing Zuri was with her estranged mother at Kadia Castle didn't sit well with me. Queen Lyvia Ariella was a thorn in the side of paranormal beings for the last two decades, east of the Belisma River and the Riodhr Forest separating the west and east sides of Quivleren. The thieving human bitch of a queen stole land given to the werewolves in the last Dragon-Wolf War hundreds of years ago, and gave it to the dragons who have no use for the timbered land, just to drive the wedge further between our races. Dragons preferred the mountain ranges or places like West OKimma with all the stone under their claws.

If I didn't know better, I'd say she was a dragon. Not only did Queen Lyvia, or Ariella as she preferred to be called, want to diminish the werewolf packs but eradicate them all together. It was well known Queen Ariella despised werewolves, witches and other beings like minotaurs, centaurs and mermaids. Although I've heard rumors of some minotaurs being in her court, I had no doubt she held something over their head to get them there. Fuck they may even be bound. I wouldn't put it past her. She had magically bound some of my own were-kin into servitude when they refused to bow to her. At least fifteen were-wolves served her at Kadia and four of them were from my pack. For some reason, other shifters like bears and lions were left alone.

My hands clenched together. Zuri was mixed in with her mother by birth. It angered me. Zuri was a woman, under any other circumstances, I would like to get to know. But I don't think I could ever get over the fact that she was connected to those who had ruined my life. Even if she was clueless, it was just too much. I stormed outside the house, going straight to Zuri's Bronco to search for more clues about her and what she was hiding.

The murdering queen should have been disposed of years ago. Justice should be delivered, but she served as a stepping stone to the even worse Empress of Dragons, Jadiza. That evil woman would stop at nothing to have complete dominance over Quivleren. She desired nothing more than to rule the world with her dragons and vampires. Humans were little more than worms to her - slaves to meet her needs. I snorted. Oh, the irony that Lyvia was human. She was simply a puppet until the empress decided she didn't need her anymore. And her actions displayed her worminess. *Typical human.*

When it came to who was responsible for what, the lines were so tangled and as loathe as I was to admit it, Zuri was caught in the middle of it all. Between the Dragon Empress's using Ariella and Ariella's power-hungry actions, the were-folk and my parents had no chance. And apparently, neither did Zuri. I hated her on principle, but I'd be lying if part of me didn't pity her, even sympathize a little at the trouble she found herself in lately. If nothing else, though, I was certain everything that was wrong in my life, and many of the lives of my fellow shifters, came back to Zuri Barsotti. Everything came full circle around her. There wasn't any way this young, naive lady couldn't possibly know of what was going on around her.

As I stomped down the drive toward her Bronco, my mind fumed. I glanced up, stopping in my tracks at her destroyed vehicle.

"Well fuck," I said, shocked at the state of her rig.

Someone had opened the hood of the converted gas-to-diesel motor, tearing hoses and the entire motor to shreds. The entire front axle sat shredded on the ground, claw marks peeling back metal like an orange peel. I inhaled deeply. I wanted to see if the wolf who destroyed her rig was one I knew personally. I leaned in a little, sniffing the axle specifically around the claw marks. The wolf was male. And he was not one of the three from inside the cabin. Other than that, I couldn't tell much. His pack affiliation was unknown to me and I didn't recognize his scent specifically.

"I wonder if I'd recognize him if I saw him."

I shrugged and walked around the house and found a freshly dug hole. Human fingermarks pocked the ground around it in long strips. A purple blanket poked softly above the dirt scattered on top. I stared at the ground, waiting to see if the dirt clumps stirred.

Curious, I bent down, sniffing it. It smelled of Luell. I quickly uncovered whatever it happened to be. Sticking my hands down inside the softly dug and easily malleable dirt, I pulled out the blanket I vaguely recognized as the one that had covered the back of Zuri's loveseat. Inhaling sharply, the scent of feline blood attacked my nose. I wriggled it.

Pulling the blanket up and holding my breath, I revealed a still Luell. I hesitated to touch her, afraid she was alive and my touch would hurt her more, yet afraid she was dead and what it would mean for Zuri who had loved this animal more than anything else in her life. Finally, I ran a finger along the cat's side and was surprised when Luell lifted her head and gave a weak mewl. I carefully lifted her up and cradled her to my chest, bringing the blanket with me as a comfort to the cat. I inspected her carefully, slowly running my hand down her coat, noticing the blood matting her fur. Several long cuts lined her head and side. She'd been mutilated on purpose, in a way to make her bleed out slowly. No wonder Zuri thought her dead.

I knew Zuri would have to pay for the sins of her mother. And my heart desired this revenge. At least, I thought it did. And even though justice would be served soon and this cat would be ownerless, I couldn't leave her here to suffer needlessly. I couldn't even claim guilt by association like I could with Zuri, even if my heart twinged every time I thought about it. I turned away from the thought and buried it deep, focusing on the bundle of fur in my arms.

"Poor cat," I crooned. "Sorry, this happened to you."

Even though I hated Zuri on principle, she'd taken time to wrap Luell and bury her lovingly. I could even smell the distinct saltiness of tears on the blanket. I couldn't not tell her. My heart was at war with my mind. This time, I'd let my heart win. No one should suffer emotionally like this. She needed to know that her beloved cat was alive and going to the vet.

Me: Your cat is alive. I'm gonna drop her off at the emergency vet before I come get you.

I snapped my phone shut, rising to my feet. There were no other clues to be found here at her house. I took three steps when the hairs on my arm stood on end. I paused at the back door and crept a few more steps to the corner and craned my neck, peeking around the edge, tucking Luell further into my chest.

A black SUV parked at the end of the drive on the other side of the gate. The window of the car was rolled down, revealing an olive-skinned man with slicked back black hair in the driver's seat. Another man sat in the passenger's seat smoking something that billowed gray smoke out of the open window.

Moon Walkers, I growled, recognizing one of the alpha's through the window. *I gotta get out of here.*

I was strong, but not strong enough to take on whomever else happened to be in the SUV. Gulping, I stared momentarily down at Luell. The sad looking animal whined in my arms. I stroked her blood matted fur, pulling the blanket further over her.

The high-pitched whine of the engine signaled to me

the vehicle left. I let out a breath, thankful I wouldn't have to deal with all those wolves in the car. Adjusting Luell in my arms once again, I strode to the front gate, to where my car was parked just outside.

Walking carefully to not hurt the cat, I slipped through the gate; my car was still parked to the right. I walked around it, checking to make certain the tires were not slashed or any part of my vehicle was damaged. Since my focus was on Zuri and then her poor cat, I'd pitifully admit, I let my senses drop. Satisfied, I got inside, putting Luell in the passenger's seat. Once I got Luell to the vet, I would ditch the car to be safe and head to Zuri on foot.

"To the vet for you, then off to find your owner."

Luell mewled pathetically.

"Poor kitty. Soon you'll be fixed up and chasing mice in no time. Hang in there sweet baby."

I checked my phone to see if Zuri messaged back. *Not delivered. Fuck sakes,* I grimaced. I called her phone but it went to voicemail. The hairs on my arms stood on end. My gut told me Zuri was in trouble, and daylight was burning.

CHAPTER FOURTEEN

ZURI

I rose stiffly off the ground, resolving to meet my mother full on. Considering how I got here, and how long it took me, I had no idea how she was here, but after her magic display, I could guess. And I was fucking pissed.

I crossed my left leg over my right, to hide the key from sight and feign having to pee. I felt the key on the inside thigh. I crossed my arms over my chest, not caring to be so exposed in front of my mother. Part of me desperately wanted to make a grab for my 9mm. However, it would be so waterlogged, I wasn't sure if it would even fire at the moment. I would have to extensively clean it when I got to another safe place.

Lyvia stared at me with calculated poise. Her upper lip curled slightly at my appearance. Her elegantly coiffed hair styled specifically for her little party, was now disheveled down her back. She'd changed from her dress into black leather biker pants and a royal blue flowing blouse. I wanted to smirk at the irony of the royal blue and her status, but the immediate danger stopped me.

Her presence rankled and worried me. I had nothing but my fists and wit to defend myself. I doubted a rock thrown or a branch swung would do very much against her magic. If it came to a fight, I was pretty much screwed, but I was going to fight for all I was worth.

Lyvia brought a kerchief to her eyes and sniffed. "I cannot believe you would want away from me so badly as to kill yourself."

Dumbstruck, I stood there. Never being put into this situation before with a cunning manipulative crying woman, I wasn't quite certain how to handle it. I never had a mom; someone there to make the worries of this crazy world seem a bit brighter. What I desired and what I got were painfully different. There was something dark and twisted in her blue eyes that cautioned me from comforting her. I guess this is what disillusionment felt like and it was a strong, breathless kick to the gut. This person, deemed to be my mother before me, wasn't a mother at all. I desired so much to have a mother-daughter moment with her that I was blinded by who she was. And it nearly cost me my freedom and life.

Lyvia came into my life right when it changed and crumbled - from moving to the outskirts of town and getting left by Lazaro - to getting attacked and security systems failing, and my cat dying. Lyvia came in, playing on my despair and grief; playing on me having no one and needing to trust someone. And instead of relying on a trustworthy creep, I put my trust in my mother.

Lesson learned; I would never trust anyone again. The only thing I could trust in anyone was that they left. *If she couldn't be a part of my life from day one, she didn't need to be a part of my life now.*

Lyvia extended a hand like one would a little child to come with them, then quickly retracted it.

I scowled at her. "I told you I was leaving and you trapped me within your walls... What did you expect, Lyvia?"

Lyvia's blue eyes narrowed. "I *expected* you to stay like an obedient child. You have no idea what is out there!"

Chortling, "I'm far from obedient and no longer a child. You would know it if you cared to get to know me," I shot back. "Whatever is out here is much better than what you could ever offer me."

Marching straight to me, Lyvia pointed a finger at my face. "Why do you think I invited you to my home? I want to get to know my daughter. I want to keep you safe."

"Getting to know me doesn't involve entrapment or authorizing over a dozen werewolves to contain me. Getting to know me doesn't involve manipulation, magic spells, or confinement. You never cared about keeping me safe before. Why now?"

"You're dangerous, Zuri. It scares me how dangerous you are to others, but more so to yourself. I have to keep you safe from yourself. That's what a mother does."

I chortled in disbelief from how manipulative and backhanded this entire event played out. This woman had a plethora of excuses, most blaming me, for why she felt the need to control me, leave me for all my life, and keep me at Kadia Castle now that I was an adult.

Like hell I was staying anywhere with her again. I have been blamed all my life for the fallacies of my parents, for the actions and manipulations of their mistakes, and made to believe I'm some sort of horrid person, just like them, but I'm not horrid... I'm lost to who I am, but I'm not horrid.

Crossing my arms over myself, I sighed. Stupidly, I went with her. Sheer curiosity for the woman who birthed me, sent my rather usual and keen judgement on a rollercoaster. I desired to know my mom, who she was and trivial things about her like her favorite color. It backfired hard; so painfully so, I now understand, I never had a mother.

Uncle Syrus's voice rang in my head with something he always said - *just because she's your mother doesn't make her your mother; and blood isn't always family...* I sighed, understanding now, what he meant. *I should have never come here. Damn it all.*

Lyvia's gaze softened. She reached out to take my hands. I continued to keep them tucked under my armpits. She scowled, dropping her hands to her side.

The sun waned farther, turning the sky above us to pinks and purples as sunset came on. There was maybe an hour of daylight left, if that at all. Evander had yet to show up, although it was entirely my fault as I wasn't where I was supposed to be for rescue.

"You're coming back to Kadia with me," Lyvia announced.

I laughed. "Nope."

"It was a statement and not open for discussion."

I took a step toward her, forcing Lyvia to backpedal. "You might be able to control your weak-minded people, but not me. I said no. And no means no. I'm never coming with you, or seeing you, again."

Lyvia held her hands out at her sides where magic pooled in the middle of them like a dry ice misting in a horror movie. I perked a brow, moving my right foot back into a sideways stance, bringing my fists up in front of my face. I was no pugilist by any means, but I could hold my own when needed.

"I don't want to do this, Zuri. It breaks my heart," Lyvia commented. No sorrow laced itself in her voice.

Lyvia drew her right arm back, with her left hovering over the orb of magic. The silver mist crackled in the orb, swirling like a fire on a brushy ground, but banging against its container like lightning.

It hurt me. I would assume my mother, or any mother, would feel some twinge of sorrow or regret; and it hurt I didn't see the emotion in her. It helped solidify my realization that Queen Lyvia Ariella wasn't my mother.

Twisting my body forward, my left fist caught her in the chest while the right followed through to her throat. Lyvia choked, falling back on her butt. The magic once swirling in her hands, dissipated. Spinning on my heel, I leapt into the water and remained submerged, swimming downstream under water until I couldn't hold my breath anymore.

Rising for air, I refrained from sucking in a loud lungful and giving away where I happened to be. I treaded water while being carried away by the current downstream. Spying a large boulder, I tucked myself back behind it in the middle of the river. Lyvia's shrill screams from shore echoing down, brought a smile to my face.

I watched for the telltale sign of magic, the fog-like appearance or maybe even a charge in the air. Thankfully, even magic had its limitations. From what I understood of the manipulative nature, magic couldn't be performed in water. Any magic cast out toward water, would dissipate and become null. That didn't stop me being watchful though. Especially since I was no expert; but judging by Lyvia's quick anger, I figured I was right. And based on her not following me, either she couldn't swim or she wasn't willing to ruin her expensive clothes. But once I got on land, I could be tracked.

Sitting there listening to Lyvia's rants and ravings, one thing I knew for certain, I couldn't make the same mistake again - hopeful trust in family. This time, I couldn't afford to be caught and brought back to Kadia.

I brushed my wet hair off my face, feeling the gems my mother put in my hair still locked onto the strands. I frowned, thinking that they would have fallen out by now with all I put myself through.

This must be how she found me, I surmised. *These gems must be trackers.* My gut swirled, a jumbled mess of emotions I had to sort through to clear my head.

I maneuvered over the boulder rock area, pulling myself onto its slimy jagged surface. Piece by piece, I combed through my hair, yanking out strands and breaking pieces off of the gems that wouldn't release. It took until damn near darkness, where the gray of the night sky announced only a few more moments of daylight, but I removed all the gems. For good measure, I took off the shoes that somehow remained on my feet, putting them beside the gems on the rock surface. I also removed my necklace and earrings. I left all of those there on the boulder so her damn werewolves would be led here and not where I was headed.

Leaning forward, I rested my elbows on my knees and gazed out across the water, allowing myself a moment to breathe. *My whole life I strove for a place to belong and I couldn't have it. And when I felt like I finally got it, it blew up in my face.* I wiped my face clear of water, taking in a deep breath. *Goes to show that maybe I should be alone.* I shuddered, shaking off the gut swirling mess of loneliness and sadness.

Checking myself over again, I found no other gems or weird marks to be tracked with. Satisfied, I plunged back into the water. The current swept me away downstream. Once full darkness came, I would get to shore and begin the tedious walk west.

CHAPTER FIFTEEN

EVANDER

After dropping off Luell at the vet, it took me a couple hours to reach Kadia Castle. I was already behind, in my self-given timeframe, in coming to get Zuri, making certain my files were documented and sent off with the overnight post, along with a final visit for clues to Zuri's place. Although getting Zuri back was important, I had no regrets in taking care of the cat.

My watch read the time as six-thirty in the evening. The sun waned, ready to go down, but still had an hour or so before it completely set. I crept along the edge of the forest, circling around to the east side of Kadia castle, staying well out of sight and earshot. I checked my phone, turning the volume on silent while scrolling through to see if I missed a call from my commander.

It bothered me that I hadn't heard from Commander Iorgas and I hoped I would merit a few more days to turn in this new information and Zuri Barsotti-Luciani herself. Even with the evidence against her, I still wanted the truth from her lips. I wanted to hear from her, from her mouth, what she had done to my family. I wanted her to own the death she dealt to them.

My hands balled into fists. To say I was furious was an understatement. I was hurt that it took this long to put all the pieces together, relieved that I finally had answers and angry with myself for wanting to kiss the bitch who killed my family.

I walked stealthily out of the forested area toward the backside of the mountainous range guarding the east side. I hopped the black cast iron fence easily, passing a bear shifter in the process who paid me no heed. My nose wrinkled at his musky scent. I carefully trekked through the crags and boulders, being sure to stay out of sight and downwind of shifters who served the damnable queen. I crouched behind a large boulder that looked like a broken nose. Werewolves patrolled the ramparts in their fully shifted forms, the size of ponies.

I was a tad nervous seeing the wolf sentries, but when it came to passing the actual gate guard, I simply walked past. The giant of a grizzly shifter didn't even bat an eye. I knew he smelled me as bears noses were stronger than mine. Not sure why he trusted me to walk in, but I wasn't about to complain. I'd never had an issue with bears, and I wasn't going to start now.

Don't think too much about it. The bear probably hates the mad queen like most of Quivleren.

From my position by the nose boulder, the back of the castle was in perfect view. A large balcony hung over the mountain with nothing below it but a sheer drop. The three-foot-tall balustrade on the balcony came out like a half oval, overlooking the sheer and magnificent drop to the fir trees and rocks below. The crags of the mountain were hundreds of feet from the castle itself, allowing no human nor shifter to leap and get to the castle. My back was to the Espowyes Mountains surrounded by the Xylia Forest making the hair on the back of my neck stand on end from knowing what lurked inside.

Growing up, my pack issued a rite of passage test when a wolf turned thirteen, in those mountains to kill a gogmagog. The wolves with the least injuries, especially the merciless rotting blisters caused by their saliva were the most honored. The less injuries, the stronger the wolf and more security they brought to the pack. And if a wolf escaped without a blister, which is almost impossible, their status was just under the alpha. Those were the wolves who were the most clever and best able to protect the pack. Thankfully, my own test, at thirteen, resulted only in a dislocated shoulder and a broken wrist. No rotting blisters and I was able to walk back home on my own. Many of my friends weren't so lucky.

I shook off the uneasiness I felt, concentrating on entering the castle from the back. The entire castle was built on the edge of a cliff itself, carefully creating a seamless edge from mountain to stone castle. There was nothing in which to grab on the side - no vine, no cracks in the stone, there was only the balcony with the balustrade.

A long scream, laced in enmity and vitriol came from the double doors leading out to the balcony. My head whipped to the left, eyes honing in on who made the sound. The woman that stormed out those doors bore a similar resemblance to Zuri with her long brown hair and petite, willowy frame. Dressed in a black leather pants and a royal blue blouse, she furiously paced the balcony.

"That little bitch!" the woman bellowed so loud my ears heard everything without shifting. "I should have just killed her when I had the chance... So many chances, WASTED! UGH! Little damned *bitch*," the queen raised her hands, blasting silver magic at potted plants and destroying them. "I assumed that with her being my daughter, she would be more pliable... Fuck! Damn, that little escaped abortion is my daughter! *Fuckkkk!*" Lyvia screamed again, her voice echoing off the castle and stone surrounding her. She picked up a chair, launching it over the balcony. "She leapt into the river! How did that living mistake know magic doesn't work in water?! WHO TOLD HER?!"

My heart clenched for Zuri at the queen's callous words. I frowned at my somersaulting emotion of pity. I rolled my eyes at myself. "Serves her damn right," I murmured to myself.

A male werewolf approached the queen, putting a consoling hand on her lower back. I raised a brow at the causal interaction.

Queen Lyvia flicked him off, rounding on the werewolf. Lyvia's red face narrowed in on the man; pointing a finger at his chest. "Find her! I want her dead!"

"Your Majesty, is the tracking system still on her?" the male asked.

Lyvia's hands clenched at her side. "No, you bumbling inbred idiot! Zuri ripped them all out of her hair. She was floating down the Zilar River. Put your wolves at *every* offshoot of the river. I want her found and killed; by any means necessary. I don't care how. Kill her and bring me the key and her head! There will be a reward."

Fucking Gods! I blinked. *How in the graces of Elohi did Zuri get to the river? Would she be lunatic enough to jump off the balcony?*

I felt someone approach from behind me. I found myself fully shifted and on top of the attacker in a matter of seconds. My body bristled and shook at the instantaneous shift, similar to stepping out of wet jeans - itchy, quick, and slightly uncomfortable.

A six-foot-tall, lithe man laid calmly on the ground under my paws. His silver eyes remained passive. My jaw snapped as I snarled at him.

"Easy," the man whispered. "Don't alert Lyvia's brainwashed wolf horde."

I wasn't about to let the bear shifter off lightly. "Where's Zuri?" I questioned.

The man squirmed under my paws, attempting to get off the hard ground. "Gone... She jumped." he grunted, trying to get my bulky frame off his chest; his eyes darting toward the balcony.

Scowling, I pressed him harder into the stone with my paws. We were a fair match for each other. The bear, once he shifted into one, had a slight advantage with weighty paws, long claws, and crushing teeth. But I also had the same basic parts. Not as weighty, but agile and quicker. I could run circles around the bear and as long as I didn't let him get too close, he couldn't crush me with his strength.

I half changed back into a half human, where fur still covered my body. Luckily, my face remained as it was. I just looked like I had a big hair deformity. It was weird looking, even to me. Every time I saw my furry reflection, I saw those strange ass monkeys in that tornado movie looking back at me. If it weren't for the amazing strength in this form, I'd never use it. And after this event, I prayed it was the last damn time. I let off of him, standing a few feet away with my arms crossed.

"What do you mean jumped?" I asked.

The bear sat up with his back pressed against the stone. "She jumped - *literally* - off the balcony to escape Lyvia. The queen was going to keep Zuri here permanently and Zuri wouldn't have it."

I fully shifted back into my human self. I ran a hand over my face, admiring her courage to stick to her guns, but also surprised at the woman's insanity to do something so utterly stupid. *If she would have waited inside, like I told her to, she wouldn't be Gods' know where. But seeing as how she is so distrusting of people, I can only imagine what provoked her.*

I growled to myself ignoring the bear for a moment. This made things so much more complicated. I hadn't expected to have to hunt Zuri down while the Mad Queen herself hunted her down. That was a complication I didn't need. I was tempted just to let Zuri go and deal with her own fate, but if my research was correct, Zuri held the key to all my questions and dilemmas. I couldn't just leave her to the whims of the Mad Queen. I had to hunt her down myself and avoid the queen's crazy wolves.

"That's not even all of it," the bear shifter began again.

"According to a human servant I spoke with, once Zuri got to the ground, she jumped off the cliff into the Zilar River."

I thought if my eyebrows rose any higher they'd become permanent fixtures in the middle of my forehead. "Fuck..."

"Yeah," the man replied with a chuckle. "She's nuts... I like her."

I shook my head. Zuri could be anywhere along the Zilar River. There were so many offshoots and so many dangers along the river, not least of all was the river city of Chay where Zuri could easily be captured by the faeries who were known to take human slaves at best or make them dinner at worst. My stomach clenched when I thought of her getting to the coast where the mermaids killed and ate anything that floated by them. Hopefully she'd avoid those two dangers, but there were countless others. And she was on her own.

The only way for me to find her was scent. Yet I wouldn't know where to start and the queen's wolves had her scent too. My time was running short and if I was going to find her, I needed to start now. But I couldn't help but hesitate as thoughts ran through my mind.

If Zuri jumped off a balcony to escape her blood, it left two plausible reasons for me. One being she was in cahoots with her mother over something like destroying more were-packs that Lyvia despises so much and got caught. Two, she was truly innocent. It was difficult for me to even believe the latter now that Zuri had been with her mother, but my gut believed otherwise - that she was innocent, merely escaping a terrible person.

"Shit, shit, shit," I grumbled under my breath.

The man beside me chortled. "You in love with her or something?"

I wasn't sure if my face rendered shock or disgust. Me being in love with Zuri was like a wolf being in love with an ogre. It would never happen due to who her family was. Even when I entertained the thought earlier, it was prior to me knowing all I knew now.

Smitten, Holdur told me... Nope, I decided, *Zuri is cute, but nope.*

The man put his hands up. "Just asking. Seems crazy to me a random wolf shows up looking for Zuri reeking of hate and lust."

Keeping my voice low, I laughed. The entire thing was laughable after the information I found on Zuri's family. Not only would she have to face justice, because making her mother pay for what she did was nearly impossible at this point, although I would pursue the werewolf laws of a death match against her later, but tainting my family with such a poor heritage was never going to happen. Her parents ensured that she'd be untouchable to any *were* family, as well as signed her death warrant with their actions.

I carefully peeked over the edge of the boulder. The wolves on the ramparts still patrolled while more gathered on the balcony all huddled together. Each male equipped with a gun to take out Zuri and shift the blame somewhere else.

"Thanks for the info," I said, maneuvering over a rock.

The trail heading down to where the base of the mountain cliff met the roaring water was a hike to say the least. Honestly, it would suck to trek down in human or wolf form. How the idiot of a woman didn't die was beyond me. If I still believed the god Elohi was still around, I'd say it was his intervention. But he'd not been seen in thousands of years. I highly doubted he'd intervene for a woman condemned to death anyways.

I felt the bear-man behind me, following at a respectable distance. I only managed a few feet down before the cliff turned into a sheer wall of slate followed by jagged stone surrounding trees at the bottom. I looked down and saw the toothpick looking trees and wondered how they grew there. My only conclusion was that magic kept them there. The air reeked of the stuff and my wolfish senses were on guard because of it.

"There's an easier way down," the bear man said, stopping behind me.

I stopped, perking a brow. "What's your aim?"

Bear shifters weren't one to willingly involve themselves in any kind of affairs but their own. Seeing as how this one worked for the queen, had me wondering what happened to him and what his aim would be. They lived in forested, very remote areas in Quivleren, keeping to themselves and their own race. If a bear happened to mate with a different being, it was for a political reason and nothing more. Having this one here, more than likely working for the Queen, put me on edge.

The bear man's bright silver eyes narrowed in on me, bringing forth such a vehemence that made the hairs on my arm stand on end. I hoped the man's ire wasn't directed at me. I loathed fighting fellow shifters. It didn't sit well with me. Shifter fights always were to the death, something I never particularly cared for as one of us would come out breathing while the other would be in a hole with a gravestone.

"Lyvia destroyed my family, binding me magically to this castle. I want her dead so I can be free."

I nodded. Hearing this made my stomach tighten in knots. It made me even more determined to find Zuri and hold her stupid human weak ass accountable for hurting me and mine, but also those beings around me, beings like this bear shifter. Her family was responsible for deaths of numerous wolves and still they wreaked havoc. Eradicating Zuri and her family would solve a plethora of issues for paranormal beings and end the control the bitch of a queen had.

If I could get enough backing by other packs to challenge the Queen of Kadia to a fight to the death, I would. It's all such a political mess because of the damn dragon in Lyvia's pocket. *And by the gods' I will get the packs to endorse me, and I will win against the human bitch who is slowly destroying Quivleren with her political lies, funding small pack wars, and racist hate.*

I clenched my fists. "I'm going to challenge that bitch," I growled, meeting Barend's steady gaze.

The bear stuck out his hand. "I'm Barend. Find my clan in Fenna on the outskirts of the Scirwode Forest. Tell them where I am and that I'm bound. Our clan will not stand for this. And tell them I will endorse you."

I perked a brow. Another paranormal, being accepted

by a bear clan was suicidal unless there was some word of safe passage or marker.

Barend reached behind his head, removing an amulet with a polished red stone paw. "Give this to my mother, Arthes."

I took it, tucking it into my pocket. "Thank you, Barend," I said, shaking his hand and giving him my name. "The queen has to fall."

Barend nodded, a quiet fire burning behind his silver eyes. "Now, follow me. We are going to head through the tunnels."

I warily watched Barend move toward a boulder on the other side of the rock crags I was hiding in. He went to a boulder shaped like a pickle, long, cylinder shaped and bumpy.

Pressing a hand against one of the bumps, the sandy stone slid to the left. A long dark tunnel emerged into view. The cold air trapped inside brought a windy surge of must and mold tingling under my nose.

"Follow this down. It will bring you even with the bank of the Zilar River. Good luck finding Zuri," Barend said.

The hairs on my arms stood on end with the temperature drop at the mouth of the underground stone tunnel. I sniffed warily, waiting for any recent scent to waft my direction. Nothing.

I turned around to thank Barend. The bear was gone. Stepping into the stone tunnel, I fully shifted into my werewolf form. A mixture of black, gray and white hairs blended over my body. I scratched my paws at the stone, sinking into the cold ground to bond, a moment with the world Elohi created; taking a deep, soulful breath to allow my inner wolf to become one with the world around me and hone my innate senses.

Trotting into the tunnel, the hidden stone door ground shut behind me. The path felt smooth under my paws. My vision adjusted quickly to the darkness. Taking off at a full run, I followed the pathway down. If the other werewolves found Zuri first, my justice, my vengeance couldn't be fulfilled.

CHAPTER SIXTEEN

ZURI

The hot sun beat against my face like getting punched with a dodgeball. I tried to move my arms and legs, hardly finding the strength in me to complete the task. A cold rush of water beat against my legs and made me shiver. My arms felt heavy like anvils. Lifting my head and wiping the sand off the right side of my face made my neck crack. I moaned at the weariness and the pain in my body. Scrunching my eyes, I slowly opened them. Every muscle protested and pulled.

Where I exactly happened to be, I didn't have a damn clue. Everything in my head was messed up, like a jumbled puzzle in a box. I lost all sense of direction the moment I first plunged off the waterfall at Kadia Castle.

I rolled over onto my back. Water lapped at my knees. I shuddered again from the chill. How I survived the night in the water, I didn't know. It scared me. Not the fact of surviving drowning, but the fact the queen hadn't found me; I had won this particular battle and that would enrage her. And *that* scared me. Lyvia would be relentless in trying to get me. I may not know my mother on a personal level, but her ruthless reputation preceded her.

Inhaling deeply, I lifted myself to a sitting position. Sand fell from my matted dried hair. I shook my hair out, feeling the itchy sandy debris cascade down my bare back and scrape the tender, sunburnt skin. Raking my fingers through my hair for the hundredth time, I felt paranoid, but couldn't shake the feeling those little gems were what allowed my mother to find me so easily last time I'd crawled out of the river.

I shouldn't have ever gone with that horrible woman, I grumbled to myself, finding no more little beads.

I patted my left thigh, exhaling with extreme relief when I felt the little telltale bulge of the key. In this moment, spandex was the greatest invention ever. However, my gun and the mags were gone. I laughed to myself as I started to think about my next move. *I had a plan yesterday. All this jumping into freezing and rushing river water though seems to have washed it out of my head.* I scrunched my eyes tight and racked my brain for any monetary plan I had.

"Vidis Forest!" I blurted aloud.

Ignoring my screaming, stretching muscles, I rose slowly to my feet, gazing around me. I was naked. Well, except for the spandex shorts with the key tucked inside. My upper half was exposed.

I knew I should have worn a tank top under that damned dress, I grumbled to myself.

A forest was to my right. The Zilar River, or whatever

part I was in, was to my left. My feet faced up the river-bank, where the river came flowing downward. I looked around for any sign of the north. I couldn't find it.

Frowning, I glanced at the sky. The sun wasn't directly overhead yet, still roughly two hours until it was. *Sun rises in the east, sets in the west,* I mused, turning around, so my right side faced east. *Now, what way is north? Moss typically grows on the north side,* I surmised, heading toward the forest warily. I'd get a true sign at nightfall when the stars emerged. I didn't know much about the stars, but I did remember that if I could find the biggest star and the constellation connected to it, it would point south, and then I would know the true north. I just wasn't sure if I could wait that long. I had to risk walking in circles for now.

My feet took me toward the forest. I hesitated at the edge, my bare feet inches from the first fern. I stared inside to the dense shrubbery of tall firs, wide, branchy maples and a few other random trees I didn't have names for.

"This is where me and my stupid shit lands me," I grumbled, moving into the forest. "I just *had* to get to know the nasty woman. Damned human curiosity... Maybe I'm part fuckin' cat shifter or something."

I shook my head. Being part cat explained my curiosity for things, like getting to know Lyvia or if cereal tastes good with chocolate milk. I should stay away from, and the tendency to do, stupid things; and get startled when those stupid things blow up in my face. I pictured Luell playing with a garden snake and jumping when the snake bit back. I smiled, forcing back the grief. I loved and missed her. But sometimes she was dumb. And in this situation, I was the dumb cat.

I blew a puff of air up into my messy, long bangs, annoyed at the turn my life had taken. I hadn't planned on 'public' nudity nor had I planned on my mother shooting magic at me multiple times. Just two months ago, I'd been planning on buying a house with Lazaro and considering venues, and content to work in medical billing. Now I was pretty sure my job was gone and Lazaro was a pretty big mistake, and I had no clue what to do next.

The immediate future would be to focus on survival. I was at a very high risk of dying from exposure, hunger or forest monsters. Maybe a combination of the three. After that, I'd need to focus on finding Elohi, giving him the key back and then I'd figure out the rest of my life.

I rubbed my arms as I walked further into the forest, my bare feet still a little numb from the frigid river water. I looked down thankful I still couldn't feel the sticks I was stepping on. If this *god* was almighty and powerful, then where the fuck was he? If Elohi had the power, the magic and everything else a god would have, whatever it may be, why not find the key himself? Why do I have it? And what the hell did he expect a human to do with it?

I grumbled, moving through the dense ferns and rhododendrons. I stopped at the first big fir tree I came to. Walking around it, I inspected the bark looking for the telltale moss that would point me north. I sighed heavily. No moss. Dumb damn tree had let me down. I started around it once more, hoping in vain that my eyes would pick something up I missed the first time around. And as I was rounding it slowly I spotted the white splotch of mold. Glancing above my head, I spied several more splotches.

Grinning, I grabbed a stick off the ground and made a compass. I needed to head west, then south once I came to the Belisma River. Vidis Forest lined the southside of Quivleren, east of the Belisma River. I figured to start at one end of the forest and work my way through it. No matter what though, I had to start somewhere.

I parted my hair down the middle, moving it forward and off my sunburn. My hair smelled of fish and dirt. My nose curled at the pungency. I liked fishing and I loved eating fish, but I didn't want to smell like them.

I wonder since I was in the water for so long, and I smell awful and fishy, if any of my mother's wolves could track me?

My nose cringed again as I caught my scent. My mind wandered to Evander, wondering if he was trying to rescue me. Part of me hoped he was, but I had no clue how that would work now that I was miles away from the castle and smelled like gross dead fish. Another part of me figured he wouldn't. Especially since he was a man, and in my experience, especially after Lazaro, couldn't be relied on. I preferred it that way. My problems were my own, and I would solve them myself.

Running a hand over my face, I groaned. *He isn't coming for me. No wolf would willingly go out of their way to save a human*, I reasoned. *Yet Evander did... He saved me with those men that one night. He was there, stalking me like a creeper, but saved me from danger.* I tapped a finger to my chin; *would that be a guardian or a prowler?*

I had no idea how to place Evander. He was kind and

considerate to me and saved me. He was also aloof, sort of a butt nugget, and constantly pissed off. On that same note, he was so handsome - the drool worthy kind where I was sure I would drool if I stared at him. He was the hand-somest male werewolf I'd ever laid eyes on.

Raising my hand near my head, I waved those thoughts off, as if this random movement would literally push them from my head. "Whatever," I said aloud to myself.

I rolled my eyes to further push the thoughts away, continuing my trek through the forest. My feet were completely numb and I couldn't tell if they were bleeding or not. I moved my hair over my boobs to help keep the mosquitoes away, but they were still coming to eat me. I growled at the annoying buzzing around my head. Hunger made my stomach sound a loud alarm alerting me and anyone within several hundred feet that I was starving.

I tried to keep my walking path as straight as possible west, keeping the sun within eyesight. I still had several hours until nightfall, but it got my mind reeling for what to do next in terms of food, shelter, fire and water. I could keep going for hours without food, not so much without water.

I walked for what I assumed had been at least a mile if not more into the forest; knowing a person could walk a mile in fifteen minutes, but with my bare feet it took a little longer. A large branchy maple caught my attention. I stared up at it, wondering if I should climb in it to rest for the night or continue on.

High-pitched tittering from behind me caught my attention. It was the kind of sound even the birds stopped chirping for. My blood froze. Part of me wondered if I should start running and head back to the water, or take my chances through the forest. The little hairs on my arms prickled.

Oh, hot damn, I thought, trying to remain calm. *Water or forest... Water. Their magic can't work in water.*

A bright streak of pink flashed to my left. I tried my best to ignore it. A chill crept up my spine causing the hairs on the back of my neck to stand on end. Tittering reached my ears from the right. Another bright flash zipped past my field of vision. Head up, I abandoned the maple and kept charging my way through the density of the forest, making a slight change in direction toward the river.

A fae zipped past, coming close to touching my skin. I kept my face as passive as possible and my eyes fixed on the destination of the river ahead. Inside, I trembled, anxious and terrified of the possibility of being dragged back to their city of Chay.

Unlike the sprites who were at Kadia Castle, the fae to the east of Zilar Lake and River were nasty. Three-foot-tall, bright pink creatures with golden hair and eyes. Wings, dark as ebony, protruded from their backs looking like Alençon lace that came up to a rounded nubbed tip. The fae looked adorable, like a doll for a little girl. Their teeth, pointed and curved inward like a lake trout and wouldn't let anything go once inside their mouth; long spindly fingers with sharp gold nails danced eagerly in the air at the sides of their body.

My body desired to shudder, but I repressed the action. Light came from the edge of the forest in front of me. The fae taunted me with their obnoxious giggling, zooming past me like they wanted to brush against my skin.

Keeping my head high, I made it to the edge of the forest, back where the river happened to be. Spindly, gnarled fingers, pressed into my bare skin on my left. Balling my right hand into a fist, I swung at the fae. The woman fae laughed, ducking out of the way.

"Human," the woman fae chattered, to the other.

I glanced at the one on my right. The three-foot male creature grinned vilely at me, revealing the inward curved pointed teeth. The fae woman grabbed my arm again. She inhaled deeply, smelling my skin while her head bobbed up the full length of my arm. I swung a fist at her again, connecting with her chin.

"Human," it squeaked.

The other fae I'd nearly forgotten, grabbed my other arm. I stopped walking, my mind reeling with any kind of plan. This fae, a deeper pink and male, didn't grin or respond. He bared his teeth, eyes pinched together with seething venom behind his gaze. Taking a quick peek down, the male was naked save for a club dangling from a strap on his hip.

Turning my attention back over to the female fae, I looked down at her side for a weapon of some kind. Nothing was there but a sheer cloth hiding her bottom half.

Bending to the right side, my left foot lashed out, catching the female in the gut. Surprised, the male flew into the air with a hard grip on my arm. I sunk my weight down, not wanting to be taken by the damn fae. The male growled, pulling me harder. I winced as his fingers dug into my skin.

"Damn it," I grumbled under my breath.

Leaping into the air, I made a grab for the foot long club at his hip. The male fae rose into the air, attempting to escape my grasp. The link on the club snapped, sending him higher into the air. The female screeched, making a bee-line for me. Bringing the club in my right hand up, I caught her in the stomach. The fae whirled backward. Seizing my moment, I took off sprinting toward the river.

CHAPTER SEVENTEEN

EVANDER

I stayed in my wolf form, trotting down the river's edge, and pausing at every suitable bank to hunt for clues. If she washed ashore at some point, I had to find her before Queen Lyvia's wolves did. Only, I couldn't detect her scent. I couldn't find tracks, any tracks - human or otherwise, and it bothered me to no end.

The bank opposite me had marks upon the soft sandy soil. I grumbled. The Zilar River flowed steadily downstream with many different offshoots and tributaries. Shaking my body free of annoyance, I leapt into the river, swimming steadily against the current to the other side. Getting closer to the bank, I spied the soft outline of slippered feet with a big toe indented in the sandy ground. Getting fully out of the water, I shook most of the water free of my fur.

I growled under my breath. Being wet in wolf form was rarely fun. It happened and I dealt with it, but I rarely enjoyed it. Being wet at night though? It was torture. And the sun was going to sink soon. Finding Zuri along the many branches of the Xylia forest that went in tandem with the Zilar River wasn't going to be a picnic either. I looked around and sniffed the ground, thankfully catching her scent. At least I was on the right path now. That would make finding her and exacting my justice immensely easier.

Approaching the footprints in the dirt, another set lay firm in the sandy shore bank. A booted set, slightly larger than Zuri's petite, narrow feet. Lowering my head to the slippered track, I inhaled deeply.

Zuri, I confirmed. *She was here, but where did she go?* Going to the other track, I lowered my head and sniffed. *Not Zuri, but female from what I can gather.*

I scanned the area behind her, seeing no additional tracks heading into the wooded forest leading into the Xylia Forest and the Espowyes Mountains beyond, I spun around, facing the river and the tracks heading back to the water. Surveying the ground, Zuri's slippered feet, did some sort of maneuvering then dashed back to the water. I perked a brow, wondering if a fight had happened given the distance of strides. The heel of her slippered foot was the only indication left of her possibly getting back into the water.

I rolled my eyes and huffed. *At least this is somewhat better than trying to hunt her through a gogmagog infested forest. She is smart... ish...* My lips pulled in a reluctant wolf grin. *She is relatively keen, I guess.*

Following the river further downstream, I kept my eyes peeled for Queen Lyvia's werewolf henchmen and signs of Zuri.

I came to a place a few meters before the first big split in the river. Boulders protruded from the water, creating a churning current below the water's surface. I caught a scent on the wind of Zuri's hair. The boulders near one of the big splits in the river, my eyes caught sight of glittering beads in the sunset. Narrowing my eyes, I spied silver slippers on top of the rocks.

Not wanting to get wet again, I paced the riverbank. The slippers had to be Zuri's since slippered prints were just two miles up the river. My gut churned with affirmation.

Where would the river take her once she plunged back into the water?

Sitting on the riverbank annoyed, I studied the river flow. I was no expert by any means. But I wanted to make certain whatever direction I chose, would be one that led me to her.

A long, hair-raising howl came from behind me, closer than I anticipated it being.

"Fuck," I seethed under my teeth.

Lyvia's wolves were on Zuri's scent and more than likely mine as well. Taking off at a full run, I sped down the riverbank toward the fae city. Somehow, I knew in my gut that Zuri had found herself somewhere near the city of Chay. I knew it. I didn't know how or why, but I did.

If Zuri was anywhere near Chay, she was in danger and my vengeance was on the line for that matter. Chay wasn't a city any normal paranormal or human wanted to go near. The fae were slavers; taking kids and adults, human or paranormal, in the night and using them as personal servants or eating them - whatever seemed to strike their fancy. To anyone who didn't know any better, these three-foot, bright pink, bumbling, child-sized creatures were adorable.

Baring my teeth, I dug my paws deeper into the soil, forcing myself to go faster. I had to get to Zuri. Not only to save her stupid ass from a horrible death by the fae, but from Lyvia's goons, all for my own selfish, personal reasons.

I wanted her, more than anything, to pay for her familial crimes against me and my pack. For that, I needed her breathing. A dead body wouldn't cut it. Dropping her off with Iorgas was going to make me sublimely happy. When she dies, my soul will be able to be at peace. After Zuri's death, I would get my vengeance on the Queen of Kadia and finally whoever Zuri's sire happened to be.

Glancing behind me, three wolves were quickly closing in. Teeth bared and howling, they called for reinforcements. As far as I knew, fifteen wolves served Queen Lyvia. I had no doubts most were following behind me. The queen did nothing small; especially when it came to her enemies.

"Shit," I grumbled to myself.

Looking to my right, the Zilar River was quickly becoming more rapid. The water churned, ripping past me with a roar; not quite sounding like the thunderclap, but loud enough to realize the current was zipping by and churning beneath the beautiful surface. Up ahead another split came in the water, leading in different directions. I skidded to a stop, facing the water. Glancing behind me again, the queen's wolves were damn near a mile from me.

Without thinking, I leapt into the water, swimming toward the right split in the river.

Lyvia's wolves skidded to a stop where I was moments before, growling, and pacing the riverbank. I growled in irritation. I loathed the water. The only good water was for drinking and showering and now this human had me humiliating myself with the doggy paddle, barely keeping my nose above water, just so I could save her hide to then turn around and kill it. My logic didn't make sense to me even, but I pushed that aside and concentrated on surviving the current and getting Zuri before these wolf-slaves caught her.

More wolves lined the opposite side of the riverbank, waiting for me to emerge and surround me. I growled, baring my teeth as I swam by. The Zilar River picked up its churning pace, taking me swiftly past all the wolves. The sun was near to setting, casting a dark shadow on those who had followed Zuri and myself.

"You two," a wolf shouted, "follow him. The rest of you, search the riverbank."

The wolves split, taking off in different directions. The river continued to pick up speed. *Fucks sakes*, I grumbled, trying harder to keep my head afloat. I wasn't sure at this point what form would be better in this ripping current. I wasn't a strong swimmer in either form. I tried to swim toward shore, but was pulled to the middle by the current.

"Dammit," I grumbled, keeping my head above water. "Things I go through to bring a human to justice."

After a minute of struggling against the current, I gave up and just allowed the current to take me. I let my body shift into human form, my head bobbing in the water. The river made a slight bend to the right, dipping downward. My legs and right side connected with a boulder leaving me slightly breathless from the hard impact.

In my peripheral, on the right, wolves kept pace with me and the river. *Shit.* I needed to get on shore soon, but if I struggled to shore, I would be too exhausted to fight them off.

"Fuckin' ouch," I said, smacking into a rock hidden beneath the surface.

My blood froze. A deafening roar came from ahead, around a bend I couldn't see. I panicked and looked around me. Neither bank was an option for me as wolves prowled both sides. But the bank to the left had fewer wolves. I paddled desperately with both hands and feet, but the current was too strong and it continued to sweep me closer to the roar. I made one final lunge at a boulder that barely stuck out of the water. Instead, my shin smacked it, causing my whole foot to go numb. I cursed and took a deep breath as I plunged off the edge.

CHAPTER EIGHTEEN

EVANDER

Opening my eyes, sunlight pelted my face with a bright, burning vengeance. I crinkled my eyes, squinting them shut as I rose to my feet. My hands held my head, attempting to cease the pounding. I dusted the sandy dirt from the side of my face, and hair.

My water clogged shoes slogged as I shuffled forward a few paces and stopped. Wriggling my feet, my lip curled in disgust at the squelching between my toes and socks. I swore I could feel the wrinkling of my feet and rubbing against the fabric of my socks. I hated it.

Opening my eyes, they slowly adjusted to the light around me. In front of me was a forest - dense, dark, and thick with vegetation. To my immediate right was the Zilar River flowing steadily, but not violently anymore.

"Son of a bitch," I said aloud, as I prepared myself to shift. My back popped and my muscles groaned as I moved. "Dammit all! This shift will be miserable. Maybe just walking a little while will loosen my muscles enough to not feel like I'm dying as my wolf emerges."

I walked along the river bank, keeping the forest to the right of me. I sniffed the air, not getting any form of a scent. I was thankful that even in my human form, my inner wolf still allowed me it's primal senses. I wasn't ready to shift yet. The grogginess in my head made it pound more. I dared another glance at the flowing river and squinted my eyes at the brightness reflected off the water.

I paused my strides, glancing behind me. No other wolves greeted my gaze, but I knew it didn't mean they weren't hunting me or Zuri. I tried to come up with a plan. My head protested any deep thoughts.

"Fuck," I groaned.

I needed to shake this if I was going to save her to bring her back to the department where I worked. Looking to the sky, I noticed the sun was to my left, which, based on my location, meant the sun was about two hours until noon. I couldn't help the groan that came out. It was a mix of elation and pain. On one hand, I hadn't lost much time. On the other, that much brain power caused the vicious drum beating creatures in my head to pound harder. I sighed as the forest to the right of me called to the wolf in me. The wolf side, like a sweet tooth needing satisfaction, begged to take over; to run into the forest, hunt and track Zuri down. The human part of me, the part of me ruled by reason and logic as opposed to instinct and desire, wanted to follow the river to see if this was the way Zuri happened to come.

Shaking my head slowly, I ignored my wolf and

continued down the riverbank. Urgency prickled at my skin. Queen Lyvia's buffoons would still be on Zuri's scent. Whether or not they stopped for the night based on the queen's orders was a different question entirely. I hoped they stopped. I imagined the fae getting their tiny fat pink fingers on them and I grinned at the image.

I lost my smile and sighed. I shifted as I grumbled under my breath. The whole situation annoyed me. Being wet was the worst. Chasing a human; a human I had liked until I discovered her association with my enemies; a human I couldn't quite hate even though I was trying; a human I half wanted to turn in and half wanted to protect. My agitation grew as I thought of Zuri and doubled when her abhorrent mother flitted into my mind. Finally, I shifted. To my surprise, the misery I expected never came. I could have slapped myself. I'd been so distracted, I'd forgotten how healing a shift could be. That in itself spoke to the amount of frustration and stress I was under. I was as tough as the next wolf, but I liked my world orderly, and this whole situation was completely outside of my comfort zone. Groaning with pleasure, I dug my toes into the soft sandy dirt. My body shook as I finally gave in to the primal instinct and edged closer to the forest.

Inhaling deeply and growling at all the scents that assaulted my nose, I caught a specific scent I loathed and terrified me - fae. Although the creatures dared not take on a pack of *weres*, for that was suicide. But I was alone.

Tittering reached my ears - light and childlike. It bothered me. There was a vehemence behind it, hidden in the dulcet tones of innocence and youth, but most knew it was there and could catch it. Only those completely ignorant or stupid missed the malevolence. Keeping my head down and baring my teeth, I trotted further downstream, away from the noise and hopefully toward the scent of Zuri.

The fae hated the water. They couldn't swim worth anything and their magic was weak in water. I smirked. For some reason or another, most magic was useless in water - except dragons. Their magic was infinite, lucky fuckers. Fortunately, gifted dragon magic was limited to the same aspects of being useless in water.

A fae peeked out of the tree line, staying well away from the water. The fae woman smiled. I cringed at the strange teeth curving in toward her mouth and her odd facial expression - a mixture of glee, terror, and hunger. The three-foot-tall creature, hovering in the canopy of the forest, licked her lips. Keeping my head down, I trotted farther down the bank, staying as close to the water as I could without actually being fully in. I kept my attention toward the forest. I didn't want to be caught off guard and I was being hunted again. The fae followed, sticking to the edges of the forest.

Scuffles around a large bend on the shoreline caught my attention. Whoever it was struggled. I heard splashes, shifting sand, and thuds as if a body fell, got back up and fell again. I paid half attention to the fae woman as I turned to the dirt in front of me. About a hundred feet in front of me the dirt was disturbed. There were indentations, footprints and handprints as if someone had stumbled, slipped on the wet sand and caught themselves. I breathed in deeply trying to catch whoever's scent it was, but the water had washed it away save for the dirt, trees and fae smell.

The fae woman at the forest's edge giggled, bobbing up and down gleefully. "Human!" she screeched, clapping her hands. The creature turned her head back into the forest, yelling, "More human!"

My heart somersaulted. *They have Zuri. I hope she isn't hurt. It would impede the rescue and getting her outta here.* Lifting my head, I sniffed the air, hoping to catch her scent in the air. All I sniffed was grungy fae and it singed my nose. My gut tingled with anticipation of getting to her. What I thought would be a quick rescue mission for selfish purposes was proving to be a horrible chore.

My eyes scanned the tree line and the shoreline ahead for any more fae that could be peeking out. So far all I saw was the woman, but like pests, where there was one, there were always more. The question was - how many? My claws dug into the soil, hoping there weren't many and that Zuri was alright. I feared for her safety, not that I was much safer.

Growling, I sniffed the tracks closer to the forest. Zuri's faint scent wafted up to my nose. Bare feet prints were left in the wet sandy shoreline. Following the tracks, she stumbled to get her bearings and made her way into the forest.

Alright girlie, at least you were alive about an hour ago, I thought. *Where are you now though?* I sniffed the ground again, lifting my head up in the direction of the prints. *And you're headed west. Why west?* Shaking off the sheer irritation, I reminded myself about the joy of seeing her death once I got my paws on her. Doubt crept it's tingling fingers in my gut, reminding me she was nothing like those who destroyed my family. I growled at myself, forgetting I had pushed from my mind of where to place her in my neat little cubicles of right and wrong. Even after I got her back, I still had time to decide before I left her with Commander Iorgas, if I did at all.

Inside the forest, branches broke. A vexed cackling of faeries chirped amongst each other. I squared off with the fae on the forest's edge. The fae woman rolled her shoulders, mouth open as her tongue licked her teeth.

"Human!" the fae tittered again, pointing in my general area.

Rustling came from inside the forest. Bushes and branches cracking. A human sounding yelp echoed close by in the chaotic din of whatever was happening inside the guarded safety of the forest.

Digging my paws into the soil, I took off inside the dense forest. Leaping over a rhododendron, my ears swiveling for the sound I heard. Bearing to the right, the fae who'd been following me on the forest's edge, barreled toward me.

Dodging to the right, I missed the fae woman's greedy grasp for my fur. The fae swerved around, charging me again. Its black lace wings beating furiously, both to propel her faster and knock me off balance.

I leapt into the air, forcing my body to turn mid-air. I made a hasty snatch for the fae's wings, getting hold of one and shearing it off her body. I spat out the foul-tasting wing, and growled at the creature. The fae cried in agony, crashing to the ground, moaning, barely moving. Gloopy blue blood oozed from the open wound I created in her back.

Landing on my feet, I charged the fae laying on the ground motionless. My teeth enclosed around her unguarded throat and crushed it. I didn't particularly like leaving something to die slowly - fae or not.

"Fuck!" Zuri's voice screeched.

The human nearly plowed into me, stumbling over her own feet, barely catching herself and sprinting off to her right with a bloody club in her right hand. I shook my head, doing a double take then looking away quickly. All Zuri wore were tight, athletic shorts. Her top was bare, and while I looked away quickly, I couldn't help but notice her breasts bouncing unrestrained and her sculpted butt jiggling in a most appetizing way. I snorted a laugh at myself, remembering I was supposed to hate her. I couldn't help it though. She was gorgeous and both the man and the wolf liked what they saw. But that was all I could allow myself. My duty was to my people, and I had to turn her in. So, I dropped the dead fae, huffed and took off after her, being sure to keep my gaze on her bare feet.

It wasn't difficult to overpower and pass her. I wanted to laugh at the sight of her petite legs pumping so hard. And I could laugh now that the immediate fae danger was over and I'd found her, but restrained myself. I had a job to do.

She would never make the track team, I mused.

Leaping forward, I used my weight to knock her to the ground. Hitting her in the back from behind, she somersaulted forward, rising to her feet, taking off again; the club still in her hand, absolutely unphased. Her sheer will and determination to survive made me proud, despite why I was here. I couldn't help but admire her. She'd been on the run for days, down a raging river, against magic I could only imagine, defeating at least one fae if the club in her hand was anything to go by and completely human, yet she was still running. I admired her tenacity. *She'd make a good wolf's mate.* I growled at the thought. *Not the time Evander. Not ever, fuckin' moron.*

Branches snapped from the left and I swerved my head that way. Two fae flitted toward Zuri at full speed and I veered off to sneak up behind them. As I turned, Zuri swung her club and caught one under the chin, eliciting a scream of rage.

With the fae occupied with Zuri, I snuck around behind. Soaring at one, I landed on its back. Before it could realize what was happening, I bit into its neck, severing its spine. With a quick shake of my head, I decapitated it.

The second fae turned on me. Zuri stood behind the creature, thwacking it on the head. The fae sharply inhaled, crumpling to the ground. Seizing my moment, I bit into the neck of the stunned, breathless fae, ending it.

Zuri held the club out in both hands like a sword. "Shift!" she snarled at me.

I laughed, softly then it became manic. The determined look on her face complete with a full-on glower in an attempt to look menacing while completely naked was too much. It was adorable on a human who barely passed the five-foot mark.

Pain radiated through my head. My legs gave out, sending me to the ground. Zuri had struck me.

"Dammit Zuri!" I shouted.

Zuri put a hand to her mouth. "Evander?"

Shifting to my human form, I rose to my feet. "Yes," I grumbled, rubbing the top of my head. "You could have given me a moment to shift, ya know."

She dropped the hard club with a thump on the ground. Warm arms enclosed around me. Her head rested on my chest. Warm water pelted my black t-shirt. I put one arm around her, giving her the comfort she needed. Part of me was absolutely relieved at her safety while the other battled with my own selfish relief of being able to bring her back alive. For the moment, I patted her back and let the emotions die so I didn't read into them.

Zuri sniffled, pulling back, blushing and wiping her eyes. "I can't believe you came for me," she said softly.

Withdrawing myself from her, I took off my t-shirt, and handed it to her. Gratefully she took it and put it on her body. I almost came to her mid-thigh, bulky to her frame. She pulled her long, blonde hair out of the back of the shirt and sighed. She smoothed it out, taking a step away from me.

"Thank you," she said, contentedly.

"You're welcome, and I told you I would," I replied.

Zuri shrugged. "My problems aren't yours though." She wiped her eyes, taking a deep breath.

I stared at her, taken by her truthfulness. My gut battled with my head and I tried my damndest to ignore it all. I opted for a nod, "Let's get back to OKimma. Ladies first."

Zuri nodded weakly. She looked forlorn, completely defeated. I pursed my lips at her expression. She had sass, vivacity and a thirst for independence and seeing her like this made me question my motives. For being a human, I was surprised and impressed with her ability to stay alive this long.

I grunted to hide my reaction and she glanced at me. I gave her a sympathetic smile. This sucked. I really liked her. She was resilient and her survival instinct was amazing. But I had a duty to my people. I had a need for justice and our laws demanded it from any blood relation. And my family was still dead and that anger burned deep. But I looked at her and couldn't help but feel sorry for her. She was such a sweet little thing that trusted me like I was her life saver. Getting her to Commander Iorgas would be simple. She'd follow me without a damned clue that I'd be betraying her. I swallowed hard and pushed the thought away.

I moved around her, taking the lead north. Glancing behind me, I saw Zuri following despondently. Her head was down, but when she glanced up, her face displayed several emotions: relief, sorrow and desperation. Her honey brown eyes were so expressive and her hands twisted her hair over her right shoulder like she needed to be distracted and I felt that twinge of guilt and sympathy again, but allowed anger to override it. I could not sympathize with her too much. I had a job to do.

"I'm so stupid," Zuri whispered. "I wanted to have a mom. A *real* mom, to know what I was finally like to have one. Ya know to bake cookies with, watch a favorite soap on tv or go shopping... Whatever mom and daughter's do; and it got me here," she cried, her voice crackly, wiping her eyes angrily. "I'm so stupid."

I perked a brow, saying nothing. I couldn't imagine what she was going through. My family was dead. Even though they were gone, I had long stopped imagining what they would be like to have. And to further drive the heartache of the 'what if's' I had long stopped listening to stories of my parents for they never did any justice to who they were; only stirred up emotions of me wishing I would have gotten the chance to know them.

I opened my mouth to say something, but snapped it shut. After all she had been through, my callous remark would serve no purpose.

Zuri took a deep breath. "Lesson learned. I shouldn't have never met her."

I pursed my lips, controlling my tongue. *The less I said, the better,* I reminded myself. *You have a job to do and justice for the pack to get.* Zuri put on a good show for those too thick to dissect what she was about. She was the type of woman who put on a brave front, a show for the world to see. Inside, she was as weak as they came. The only thing setting her apart was her sheer honesty and loyalty to those she loved.

At least this human is capable of such, I thought. Most I had encountered were quick to pass the blame or were scheming for personal benefit. Zuri had several qualities far and above what I figured a typical human could possess and I appreciated that about her.

I trudged through the forest, making a path easy for the

bare footed human following me obediently. I felt bad at her lack of shoes but selfishly I also didn't want to listen to her whine. The forest opened up a touch, giving way to spaced out trees and less vegetation, making the floor dirtier and easier for her. She softly grunted behind me. Peeking over my shoulder I saw her lips curled in, eyes and face wincing as she stepped on a stick. Her eyes met mine and she smiled wanly. I reciprocated, admiring her spirit to push through her hurting feet.

My eyes scanned for signs of Queen Lyvia's horde of wolves now that we were in the open. Sniffing the air, I couldn't smell anything nearby. Zuri suddenly paused, feeling the inside of her left thigh.

"What are you doing?" I asked, curiously.

"Making sure the key is still there."

I laughed. "You're not going to be going back to your house for a while."

Zuri shook her head. "Not that key," she said sharply. "This key."

She pulled it out from the inside of her thigh. The small silver metal key rested softly in her hand. On one side of the key was the tree of life. Coming toward her, I picked it up out of her hand, turning it over. On the other side was an hourglass and goat. Taking it from her, I held it up in my hand, reading the inscription around the shaft and collar - *For those that shall seek, will find and those that shall protect, will endure.*

"Is this...?" I asked, unable to fully get the words out.

Zuri nodded, plucking the key back from my fingers

and sticking inside her bike shorts on the right side of her thigh this time. "I have to find Elohi and give it back."

The urge to laugh warred with my anger. I took a step back to put some distance between us. This key and this woman's family destroyed my pack, destroyed my parents; all over control of Quivleren and manipulation to get it. The paper I had from her Grandma Kaethe confirmed to me, Zuri and her family were involved with the destruction of mine. This bitch's family ruined everything in my life. In a flash my hand enclosed around her wrist, locking tight.

Shock and pain registered on her face. "What the hell Evander!"

"You!" I seethed. "You're coming with me."

Zuri dug her heels into the dirt. "What is your problem?" she shrieked, her face mottling to confusion and hurt.

I yanked her forward. She flew through the air and would have face planted in the ground if I hadn't been holding her. I lessened my grip, guilty at the unnecessary roughness I used, but still holding her firm. *For my pack and justice, for my pack and justice.* I breathed out, my eyes locking on her and I growled low.

I locked both her wrists in one hand, holding her close to me so I could punctuate each word I said and so she could hear the venom in my voice, "*You* are my problem. You and your family damn near annihilated my entire pack. Your family stole the key we were guarding. Because of you and your blood, other packs like mine are decimated too, all because your blood wanted a key it should never have possession of. You and your blood should be eradicated from the entire world of Quivleren," I snarled.

Her pathetic hands tried to wriggle free of my grasp. She attempted to throw an elbow and failed. She tried to kick out, but I would not be swayed. She was too weak. I swept her legs out from underneath her, where I helped her fall to her back. I held her there with a foot on her chest.

"I haven't killed anyone," she cried, hurt lacing her voice.

Standing over top of her, I watched Zuri's body shake. She was a keen enough woman to understand fighting my wrath would be pointless. Instead, silent tears tracked down her dirtied face. Her eyes reflected fear and a hollowness.

"Not directly," I agreed. "But your mother killed and your sire did as well. My parents were killed. My pack was killed and the remainder were enslaved to your cunt of a mother. The only reason I wasn't killed is because I wasn't home when it happened."

Zuri shook her head. "I don't," she stammered breathlessly. She became silent. Her entire body stilled. "Are," she swallowed. "Are you evoking the werewolf Rights of Justice?"

I yanked her to her feet, my hand still clamped around her right wrist. Getting in her face, I stared into her beautiful, scared eyes. "Yes," I growled.

CHAPTER NINETEEN

ZURI

It was pointless to fight against him. Evander wouldn't have it. His strength was too much and if I struggled more, no doubt he'd knock me out and carry me. And I couldn't look for an escape if I was unconscious. I knew I had no chance to overpower him. But maybe, just maybe, I could outwit him somehow and give myself a fighting chance. That chance was not right now. The hatred and anger pouring from him reflected the malevolence in his eyes. I thought, for a brief second, I'd seen pity, but considering the hatred I saw now, I must have imagined it. A figment of my hopeful imagination. And now, he was on high alert, watching my every move. I'd have to wait.

His one-eighty personality switch gave me whiplash and the shock numbed me. I'd spent days trying to survive and I knew I hurt under all this numbness. For now, I couldn't feel a thing - no hunger, no arms, no legs. Everything in me went blissfully senseless. I couldn't even wrap my head around my own death. Whatever my family had done to Evander, the laws of Quivleren couldn't save me now.

Evander came for me. Not as a concerned friend. He was on a mission and I was his target. His evoking the Rights of Justice would see me dead. The werewolves who would oversee my trial would be biased. They were notorious for being thorough in their investigations, and that may be my saving grace. But they were also known for their biases and while not overlooking evidence, spinning it toward their favor. And the Rights of Justice could take a non-guilty party and make them responsible for past generations' mistakes. I was fucked. But, thinking about it, I was not surprised. This was typical Zuri luck. And if it were me in Evander's place, I'd want justice too. If my deranged mother and unknown father were responsible, I felt a strange responsibility to make it right. I just didn't want to die to do that either.

I looked down at my still numb arm. My wrist lost color, being clamped down hard by Evander. He vehemently trudged through the forest, his eyes fixed forward and I imagined a snarl on his lips.

"I'm sorry," I whispered.

He snorted, pressing on, and refusing to look at me.

I was sorry for everything done against him. I hadn't a clue about what had happened. I felt bad for him, because like me, he lost everything and had no one. Whoever did this to him, be it one of my parents, needed to face justice. I completely understood and agreed with it. And I understood his anger toward my lineage since he clearly thought my parents were responsible, but I couldn't help who created me though; and I shouldn't be held account-able for it either. Not in this extreme. Maybe if they asked me to help set up a charity or a fund for the orphaned or to seek justice from the actual guilty parties, I could totally be on board. But death in their stead was too much.

The werewolf Rights of Justice to me were a bit ridicu-lous. To bring me in, have me tried for something I did not do, or wasn't around to do, was unjust. But there was nothing I could do. The laws of different beings in the entire world of Quivleren did not overlap. A human lawyer couldn't save me from this. Nothing could, but werewolf overseers of justice themselves; and they hardly ever came to the verdict of 'not guilty' according to Lazaro and those of his pack.

Evander's hand clamped tighter around my wrist. I gasped at the pain he put behind it. He hung his head and sighed, lessening his grasp.

"Sorry," he offered.

"Can you ease up a bit," I asked. "I'm not going to run away."

Evander yanked on my arm. "Come along."

"Seriously," I grouched. "Ease up. It hurts!"

He rounded on me, standing toe to toe with such a ferocity that grayish-black mottled fur was shifting onto his skin. I gulped. His eyes brightened to an intense gold. A snarl split his handsome face as his lips curled to reveal sharp pointed teeth.

He dropped my hand, perking a brow as he did so. "I'll ease up, when you pay for what you've done," he quipped.

I rubbed my wrist, flexing my hand to get the feeling back. "I'm not gonna run away."

"Trust me, I know," he seethed, his wolf going back into hiding.

A howl permeated the thick forest. Evander growled low in his throat. Taking my left hand this time, he yanked me through the forest heading west.

"Keep quiet," he whispered.

"What's going on?"

Evander groaned softly. "You're doing the opposite of what I just told you to do."

"Sorry, I'm *really* hard of hearing... Answer my question. What's going on?"

"You're being hunted by *your mother's* wolves," he replied, spitting out the words 'your mother' with malice.

I let out an irritated sigh. "Good gods I despise the woman. I should've listened to my gut about her."

"Why didn't you?"

I shrugged. "I wanted to know what it was like to have a mom."

He nodded, yanking me along behind him. He plowed right through and over any debris or vegetation in our path. My feet hurt more fiercely now that we were hurrying. It was pointless to say this aloud. Evander wouldn't care. It was just a mission and as long as I arrived wherever we were going alive, it didn't matter if I was hurting or not.

My skin prickled with the anxious inkling that I was being watched. Evander's head swiveled on his shoulders, his eyes vigilant. I shuddered. Getting taken back to my mother's castle was terrifying for me. If she had the gumption to try and keep me there with magic and force, there was no telling what else she wouldn't do to get her way. And I would rather face the Rights of Justice over my mother, stupid as it was.

My mind wandered as I was dragged by Evander. I couldn't help the nagging question that plagued me. How did everyone know where I lived? Beyond the necessary paperwork for a move change, I'd told no one my new address. Save Uncle Syrus and he would NEVER betray me. I prayed it wasn't someone at work. I prayed that the database hadn't been hacked. I may keep myself at a distance, but they have always been friendly and I just couldn't imagine anyone giving me up so easily.

It bothered me that I moved and suddenly, I'm a target. Granted, me moving isolated myself from people, making me a perfect target. However, no one bothered much with humans. We had nothing special going on. And theoretically, a move shouldn't cause so much attention. How many single women had moved and been ignored? What made me so special?!

Something rushed by on my left, making the foliage rustle. My heart raced. Fur caught the corner of my eye as it disappeared into the vegetation. I licked my lips.

"Evander," I whimpered.

"Shhh," he said softly, his eyes locked on a destination ahead.

He stopped. My body shook. Sweat peppered my upper lip and my hands became clammy. I moved closer to Evander. He glanced at me over his shoulder, then promptly returned to the bush with his vigilant gaze. Even with his resolute promise to take me back to receive justice, he was still safer than what was around me. His justice would be swifter than what any other wolf might have in store for me.

Call me a damn moron, but I would rather take my chances with Evander than my own batshit mother, I thought. *Good God Elohi, maybe I'm the crazy one.*

I pressed myself against his back, taking what little comfort I could from his hot, smooth skin.

"Don't do that," he growled.

I backed off a touch. "I'm scared."

"They won't harm you."

Despite his firmly voiced reassurance, I cowered. I put on this big bravado ego to deter would-be jerks. I was trained to defend myself by my uncle because, as he pointed out, women don't have the muscles men do.

Women are made to do specific things men can't and vice versa, Zuri. The least I can do to help you even the odds if you find yourself alone, is to teach you self-defense and basic vehicle maintenance, Syrus constantly said to me.

He was right. I learned to defend myself. I learned what I needed. And in learning, I was constantly on high alert, hyper aware that I was the prey, the easy target in a world filled with paranormal.

Low growls emanated from the bushes around us. Evander let go of my wrist and fully shifted in a blink. He was a tall wolf, his shoulders coming to the middle of my stomach. His fur, a beautiful long-haired mottle of black, dark gray and white adorned every inch of his wolfish muscular build. Evander spread his front paws wide, his shoulders and head lowering near the ground, in a challenge.

A wolf snarled, coming out of the concealing bramble. Three more closed in around us.

"Back off and live," one white wolf advised.

"She's mine," Evander replied. "Rights of Justice."

The wolves stared at Evander for a quick moment; their faces transforming from surprised, back to determined, in a quick shift of their wolfy eyebrows. I bent down, picking up a hefty branch of a fir tree that snapped in a storm and fell to the ground. Holding it in my hands like a staff, I readied to defend myself.

Evander turned his head slightly, staring at me out of his peripheral. I couldn't read the expression on his face. My eyes went back to the wolves, each one blocking a cardinal direction.

My fingers enclosed tighter around the branch, ready to strike at whomever charged. My breathing became shallow as nervousness took over. It felt like I forgot how to breathe properly and everything was building inside my body.

A gray-white wolf briskly trotted forward, daring a bite at my bare left calf. I whacked it on the head with the top end of my self-made staff while the bottom end deftly came up under his chin. .

"Not today, puppers," I quipped.

"Come home to your mother, Zuri," the white wolf beckoned in a friendly manner. "And we won't kill your friend."

The bravado I felt returned, and I shrugged at his command. "Kill him. I still won't go with you."

The hairs on my arm and neck stood on end. I spun on my heel, facing the other direction. I gritted my teeth stopping a shudder from wracking my body. I looked hard, pushing aside the thought that death was inevitable. I was going to fight to the bitter end. Most people underestimated my grit and determination. That is what I had going for me and I was going to use that to my advantage.

Whirling my staff around my head and slamming it down on the hard ground, I hoped my short display of finesse would be enough to get the werewolves to back off. It didn't work. Slowly, like they took pleasure in making me nervous, they stalked forward.

"Zuri," the same wolf called. "Last chance to back down."

"If I threw a stick, would you leave?"

Evander snorted.

I turned my head, glaring at Evander, "You included," I hissed.

I snapped out of my despair of being taken to receive justice. I either got fucked over from him or my mother. I chose Evander because at least he was honest. I was currently stuck being near Evander for protection against my mother's brainwashed wolf pack, but I wasn't going to make anything easy on him either. Evander was certainly the better option at this moment. With him, I at least had a fighting chance to escape later. He didn't have magic that could bind me and until I was on the wolf council's doorstep, I had a chance. And I had scraps of a plan too. But those involved getting away from these Kadia wolves.

From the right, a wolf lunged at my legs. With a sharp crack, I brought the staff up from below; getting the wolf under the chin. The wolf's head rocked upward, falling to the side. Dazed, it shook its head and sulked back to the rest of the pack.

A smaller gray wolf charged me, going for my legs. I repositioned, standing sideways to make myself appear slimmer and less of a target. The wolf lunged, using his hind legs for leverage. Swinging my staff down, I poked the top forcefully into the wolf's chest, shoving him away from me.

I'd been so caught up in keeping myself standing against my own two wolves, I'd lost track of what was going on with Evander. I'd pushed him aside in favor of surviving in the moment when snarling and violence erupting from behind me, I almost turned to look. I desperately wanted to watch Evander, out of stupid curiosity, beat the other wolf, but I couldn't. Taking my eyes off my own enemies would kill me.

Wolf fur brushed against my leg. Glancing down, my body tensed to strike whoever it was. I let out a breath, recognizing Evander's mottled fur.

"Leave," Evander snarled. "Or die like your friend there."

The three enemy wolves took two paces forward at the same time; heads lowered and fury in their golden eyes. A small gray one snarled. Evander leapt at the smaller gray one. Their bodies collided, Evander fell on his back, but kicked as he landed, knocking the gray wolf off to the side. Evander leapt to his paws faster than the gray wolf had a chance to rise. The gray wolf yipped as Evander sunk his teeth into the enemy's side.

One second I was watching Evander sink his teeth into the enemy, the next I was on my back struggling to breathe. Instinctually, I lifted my hands, thankful to whatever gods were watching me that I hadn't dropped my staff when I'd fallen. As I brought the staff up, it caught the furious mottled gray-white wolf in his throat; his snapping jaws missing my throat by inches. I kept moving my staff up, shoving one end in the mouth of the wolf as he repositioned and lunged again. The wolf, surprised, wrenched his head back and forth, trying to dislodge the staff. I smirked internally, *puppy is damn genius*, I quipped. *All he has to do is get off me and no more branch.* I refocused and shoved harder, ensuring the branch lodged farther into the wolf's throat. His weight crushed me as he thrashed, twisting back and forth to break free. My amusement was short lived as I fought to breathe, realizing that, while this wolf's teeth couldn't get me, he may still kill me by crushing me.

Evander's paws struck the wolf on my chest, shoving it, and me, sideways. During my struggle, Evander had dispatched the rest and now the one currently crushing me was the last. The look in Evander's eyes promised pain - lots and lots of pain.

I took a deep breath now that the wolf was off my chest. I released the branch and rolled in the opposite direction, careful to keep an eye on Evander and the gray-white wolf. Unsteadily, I rose to my feet.

The gray-white wolf had the branch stuck in its face, swishing its head to free the burden desperate to defend itself from Evander. Evander watched the branch; not wanting to be struck. Seizing an opportunity, Evander leaped onto the last wolf's back, sinking his teeth into the back of its neck. My ears rang as the wolf gave one last agonizing howl.

As the last enemy werewolf died, the body shifted into human form. Looking around me, all four men lay bloody and dead. Evander growled, shaking his body and shifting back.

Cuts and bruises formed on his bare muscled chest. I swallowed. Seeing him like this was attractive. He ran his fingers through his skater-boy mop of brown hair as his emerald green eyes fiercely met mine.

"Just because you... helped," Evander spat, "doesn't mean I won't take you back to receive justice."

I bent down, making certain the key was still in my pants. I let out a breath of relief when I felt it's outline on the inside of my right thigh.

"You're a bad dog," I growled slowly standing up.

His left hand lashed out, catching my face in his palm. He squeezed my cheeks together, making my skin stretch as my lips puckered like a fish and my face hurt from the ferocity of his attack. Bringing my cheeks together, the palm of his hand went under my jaw as he lifted me off the ground with one hand, my darn, short legs dangling uselessly.

He studied me for a second, the anger radiating from him. Again, for a split second, his expression changed and I swore I saw remorse in his eyes. But again, it was erased quickly, the anger turning into hatred once again. These little flashes of conflicting emotion confused me. Did he truly hate me or was that a front for something deeper? I wasn't sure I'd ever find out. But I shivered at his next words.

"I would love to kill you now," Evander snarled, his teeth becoming wolfish points. "Nothing would bring me greater pleasure in seeing you dead. But I need you alive for the council."

He tossed me away from him, his expression morphing to disgust. My legs failed to catch me, and they folded under me, as I crumpled to the ground.

"Let's go. We have miles to cover before we can rest," he said, walking ahead of me.

I glared at the back of his head. Earlier I promised to go easy with him. Now, he could just fuck off. I wasn't going to make this easy. I wasn't going down without the best fight in me. Without any forethought of what to do next, I scrambled to my feet, and I took off sprinting in the other direction.

CHAPTER TWENTY

ZURI

I dashed through the thick brush, trying to put as much distance between me and Evander as possible. Growling reverberated from behind. Forcing myself to go faster, I maneuvered through the forest with ease.

Fists pumping and bare feet pounding the hard ground, I had never worked so hard in my short life. I zig zagged in a wide circle, trying to make following me as difficult as possible while making my way back to the river. Hopefully swimming would be better than trying to navigate through a monster infested forest.

My throat burned from the constant running. My skin felt stretched and strained against aching muscles and tired bones. Overall, I was physically exhausted and emotionally overwhelmed. But I refused to give up.

Keep going. Run, Zuri. Gotta get away.

Vegetation and branches slapped my bare shins and forearms. Thank goodness for my spanx and Evander's shirt because I could have been hurting more. The rushing gurgle of the river reached my ears. Mechanically, as if I was not in control of my own body, my bare feet urged me forward as I almost closed my eyes in relief.

Without realizing I was being tackled, my body crashed to the ground. Hands out, I barely stopped my chin from striking the ground and jarring my face.

"Not today, Zuri Barsotti," Evander growled in my ear from his perch on my back, his bare chest pressed against my heaving back. "I will do whatever it takes to force you back. I will stop at nothing until justice is met."

Evander rolled me over to my back. His eyes bore into mine, the depth of emotion there capturing me. I was helpless as I watched the anger, hurt, loneliness, even respect, pity, remorse, and admiration swirl in those green depths. His eyes didn't match his hateful words. He looked conflicted and I was confused. I bit my lip waiting to see which emotion won out. I prayed that remorse and admiration would win out in the end, but emotions were tricky and I, of all people, understood how someone could go against what they truly felt when they thought they needed to. Evander's eyes settled on anger with a hint of remorse and pity as he rose to his feet, bending over and grabbing my upper arms like a child throwing a tantrum, forcefully yanking me to a stand.

"Rights of Justice will prevail. I will have my vengeance on your blood."

I didn't know what to say. He had every right by werewolf law to do this. I had every right to try and get away.

I shrugged and pretended this situation didn't bother me, "I had to try."

Evander snorted derisively. "You must have failed in high school track."

I nodded. "Sure did. Short legs don't make for track stars. But I got an A for effort. Just in case you were wondering though, I'm really, *really* jealous of all the people who have never met you."

His emerald eyes narrowed on mine and cryptically replied, "Same. I truly wish I'd never met you."

Latching his hand around my wrist again, although not nearly as tightly as before, he dragged me back up the river, heading north. Evander was silent as he dragged me, shoulders hunched in what I thought maybe resignation or defeat, if what I'd seen in his eyes was accurate, while grumbling under his breath.

Broody damn werewolf. His stupid emotions are giving me whiplash. He waltzed into my life as I had started over. All I had wanted was to move to a tiny safe place where I could start over after the Lazaro disaster and truly find who I am. If nothing else, another failed relationship showed me I still had some soul searching to do before I could find the partner who would compliment me. I looked around me and huffed silently. *Guess that's out for now. Weeks later and my life's in ruins.* And try as I might, I couldn't figure out why my life was in tatters. The when was easy to pinpoint. The how was dubious, but the why was impossible to figure out.

Evander jerked hard on my wrist, tugging me forward along with him. "Come on, Zuri," he sighed. "I don't wanna be around here for more fae or wolves to come. Do you?"

"Not quite sure which I would rather choose at the

moment. When choosing between evils, I prefer the one I haven't tried and might possibly survive through."

Evander swore under his breath.

He seemed in an amiable mood. I smirked and shrugged to myself. I might as well start a conversation when he's talkative, even if his mood is sour. "How did anyone even know where I lived?" I queried. "How did they find out when I only told my work my new address?"

Evander stopped, turning around to face me full on. Werewolves, thankfully, were not skilled liars. They were too dominant and forthright. It was hard to find a werewolf who could lie without giving something away like a smile or a quick darting of the eyes. An ancient scribe once said that lying was like murder. It could ruin lives and it seemed that this truth was ingrained in werewolf DNA. It was almost impossible for them to even fib, let alone flat out lie. Made me wonder how Evander could have been so nice to me when he'd first started stalking me. Looking at where we were now, his friendliness seemed to be a flat out lie and made me wonder if I could trust anything he said or did now.

"Your company, Inner Connections, was bought out by a larger medical billing company owned by the Moon Walkers," Evander explained. "Each werewolf pack is a subpack of either the Moon Walkers or the Vilkas. I belong to the subpack Bardou which is part of the Vilkas. And as you know, or must have since you dated one of the Sandalio mob, Vilkas and Moon Walkers don't mix. Finding you at my family home was merely coincidental."

I stared dumbfounded. No *were* has ever told me this

much information about packs or even subpacks. I knew it was all political and everything in the werewolf community was kept hush.

I pursed my lips, wondering what else he was going to disclose. His answer was not much of one. It explained the coincidental part of finding his familial home. I glowered, my mind tinkering over possibilities of what was really happening.

Evander glanced to the sky in between all the bright green foliage and branches. The golden sun was directly overhead, poking sunbeams through the trees, the beams turning the ordinary forest into a mystical place, making the air dance with light and shadows. I pushed out my troubles for just a second. Taking in a deep breath, I relished the peacefulness it made me feel. Despite my predicament, I loved the forest.

Wriggling my toes, I let out my breath. My feet ached, but it wasn't unbearable... yet. The tenseness in my body slowly dissipated. I was tempted to make a break for it again. My tired brain kept turning to escape plans when it wasn't going over my mother's betrayal, Evander's betrayal, and the new information he'd just given me. I even went over ways to beat the tar out of my captor, the image of him unconscious making me want to laugh hilariously. But I knew, despite the many rational and ridiculous plots my brain had gone over, running right now would be useless. I'd tried once when I'd hoped he was too tired to chase me and I'd been wrong. Knowing his speed and strength, I'd never make it very far. I'd have to just bide my time so I could catch him unawares.

I refocused on Evander's little info bomb, "The Moon Walkers then found me when I updated my residence," I confirmed. "They would have gotten to me no matter where I was."

Evander nodded, letting go of my hand. "Yeah... they would have."

"So, my mother," I brushed my hair back out of my face with my free hand. "Is she working with the Moon Walkers? Is that how she found me?"

"I don't know. It's possible. But then again, all paranormal and human information in terms of residency is made available, unless you pay a ridiculous amount to remain private."

I'd forgotten about that piece of information. All information about everyone was made public in terms of names and locations. I made an 'oh shit' face and rolled my eyes at myself. *Like right now, smarty pants. Ugh, if I get the chance to change anything, it would be everyone's privacy.*

Evander reached out for my hand, but hesitated. His rough, calloused, sun-kissed hand paused inches from mine. I shoved my left wrist into his hesitant hand and closed his fingers around it with my free hand.

"It's ok... I understand."

His sharp green eyes bore into my soul as he searched my eyes for something. I didn't know what, but my guess was he was searching for lies or some sort of deceit so he could hate me more. I wasn't about to give him another reason, a legitimate reason to hate me.

I searched his eyes back. For what? No clue, but what I saw there surprised me. Yes, I saw anger. I saw hatred. But

I also saw loneliness and defeat buried way down. I saw his need and determination to take me in, whatever the cost. I knew the feeling. I knew the desperation. I resigned myself to being dragged to OKimma to receive the Rights of Justice. I still wanted to escape, but I doubted any attempt I made would work. And technically, legally, they were in the right to try me for what my kin had done; whether I agreed with that law or not.

I inhaled deeply again, savoring the richness of the forest soil, fir trees and sunshine. If I were to die soon, I wanted to be able to remember the forest and peacefulness in my final moments, however it was to come. I sighed, *just enjoy the time you have left, Zuri.* I nodded at myself, as if I finally decided it was the thing to do. There wasn't much else I could do. I was tired, hungry and my brain was a jumbled mess. Outrunning Evander was stupid. I ran a hand over my face. *Enjoy the time you have left,* I reminded myself.

Glancing at Evander, I saw him watching me, his emerald eyes locking on my face, scrutinizing it as if he looked for a flaw or any inkling I was being a jerk. His eyes softened then hardened, turning his face to match the whims of his eyes.

"Before you take me to whoever to receive justice, may we stop by a lawyer's so I can make a will to pass the house onto you?"

Evander ran a hand over his face. "Let's get going. I wanna be back in OKimma by Monday since it's Saturday."

His fingers adjusted on my wrist, feeling softer in comparison to earlier. It sent a chill down my spine.

Companionably, side by side we walked through the forest of Chay.

He sighed, pulling at the skin on the back of his neck as he finally nodded. "I will let you do that," Evander finally said.

I nodded, staring ahead. "Thanks."

CHAPTER TWENTY-ONE

EVANDER

D*ammit all!* I was so fuckin' pissed! I couldn't figure her out. And this aggravating woman was getting beyond my defenses. I wanted to be angry. I wanted to hate her. But her kindness, humility, resolve, and courage made it really hard. In order to stay pissed I kept reminding myself she is the enemy. She and her family. Her family was the reason my family was dead and my pack enslaved. And I would have my revenge and my pack justice. I'd come too far to let myself soften toward her and I could not let anything stop me now.

Not even her, I decided, taking a peek to my right. She walked with her head up, honey brown eyes keen and alert scanning the forest with her sunshine hair swept off to the right side. She walked with resolution, taking in the forest with a wan smile and long, deep breaths.

Everything about the woman was just... more than my previous wife, Catronia. I couldn't help but pity and admire her, despite her finding herself in this situation. I know she couldn't help who sired and birthed her. Heck, what child could? Yet she was in this situation nonetheless and she was handling it like few would. I couldn't afford to let her go, even though her bravado hid a heart of kindness, bravery, ferocity and loyalty and I respected that like nothing else.

And I'd be blind not to notice her perfect body. Hot damn. I was an ass guy, and Zuri's was perfect and those curves around her hips made me salivate. Considering how I'd found her, I couldn't help but notice her tits, although I tried to shove those out of my mind. I tried to be a gentleman, most of the time. Regardless of my attempts to not think of them, their perfect pertness kept entering my mind and my body responded despite my best attempts to make it behave. Most of the time, the red heads caught my eye, but Zuri's sunflower blonde and honey eyes had captivated me since I'd laid eyes on them. All this and my grudging respect for her just angered me more. I didn't want to like her and here I was sympathizing, pitying, respecting and lusting after her. Too bad she'd be dead in a week. My wolf mourned at the thought and I comforted him by mourning with him, reassuring him we'd find a worthy mate someday. Not sure if either of us believed it, but I gripped the thought and hung on tenaciously.

Running a hand over my face, I attempted to swipe away any favorable thoughts toward her.

"You do that a lot," Zuri commented.

"What?"

"Run a hand over your face, then take the same hand

and pull at the skin at the back of your neck," Zuri said, keeping her eyes forward. "What's wrong?"

I snorted. "Nothing you need to concern yourself with."

"You're such a thundercloud."

I laughed. The comment was so quick and to the point. "Life is hard, Zuri. It's unfair, unkind and difficult. You wouldn't know that, would you?" I mocked her, but I had to do something to keep the soft emotions at bay and at the moment it was the best I could do.

"But I'm not a thundercloud."

Her casual comment helped swipe those soft emotions away and I seethed out, "I have EVERY right to be a *thundercloud*," I air quoted with one hand. "Your disgusting kin killed my pack and enslaved the rest. The only reason myself and a handful of others escaped was because we were hunting. I came home to ruin and death." My voice broke. Damn. I had to reign in my emotions. "I have every right to seek justice and avenge them. No one should ever come home to that sight. And if I have any say in it, they never will."

Zuri's lips pursed and moved to the right of her face, slowly forming a frown like she was about to cry. Her honeyed eyes narrowed on a fixated spot in the forest. They shone with unshed tears whether for her own neck or mine, I couldn't place. Knowing her, it would be for me, and that irritated me. I didn't want her sympathy. She opened her mouth to reply then snapped it shut.

"Nothing to say?" I prodded.

Zuri shook her head. "Nope."

"Just like you humans," I snorted derisively, spitting to

the left. "Lying, sneaky, backstabbing curs. The lot of you are all the same. No wonder every race wants you all enslaved."

Zuri stopped walking, turning to face me with narrowed eyes and a snarl on her lip. I immediately regretted my words. This angry, hateful wolf wasn't me and honestly I was embarrassed at myself. But this whole situation just ticked me off and my confusion, my duty, and my desire for justice only muddled my mind. So, I grinned, to hide it all and to attempt to keep her off balance. If I was confused, I would be damned if she wasn't.

"You're an idiotic conundrum, you know that?" she seethed and I allowed her to wrench her hand back. "Hate me or like me. Keep your tone and level the same for good-ness sake. This back and forth isn't working for me."

I paused, thinking about her words and their truthful-ness. It made me bristle. *I hate you*, I hissed inside my head, but couldn't make my lips say it. I opted for a growl. This disgusting waste of flesh dared to challenge me, but I had to keep myself in check. I wanted to shift, to feel my teeth sink around her neck and squeeze. I wanted to feel her dying breath and taste her blood on my tongue, to know she died.

I had to bring her back as was part of the deal struck between Commander Iorgas and myself. I ran a hand over my face.

Zuri gazed at me sympathetically. "You're so caught up in hate," she shook her head. "I feel bad for you."

Laughing, I shook my head. "Shut up and keep walking."

I took her wrist in my hand, my fingers enclosing around her soft flesh. My wolf liked the way she felt in my grasp. I growled at myself, walking forward toward the northwest. Zuri dug her feet into the ground.

"Ya know, we're so similar and I think that terrifies you," Zuri continued. "We both lost our families. We both are alone. We both-"

I rounded on her and snarled. Surprised, Zuri took a step back then rose up to meet me head on. She was small, barely coming to my chest. Even standing on her tippy-toes hardly afforded her anything extra to face off with me. I struggled to hide my amusement and admiration at her standing against someone so obviously above her might. I huffed a laugh hoping it came across as disgust and rallied my attitude.

"Shut. Up." I growled.

Zuri's eyes narrowed, "No."

My other hand shot out, resting on the base of her throat. I felt her swallow harshly; the beat of her heart radiating through my hand. I stroked her throat with my thumb, softly pressing inward. Zuri stood there, quiet, defiant, sucking in a quick breath to brace herself for something I couldn't bring myself to do.

"I hate you," I breathed.

"Prove it," Zuri dared, hiding her fear behind her sheer bravado.

I pressed my thumb inward on her throat. Zuri closed her eyes. Sunlight streaked across her face, enhancing her beauty like no makeup ever would and my heart twisted in my chest.

"Damn it! I hate you and like you. I'm not sure if I want to kill you or kiss you. Damn you!" Snarling, I let go. Taking her wrist, I overcompensated for my softness and yanked her along a little too harshly. "Come on. I want to be in OKimma by Monday." I threw her over my shoulder, taking one last look at her before glaring at the trees.

CHAPTER TWENTY-TWO

ZURI

I huffed at being thrown over his shoulder like a doll. The only good parts about it were - he was warm and my feet didn't hurt. Evander sighed, walking steadily through the forest not even bothered by my grumbling.

"I don't like my blood either," I finally said.

Evander snorted dryly. "Oh yeah?"

"Yeah... Growing up, I was shoved around from place to place. No one kept me for longer than six months or wanted me around because of who my mother happened to be. It was lonely, and," I paused, forcing the hiccup in my throat down, not wanting to cry in front of him. "And I just want someone to love me. Guess it's why I clung to Lazaro even though he was terrible to me. He was always controlling how I ate or dressed, going as far as to who I spoke with, and I went along with it because he was there."

Evander chuckled mockingly. "Lazaro is a horrible person. It says a lot about you though."

"Like what?" I snapped.

He shrugged, the movement jostling me on his shoulder. "Sorry," he said, then sighed. "You're easy and willing to take love however it comes."

I bristled, my free hand itching to slap him across the face. I sucked in a breath through my teeth and grit my teeth. *Not worth it. He's being a butt to get a reaction out of me. Probably to justify his hatred. I will not give him a reason to hate me.*

Growling to be free of him, I wriggled on his shoulder. He chuckled, bending down to set me on the ground. I brushed off his shirt and my bare legs. Checking to make certain the key was still tucked on the inside of my right thigh, I let out a breath thankful it was there.

Evander rose to his feet, taking the lead without grabbing my wrist. He followed a faint trail in the dirt heading northwest. I hated that Evander had come for me just to condemn me to death. The last thing I wanted was to die. But despite his reasons for coming for me, I was glad he was there. There's no way in hell I could have survived much longer. Not with both the fae and my mother's wolves after me.

His words, though, tumbled around my brain - *easy and willing to take love however it comes.* I hated to admit it to myself, and I'd never admit it to him, but he was right. I'd jumped at any opportunity for love. Not sex, but love. There was a distinct difference for me. I longed for love, to belong, the intimacy of being someone's and them being mine.

Recently, I'd wanted Lazaro to be that someone. Then my mother. I shook my head at myself. I knew there had been flaws to these relationships, or lack thereof. Lazaro was a wolf. And inevitably all wolf/human relationships ended because wolves just wouldn't make humans a permanent part of the pack. But I'd hoped still. Hoped that somehow we'd be the one that made it. Hoped that we'd figure out how to work around it. But he'd been a jerk by keeping me a secret from his family, dating a female wolf, and then ending our relationship via email. The epic failure of a relationship made me wince and wish Evander hadn't been so right.

I felt my brows pull down and my face furrow into the pulling desolation I felt. All I wanted was love and that desire, made me dumb. I stared at the back of Evander's head, how his wavy mop of brown hair tended to have a slight curl at the end and flip out like a sexy old school skater. Evander turned his head slightly and his eyes narrowed.

"What?" he grumbled.

"Nothing."

He snorted his disbelief and disgust. His dislike of me was palpable. The silence went from comfortable to tense as his dislike emphasized that I was simply a mission for him and he was more determined than ever to end his suffering by ending my life. I thought about pleading and begging, but his disgust and the tension told me that it'd be no use. And I still had some pride. I refused to spend the whole trip to OKimma begging.

My feet followed Evander on their own as I stared at the small path we followed. My lips pursed to the side as I racked my brain for any moment where I was a jerk given the fact Evander hated me so. I must've been an asshat at some point to him or someone else, only I couldn't think of an instance. I usually kept to myself. And my snappish remarks to him were justified by him being a heroic creeper. I wasn't a bad person, tightly wound and terrified, absolutely. I learned from a young age to be tough, to act it, and follow through if I wanted to survive bullies. It didn't make me a terrible person. It made me a survivalist.

My foot stepped on a sharp rock. I inhaled sharply and winced. "Dammit," I cursed, continuing to keep up with Evander.

Evander stopped mid-stride. My face pelted into his back. I reeled backward, about to fall when he caught me, grabbing my hand while the other wrapped around my back. He set me to rights, taking a step back and sighed.

He ran a hand over his face. "Zuri," he called, standing in front of me, rigid as stone.

"Yeah?"

His eyes swirled with anger, curiosity, and dare I think it, kindness. Shoulders hunched, his muscles tensed then slowly relaxed. He threw his head back and worked his jaw. I strained to watch his face and his eyes to see what he was feeling. Shaking his head, he brought his head back down and pressed on. I perked a brow, wondering what he was about to say then snorted it off. It was probably more of the same line - *I like you, hate your family, and so you must die* - routine.

We made it to the other side of the forest where the rushing of water made my skin crawl. After my harrowing trip down the river, and being waterlogged for so long, the last thing I truly wanted to see was another huge river crossing.

My heart pounded. Staring at the cold whooshing of the water made my gut swirl. I feared yesterday would repeat itself. I looked at Evander's now dry shirt and my messy, but dry, hair that fell across my chest. I was tempted to whine, but schooled my voice into what I hoped sounded like a reasonable tone for a discussion.

"Can we look upstream for a better crossing?" I asked, biting my bottom lip.

Evander pursed his lips, eyes scanning the river. "What do you think I'm doing?"

The water whizzed by; on any other day, white rapids and the swirling of water behind huge boulders was enchanting to sit and watch. But watching it now, thinking about getting in the churning liquid was a different story.

After snipping at me, Evander watched the water for a minute or two, as if he was just as enchanted as I would have been. Then he turned left and we walked silently upstream. My bare feet finally got a reprieve from the branches and difficult terrain of the forest. My short legs struggled in his long strides as I stepped in his footprints where the sand was already compacted and easier for my bare hurting feet. It was probably stupid of me to get rid of the slippers, but I was fearful of them being magicked so my mother could trace them to me. However, I would rather be uncomfortable like I am now than dead.

A blackberry bush about the size of a door was to my right. I was thrilled. The untamable weed loved easy ground to grow. Pausing, I plucked some, stuffing them into my face. Evander whirled around, his keen ears picking up that I had stopped and stared at me in annoyance. I held out a berry.

"Thanks," he stated begrudgingly, popping it into his mouth.

We stood side by side, eating the small morsels. My belly's fierce protesting started to quiet down and my fingers turned purple. I stared down at my discolored fingers for a second while I chewed slowly and I had the sudden urge to poke Evander and stain his skin. My inner two-year-old wanted out and Evander was my next victim. I smiled on the inside. At this point, I didn't care that he was marching me to my death. I'd seen the good guy inside him, and I decided to make it my mission to find him again. Glancing over, I perked a brow and reached out a finger.

"No," he said, fighting a grin through a mouthful of blackberries, swatting my hand away.

I smirked, going back to plucking berries. We picked the bush clean, both of us with black berry juice running down our chins and across our cheeks. Considering the last two weeks, that thirty minutes were pure bliss. No murderous, raping wolves; no cannibalistic fae; no mysterious, evil key; no evil mothers; no werewolf law. Just me and a handsome wolf enjoying sweet berries. I even managed to get a few smiles out of him. I almost cried when I saw the bush picked clean.

"Come on," Evander commanded, turning back toward the river.

Evander's long strides made it hard for me to keep up.

We walked in silence, keeping close to the river. His alertness put me on edge. My eyes darted from one side of the river to the other for any sign of the queen's wolves or another horrible pink faerie.

The calming gurgle of the river and our breathing were the only sounds to come into my ears. Trees swayed in the slight breeze. In all, it was a peaceful afternoon if it weren't for the fae trying to eat me or a pack of wolves trying to take me back to Kadia. Chills ran up my arms at the thought. I shook my head and jogged to catch up with Evander, who'd surprisingly, in a non-jerk move, given me a little space. The sand was a blissful carpet to my battered feet and I almost cried when I stepped on a sharp twig. I couldn't help the hiss that escaped.

Despite my attempt to smother the hiss under my breath, Evander heard it and glanced back at me even as his feet and body angled north, heading up river.

"Do your feet hurt?" Evander said, almost sounding like he cared.

I didn't want to push my luck or his sudden show of kindness so I just shrugged and clipped out, "Yes, but walking on the sand helps."

I watched as emotions escaped Evander's mask. I could have sworn I saw guilt and maybe an inkling of pity and compassion flit across his features before he schooled his face again.

"Can't afford to lose any time. If they're hurting too much and they start to cause us to fall behind, I'll carry you. We both know you have soft human feet and I have to get you back to the Council before sunset Monday."

Evander's gruff tone almost sounded amused. I studied him from beneath my lashes, choosing to ignore his comment on soft human feet. My guess was he was trying to be nice. I'd give him the benefit of the doubt. I narrowed my eyes and gave just a bit of attitude. I was still his prisoner.

"Thank you," I mumbled.

"Don't get any ideas," he replied.

I laughed inside. What ideas did he think I'd get? That he was more human than he let on? That maybe deep down lurked a nice guy? I already knew it. But he was also taking me to my death because of his grief, anger and some archaic werewolf law.

I rolled my eyes and asked, "After you give me to the council, then what?"

A light breeze along the river tousled my long blonde hair. I moved up beside him, watching him struggle to gain a modicum of composure. His eyes betrayed him, acknowledging his pain, suffering, but also the tiniest whisper of kindness toward me.

Wolf hairs appeared on his arm. "Taking down your mother."

The ferocity in his eyes made me tremble. There was an animalistic nature to them, flashing between green and gold. I didn't blame him for the hatred he felt toward the person who birthed me. She was a monster, someone who killed indiscriminately on a whim. She was someone who needed to be destroyed.

I smiled at him, hoping to appear genuinely grateful he was going to take my mother on and win. I knew he would.

And if he was seriously going to take down my mother, I would back him.

My heart hurt briefly for the desire of wanting to know a mother's love - to have it and feel the embrace. I never got it and I never would. Tears stung behind my eyes making my nose burn. I wriggled it, attempting to get the sensation to stop. Between losing Lazaro, my cat, job, house, mother and now my life, I wanted to cry. But crying in front of this alpha wolf wouldn't help my cause.

I sucked in a shaky breath, plastering a wan smile. "Thank you," I finally said, moving past him and toward the water to cross this shallow part, "for coming to get me."

Evander caught my wrist in his calloused hand. *Crap! He just stopped holding my hand and now he's got it again.* I couldn't help but chastise myself. I'd given him a peek at gratitude and he seized my wrist at the first moment. No doubt to remind me I was his prisoner. I stopped, peering over my shoulder, surprised to see his face open and vulnerable.

"I..." he stammered. Rolling his eyes and looking skyward, he paused before bringing his head down level with mine. "I forgot to tell you, Luell is at the vet. She lives... somehow."

I put a hand to my mouth, tears flowing freely down my face. Evander pulled me toward him, wrapping his warm muscled arms around me. His comfort surprised me, validating in my mind, he wasn't the total asshole he made himself out to be. I knew in my gut he found Luell and took her to the vet. He saved her, proving he wasn't the jerk-face he tried so hard to convince himself and me he was. My face pressed against his chest, I relished the warmth and security he offered in this moment. Without thinking, I wrapped my arms around him, lacing my fingers together, snuggling him just a bit tighter to me.

Evander stiffened when I tightened my grip, trying to pull himself away. "Ok human," he said irritably. "We're done."

"Five more seconds."

Evander grumbled, his hands dropping to his side. But he didn't try to pull away. And I swear I heard him sniff a little.

I stifled a grin and pressed my face into his chest, breathing deep myself. In this moment, my mind allowed me to forget. All of it. I just was. This hug from Evander, despite his insisting on turning me over to the Werewolf Council, meant more to me than I could ever say.

"Human," he called with a raised tone at the end. I smiled at his awkward tone. "We're done here. Keep moving."

In a motion so fluid I didn't know was happening, he untangled himself from me. He moved around me, leading the way.

I sucked in a deep, shuddery breath, squared my shoulders and set out after him.

CHAPTER
TWENTY-THREE

ZURI

Night came on quicker than I ever anticipated it could. The sun began to transition from shine to glow, bringing out brilliant purples, oranges and pinks. Before I had the chance to even admire the splendid colors, the sky morphed into the gray darkness signaling evening. Luckily, there wasn't a storm cloud in the sky. I was thrilled it wouldn't rain. My anxiety heightened, and along with it, fear of creatures lurking.

We had crossed the Zilar River hours ago, heading our way northwest. My legs still felt icy from the quick dip in the rushing river waters. Evander crossed with his pants on. I couldn't figure out if he'd forgotten till he was butt deep in water, didn't care, was modest or if he'd kept them on out of respect for me. I scoffed internally at this last thought. He'd been standoffish and aggressive since our hug. Arguing at every little thing and throwing evil laughs at me when I struggled to keep up. I was officially pissed.

No matter how angry, hurt and grief-stricken he was, this back and forth was uncalled for. I wasn't a toy to be played with and he couldn't make up his mind whether I was the spawn of a demon or a decent person with feelings. And I was tired of it.

"Come on *human*," Evander called to me yet again.

I grumbled under my breath, tripping on an unseen tree root. I grunted, "Can we stop?"

"Hmmm?" he goaded, his voice echoing from somewhere ahead. But in this creepy dark, I couldn't tell where it came from and he'd disappeared.

I shrieked, feeling fur brush against my left leg. Instinctively I crossed my arms over myself and ducked my head in anticipation of the blow to the head I knew was coming.

Evander's rancorous laughter erupted bouncing around the otherwise still forest. "You humans are ridiculous. All the same, terrified!"

I straightened and bit back all the curses. "If I give you chocolate will you die?"

Evander sobered. "No, but aren't you funny."

"Pity."

"Come on, *Zuri*," he spat.

I moved forward, blindly swatting away any branch that might be smacking my face, "Does the sound of my name really piss you off?"

"In fact, it does."

I grinned as a plan formed that I hoped pissed him off as much as he was pissing me off. "How wonderful! I may start speaking in third person."

Evander snorted. "Hop on my back and I'll carry your blind ass."

I swatted around until I felt his denim pants and I pinched it out of spite. "Zuri would be most thankful."

He grumbled while I clambered on his back, making sure it was the most awkward, failed attempt possible. Evander grunted, mumbling profanities under his breath. He looped his arms between my legs, hunched over and carried me. I lay on his back, the top of my head barely coming to the base of his neck. My legs stuck straight out in front of him. But after the grueling walk and my last couple days of hell, this awkward position felt heavenly. I almost sighed.

"Zuri appreciates this."

Evander sighed with annoyance. "I'm sure the *human* does."

I nodded like the idiot I was pretending to be. Making sure he felt it on his back. "Human Zuri does."

Evander cracked a semblance of a normal laugh and I relished my victory.

"Zuri likes real laughter," I said grinning.

"*Human* can stop this now."

"*Zuri* doesn't think so; until the doggie really laughs."

Evander suddenly leaned back and dumped me off. I fell to the ground flat on my back, breathing in sharply. A rock pressed into my shoulder blade. I moaned, rolling to the side.

"Zuri did not appreciate that."

"Huh, I would imagine not," Evander said, amusement lacing his tone.

I got off the ground, rolling my shoulders to work out the painful knot forming in my shoulder muscles. "I'm sorry."

The night was silent until Evander's draft horse-like footsteps warned the whole forest he was there. I was pretty sure he was throwing a temper tantrum. The crashing of twigs he'd gathered for the fire sounded like an elephant stomping through dry tinder. I couldn't help my annoyance. His bad attitude was interrupting my first peaceful evening in days. While I was with butt-hole extra-ordinaire, I was safe from outside threats and that was enough for now to set my mind at peace. So as Evander stomped around, I threw my best glare at him.

"Chill," Evander commanded.

I rolled my eyes. Sitting down, I pulled my feet to my chest and stretched his shirt over top in an attempt to preserve body heat. Sparks cracked the darkness, and my eyes followed them up as they illuminated Evander's face for a brief moment. My mouth dropped at how sexy he happened to be at this moment. His striking green eyes reflected in the tiny sparks made his emerald orbs livelier and sent chills through me. Evander was handsome, and I'd fought my attraction since the first moment I'd met him, especially after this whole Wolf Justice fiasco. But in the fire light, Evander was enchanting and I was in big trouble.

He sparked again at the tinder, a soft blow of breath engorging a weak flame. I wondered at how he had a tinderbox or even a striking tool to be able to create a flame. But at the same time, I didn't care. In a bit I would be warm. The ember caught on the moss, illuminating the darkness with its captivating gleam. The dead sticks soon caught.

"Thank you," I whispered.

Evander perked a dark brow and I saw pity and compassion flash across his face before his expression settled into his snarky eye. "Don't get any ideas. I like a good fire as much as the next person."

I let my lips curl a little. He may not want to show me his softer side, but I still caught glimpses of it. I shrugged and made sure my voice came out even, "You keep saying that."

Evander's face twisted with sarcasm, "Really? Can't imagine why I would."

"Zuri doesn't appreciate your asshole-ism."

"*Human* should probably get some rest."

Evander strode off into the darkness muttering under his breath about how awful humans were. One human in particular. I rolled my eyes. I laughed a little inside at his lack of originality. It was well known in the supernatural community that humans were scared of their own shadow and had a tendency to act before thinking. It didn't mean we were all terrible though. In fact, most of us, when we weren't scared, were pretty amazing people. Some of us even used our fear to become better, I liked to think I fell into that category. But really, we weren't so different from other paranormal races. Point in case - Evander. He may not be scared, but he definitely was using his grief to do a terrible thing. How was he any different than humans in general? From where I was sitting, he wasn't. But I dared not say this out loud. I didn't want to provoke him further. Especially when I kept seeing glimpses of the real Evander.

My mind wandered to my situation and I scrunched into myself more. I felt so alone right now. My mother was a whack job, my family was practically non-existent and while Syrus was in my corner, there was only so much I could expect him to do. And going against a werewolf pack was not one of those things.

"I wanna go home," I whispered.

Evander trudged back, dumping a load of sticks by the fire. "Well, you aren't ever *going home*," Evander said. His voice was hard yet his eyes held a glint of softness. Still, it irked me how he was being so callous.

I glared at him. Letting my body fall to the right side, my knees remained tucked inside the shirt, I just plopped to the ground. The warmth of the fire warmed my tired, aching body. I was more worn out physically and emotionally than I ever thought I could be.

Drowsily, I closed my eyes, listening to Evander shift. It was odd listening to the transformation. A mix between shaking blinds and tearing jeans with a quivery feel to the air. I pried my eyes open hoping to watch the transformation before it was over since I'd never actually seen a wolf transform. Lazaro never let me watch and I was hoping to catch Evander's shift. Unfortunately, even though I'd opened my eyes as soon as I realized what he was doing, I missed it. I closed my eyes, stifling my disappointment.

"Night," I mumbled.

Evander blew his wolfy lips out, padding closer to me.

He laid down at my head, close enough I could feel his heat. I swore I heard him sniff my head before he grumbled, "Night."

CHAPTER TWENTY-FOUR

EVANDER

The gray light of impending dawn would have roused me from my sleep had it not been for Zuri's sniffling getting on my nerves first. They made me feel bad and I had no idea how to handle tears. Never had. Under normal circumstances, I'd reach out and pat her back. Probably in a super awkward way. But these weren't normal circumstances. I couldn't comfort the woman I had to turn in. I couldn't afford to get close to her. I'd already made the mistake earlier and I could feel her start to worm her way into my heart. It's why I'd doubled my efforts to be a jerk. But sitting here, listening to her now, I couldn't deny to myself that she'd affected me. I felt sorry for her. And I couldn't muster enough energy to be angry.

I blew my wolf lips and moved my head further onto her soft blonde hair. I understood her plight to be loved more than I would ever admit toward her. Werewolves had their own system like the humans did for foster care. For me, I was taken in on pack obligation, always reminded of it. Losing my family and discovering it was her and her family who did it, ate at me. Zuri and her family destroyed everything I loved, everything I held dear to me. And she lost everything too. Her comment earlier today about us being so similar was true, loathe to me to admit it.

My ears swiveled on my head, listening to the sounds of the early morning so she could sleep. My wolf form was so much more sensitive than my human form and as I laid at Zuri's head, I could smell the tears tracking her face. My shriveled-up heart broke for her even as I attempted to steel myself against her. This silent crying stuff would take her ages to get out of her system. I'd much rather her do the ugly cry thing, I'd heard the females call it, and get it over with than to sit here for eternity while the silent tears rolled down her face.

Irritated, I rolled my eyes and huffed as I laid my head on my paws and tried to get comfortable. I planned on staying in my shifted form all night just in case the queen's wolves showed up. Plus, the night had a chill that my thick pelt would keep at bay. My conscience twinged a little. Zuri will be cold tonight. I scooted my body so my supernatural heat would help ward off the chill she'd feel. But I played it off as if I was repositioning to a more comfortable spot. I couldn't afford to. look soft with her. Not when she was going to die soon.

Trees rustled in the slight wind, moving the fading moonlight softly around. Dawn would be coming in around twenty minutes. Zuri sniffled, curling up in a tighter ball.

"You can just cry," I said, more irritable than I meant to sound.

Zuri startled, shaking at the sound of my voice. She rose up on her forearm, glaring daggers at me. "You can just fuck off," she sniffed.

I shifted, standing over her as a human. She wiped her eyes with the back of her hands and stood, glaring at me.

"What," I asked, staring at her blazing brown eyes.

The fading firelight cast soft, playful shadows on her delicate features from her oval face down across her ample chest hidden by my shirt. Tears left a trail down her cheeks, allowing me a hint of her hidden beauty behind dirt.

She pursed her lips, moving them back and forth. "Since you wanna see me die so badly, just end it now. But if I'm allowed a final request, will you take care of Luell?"

I blinked, caught off guard with where her thoughts were. In my experience those facing death didn't think of others. All they thought of was their need to escape and preserve their own life, going so far as to grovel and make fools of themselves. Her concern for her cat was refreshing and I couldn't help but respect her a bit more.

I grumbled, *she's... okay...* I finally allowed myself to acknowledge. *I'm just doing my duty at this point. She is... she's,* I mumbled at myself, not being able to say the word I thought of her. The wolf inside of me whined. I closed my eyes so Zuri wouldn't see my eyeroll. *Fine, persistent ass, she is good. And I'm just doing my duty at this point.*

Zuri moved behind a tree and crouched down. I turned to face upwind of her scent and gave her some privacy. She came plodding back like a bear - yawning and groggy from what I could figure was her first decent night's sleep in a while. Spinning on my heel, I went to relieve myself.

"Let's get moving," I commanded.

Zuri fell in step behind me. "Zuri wants to know what will happen to Luell."

"Really? Already?"

I could feel the smirk on her lips without turning around.

"If doggie is gonna start the day being crabby, Zuri will start the day being snappy. So, change the 'tude and don't be rude or Zuri will rhyme the entire time."

"You're despicable."

Zuri laughed. "Awww look at you finally using a different word for me."

Grumbling, I set a fast pace, knowing the human couldn't keep it up for very long. Already she was huffing, yawning and making weird noises as she attempted to keep the pace directly behind me.

It was still early enough in the morning that the sun's rays were weak and cool, for which I was thankful. Birds chirped, flitting from branch to branch. It was peaceful. I listened intently for any sign of the birds stopping their morning songs. Not even birds cared for the fae.

Up ahead, the trees broke apart becoming spacious and not so condensed. Ivy clung to the base of trees, steadily climbing higher, reaching for sunlight. Maples and birches sprouted up in between the towering firs. I loved the forest when it was like this - concealing yet revealing; a place to be able to hunt and stalk prey, open enough to see yet enclosed enough to hide and lurk.

Zuri yelped, tripping over a rock. She hissed loudly, whimpering over her stubbed toe.

I went back to her, kneeling down while she examined her foot. "Are you ok?"

She nodded. "Yeah," she said, offering a winced look while her shoulder shrugged like she didn't care.

I rose, then helped her to her feet. Spinning on my heel, I picked a less rugged path for her to follow on.

At least we are getting closer to being done, thank the good god Elohi, I thought, pulling at the skin on the back of my neck. *The more time I spend with her, the more I'm allowing myself to like her.*

Her ogre-like footfalls sounded behind me. Without any sort of warning, I was being thrust toward the ground. I fell, catching myself from smashing against a rock. *That's the last time I think and walk with her around,* I acknowledged. Zuri landed on top of me, groaning dramatically and I wondered how hurt she was.

"Sorry," she said, her voice deep with a mock imitation of my own voice, as she scrambled off me. "I tripped."

I smirked. "Ahhh really? I couldn't guess for myself."

Zuri stomped past me, throwing over her shoulder, "I didn't think you could, which is why I said something."

She stopped in front of a large bush blossoming with large coral covered berries. Plucking one, she turned it over in her hands before popping it into her mouth. Closing her eyes, she moaned as she savored the flavor.

"Salmonberry," she explained, holding one out for me.

Dusting my bare chest and jeans off, I shook my head. Zuri shrugged. Holding out the shirt she wore, Zuri began filling it full of the plump salmonberries. Idly, I stood by, watching her quickly pick handfuls tying them up for later. *Damn. Wish I'd thought of that. Her forethought is admirable. And incredibly sexy.* I would not allow myself to go there. But it didn't stop me from being intrigued or admiring her from afar.

What I expected of her was to be a blithering mess. Prior to Zuri, I had brought several other traitors in connection to the night my pack was nearly annihilated before the council to receive judgement was a mess. Anyone - human or not. Zuri wasn't a mess and I couldn't for the life of me figure her out.

I leaned against a tree trunk and grumbled. I liked her, despite how I treated her. Her banter was irritating, but fun. She was one of those rare few who could take whatever she dished out and damn if I didn't admire her for it.

After you take me back, what's next, she had asked me. Honestly, I wasn't sure. Taking down the Queen of Kadia Castle was certainly on the list. But after all was said and done, I had no clue who I'd be or what I wanted to do with my life.

Eventually, I would like a family of my own with an alpha to rule at my side. A pack of my own creation within the pack Bardou since all who lived were enslaved by the queen of Kadia. Regret stabbed my conscience at the same time as relief for dodging a major bullet. I could have started a family with Catronia, but because I was wrapped up in seeking revenge for my family, I'd missed the opportunity. Yet, finding out she'd been cheating on me the whole time, alleviated my guilt. I'd missed it for a long time, possibly because my whole mission had been to exact revenge and I was consumed by the thought. I was just glad now that she was out of my life and I didn't have to worry about her lying and cheating while we had pups to raise.

I ran a hand over my face, then pulled at the skin behind my neck.

"What's wrong now?" Zuri asked, muttering between mouthfuls of salmonberries.

I snorted, ignoring her question I cared not to answer yet. Everything was wrong. I lost my pack, my family because of what hers did to mine. I lost my wife because I was so caught up in getting justice. Even though we had divorced well over a year ago, the wound still felt fresh to me. I lost my world because of Zuri Barsotti, the Queen and whoever sired her. Yet, I couldn't bring myself to hate Zuri anymore.

Zuri strode up to me, the shirt she wore heaped in berries. "Eat," she commanded, holding one out.

Turning on my heel, I strode away from her. I needed to drop her off with the commander and fast. I couldn't take the battling in my head between wanting to hate her and wanting to know her more.

"Hey!" Zuri yelled, catching up to me. "You have to eat something," she nagged.

"If I eat a berry will you shut up?"

Zuri huffed, jogging beside me to keep up with my fast pace. "Only if you eat ten berries and smile while you do it."

I stopped dead in my tracks while Zuri swerved around in front of me. Reaching into her shirt, I cupped my hands like a shovel and scooped berries, shoving them all in my face. Zuri's beautiful honey brown eyes narrowed on me. Returning her look, I perked a brow.

"Satisfied, *human*?"

"No, Zuri is not. Doggie did not smile while he ate."

My upper lip twitched. "*Human* will be quiet now. We have one last part of the Zilar River to cross then the home stretch to OKimma. We will be there today."

Zuri popped a berry into her mouth, glaring at me. There was humor behind her eyes instead of the ferocity I was used to seeing. Or maybe I never saw the humor because I had been doing my best to ignore her.

I liked the challenge and mischief I saw there. I grinned, forcing my wolf teeth to show to see what she would do. Zuri took a giant step toward me, shirt still up holding the remaining salmonberries inside, offering a small peek of skin.

I put my hands on my hips, lowering my head toward her. "Yes?"

Zuri grinned. "Zuri would slap you, but that would be animal abuse."

Blowing my lips, I bit back a laugh. "Come on, Zuri," I commanded, striding toward the last section of the Zilar River.

She fell in step behind me, munching on the remaining berries. "All right," she preened, grinning triumphantly behind me.

In everything that transpired between us over the

course of a couple weeks, her resilience and bravery weren't something I expected of her or let alone a human, yet after her constant displays of these and other traits, I couldn't help but admire her a little more. And here she was, brave and strong while I led her to stand trial and die.

Glancing over my shoulder, a wan, sad smile caressed her plump pink lips. A type of contentedness graced her tan face as she gawked around the forest, taking in the serenity.

Righting my gaze, I led the way through the last part of the forest. For the first time, I was truly beginning to question exactly what I was doing since realizing these emotions she was eliciting were linked to me and her impending fate.

I swiped at my face with a hand, *shit...*

CHAPTER TWENTY-FIVE

ZURI

Crossing the last part of the Zilar River was surprisingly easier than I anticipated. There was a bridge ahead of us. Out of nowhere, the forest unfurled into open land with dark green grass up to the ankles. The luscious grass swayed in the light crisp breeze and my feet thanked me as they brushed the soft meadowland. Marigolds and Pacino sunflowers grew sporadically in spots in the grass, bringing colorful warmth to the pretty open landscape.

Bending down from Evander's large back, almost losing my balance, I plucked a sunflower and smelled it. It would probably be the last time I smelled my favorite flower. I wanted to remember the scent, to savor it.

Evander turned his head, watching me intently; tilting his head to the side as if he was trying to figure out the reason why I stalled. Ever since our sarcastic quips back and forth earlier this morning, he'd been dead silent only now mumbling. Wanting to make, as he called it, excellent time, he'd begun to carry me on his back in his wolf form about midmorning.

"Everything ok?" he asked, though annoyance and anxiety were in his tone.

Still clutching the flower, I slid off his back to give him a break as I followed him toward the bridge, staying in the grass for my feet's sake. Evander shifted, shaking out the shift and ran a hand through his hair. The steel framed structure appeared entirely displaced in the beautiful scenery. Stepping onto the hot, expanded metal bridge hurt my bare feet. There was nowhere else to walk though. Everything was a giant grate that reminded me of a cheese grater. The cuts on my feet ached, my feet ached in general, but the ache was now going up my legs.

I closed my eyes, hissing with each step I took; I walked slowly, picking my feet up in exaggerated, careful steps, trying not to trip or do anything that would cut my feet open wide.

He stopped, turning to look back at me. "Are you ok to cross this?" Evander asked.

"Yeah."

Without warning, he threw me over his shoulder like a fireman with one arm through my leg and his other arm hooking my left arm. My head rested on his upper right bicep.

"You're heavier than you look," he commented.

"Wow... you certainly know the way to a woman's heart."

Evander smirked, rolling his eyes.

"I saw that," I grinned.

"Really, I was hoping at this close a distance you couldn't."

"Me too. I would prefer a change in scenery, but I won't complain about what I got."

"So, it's not terrible?" he asked, perking a brow.

I tried to shrug. "Not entirely. The words coming out of a gaping hole in the middle, tends to put me off though."

Evander blew his lips. "Human," he paused, stepping off the bridge.

He set me down gently on the grass, looking at me with a conflicted expression. His swirling emerald eyes held mine for a brief moment, then looked away. Holding his head high, he began walking on the edge of the road, following it northeast.

I followed him, staying on the outer edge of the grass. I took a deep breath and caught a whiff of BO and almost gagged. Gosh, I couldn't wait for a hot shower. And an actual meal! I hope they allowed me that luxury before offing me. I chuckled darkly to myself. I couldn't guarantee anything now, but I could hope for small kindnesses.

I frowned, my cat was more important in comparison to a hot meal and a shower. I would take getting to see her if I could over anything. My frown deepened, as I wondered if I would get to say goodbye to my cat. I already did once when I thought she was dead, but now, I wanted to say goodbye for real, on my own terms.

"Can we stop and get Luell?"

Evander nodded. His head swiveled. His body tensed as he looked around. I stopped moving, turning in a slow circle. I saw nothing. Scowling, I took a tentative step forward, coming to Evander's side.

"Stay there," Evander whispered, extending a hand behind his back.

Quicker than I could blink, Evander shifted into his wolf form. His black fur, all splotchy with gray and white bristled. Evander took a small step forward, growling low in his throat. His ears swiveled on his lowered head. Carefully, he paced forward, moving to the right.

I glanced around for anything I possibly could wield as a weapon to defend myself. There was nothing but grass and small pebbles.

"Get ready to run," he whispered.

My body tensed. I felt like an antelope on a nature show where the animal couldn't decide which direction would be best for fleeing - and then it died

"How you humans live past childhood is beyond me," he grumbled, backing up to stand by my side.

"I'm really upset chocolate doesn't kill you," I teased.

Evander snorted. Glancing down, I thought I saw a grin, but I wasn't sure. I couldn't tell if it was a smile or his flopping wolf jowls.

"Run down the hill toward the trees."

Without hesitation, I took off down the hill toward the trees. A small cluster of maples met my eager retreat. Snarling sounded from behind me. Curious, I glanced over my shoulder. Evander battled two large white wolves that were nearly bigger than him, and Evander was a large wolf. It looked like he was getting his ass kicked. While I couldn't be one hundred percent sure, common sense told me Evander wasn't doing well.

"Shit."

Pumping my arms and legs faster, I made it to the bottom of the hill and picked up a fallen tree branch. Peering up the hill, Evander was pinned on his back by one wolf while the other tore into his chest with its teeth. Evander yipped, kicking his attacker and successfully removing him. Evander spun, catching the other wolf by the throat and whipping him to the ground like a snapping of a tree branch. The bloodied wolf leapt onto Evander's back, tearing a gaping hole into his left shoulder. Evander swerved around to face the aggressor, lunging at him with paws and teeth, getting the asshole wolf on the side of the face. Even with Evander successfully on his feet, the odds were not in his favor.

I mockingly whistled. "Here boy! Wanna play fetch?"

The white wolves stopped. The one attacking Evander was covered in blood around the mouth. Heads lowered, they trotted toward me, grinning at me in a fear inducing way only a werewolf could. Swiveling the branch in my hand, I pointed the sharpest end toward the other wolf.

"Zuri," the cleanest white wolf snarled. "Come with us."

"To the pound?"

The clean-wolf snapped its jaws, nodding its head at the other wolf to do something in silent agreement. The blood covered wolf trotted to my right, head lowered, assessing me with keen golden eyes. Evander went up on top of the hill, trying to keep the limp from being noticeable.

I moved my head slightly to keep an eye on the bloodied wolf stalking closer to me. *Screw it! I'm not waiting for him to attack.* Sharp end forward, I plowed straight into the wolf's side.

Dammit, I want to stay breathing. Anger and fear just fueled my desire to live, I channeled it into my spear thrust. The wolf whimpered, falling to its side. Blood pooled around the entrance of the wound.

Before I got a chance to sigh in relief or gloat like I wanted to, the air in my body was knocked out of me. Falling to the ground, I barely caught myself. Pain registered in my brain to scream, but I could not make the sound come out. The wolf I ignored, clamped its teeth around my ankle and shook its head.

With my free ankle, I began kicking, trying to connect to its face and missed.

"Evander!" I heard screamed, only vaguely aware that it was my voice doing the screaming.

Everything slowed down. Time itself seemed to limp by as I watched Evander stumble down the hill, almost as if he was on a leisurely walk. Although, logically I knew he was hurt and he was trying to get to me; this slow as fuck time made me angry and afraid something would happen in this weird in-between moment. I lashed out with my foot again, this time connecting with the wolf's jaw. It yelped and released my foot and I scrambled back as best I could.

I lost sight of Evander while getting unsteadily to my feet. I faced the wolf like I would a wrestling opponent. Of all the skills Uncle Syrus taught me, wrestling was one of his musts for women. I wasn't sure if a double-leg take down would work on an animal, but I would try.

The now bloody white wolf paced in front of me in short strides. I bent down low and swiped at the shifter's paws and missed. The wolf dodged and went behind me. Rising to my feet as quickly as I could, I spun around to face him, but immediately realized I was not fast enough.

In a blink, the werewolf transformed into a human. His ebony black hair slicked back on his head. Hard blue eyes bore into mine with hatred and promised malevolence making me shudder. The giant of a man waggled a finger in front of my face.

"Zuri, Zuri, Zuri," the man tisked, shaking his head.

I refused to show my fear as I sassed back, "Yeah I heard you the first time."

The man laughed arrogantly. "Pathetic human," he spat. "Gimme the key and I will let you keep breathing."

"Pathetic human just whooped your boyfriend's ass. Your use of adjectives is horrendous."

The man brought a hand up to his jaw, rubbing it against the dark stubble. He tapped a finger against his jaw. His careless disregard of me was going to bite him in the ass. I inadvertently giggled at the thought of - bite him in the ass - since he was a werewolf and he probably did bite his ass to get the fleas.

Seizing my moment, I football tackled him; shoulder down and into his side. The force of my assault knocked him off his feet. I maneuvered behind him, throwing him into a headlock and wrapping my legs around his abdomen. I squeezed with my arms and legs as tight as I could. The man pulled at my arms, but I was damn proud of myself for not letting go. He knocked me on my back, hoping his weight and the force of colliding with the ground would make me break loose. Fuck if I was letting go! Closing my eyes, I ground my teeth, grunting as I struggled to keep the upper hand.

"Zuri," Evander called.

The man stopped struggling and I wonder if I had successfully made his stupid head pass out. Opening my eyes, Evander stood before me with a handgun pressed against the man's head. His lip curled as he pulled the hammer back, piercing the anxious silence. He was covered in a thin sheen of sweat. He straightened his back, holding the gun steady as his free hand covered the open wound.

"Let him go," Evander commanded.

My entire body felt like soupy pudding - all gross and jiggly. I uncurled my legs and arms from him and scooted away. Taking a moment to breathe, I rose slowly to my feet. I stood behind Evander and off to the side.

"Let us leave and I won't put a silver bullet in your head," Evander threatened.

The man spat on the ground, "How dare you side with a human over your own kind!"

"Who said I was 'siding' with her? Whatever I'm doing is none of your business. I have my reasons for what I do. And they do not include losing her to rabid wolf scum like you."

"Rabid wolf scum? I'm an esteemed member of the

Moon Walkers. There are no scum in my pack. And we have plans for her. Hand her over." the man countered.

I blinked, wondering how many packs wanted my head. I sucked in a breath and dared a glance at Evander. He didn't look at me and I couldn't gather anything from his facial reactions. He just stared hard at the man on the ground.

Taking my eyes off the staring contest between Evander that dipshit wolf, I peered around for the wolf I impaled. The werewolf lay still on its side, breathing shallowly. Watching him labor to breathe, I couldn't help feeling guilty. I knew the guilt was misplaced. It was a fight of survival and I did what I had to do to survive. But I hated seeing him suffer and my heart clenched at his pain and inevitable death.

I squatted down low, next to the wolf's head, out of reach of possible snapping jaws, and whispered, "I'm sorry."

A bright blue eye opened and focused on me. The were-wolf closed that eye, but not before I saw something pass across it. Respect? Resignation? Acceptance? That blue eye opened again and he took one last deep breath and his chest stilled. I sucked on my bottom lip, biting down to keep from crying.

"I'm so sorry," I whispered again.

"Zuri," Evander called, a hint of urgency in his voice.

Rising from my crouched position, I hurried over to Evander who strode toward me. He extended his hand and I took it, being whisked away briskly from the scene.

"Follow me," he said, offering his hand.

Taking it, he dragged me off up the hill, leaving the

Moon Walker behind us. My eyebrows furrowed. Glancing over my shoulder, I watched the other wolf pull the branch out of the dead werewolf's side. *How in the hell did I manage that*, I wondered. *From what I knew only pure silver or complete decapitation took out a wolf.* I glanced back over my shoulder and scowled, wondering if I had even killed it at all.

"Is he really dead?" I asked.

"Yeah, he is," Evander confirmed.

"How?"

"It wasn't a full wolf yet," Evander explained. "He was created and could still be killed without a silver bullet, decapitation, or another wolf or creature killing it. The other wolf was also created. And when created you have to wait until a full moon for the lykan powers to fully take over - to shift at will and stay shifted for long periods of time instead of maybe twenty-minute intervals," he paused, waiting to see if I was following him.

I nodded my understanding.

"And so you know," he continued, "born wolves will *always* have green eyes. Created wolves will be different. The dead wolf would have been a *were* in four days."

"Oh," was all I could seem to mutter out. I licked my cracked lips. "Are you ok?" I asked, staring at him concerned.

Evander smiled at me. "I'll heal quickly. Are you?"

I pursed my lips and shrugged. I wasn't sure. Evander nodded, not pressing me for a further answer. My mind reeled. I was being hunted by numerous people and the only person remotely safe was Evander. Which meant I was stupid because I knew he was taking me back to be killed. He may call it standing trial, for a crime I hadn't committed, but we both knew it wasn't really a trial. It was a sentencing. And my fate had already been decided. Still, Evander's pack would guard and seclude me until the trial date, so even knowing this, it was still safer than any other pack and being subjected to their whims, however sadistic and tortuous they were.

We got to an older car that had seen better days. The bumper was almost on the ground, being held together by a bungee cord and zip tie. Sun damage peppered the hood and roof. The interior was clean except for the numerous claw marks on the back seat and dash.

"Looks like you get pretty wild," I said, going to the passenger side and getting in. "Remind me not to party with you."

Evander snorted, shaking his head and getting inside. "This isn't my car," he said, slamming the door and locking it now that my door was shut. "Thank you... for what you did back there," he said, buckling.

Evander turned the engine over.

I buckled. "Manners? Coming forth from a gaping hole?"

Evander smirked, "Yes, Zuri."

Soon as the seatbelt clicked, he sped off. My body was slung back into the seat and I felt myself gasp. The air came delayed though and for a second I wondered if this was a clunker or a jet. After my body adjusted, I looked over at the speedometer and worked hard not to let my jaw drop.

"150, hot damn! I didn't think this car could take that kind of speed."

I inhaled again, this time a little deeper as I tried to relax into the ride and the rancid smell of wet dog and stale burgers hit my nose and I dry heaved as nausea rolled over me. I frantically pressed buttons to get the window to roll down, but nothing happened. The damn window was stuck. I grabbed the borrowed shirt I was wearing and took a tiny breath. All I smelled was me. Not particularly pleasant, but much better than the stench of dying burgers and drowning dogs.

Evander glanced over, smiling genuinely and dipped his head. "You saved my hide."

"You're welcome."

The tension between us had slowly started to relax. Although I was still on guard. He'd done this whiplash thing a few times already and I wouldn't put it past him to get hostile again. But ever since finding the road this morning, he'd started to relax and the tension had loosened a bit. My saving his life had only seemed to loosen it more. I hoped I'd seen an end to all the hostility, but I wasn't going to hold my breath. But for now, I'd enjoy the tiny bit of comradery we were experiencing.

The tires beat pavement, passing by manicured grass that met forest a hundred or so feet from the paved road. The car was silent, save for the air coming through the vents. I shifted in my seat, turning toward Evander, smiling at him. He was a handsome wolf, a good-hearted person with a bad guy persona.

"Thank you," I said, breaking the silence.

Evander glanced over to me. "For what?"

"Saving me all the time."

I reached out and took his vacant hand in my own. I didn't want to be alone, to feel alone. I wanted to hold something. Evander didn't balk at my touch as I assumed he would have. He held my hand, loftily in his, rubbing a thumb over the knuckles.

"You're welcome."

CHAPTER TWENTY-SIX

EVANDER

Something was changing between us and I wasn't entirely certain what to think about it. I feared I was the one changing. The more I got to know this woman, the more I admired her. She'd saved me from those wolves when most would have seen that as a chance to run and save their own hide. She was absolutely gorgeous, sarcastic, witty; something I enjoyed in another person. Zuri was even braver than what I had originally given her credit for, and I'd always known she was no coward, despite what I told her to her face. She faced the Chay Faeries, her mother's wolves, and now the Moon Walkers with a determined resilience I had to admit I admired.

I mulled her most recent behavior through my mind, pretty sure she had no idea what saving me meant not only to me, but in general - I now owed her one - as the saying goes. Wolves were notorious for their dominance in fights. I'd been in a few myself and won them all, some by the skin on my teeth. A wolf could kill another wolf with teeth and claws, or another paranormal could via silver bullet or decapitation. And when those two had shown up, I'd been in no shape to fight - tired, hungry, and distracted.

She saved me; my inner wolf decided to repeat annoyingly. I pushed the thought from my head for now. I would have to think and consider it at a later time, although I felt myself softening toward her more than I anticipated myself doing. And even now, with taking her back out of sheer duty to my pack, I felt more and more like not doing so.

My nose crinkled. The smell of the car was horrid. Glancing over at Zuri, she was still breathing into my shirt. I smiled, amused at her hiding and captivated by her at the same time. She leaned her head back, scooting closer to the console and toward me. Her eyes slowly drooped, content with the gentle touch of my hand. I held her dainty hand softly in my own, still rubbing a thumb over her knuckles. Her head dipped low and bounced with a bump in the road. I held back a snort of laughter, not wanting to wake her up.

She's cute, I thought, then changed the thought to something else. It had been about an hour since the encounter with the wolves. My body healed itself rather quickly, something I was thankful for. I kept checking the rearview, no other cars or persons were following us at the moment. It didn't mean someone wasn't. I maneuvered and took corners at random, zipping down back roads, if there were any, while making a steady pace toward OKimma. We still had a bit to go.

I refused to let my mind wander to Zuri, not wanting to

think about her and how she wheedled into my thoughts. Instead, I opted for home. After all of this, after turning her into the department, taking on Queen Lyvia and finally handling whoever sired Zuri, I wanted to rebuild my pack home - put up new houses, trim up tree branches, secure the area with fences and cameras - basically make home feel safe and secure again so what was left of my pack could return to it.

I ran a hand over my face. It was a lot to take on and accomplish, but I was prepared to do the dirty work. My eyes darted over to Zuri, her head sliding off the side of the seat and resting on my arm. Her head was rocked forward so I couldn't see her face while a light snore came from her mouth.

Silly little human, I mused then checked the rearview again.

Outlying buildings were coming into view as we travelled closer. I slowed down to match the speed limit and drove toward the veterinary clinic I had taken Luell to. It had been two days since I left Luell. For Zuri's sake, part of me hoped her cat didn't make it. Not that I was cruel, but it would be cruel to Zuri to see her cat be alright and then be forced to say goodbye again. Painful for the cat to overcome the loss of it's human as well. Pulling into the parking lot had me torn between wanting to wake Zuri or allow her to sleep. The practical side of me won. Since Zuri was being hunted by different packs, she needed to be safe-guarded.

Nudging her arm, I whispered softly. "Zuri, it's time to get Luell."

Zuri startled, jumping up and wiping the drool off the side of her mouth. "I want breakfast."

"Yeah me too, but we're here to get Luell."

Her honey brown eyes alighted with sparkles. "Really?" she asked on the verge of tears.

"Yes."

Once I unlocked the door, I couldn't get out of the car fast enough. Zuri beat me not only out of the car, but to the front door of the clinic. It hadn't dawned on me how we appeared until we both stood in front of the solid glass door and the technicians inside stared at us.

"Lemme see if there's something inside the car," I said, jogging back.

Zuri's cheeks heated crimson as she waited off to the side. I ignored how beautiful her blush made her look. Checking the backseat, an old ratted red shirt lay discarded on the floor board. I shrugged it on, ignoring the scent of body odor and car grease.

Underneath the disgusting shirt were bright neon green gym shorts and flip flops much too large for Zuri. It would have to do for the moment if she wanted to see her cat. Peeking over my shoulder, she stood where I remembered her last, arms crossed over her chest, to hide her ample breasts.

Slamming the car door shut, I strode purposefully toward her. Her eager, grateful eyes reached mine. Her hands shook as she tried to put on the pants and shoes. Tears coursed down her face and I tried hard not to think about why. Kneeling down, I helped her step into the shorts and put the shoes on her feet.

"Thank you," she sniffed.

"Let's go get Luell," I said softly, guiding her by the elbow to the front door.

The technician behind the counter eyed me disapprovingly. Ignoring her stink-eye, I approached the counter.

"I'm here about the cat Luell."

The sour look on the lady's face stayed put until she tapped a few keys on her keyboard. As she stared at her screen, her eyes widened and she paused before turning to me and taking a breath. Then in what I assumed was supposed to be her professional voice she said, "That will be eight hundred ninety-three dollars. We had to do surgery, but she is ready to go home. She'll need lots of rest for a few weeks. She has a long recovery ahead of her. How would you like to pay?"

"Please call Commander Iorgas," I began listing the phone number and explaining details of why I couldn't pay her with a credit card at this moment, leaving out the actual truth about leaving my wallet in my car as I went to hunt the woman in front of her. After five minutes of negotiating and signing a document stating I would be sued if they weren't paid in a week, I turned to Zuri. Every little bit of hassle had been worth it.

The vet tech came through the swinging door from the back part of the clinic carrying the cat wrapped in a soft teal blanket. Zuri immediately started crying as the tech passed over Luell and she held her cat close to her chest. She cried like someone broken getting a piece of their heart back - blubbering and uncontrollable. Despite the previous animosity, I was glad I hadn't missed this moment.

I just stood there for a minute, drinking in the sight of her and letting her cry her relief out. Then, putting a hand on the small of her back, I led her outside to the car. I opened the door for her and gently helped her inside. Getting in on my own side, I turned the engine over and began the drive back to my apartment.

"Thank you," Zuri hiccupped.

"You're welcome," I said softly.

Zuri wiped her eyes with the palm of her hand, holding onto her cat for dear life. She nuzzled the cat with her nose. Luell let out a weak mewl in response, but I caught the cat's responding nudge from the corner of my eye.

"Thank you so much, Evander," Zuri whispered.

My hand reached out on its own, stroking the hair on the back of her head. Her hair, dirty and greasy from her escape and our adventure, felt nice in my calloused hands. She smiled wanly at me, a sparkle igniting in her eyes.

I swallowed, focusing on the road again. *I don't need this. Mission. She's just a mission.*

Zuri took a few slow deliberate breaths and watched the scenery leaning against the back of her seat and the window, careful not to jostle the cat. I was grateful for the comfortable silence. I weaved my way through the east end of OKimma, going in a blurring, zig-zagged, confusing way to throw off any would-be followers.

I put the car in park out in the open, next to a food cart and across the street from a bank and right next to a tow zone. I didn't care. It wasn't my car. Guiding Zuri by the small of her back, I led her toward my gated apartment complex, a block and a half up the road.

"I almost got an apartment here," Zuri commented.

I perked a brow. "Why didn't you?"

She shrugged, adjusting Luell in her arms. "I'm human. Something would have happened to me or at my apartment. It is safer for me and my kind on the west side."

I nodded. She wasn't wrong. Human homicides were frequent on the east side. "You'll be safe here," I replied, hoping to sound assuring, ignoring the whole reason I'd brought her here.

I punched in the code to get inside the gated complex, the beeps low and understated. The gate swung open without a sound. Zuri entered and waited to the side. Soundlessly the gate shut without a clank.

Off to the side, we ascended the stairs and strode down the small hall toward the fourth door on the left. I entered in another code for a key to pop out. Heading down three more doors, I unlocked my apartment.

"That is quite a system," Zuri commented.

"It's what happens when you work for the werewolf government," I replied.

The Department of Paranormal Justice, who I happened to work for, owned the entire complex. An employee could rent an apartment for a discounted price. Being a bachelor and seldom home, it was worth paying for, instead of a nicer place more downtown or even staying at my pack home, the commute to work and fixing the place up.

Zuri entered and gently set Luell down on the couch. I

let out a breath, relieved to be home in my small one-bedroom abode. I clanked the key on the counter and strode back to the door to set all the locks. Flashing of the answering machine caught my attention but I wanted to wait until Zuri was asleep or in the shower to listen to the messages.

Glancing over my shoulder, Zuri waited awkwardly in the living room. Her dirty blonde hair swept behind her ear. Her right arm crossed over her body to hold her left elbow.

"What?" I asked. "Make yourself... comfortable," I said, mumbling the last word. Anything else would have been callous given her compliance with all I had put her through and I wasn't sure compliance was the right word.

Zuri nodded, offering me a delicate and drawn smile. "Thank you... again. I know this whole ordeal is putting you out and you could have left me to the Moon Walkers or my mother." I watched her shudder ever so slightly. "So, I appreciate it."

I scratched the back of my head. "Welcome." Walking the five steps to the fridge, I grabbed a beer. "Want one?" I asked, waggling one.

"Yes please!" she said brightened a bit then sobered.

I tossed her a can. Zuri immediately opened it and guzzled the contents.

"Thirsty?"

Zuri nodded. "Thirsty, hungry, dirty, weary... All of it," she said, polishing off the last bit.

"Head down the hall and take a shower. I'll order take out."

"No curry for me please."

"I remember."

Zuri smirked. "Is this our date?"

I scoffed. "No, I take women on better dates than a night in."

She shrugged. "I wouldn't know about your kinda dates, but I like night-in dates."

"This is *not* a date."

She strode down the short hallway, turning right into the bathroom. "Ok," she said, her voice lilting, "whatever you gotta tell yourself."

The door to the bathroom shut gently. I snorted and shook my head. Going to the landline, I picked up the phone and began dialing the number of my favorite place.

"It's *really* not a date?" Zuri called in what I would categorize as a hopeful tone, poking her head out of the door.

"No... I do better dates than this, so don't worry yourself, *human*." I teased.

Her face scrunched and her lips pulled down. "*Zuri* will believe it when she sees it."

"Take a shower," I shot back, giving a half grin.

She smiled genuinely, shutting the door, but not twisting the lock. Desire swirled inside of me. I pressed it down. There could always be later or not at all and I caught myself second guessing everything again. I ran a hand over my face and became relieved when I heard the water in the shower start to take my thoughts away from her. I turned back to the phone call I had to make before I ordered dinner.

CHAPTER TWENTY-SEVEN

ZURI

I stripped down in seconds, putting my grandmother's key on the countertop. The hot water massaged my sore and tired muscles, almost as well as a masseuse. At least that's what I told myself. I let out a low groan as my muscles began to unwind. Using Evander's loofah, I scrubbed every part of me I could, saving my hair for last. His soap smelled of cracked black pepper and juniper berry and I took a couple of good whiffs, enjoying the scent I'd caught off him several times.

Like the woods outside my house. I scrubbed every inch of skin until the dirt and grime were gone and my skin felt tight. Spying a razor, I grabbed it.

"I'm using your razor!" I shouted.

I didn't care if he cared or not, looking like a bear wasn't on my agenda even if I only had a day or two to live. I'd go to my death looking my best. I shaved my underarms and legs, only up past the knee by an inch. I laughed when my Aunt Espe's screechy voice echoed in my head - *don't go past the knee. You don't want to look like a hooker!* I put no stock in that nonsense. But my hair was blond enough to blend into my skin and I figured if no one could see it without a microscope I wouldn't put any more effort into it.

Taking a deep satisfying breath, I turned off the water and stepped out, feeling revigorated. Wrapping a towel around me, a soft knock came from the bathroom door.

"Come in," I called.

Evander stuck his hand in, holding out a pair of black sweatpants and a dark teal shirt. "Here," he said.

Gently I took them and set them on the counter. His hand poked through the door again, handing me a dark red bottle.

"It's lotion... Thought you might like it."

"Thank you," I said, taking the bottle. I popped open the lid and inhaled sandalwood and cinnamon. "This smells great."

"I ordered us burgers, strawberry milkshakes, and fries," Evander said through the door.

"My favorite, thank you."

"Yup. I will be in the living room when you're done," he said, shutting the door.

I took off the towel and wrapped my hair up in it. Beads of water rolled down my legs. I rubbed lotion all over the bottom half of me then wriggled into the sweatpants. A contented sigh loudly escaped my lips. The sweatpants stuck to my wet legs. They were a touch large and falling off my body. I had an ass, but not much in the way of hips.

"No ties," I grumbled.

I crossed my legs, hoping it helped to hold up the sweatpants. Taking the lotion again, I put it all over my upper half, wherever I could reach. My skin loosened, and I felt less like I had barbequed chicken skin. The thought of food made my stomach rumble. I grabbed the key and shoved it into the deep pant pocket on my right.

Putting lotion on my face, I smiled rubbing it in. There was something to the crisp freshness I loved about this part of hygiene. I took the teal shirt and shrugged it on. The v-neck came down low, displaying a touch of cleavage on my 'C' cup sized breasts. I rolled the sweatpants over a few times, hoping the fabric bundle would be enough to help my pants stay up.

A loud knock came from the front door. Panic swirled inside of me. I was scared it was the Moon Walkers or my mother. I heard Evander's mumbled voice at the front door and my heart kept thundering. Gently I locked the door, keeping myself inside the bathroom. Digging through the drawers and carelessly invading Evander's privacy, I attempted to find anything to defend myself with.

A 9mm pistol lay in a vacant drawer. Grabbing it, I checked to see if the mag was full. It was. Jamming it back in place, I fingered the safety off. With a deep breath, I opened the door and came out with the gun drawn level, finger next to the trigger.

A delivery boy in a bright turquoise shirt raised his hands. "Whoa lady! I brought you food."

His blue eyes darted from me to Evander. His blond hair swept over the side of his face like he stuck a giant fruit bowl on his head and cut around it.

Evander turned around, staring at me with an understanding gaze. "Zuri," he said, soothingly, putting himself between me and the kid. Evander handed the kid money behind his back while coming to me with a hand out. "I ordered food, remember? You're safe. It's ok."

The boy was maybe sixteen and he stared wide eyed at me. In bright purple letters across his turquoise polo shirt was the local burger joint slogan - *Were-Burgers, where burgers are anything but normal*. My face burned. I gaped like a fish. I lowered the handgun, backpedaling inside the bathroom and quietly shutting the door. My heart beat thrummed in my ears, feeling guilty about what I had done to the kid, Evander let in to bring us food.

I heard the front door slam and the heavy measured footfalls of Evander approaching the bathroom. "Zuri," he called, his voice soft, low and sympathetic. "You all right?"

"No," I squeaked out.

I had never pulled a gun on an innocent person before. I pulled a gun on intruders, and those wanting to do me harm, but never in my life on just a random, normal, innocent person. My skin crawled anxiously. The room felt like it was swaying and closing in. I leaned against the bathroom countertop with a hand over my face.

Large arms encircled me and I didn't hear the door open. "Hey," Evander soothed. "It's all right. You've been through hell the last several days between everything and myself included."

Tears coursed down my face of their own accord. My usually put together, hard outside self-crumbled like concrete buildings being demoed. I leaned into his embrace, throwing my hands around his waist.

"I'm sorry. I thought he was here to hurt you… to hurt me and I got scared. I forgot you ordered food."

Evander held me tight against him. He stroked my wet hair, kissing the side of my head. My eyebrows drew together and I blinked rapidly.

"Sorry," Evander said.

My mouth became a desert. I opened it to say something yet no sound emerged. Instead, my hands moved to hold the back of his neck and I pulled him down to my level, kissing him lightly on the lips.

Evander's full lips met mine with fervor. Soft. Tender. Everything I secretly imagined they would be like. I held my lips against his, savoring his husky, masculine scent like woodsy cologne. I moaned, my own arousal building, but I held it off.

It's just a kiss, I repeated in my head. *A kiss. It's a kiss…*

He put a hand on the base of my neck on the side, holding me. Pulling me toward him, his lips crushed mine; powerful and hungry. And I gave in, pulling him toward me. I couldn't get my lips close enough to his.

His lips parted mine, slipping in his tongue. I pulled back from his sweet kiss, jumping up, and wrapping my legs around his torso, pressing my body against his. The sweatpants dropped off my hips a little. My left hand broke off from being around his neck, and pulled up the pants, not breaking our lips apart. Biting his bottom lip playfully, Evander emitted a low growl.

He spun, pinning me against the bathroom wall. His

tongue danced with mine and I moaned. My lips cascaded down the side of his face to the base of his collar bone, leaving kisses in their wake.

His hand snaked up my shirt, grabbing a handful of my breast and kneading the nipple with his fingers. My hands tugged at his shirt, silently begging for him to remove it.

Evander's body shook. Wolf hairs emerged from his skin just to get sucked back under. His lips descended on mine, taking charge and becoming possessive. I craved it.

A morbid thought popped into my head as Evander took charge. If I died soon, probably tomorrow, I wanted this to be my final kiss. I'd remember this kiss if I lived another fifty years, let alone a day or two. The perfect final kiss. I shoved the thought aside and continued to grope at his shirt, hoping for a bit more than a kiss. As my hand grazed his raised nipple, he broke away abruptly. I gasped, and tried not to look disappointed. Especially when he set me down with dark wanton green eyes and a deep frown, leaving the bathroom as if it were on fire.

I touched my lips, tears brimming in my eyes. That kiss was magical and I tried not to read into it. If I let it, the kiss would fuel my dreams of being wanted, desired, a home, a place to belong. Whatever synonyms popped into my head, it all included one thing: a person who loved me for me, who wanted to take care of me and would allow me to take care of them. That kiss was powerful, and I had to shove all the desire into a small compartment in my brain. I sniffed, tucking it all inside, tight and secure.

I'm his task. His mission. Even though these feelings for him keep growing for him, I have to stop it. I have to stop the banter, the connection, and the desire to be near him. I closed my eyes, my head tilted back toward the ceiling. *Suck it alllllll back in Zuri. Evander will never want you. At least not for more than a tumble; you're worth much more than that.* Checking myself in the mirror, I strode out of the bathroom like nothing was wrong.

CHAPTER TWENTY-EIGHT

EVANDER

K issing her was like alcohol or something more addictive. I could have gotten drunk off her easily and not cared. But I did care. I cared a lot. Her being a human was a giant drawback for me, mainly because of who she was related to and my thirst for vengeance against her family. I growled, my mind battling with my gut over how she was nothing like them, she was better, better than most female wolves I knew.

Fuck, I thought, my gut winning over.

I hated breaking away from her sweet soft taste and the tenderness of her body. As I walked away, I cursed my hormones. I cursed the day her family killed mine. I cursed all the things standing in our way. It would have been so easy to have taken her right there. But not right. I couldn't do it with everything hanging between us.

The disappointment and lusty haze in her honey brown eyes haunted my mind every time I blinked. I shook my head to clear her image. All it did was give me a mild case of whiplash and a headache as I slammed my bedroom door behind me. Thankfully, I'd had the foresight to grab my dinner on the way into my room. My mouth salivated at the smell of burger and fries.

Zuri's sniffles sounded even through the door. *Walls are too damn thin.* I sat on my bed, stuffing my face full of fries in between a large gulp of strawberry shake. I didn't even care to taste the food, only that it was in my mouth. Shoving the burger in my face, I cursed myself for only grabbing one of the six I bought.

I want her, I smirked. *But I can't let her into my heart and head. Sure, she is alluring, brave in a crazy dumb way and loyal to me for some damned reason. She's even chosen me over other dangers and fuck me for knowing why... What the hell is going on with me?!*

Polishing off the fries and shake, I opened the door to go get more burgers. Zuri sat with her back to me on the couch, facing the wall with no television on.

I peered over at her. Her feet were crisscrossed under her. She slurped on the strawberry shake and pet Luell at the same time. In the middle of her crisscrossed legs, she held her fries and half-eaten burger.

Running a hand over my face, I scowled, immediately dropping my hand to my side. She was someone I wanted, and someone I couldn't bring myself to have.

"Hey," Zuri said, without turning around and holding a fry out to the side she was about to eat. "You gotta laptop around here? I need to handle some finances and make a will."

I blinked, staring at the back of her blonde head. Her

voice was raspy, like something got caught inside and she tried to hide it. Maybe not raspy, but constricted. She cleared her throat, leaning back against the couch and not turning around to face me.

Dumbstruck by her start of a conversation, I went back to my bedroom for the laptop. Lifting the mattress, I pulled the small compact device out from where I kept it for safe-keeping. I turned it on for her and opened the screen up.

Plopping the laptop beside her, I said, "There's no password."

Using her right hand to scroll and click, she murmured "Thanks," in between a mouthful of burger.

The sharp ring of the phone brought me back to the present from watching Zuri. Her head whipped around at the sound, staring hard at the phone on the wall next to the front door. I could only surmise by the expression on her face, that she thought it was someone to take her to the council.

Walking over, I picked up the wireless phone, spying the caller id as unknown. "Hello?" I answered.

"Evander, Commander Iorgas. I got your message. Bring her to the south entrance."

I frowned. "You think it's necessary?"

South entrance was used for disturbed, high security criminals. Zuri wasn't one of them. She was sweet. I shook my head, putting my free right hand to my forehead. *What the fuck...*

Commander Iorgas cleared his throat. "If she has the key like you called about, then absolutely the Southside."

I was silent for a moment.

"Don't let some human sway your good judgment Evander," Iorgas commanded. "They cannot be trusted. Anyways, I got news for you; in person tomorrow. Eight in the morning. Sharp."

Commander Iorgas clicked off the line. I hung the phone back on the receiver. The furious clicking of keyboard keys reached my ears.

I ran a hand over my face. The only words going through my head continually were - *what in the fuck.* What in the fuck was I doing, why was I becoming so invested in her and if I even wanted to turn her in? This is what I wanted. This is all I had lived for since I'd found my family dead when I was eleven. All I'd lived for was justice for my family, my pack. Commander Iorgas was right - I shouldn't let a human sway my judgment.

I was right about Zuri all along. She was connected to the ones who killed my pack and family. Only I couldn't find a darkness in her that I wanted to see. And try as I might, it just wasn't there. I glowered at myself, figuring that was probably why I was so pissed. All I had against her were two things - her lineage to prove she and her kin destroyed my pack and the key she hid in her spandex, now in her sweatpants pocket along with the note from her grandma.

A scowl deepened across my brow as I stared at the back of her blonde head, not moving from my spot by the front door. The clacking of keys paused and about thirty seconds later, I heard soft sniffles. Zuri hung her head, her left arm reaching out to pet Luell. She pushed the computer aside to reach fully for Luell then stopped herself, probably from not wanting to hurt the healing animal. The saying of - curiosity killed the cat - should have gone for werewolves too.

Blowing my lips, I went to the couch, standing over Zuri. Her head was down, staring at her lap. Her garbage from dinner, crumbled and to her right. The computer, now in her lap, her hands hovered over the send button.

"I finished the will. I'm gonna make a copy of it first then send it in for filing at the human services office," she stated in a dead tone despite the tears running down her cheeks.

In a couple of fluid motions, a copy was saved to the hard drive of my computer and she sent in her will to the human services office in west OKimma.

"I'm going to pay bills, then I'm done," she stated, taking in a shuddering breath, still refusing to look at me.

I didn't say a word. I watched her zoom through different websites, setting everything up on autopay stating doing so just in case I had a hard time getting my grand-parents' house. I walked back to the kitchen, sitting at the dining room table. I didn't want to be creepy and hover over her, instead I watched her every so often bring up the back of her right hand to wipe the tears away. Within fifteen minutes, she was completely done.

Zuri silently closed the laptop and handed it to me over the back of her head. "Thank you."

I got up and took it from her, setting it on the kitchen counter. A tense silence built between us. I felt like sticking my tongue on a dead battery just to get some feeling back instead of this. I went to the fridge and made a grab for another beer. Feeling her eyes on me, I looked over my left shoulder, Zuri stood a few feet away.

"Yeah?" I asked, a touch harder than I meant to.

"May I call my Uncle?"

My eyes narrowed in on her.

Zuri quickly opened her mouth, adding, "I won't mention this and chances are he won't answer."

Silent tears rolled down her cheeks. Her eyes, red-rimmed, stared at me, waiting for any hope of an answer beyond my hard stare. I wasn't sure I was going to give it. Grabbing a beer out of the fridge, I handed it to her and got one for myself. I sighed, feeling myself caving because all her requests so far have been not for herself, they were uncomplicated compared to some others who wanted to skydive or go to the strip club. Zuri's requests were practical and not one was for herself, in a selfish manner that is. I ran a hand over my face and nodded.

"Quit your sniveling, compose yourself, then call," I grumbled.

She nodded, drying her eyes on the end of her borrowed shirt sleeves. "Thank you."

Cracking open the beer, I took a large gulp and grumbled, "Not even the creatures on The Most Wanted list have been as needy as you."

Zuri stared at me blankly. Turning on her heel, she went back to the couch, sitting beside her cat. I emptied the contents of the beer and made a grab for another. Popping it open, I watched the back of her head dip a few times and her hands go to her eyes. At least she was silent now. And I felt a tinge of guilt for being abrupt with her. I just couldn't let her wheedle into me anymore.

I glared at the back of her head. I couldn't help it. In just over twelve hours, I'd have to bring her in and accuse her of crimes she didn't commit. I'd have to lay the blame for her family's sins at her feet. I would have to prove these claims and I'd have to prove she had the key in her possession. That damn key was enough to condemn her. And I was struggling with it because even though who she was linked to was terrible, she was not. Zuri was everything I didn't expect her to be and more.

Downing the entire contents, I hesitated getting another. Instead, I began washing the few dishes I had and set them in the rack by the sink to dry. It annoyed me to no end, I couldn't find other reasons besides my pack, family, and a key to damn her to die.

Even from looking and going over every inch of her files I obtained before going after her, there was nothing to link her to anything noteworthy - no murders, police run-ins, not even a parking ticket.

She's stubborn, I thought with a smirk. *Well, not really stubborn... She's vibrant, alluring, everything a woman should be - brave, but knows limitations. Smart, but not conceited...* I slapped a wet hand across my face. *Fuckin' hell dude. I'm taking her in tonight and being done with it. Commander Iorgas was right, I need her outta my life and head.*

With dishes finished, I dried my hand off and caught Zuri moving out of the corner of my eye. Rising off the couch with a determined hard look, Zuri went to the landline and plastered a fake as shit smile to her face, dialing a number.

She stood by the front door, hand on her hip waiting for her Uncle Syrus to answer still as her wobbly knees would allow. "Hey Uncle Sy, it's me. Just calling to let ya know I will be out of town for a while on a getaway with Luell. Work has been a *huge* butt since the company switched, so they are reconfiguring a new system and I wanted to escape from Lyvia since she showed up. I left my phone at home. Don't want any calls from idiot facilities or *her*. So, I'm calling from the hotel I'm at to let you know I love you very much, I'm safe, and I will see you when I get back. Love you. Take care and tell Aunt Espe hi," she hurriedly clicked off the phone.

I stared at her dumbfounded at how a person who could look so somber, managed to be chipper for all of thirty seconds; and kept it together for the entire call without breaking stride.

"Thank you," she whispered, staring at the phone and taking a shuddering breath. "Uncle Sy is all I have." She put the phone back on the receiver.

I perked a disbelieving brow. "Don't you have friends?"

Zuri shrugged. "I have one - Adiva, but she is busy most of the time. I text her weekly and never hear back... So, I guess it's not friendship at this point."

"Guess not."

She shuffled back over to the couch. A knock came from the front door, heavy handed pounding and loud, rattling the lock and knob. Zuri's eyes went wider than dinner plates. She stood firm in front of her cat, fists balled at her sides and ready.

"Akselsen," the person's deep baritone voice on the other side bellowed.

Commander Iorgas. I let out a breath I was holding. Looking over at Zuri, I held out my hand and whispered it was ok. She untensed slightly, fists still balled at her side.

I cautiously undid the chain on the door and opened it just a bit. Spying the dark brown haired, green eyed tall man, I opened the door further.

"Commander," I greeted.

Iorgas stepped forward. His pristine dark navy suit and cream undershirt snuggly fit his hulking frame. How anyone found a suit or let alone made one for this man, was a master craftsman. Iorgas ducked coming in the doorway. His seven-foot frame took over the entire entryway.

He paused as he entered and scanned the living room and kitchen, his gaze landing on the petite blonde defending her cat. "Zuri Barsotti, you are arrested under the laws of the Vilkas for crimes against Homicide Detective Evander Akselsen and his pack Bardou. The great Council of Alphas will see evidence against you and your kin and hold a trial. Upon which, if found guilty, you die by firing squad. If found not-guilty, you shall go home."

Zuri knelt down, kissing her cat on the head. With tears tracking down her cheeks, she came toward Iorgas, arms out in front of her and hands splayed, showing bare palms.

"I understand," she said.

Iorgas stepped to the side, allowing two other werewolves entry. The slender young men, dressed in black camo and utilities from head to toe, held shackles in their hands. Bringing out iron shackles in case Zuri had magic, they bound her at her hands, feet, waist and neck. One blonde wolf was kind enough to move her hair out of the way before the iron clasp was shut and locked with a padlock. Fury boiled inside of me. She wasn't dangerous by any means. But I was even more pissed at the Commander for usurping my authority to bring her in.

Zuri glanced in my direction, a wan calm smile on her lips, and nodded at me. I frowned, not really under-standing her need to reassure me. Since getting to know her, it was who she was and it pained me a little more to see her chained.

"Anything you say will be held against you," Iorgas's voice boomed over the clasping of the shackles.

Zuri nodded.

The werewolves who I didn't recognize patted Zuri down, pulling the key out of her pocket. The same blonde wolf handed me the key. I tucked it into my ratted jean pocket.

The large commander turned toward me. A smug smile creased his lips. Zuri was led away by the two other were-wolves out of my apartment. Zuri's loyal cat mewled angrily, having trouble raising her weak head although she seemed to understand what was going on.

"Excellent work, Akselsen," Iorgas praised, shaking my hand. "The Council has decided to make you one of their top investigators with all the perks."

I put on a pleased expression even though I was still

pissed the commander was even here. "Thank you, Commander," I said evenly.

"Iorgas now," the giant of a man stated. "You're now a commander yourself. Congratulations."

I pointed toward the door, making my stance more casual by putting my left foot slightly ahead of my right and leaning back. "When is her trial?"

"Tonight in a few hours. The Council couldn't wait to see this one. Even Royan Pright will be in attendance."

I couldn't stop my brows from going into my head. The leader of the Vilkas - Royan Pright - would watch her stand trial. I blinked, not able to wrap my head around it.

The Council must already deem her dead to bring in Royan... The Council of Alphas of numerous large packs hardly ever brought in the middle-aged leader for anything outside of a for sure judgement and death penalty.

Ten members sat on the Council of Alphas. Six votes were needed for a final decision, unless Royan decided to overrule them all. The Commander clasped me on the shoulder, almost knocking me off my feet.

"Sorry for intruding, the council overruled and wanted her now. The council also wants a detailed report in front of them in a few hours. See you soon, Akselsen," Iorgas said, slamming the door shut behind him.

I ignored the slamming of the door, taking a deep breath. "It's all over."

Well part one was anyways. Part two would be challenging the Queen of Kadia. But this was the step in the right direction I needed. My pack and family would be avenged; my vendetta almost completed. I grabbed the laptop, opened it and turned it on.

Heading back toward the couch, Luell mewled angrily. At the end of the poor angry mewl, it held a twinge of pain. Sitting down, I opened up my work portfolio to begin my documentation. Luell hissed at me.

"Laws are laws, cat," I retorted, rubbing a spot on my chest. "No one is above them."

CHAPTER TWENTY-NINE

ZURI

I kept silent during the ride. Two towering males sat on either side of me. Both were dressed in all black camo with military utilities, combat vest, helmet and a belt of tactical tools and various items I didn't know, complete with shin-high black combat boots and a machine gun across their hands with the barrel pointed at the floorboards. I swallowed. I was absolutely fucked.

The blond one seemed to show me the most compassion. He helped me into the car by putting a hand on the top of my head so I wouldn't hit it on the car door. He also helped move my hair before clamping the neck shackle on. He never met my gaze so I couldn't see his eyes beside his stone locked, expressionless face.

The other towering, hulking male with dark brown hair and green eyes, faced forward, gripping the chain ends of my shackles tightly like he was afraid I'd suddenly turn supernatural and try to escape somehow. Despite the circumstances, I stifled a snort. There was no possible way I could get away.

The man in the front passenger seat was Commander Iorgas according to my guards and Evander's surprised greeting when the man showed up at his door. The overly tall wolf was intimidating in his human form and my imagination shuddered when I pictured a giant wolf. The petite male driver gripped the steering wheel at ten and two, maneuvering the barred, tinted windowed SUV toward the department of paranormal justice's headquarters.

Sitting in the middle, I started through the barred space and out the windshield, swallowing every few seconds to give my throat and mouth some moisture. It was pointless.

Industrial buildings passed by in a gray blur. Everything was too fast to focus. I leaned back on the seat and closed my eyes. Everything I wanted to have taken care of was done. Bills, house, Luell and Uncle Syrus, all of it was completed. Evander was kind enough to let me handle my affairs and feel that I had some semblance of control of *something*, even if just for a moment. Not many would have been so benevolent.

I opened my eyes when we slowed down and stopped. My body was pitched slightly forward and the same blond male stuck out his arm to catch me. I wanted to say thanks, but since Commander Iorgas said anything I said would be used against me, I kept my mouth shut.

The driver leaned out the window pushing a few buttons on a black panel.

"Statement?" the female person behind the speaker stated.

I jumped out of my skin. The brown-haired wolf smirked and snorted. The blond patted my shoulder and I smiled a thanks.

"Seeking security clearance to enter Southside," Commander Iorgas's voice thundered.

A twenty-foot gate shrouded in barbed and razor wire slid open on screeching wheels. Five men armed with machine guns came jogging out. My mouth dropped open. I began shaking and I couldn't control it.

Everything hit me again. The enormity and reality of the situation overwhelmed me and tears tracked down my face on their own accord. Their warm saltiness entered my gaping mouth. I couldn't care. Here is where I died.

Before I could remember to blink, I was forced out of the SUV by the chain around my neck. *How ironic. Led around like a dog on a chain by wolves.*

"Zuri Barsotti," Iorgas barked at another person holding a clipboard. "Trial is at 2130. Cell 1112."

The man wrote it down on the clipboard. His slicked back ebony hair glinted under the waning sun. Five other men levelled their machine guns at my head.

Clipboard man moved toward Iorgas, writing down something on his sheet. "Commander, charges?"

"Complete eradication of Vilkas sub-pack Bardou. Complete eradication of Vilkas sub-packs - Mingan and Fenris."

A few growls emanated around me. I opened my mouth to say something then tightly shut it. It didn't matter that I'd been a toddler when it had happened. It didn't matter that I'd seen my mother all of maybe ten times in my life.

All that mattered was werewolf law said I was guilty by association.

"Vendetta," Iorgas spoke. "Bardou and the others will be avenged," he finished sneering at me.

I nodded. My heart thundered in my chest and ears. I wanted to openly sob, have wrenching sobs overtake me, but everything felt so surreal, like I was above myself, watching me be dragged away inside the thick security doors toward my cell.

The black reinforced steel beeped red and green. Decompressed air shot out through the hinges making me jump. The blond wolf held my upper arm with one hand and the chain with the other.

My eyes, wide like saucers, finally met his pale blue.

"We are going to head through two more doors like this one," he said.

I bit my bottom lip and barely gave a nod, following mindlessly. Security lined the hallways every twenty feet or so; all dressed in the same all black camo and utilities. Their hard faces sneered at me as I passed by.

I couldn't think of anything other than how far away my final moment would be and whether it would hurt to die. Firing squad seemed a tad much. Twelve people lined up only to fire one shot each, at the same time. *I hope one hits true. And quickly does the job. It would suck to have twelve worthless shots.* I took a deep breath, settling my nerves a little and concentrated on one foot in front of the other. Whatever was to come, I was settled. All my affairs had been completed.

The last door whooshed open revealing a large open

room. Cells lined the left side of the hallway and the dark gray concrete wall to my right. Each door was the same security metal as the doors we'd just walked through. Foot thick plexiglass allowed the inmates to see into the room and the guards to see into the cells. Above the glass were little holes that reminded me of kennel holes. I gulped again, trying to calm my heart and wet my throat.

It was ghastly how many people, paranormal or otherwise, were held inside the cells. A giant blue ogre occupied one of the larger cells. Tusks came out of his bottom jaw. Large ears with hairy tips protruded directly sideways out of his head. Its feet fascinated me and all I could do was stare at pancake-like pads with four finger type protrusions.

One cell held a witch. I pursed my lips. Eggplant eyeshadow and lipstick adorned her face with contoured make-up to match her beautiful caramel skin, complimenting her high cheekbones. I recognized her from the Black Ash Coven and my eyes widened, wondering what happened to her.

She stared at me a moment, head tilted to the side like she recognized me as well and then burst out laughing. "Vilkas think human powerful. Feenat finds this 'larious. Humans like snails - puny little - no power."

I blew my lips. "I'm not a snail."

The dark-haired man on my left chuckled deep in his throat. "Snail," he chortled, his voice sounding gravelly. "Fitting for a human."

The entourage stopped in front of a smaller cell with just a sliver of the giant foot thick plexi-glass. The black door opened with beeps and a whoosh of air. I was shoved forward from behind. Walking as fast as my shackled feet would allow, I shuffled into the middle of the cell room. The blond-haired wolf followed me inside the cell with keys jingling in his right hand.

"Stand still for me," he instructed. "So, they won't shoot you."

I nodded, feeling icy prickles rush all over my skin. The wolf started with my feet, then went to my neck. I closed my eyes tight. *Please let this be all a dream.* Upon opening, it wasn't so.

He unshackled my waist, hands and neck. "Stay there. Do not move," he commanded.

"I understand," I whispered.

My voice didn't even sound like me. At nine-thirty tonight, in four hours, I would be in front of a giant Council of Alphas. And shortly after that, I would be dead.

CHAPTER THIRTY

EVANDER

I stared at the computer screen. I wracked my brain for *anything*. I knew the commander expected specific details. And soon. But all I could think of was her sarcastic wit, her loyalty, her love for her cat, her sweetness, her fierce courage, her intelligence and the fact she saved my hide when she could have run and saved herself. All my mind could seem to want to do was exonerate her. She never did anything to me or my pack. Her family did that.

Scowling at the computer screen, I willed myself to complete my duty to my pack. I had to complete this report. My fingers hovered above the computer keys and I shook my head. I sighed, laying my head against the back of the couch. I couldn't type one damn thing about her. I just couldn't bring myself to do it.

I snarled, slamming my fist against the couch. The urge to slam the computer closed boiled within me. *Fucking shit, I like her.* I growled aloud in frustration. *I like her.*

Feeling a surge of emotions from guilt, pity, to anger,

annoyance - basically everything all at once and nothing at all - going through me like a charging bull, I went through the report. I left out her grandmother's note linking her further to the crime by association, even though I sent it to Iorgas before I left to get Zuri, it may not come into question since Zuri was not his direct case. I even left out the fact she had the key. If I were to be asked, I would tell the truth about the key and the trip to get her; until then, this report, with the barest of details, would suffice.

I submitted the report via email to the council's email and printed out a paper report to bring in later in case it got 'lost'. The Council of Alphas would make their decision, then Royan would put his seal on the paperwork to make the decision absolute.

Hopefully the Council will allow me to challenge Queen Ariella since she has backing from other paranormal, I need their blessing to pose the challenge.

The printer's annoying beeps and sliding of paper snapped me from my thoughts. Forty-two pieces of paper spit out and sat on the table in front of the machine, some of the sheets kiddy-wampus. I sighed, getting off the couch, leaving the laptop where it was. I pet the cat on the head as I passed by to go toward the bathroom. The feisty thing hissed at me.

The wall clock chimed like a country dinner bell eight times.

"I have an hour to get cleaned up and down to Southside," I said out loud.

The cat growled low in its throat ending in a whine of pain.

"Shit," I groused, remembering the cat needed meds.

I needed to do something with the damn cat. Not knowing how long I would be gone, Luell needed someone to take care of her and give her care and medicine. Storming out the apartment door, I turned left down the hallway. I stopped at a door with a crocheted cat on the door knocker. Around the outside of her door was a braided cat doormat with a few statues of kittens with fae wings.

Without even knocking the door burst open, revealing a small woman; barely four feet tall in a dark plum velour tracksuit. Her bright robin's egg blue glasses with a diamond chain adorned her pug-like face. A shampooed set hair-do held her black hair flecked with silver in a hair-sprayed bulbous curly mass.

Plastering a smile on my face, I said, "Hello Ms. Gurtzski."

She leaned back on her robin's egg blue tennis shoes, craning her neck to look at me and smiled broadly. She clicked her teeth back up into her gums. "Why Evander, what a treat it is for me! Please come inside."

Three cats swirled between her legs. I looked over her tiny shoulders and spotted two more on the couch. I discreetly sniffed and was surprised not to be overpowered by the odor of cats. Her apartment was no bigger than mine. Probably smaller based on her location in the building, and this many cats should have overpowered my nose. I figured she hired a witch to hide the smell or maybe she was on top of the cat boxes. I shrugged internally and directed my attention back to her.

"Sorry Ms. Gurtzski, I don't have much time before I head into work. I inherited a poor kitty on my last job and I need someone to look after it."

The old woman put a hand to her mouth. "I would love to take care of the cat for as long as you need, my sweet boy. Does it have a name?"

"The owner called it Luell," I said, feeling my chest constrict. "With my job, I won't be home for a bit to take care of it and the poor cat's in need of some extra TLC. Someone tried to kill it and it's pretty weak."

The spry old woman vigorously nodded, scrunching her face to swallow up her eyes. "Leave it to me." She went back into her apartment, leaving the door open and talking to her cats about the next friend coming to stay.

Seizing my moment, I scurried back to the apartment. Grabbing some cash from a kitchen drawer, and the cat's medicines, I hurriedly went to the couch. I scooped up the bitter Luell in my arms; the cat attempted to stir. Holding Luell close to my chest so she didn't move too much, I brought her to Ms. Gurtzski.

I waited patiently by the front door for her to allow me entry in case of witch's spells. The old woman glanced over and saw me standing in the doorway and raised her hands up in the air like she forgot what she was doing.

"Come in Evander," she called from the kitchen where she had several bowls out and a large bag of cat food on the counter.

I walked in, setting Luell down on her plastic covered purple velvet couch. Ms. Gurtzski came over, making pitying babbles sounding like a dying piglet. I flinched at the noise.

Luell stared at me for a moment, ears back and growled. I felt terrible for a moment. The cat couldn't be left alone and I had no means to take care of it.

"Here, Ms. Gurtzski," I said, handing over a few hundred-dollar bills. "This next task I have been assigned; I don't know how long I will be gone. I hope this helps with food and litter."

The old woman's eyes widened to an alarming size. I smiled wanly at her. Luell opened her eyes slightly, offering a low growl in my direction.

Ms. Gurtzski reached out and patted the back of my hand, "Thank you, my dear boy," she praised, smiling. "How thoughtful."

Putting my hand over the top of hers, I replied, "Thank you. I appreciate it."

Walking out of her apartment, I quietly shut the door and went back to mine. Report was sent, the cat was taken care of, now all I needed to do was shower and be there in time for *her* final judgment.

Glancing at the wall clock, I had just under forty minutes. My skin prickled as I went into the bathroom, wishing time would speed up.

CHAPTER THIRTY-ONE

ZURI

I sat on the small cot in the corner and shook uncontrollably, but not from the cold. No blanket would help me. Two giant fluorescent heated lights were above me, shining bright and bringing heat down upon my head. How long I stayed fixed in my position, I didn't know. Hard, poky pieces of the woolen indigo blanket on the metal framed cot poked through the thin sweatpants and made my skin itch.

Sitting on the edge, I shivered and waited. *I should've used Evander's deodorant*, I thought, checking the armpits on his shirt and finding them soaking. I wiped my hands on the pants and then on the itchy woolen blanket to no avail. My hands were still wet when I lifted them to my chest and crossed them again.

Waiting is going to kill me before the firing squad does.

I closed my eyes, contemplating committing suicide. By the laws of the wolfpack, I was as good as dead anyway. The Council of Alphas would hear my plea and whether I claimed I was guilty or not, I would still die. They'd already made up their minds. The trial was just formality. And now, discovering I was the Queen of Kadia's daughter, the same woman who'd destroyed the pack Bardou, Mingan, and Fenris, my fate was sealed.

Part of me was glad I'd die by firing squad. The whole way back to OKimma, I'd imagined being dismembered by werewolves, much like I imagined reading the history books in high school about werewolf wars and how vicious they were. It was a slow, cruel way to die since I'd be alive to feel all the pain. Firing squad should be much quicker, especially if someone's head shot didn't miss.

Glancing up at the lights on the ceiling, I tried to find a way to wrap a blanket around a holding of some kind in the ceiling to just end my life now. The fluorescent lights were flush with the concrete ceiling.

Well, that ruins things.

The jitters inside my body urged me to use the bathroom. Scanning the small cell, there was a concrete pedestal sink fixture low to the ground and a button on the wall just behind it. Upon closer inspection, the structure was indeed a toilet, not wide enough for my head to fit in either.

My mind wandered back to the blanket I was sitting on, wondering if I could fashion a noose of it. Never before in my life had I contemplated suicide. But then again, I had never been faced with this kind of mortality. I had so much life left to live. Thinking of my death made me sad. I still wanted to get married, walking down the aisle and seeing my groom's face light up. Watching my baby's first breath, hearing the sweet sound of 'Mama,' watching sports events and being the proud mommy of the little tyke who scored the winning goal. All the scraped knees, school dances, yelling matches, and falling more deeply in love with my husband. All those holiday dinners and grandchildren. My heart ached as I thought about what I was going to miss. The only advantage to dying right now was I didn't have to find a husband who would love me like that. Yet most of me still wanted to try.

My attraction had always been to werewolves. Humans were two faced, where *weres*, if they didn't like someone, said it truthfully. I adored *weres* vitality for life, their protection, their security. Not having it in my life, it was like quenching to my insatiable thirst; evening knowing it wouldn't ever last since *weres* married *weres* not humans.

I sighed. I had commitment issues. I knew this. I also saw how strong I was. Getting passed around my entire childhood had molded me into an insecure, but strong woman. I didn't need anyone. I was independent. But I was lonely. I didn't have the desire to seek pleasure in drugs and men. I could have easily succumbed to addictive substances and behavior, but whether by divine intervention or sheer stubbornness, I had come out a strong, functioning adult whose issues were something I was hoping I had time to overcome.

Evander's description of me still stung - *you're easy and willing to take love however it comes*. It was true. One hundred fifty percent, nail on the head, true. I was so desperate to have someone love me for a moment; I would bend over backward - buy gifts, constantly apologize, do whatever was asked to get a 'thanks Zuri' or even a 'how thoughtful' comment; something showing what I tried to do wasn't in vain. Now though, it all didn't matter. No one would love me and I would get love from no one. Truly, a fitting end.

I touched my lips, remembering the tingling sensation of Evander's kiss. Warmth and security had spread through me like a hot cup of cocoa when remembering that kiss. The heat, passion and hunger I felt was something I would not forget, even if I'd lived to be 100 years old.

Tears welled in the corner of my eye and I fought them back. I'd cried enough already and no tears would save me from the death about to come. Shaking my shoulders and rolling them back, I stared at the thick black metal door, waiting for it to open, figuring they'd come for me soon.

A guard stood outside the door where I could see him through the tiny sliver of thick glass. He peeked over his shoulder at me, fangs dropping down over his bottom lip as his head morphed into a grayish red wolf. I blinked, eventually looking away.

I stared at the gray concrete floor, my mind blissfully blank. The door to my cell buzzed, making me jump just as I had lost track of time. Whizzing and jolting of locks releasing sent shivers up my spine. When this moment came, I assumed my heartbeat would quicken, but it remained steadfast. My palms went cold and dry.

Evander came in. His dark brown hair was nicely styled, slicked back on his head. Dark brown shadowing of a beard freshly shaved lined his jaw. A black suit, complete with a slate gray button down underneath, a gray kerchief in the pocket, and silver cufflinks adorned his body and accentuated his masculine figure. Evander held an orange file in his left hand.

His piercing green eyes stared hard into mine with a firmness I hadn't seen since he first came for me.

"It's time, Zuri Barsotti, to face the Council of Alphas," he said, eyes narrowed and his voice cold.

I rose from my position, walking mechanically over to the door. I stopped before him, arms out like I had seen in tv shows as I waited for someone to cuff me.

Evander perked a brow. "What are you doing?"

"Aren't I being cuffed?"

"No. You're deep inside werewolf territory. You're not escaping alive." He stated coldly and walked out the cell door.

Biting my upper lip, I followed Evander out of my cell. Cell holding containers were to my left. More thick concrete lined the right side of the hall with cameras and metal doors every ten feet. I dared not wonder what was behind the metal doors. This place had a feeling like it was more than a prison; more like an execution garrison I had read about before - holding cells of various peoples having done deeds so terrible they waited to be killed.

Twelve guards, six men on either side of me, walked with hands on machine guns. I stared ahead, willing my mind to empty everything. I didn't want to look around and see the faces of all the other creatures here because of some vendetta or real crime. And I certainly didn't want to dwell on what waited for me at the end of this walk.

Evander rounded a corner to the right. The hallway

opened up revealing oaken double doors at the end. I let go of my upper lip, taking a deep breath and shaking my shoulders.

I strode past Evander, grabbing the door and pushing. It didn't budge.

"It says 'Pull'," Evander smirked.

Glaring at him, I pulled it open and strode in toward the middle of the room.

CHAPTER THIRTY-TWO

ZURI

The wide room was dark. A wooden table and chair sat in the middle. I walked toward it, taking a seat and folding my hands on the table. Guards standing three feet apart lined the perimeter, hands ready on their machine guns.

A large seal was in the middle of the floor. Half of the circular seal was a moon and a man standing under a tree in a stoic, thinking position. On the other half was a werewolf, jaws open revealing large sharp teeth and paws up with long claws.

I put my hands palm down on the smooth wooden surface of the table, keeping them visible. I stared at the table for a moment, staring at the lacquered wooden surface. Looking up, a semicircle of ten alphas sat behind a solid polished oak elevated five-foot platform desk thirty feet from where I sat. I felt miniscule in comparison to being down here on the ground while they literally looked down at me. Vaulted ceilings made the room appear a touch larger than it truly was.

From left to right, every other Alpha was a woman, all eyes on me, I'm sure watching to see what kind of terror I would bring. I glanced at the door where Evander took a seat on the side of the elevated Alpha platform, hands clasped together and the orange file in front of him. To the far right of the semicircle a slightly higher platform, seating one person, remained empty.

One of the guards opened a door to my right. A man stood in the doorway; hands clasped in front of him. A dark gray suit and teal button-down shirt hugged his husky frame. Salt flecked his greasy slicked coal black hair. Light brown eyes, almost golden glared hard into my own. A long scar trailed horizontally from cheekbone to the bridge of his nose on the left side of his face.

A male alpha stood. His long silver hair combed over and tied at the nape of his neck. His wide shoulders matched his beef size head. "Stand for the leader of the Vilkas - Royan Pright!" the male alpha boomed.

I stood, locking my gaze with one of the other alphas. Each council member wore the same uniform - some kind of dark indigo pants or dress suit with a dark maroon cape on their shoulders. Women had their hair tightly coiffed at the nape of their neck. Men styled theirs in a parted comb over or slicked completely back.

"You may be seated," the same alpha announced as Royan took his seat at the highest dais.

I sat in my wooden slat-backed chair; thankful it was

there. My legs shook uncontrollably, threatening to give out. All eyes stared at me, judging me for a crime, I was too young to even commit.

The same alpha who spoke banged a gavel. He cleared his throat and boomed, "Zuri Ariella Barsotti-Luciani you are hereby charged with genocide, murder, and the actions to eradicate werewolf pack Bardou, Mingan and Fenris. How do you plead?"

I perked a brow at the added last name. I never heard of it before, but it truly didn't matter now. "It really doesn't matter how I plead. I'm still dead," I replied evenly, shrugging.

The same man narrowed his eyes at me and leaned forward. "For formality's sake then, how do you plead?"

"Not guilty."

A woman rose from her seat. Her ebony hair glistened under the low yellow lighting, shrouding her in elegant mystery. "Zuri," she began, flipping through papers, "Twenty-one years ago, when this attack happened, how old were you?"

I perked a brow, "Three."

"Do you remember your parents; who they were or where they went?"

I could have snorted. "No. I do not. If you have any transcripts about my life, you would know I was in foster care at the time. I don't know anything about my father. Who or what he is remains a mystery. And while I'd heard whispers of the woman my mother was, she'd appeared in my life maybe ten times and for about fifteen minutes. I barely knew her name until about a week ago. So no, I don't know them."

"Watch your tone, Barsotti," Royan snapped from his dais. "We could let you go or kill you now."

"You're going to kill me regardless," I quipped back. "This is all for formality's sake so there is a paper trail to cover your ass with the human legal system."

The woman's jaw tightened. "Watch yourself, Barsotti!"

I glowered at her and shook my head. "Hate the truth?"

Another alpha rose, "Your father is Uther Luciani of the Moon Walkers," the man seethed vehemently like each word was hard for him to spit out of his flaming red face. "It is known that Uther desires to kill all Vilkas packs."

"It's news to me!" I shot back trying to rein in my shock and anger.

It really was. I had taken a blood test to discover who I was, but now, with all this going on, it's not like I had a computer handy to check to see the results myself. With these wolves though, at least I had answers as to why certain people were after me. It made sense. It also hurt like hell.

I scowled wondering how this was going to go now. *If Uther is a Moon Walker, did it mean that I carried were-blood?* I scoffed. *The bugger was probably a created wolf which makes sense as to why he wants to eradicate born wolves, but makes no sense as to killing me.* My leg bounced anxiously. I had nervous energy that I desperately wanted to release, but I forced myself still. My mind reeled at the news.

"She didn't know. You can smell the truth from her," the

woman stated, taking a seat and strumming her fingers on the table top and hard glare fixed on her contoured made-up face. "Uther is a created wolf, which explains why you are not one," she explained. "Still judgment will be made upon you for the destruction of pack Bardou and the others in the absence of either Uther or Lyvia."

"Oh perfect," I snapped back. "Blame them then, a three-year-old human toddler for what you cannot fight for yourself. Can't take down a created wolf? Can't take down a lunatic queen? But sure, let's all take down the human daughter, the *innocent*, human daughter, because she's an easy target. Here, lemme get you all a participation trophy for bravery."

"Young lady," another alpha, one foot in the grave already, stood hunched over the desk top. A large hunched curve rounded his back. The only thing not looking dead and dying were his hard-blue eyes. "Young lady, you stand before a council of alphas and dare to back talk so rudely, carelessly? We hold your existence in our hands!"

"Yes, I do," I replied, scowling, and my jaw tightening. "I don't sugarcoat my words. I'm not a bakery." The man went to respond, but I held up a hand. "I understand a vendetta, but even those who have one only attack the person who did wrong, not a child with no involvement at the time of the crime. And we all know here that despite the title 'trial' this is simply covering your asses. If you didn't have to have a paper trail, I'd be dead already. So why should I hold my tongue? This is wrong!"

The man's eyes narrowed on mine. "Even so, this council will be the one to judge. You have no right. The mere fact Akselsen brought you here alive is a kindness. The crime you're here for is so heinous, no one would think twice if he'd lost control and killed you himself."

I rose, putting my hands on my hips. Some of the guards took a step forward, guns raised and at the ready.

"Seriously?" I jabbed. "Like I can do anything, brainless dogs!"

Royan Pright stood, pointing a finger at me, "Watch yourself *human*, I've had about enough of you."

The woman from before, still standing, glared at me then turned to her right. She looked down at Evander, holding out her hand and bidding him to rise.

"Akselsen," she said firmly, "what report have you brought us regarding this *human?*" she snarled.

Evander stood, straightening his suit jacket and handed over the orange folder. "This, my alphas," he replied with a slight bow of his head. "Evidence proving Zuri Barsotti-Luciani inherited the key to open the portal to Diomedes. The same key her parents were after when they annihilated my pack and the others."

My eyes narrowed on him, wondering why he left out the note from my grandma. At the same time, it hardly mattered. I was super dead now. The entire room went eerily silent. No one breathed.

Royan stood, eyes wide. "Do you have this item?"

Evander pulled the silver key from his pocket and walked it over to the Vilkas leader. Royan snatched it from Evander, holding it in shaking hands. A gleam of shock and power flashed across his face and eyes. My body went cold.

He is going to open the portal...

Royan licked his lips, turning the key over in his hand's multiple times. He glanced over at me, a deep scowl on his face and snarl on his lips. "How did you get this?!"

I shrugged, feigning indifference. "My aunt gave me a box that was my Gramma Kaethe's. The key was in it. I have no idea how she got it."

Royan held up the key in front of his nose, mumbling, "A tree of life on one side of the bow and an hourglass and goat on the other. Around the shaft and collar - *For those that shall seek, will find and those that shall protect, will endure.* This is the key to Diomedes. This is the key to end the Moon Walkers!" he turned to me pointedly, "And your father!"

Royan leapt off the raised platform to the ground. He briskly went to the middle of the council room floor to where the seal was stamped into the concrete ground.

I glanced around, staring at the men in uniform. Their eyes hardened along with their grip on their guns. The council members stood gaping at their leader, waiting to see what would shoot out of the seal on the floor, no one moving to stop him.

With shaking hands, Royan stuck the small silver key in the middle of the seal in a tiny key hold near the tree. The silver key lit up brightly, a blazing silver forcefield of light surrounding the seal. Royan was forced back. The key turned itself in, what I now realized was a lock on the floor. The light disappeared, seeming to delve down deeper into the ground, taking the forcefield with it, leaving a faint glow around the seal.

I stood up, inching slowly closer to the only person I thought, hoped, would protect me. Before I could reach him, Evander came striding up to me, setting a hard hand on my shoulder; his fingers digging into my collarbone, holding me still.

The Council of Alphas came down off their raised platform, staring with a mix of fear and awe at the seal on the floor. My entire body shook; eyes riveted to what might emerge from the seal.

"We have to get out of here," I whispered over my shoulder to Evander.

His hand enclosed tighter on my shoulder making my legs buckle and I sat hard on the chair I hadn't quite gotten far enough away from. "You're not going anywhere," he growled.

"We have to leave, you overgrown idiot!" I urged. "We don't know what will come out of there."

"I have a duty to my pack to see this through."

I stood up, reaching around, and smacked him upside the head. "Have your vengeance on *that*, dumbass. This is more serious."

Evander's green eyes flashed to mine, his lips pulled down and tight in a weird upset way.

I smirked. "There, now I actually *did* something. I smacked you."

"*Human*," he seethed.

"Puppers," I quipped rather merrily, hiding my fear. "We have to get out of here."

Silver hair on a humanesque head began to emerge

from the seal on the floor. Vivid silver translucent eyes scanned the room. The God's cream-colored face swiveled all the way around his body like a demented owl.

"Running away, ticket for two?" I whispered to Evander.

"Like hell," he seethed back, gripping my shoulder so intensely, I was forced back into my chair again.

"Hell is right there," I whisper-hissed back, "And I want to leave!"

The giant of a god towered in the room above everyone else. A pure white suit adorned his body with a blood red tie and pocket kerchief. Blood red cufflinks held the cuffs of his suit together. If he was a normal person on the street, one might find him attractive. Seeing him finish emerging from the ground with two small thorny creatures at his feet, made me want to sprint in the other direction.

"Zuri," the God's voice boomed sweetly. "How funny my brother Elohi put trust in such a weak being to guard my enclosure."

I crossed my legs to keep from tinkling. Eyes wide, I stared at him. I would have shrunk back against Evander if I wasn't being forced to my seat by his hard grip. Even now, Evander ceased to let me go.

Royan took hesitant steps toward the god. "My liege," the alpha bowed. "I'm honored to be graced by your presence. I need your-"

Diomedes flicked a hand. The Vilkas leader went flying back toward the wall and smashed into the guards in front of one of the only exits; the guards rushed to help their leader back to his feet.

My body shook. I licked my lips nervously, unable to tear my eyes away from Diomedes.

"How about now?" I asked Evander.

Evander yanked me to my feet. "Now, seems good."

CHAPTER THIRTY-THREE

EVANDER

I yanked Zuri to her feet. She pressed her quivering body into my own for a moment; her gaze locked on Diomedes. The god of the underworld laughed, turning on his heel to face the council of alphas. With one hand, he elevated them all off the ground. Clenching his fists, the alphas sucked in a breath of air, kicking their feet and grabbing at their throats like it mattered. Their eyes rolled in the back of their heads while maniacal laughter emitted from the god. The bodies of the alphas ceased moving, turning limp. The guards lining the walls let loose a volley of bullets, none piercing Diomedes as the metal rounds went through him like a knife through butter, having no effect on the god.

Dashing forward, Zuri made for the key locked in a hovered suspension above the portal in the floor. I sprinted behind her, catching her arm and yanking her back from the open portal. Zuri wriggled out of my grasp, her fingers stretching to grab the silver key hovering above the portal.

Silver-blue magic whirled circularly. Her slender fingers stretched through the whirling magic wrapped around the cold metal of the silver key. The alphas once suspended fell dead to the floor. Diomedes turned his attention to the guards continuing to barrage him with a flurry of bullets.

"Try again!" The god's voice boomed.

Zuri tripped on her way back to me, scrambling to her feet, key in her right hand.

"Not so fast, Zuri," Diomedes purred, extending a hand.

I reached her, holding her hand. Zuri yelped and was pulled out of my grasp. I reached around and latched on to her foot. Her brown eyes locked with mine, wide and full of terror.

"Evander!" her voice shrieked then garbled.

Zuri's eyes rolled in the back of her head. Her left hand went to her throat while her right hand was being forced to open. Zuri wouldn't let the key drop.

Diomedes came closer, his face furrowed. "Give me the key!" he bellowed.

Zuri shook her head. Climbing her leg with my hands, I attempted to pull her toward me. Diomedes had powerful control of her body and Zuri wouldn't budge.

"Girl!" Diomedes fumed.

I scowled, not understanding why this almighty powerful deity couldn't shake a mere human. Zuri wasn't special. She wasn't immortal or had magic, yet somehow by either unbridled tenacity or being a complete dumbass, she was besting the god of Darkness.

"E-van-der," Zuri desperately choked out, sucking in a breath.

Her right hand shook as her fingers were being pried open. Zuri's mouth opened to shriek; no sound emitted. Her pointer and middle fingers snapped the other way; still, she wouldn't release the key holding tightly with her thumb, ring and pinky. Tears snaked down her face. Diomedes's power over her body had folded her right wrist against her forearm.

Daring a glance over at Diomedes, I noticed the god's face mottled with red. His eyes changed from translucent silver to a swirling mixture of silver and red. Royan Pright stood on his feet, bellowing incoherent orders at the men still lining the walls. Slowly, the small squadron of were-wolves steadily came forward, enclosing Diomedes and the open portal.

My heart beat trying to decide exactly what Zuri meant to me. I'd struggled for days vacillating between affection, desire and loathing. Finally, without my conscious thought, my heart committed to caring for her. Affection won out, and in a split second, I let go of her leg and shifted, allowing the hunger of the wolf to win.

The black fur on my body shook with the shift and fury. I stretched, committing to the shift and the desire for blood. I barreled toward Diomedes. The god broke his concentration on Zuri and jerked his head toward me. I was forced back from Diomedes by a forcefield I couldn't see. My body skidded across the concrete floor. Quickly, I righted myself and got to my feet. Shaking my body, I charged again; only to be deflected.

A guard shifted. Her mottling of gray and red fur covered her hulking frame. Boldly she charged, pummeling into Diomedes. The god stood unwavering by the strike, but the forcefield broke when the guard struck. Another guard shifted and charged the god, jaws wide to bite. Diomedes was thrown back a touch by the charge.

Zuri's lips turned blue, her body appeared as if it was compressing in on itself - cheeks shrunken in and her skin stretching tightly over bones. Charging together, the guard and I raced toward Diomedes. My jaws ached to sink into flesh. As we both charged, Zuri crashed to the ground in a gasping heap. Diomedes turned, facing me fully and laughing maniacally. I leapt, latching onto his left hand. Diomedes took his right hand clasping me by the throat and threw me across the room.

"You think to imprison me?" he bellowed sardonically.

Rising to my feet, I growled, stalking Diomedes in a slow, deliberate circle. I got in front of Zuri and lowered my head, guarding her by putting my body over hers.

Diomedes laughed almost uncontrollably and slapped a knee. The other guards in the room shifted. Their wolf forms took up more space and bulk, and with the giant god in the middle, the room shrank considerably. The only one who didn't shift was Royan Pright, standing in the corner and shaking like a little bitch. He opened the door and bolted from the room. Shocked wolf faces stared at the door where their heroic leader fled.

Diomedes levitated off the ground, arms out at his sides. Once about ten feet in the air, he brought his hands together, one over the other like he was holding a football close to his chest. Magic, a silver-turquoise swished in his hands. His face stayed fixed in an overly pleased, sadistic manner. Holding the magic above his head, Diomedes, let out the stream of magic, watching in amusement. The magic launched into the air, blasting through the ceiling, revealing the night sky, only to come plummeting back inside and down into the open portal.

"This room cannot contain my infinite power," Diomedes roared, ending it with a dark laugh. "Now... *watch*," he gleamed.

I perked a brow, wondering at how infinite his power truly happened to be. The god easily killed off the older, weaker Alpha council members, but could not kill a human. Either Zuri was a null and not affected by magic the way other paranormal beings were; or she had some kind of magic she didn't know of counteracting the effects of Diomedes.

Her brown eyes met mine for a moment, lighting up with affection and security. Even after all I put her through, she went to me for comfort. I swallowed. Her loyalty to me was astounding and possibly the most stupid thing she could have done.

"Puppers," she rasped, her lip curling upward.

I bent my head down to her, my wet nose touching her cheek affectionately, "Human."

Gnarled hands began emerging from the open portal. Shifting into my human form, I scooped Zuri in my arms, being mindful of her broken wrist and fingers. The other werewolves around me backed away. The alarm to the building blared raucously, screeching and fizzling out at the end of the warning call. The buzz of cell doors opening blasted through the tunnel and into the room.

Like an ant hill submerged in water, the guards in the council room scattered frantically toward the exits. Giant, horrendous monsters only ever seen in the Espowyes Mountains called Kludde, materialized from the darkness of the portal; large creatures resembling horrible monstrosities of deformed half wolves/half humans with ebony bat wings protruding broken and painful from their backs. Bear like claws, and an eagle beak with teeth added to the perverseness of the demonic creature. Green glistening dragon scales covered the kludde's entire human half while the wolfish resemblance was green-black glistening fur. Around the Kludde's left ankle, a long black chain rattled as it stalked forward. Dark maroon eyes stared into the wolves who remained, making a barreling line for one unfortunate wolf as more Kludde poured into the room from the open portal.

"My pets!" Diomedes purred. "Unleash your hell and devour souls."

The kludde rented a piercing high-pitched howl. I dashed for the door, jostling Zuri in my arms. Her face bunched up tight, holding in the pain I was causing her. A guard held the door open, and we slipped out. I ran to the right while the others went left down the hallway toward the quickest way to freedom. I took a chance on being able to get ammunition and an armored car.

"Van-der," Zuri rasped, her gorgeous honey brown eyes wide as she glanced behind us.

I couldn't glance behind me. "Are you ok to run?"

Zuri nodded.

Sooner than I believed she was ready for, I set her down while sprinting and shoved her forward. Zuri stumbled, catching her footing. Taking her left hand, I pulled her along down the twisting maze of corridors, hoping I would lose some of the demonic kludde behind us.

"Do you have the key?" I asked, glancing at her over my shoulder.

Again, Zuri nodded, her brows furrowed at the pain in her hand. Turning swiftly left, I burst through the door, holding it open long enough for Zuri to enter. I slammed it shut, throwing the manual lock and punching in the override code for the door to lock fully. With a whooshing buzz, the door adjusted and locked. A kludde following us snarled on the other side of the thick glass with iron bars.

Zuri shook. She hardly made it to a chair before collapsing in a heap of tears. Ignoring her for a moment, I went to the gun safe, pulling out whatever I could strap on my back and carry on my person. I grabbed a backpack, stuffing as much ammunition, grenades and whatever else I could manage to force inside.

Zuri wiped her eyes, inhaling a raspy sharp breath and letting it out through her nose. She shook out her left hand, freeing herself of unseen nerves. She held her right hand close to her body, curling it upward toward her chin. Her left hand went to her throat where Diomedes magically suffocated her and she cleared her throat.

"It's gonna be alright," I soothed, shoving a smoke grenade in the side pocket.

She nodded, her face bunching in confusion. "I'm not dead?" Zuri finally rasped. "Alpha justice?"

I shook my head. "No," I replied firmly. "I absolve *you*. Anything I do now will be strictly against your parents."

I stared at her, watching the human come to grips with not being dead. She was right in what she'd said before Royan opened the portal - I couldn't hold a three-year-old responsible for what her parents did. And after reading her transcripts, she was in foster care at two years old, and nowhere near her parents and what they were about to do to me and mine. I just didn't want to accept it until now.

Zuri nodded, hanging her head. Her silky blonde strands of hair falling in front of her face. I slung two long rifles and two machine guns over my shoulder and a back-pack filled with handguns and ammo over my back. I motioned for her to rise, not wanting to remain here longer than necessary.

She walked briskly over to the open pistol drawer, taking out a glock with her left hand. Popping out the mag, her lip ticked upward, clicking it back inside the gun, all one handed and surprisingly adept, especially since she wasn't left-handed.

Zuri cleared her throat, closing her eyes as she did so and brows furrowed. "Can't," she said, motioning to the gun and tapping her side.

Realizing she wanted a holster, I nodded. "It's ok, let's go," I said, holding a hand out for her. "I'll protect you."

Zuri put her elbow in my hand with a wan smile on her lips. Fear danced behind her eyes, as she stared at my face, but not truly meeting my gaze. I realized in this daunting, intense moment, how much I wanted to hold her; to wrap my arms around her and whisper about how everything was going to pan out and be all right. Her quiet confidence, sarcasm, and charm were breaking down my walls faster than I cared to admit aloud. Her inner beauty outshone everything I could ever remember finding attractive in a mate. Zuri was glorious with her honied eyes and sunflower golden hair; the most beautiful being in all of Quivleren. And my walls were crumbling possibly faster than I realized.

Shaking my head, I walked up to a wall and pushed on it. The wall moved, shooting upward into the ceiling and revealing a door that whooshed open to the right side. With Zuri behind me, I took off at a jog down the tunnel, hoping the armored vehicle would be at the end with keys in the cup holder. The door whooshed close behind us, enveloping us in darkness. The tunnel went slightly down-hill and eventually levelled out. I urged Zuri on with whispers, as I navigated easily down the tunnel. A screen in the upper left-hand corner fizzled on, showing a gray murky display of an open parking lot with two armored cars available.

The area was eerily vacant. No wolves patrolled the grounds. Kludde was nowhere to be seen. I couldn't tell through the colorless screen, but the sky appeared to darken.

"Ready," she rasped behind me with a hard nod. "Here," she flinched, opening her right hand unveiling the silver key that somehow remained in her possession and in her very broken hand. My admiration grew again.

I took the key from her and stuck it in my suit pocket on the inside. Her grip tightened on the pistol. Bringing her right arm up and out, forearm level with her eyes, the pistol rested in the crook of her arm. I perked a brow, but said nothing.

The ferocity behind her eyes sent a surge of admiration through me. Zuri was brave, at times, abhorrently reckless, but her heart never strayed from her decision. Another quality in a female I desired to call my own.

Pushing the thought aside, I turned my attention back to the screen, the two vehicles remained parked out in the open. No one was around to impede our departure from the tunnel or our arrival to the cars.

Opening the door, I burst through with Zuri hot on my heels.

CHAPTER
THIRTY-FOUR

ZURI

My body trembled as I ran toward a vacant car. Somehow on the outside the shivers didn't show. My wrist and fingers hurt something fierce. I had never broken a bone before and didn't care to again. Thankfully everything was numb to a point, but any movement sent shocking pain through my arm and body. Every jostling step was excruciating and I longed to be still.

Outside, the sky seemed surreal. Darkness, gray and patchy like a winter storm swirled in the sky. The moon shone bright from the east, but was quickly becoming covered in the darkness Diomedes was bringing. The stars lost their brilliance as Diomedes's powers took over the heavens. A beam of bright silver-turquoise light ruptured from the building we previously occupied, shooting into the sky and back down into the still open portal.

Diomedes rose above the chaos he was bringing, arms out at his sides and head tilted back. In the middle of the swirling vortex, his body turned. Silver translucent eyes scanning the new world around him.

Evander jogged to the passengers side, opening the unlocked car door for me. I got in, slamming the pistol on the dash in front of me and closed the door with my left hand.

Evander sprinted to the other side, opening the rear door and shoving the two rifles and two machine guns, along with the pack of munitions inside. He looked down, rifling through his pack.

Looking to my right, wolves dashed from the side of the building with numerous kludde trailing them. "Come on!" I yelled at Evander as loud as I could.

His head shot up, peering through the glass window. "Shit."

In a fluid motion, he had the back door slammed, the front driver's door open, slammed it shut, while taking the keys from the cup holder. The car turned over, automatic locks barring us safely inside.

"Fucking great!" Evander cursed.

I narrowed my eyes on him.

"Someone didn't put gas in it."

Evander sped off. I let out a breath I was holding, sinking back in the seat. My hand and wrist pulsated, throbbing something fierce. I put my broken wrist over the top of my head, resting on my hair to alleviate the swelling.

"You ok?" Evander asked.

I shrugged. I really had no idea if I was alright or not. My body hurt, everything in me wanted me to close my eyes and sleep for a year and I was shaken that I was still breathing. My mind couldn't wrap itself around the tumultuous emotions thrumming through me.

And how I wasn't dead made no sense. How? Diomedes crushed the throats of the Alpha Council members like they were rotten bananas. Yet I lived? It made no sense.

I stared out the window. Gray clouds continued to move to cover the stars and brightness of the moon, swallowing the heavens in ashen plunder. It made my skin crawl.

Evander drove like a street racer, drifting around corners with a blatant lack of concern for the speed limit or safety. I went to grab the 'oh shit' bar but braced against the dash instead since my right wrist still hurt like crazy.

"You ok?" Evander asked again. "Your lips got all poofy."

I perked a brow, mouthing, "Poofy?"

"Yeah, you pushed your lips out and to the side."

I nodded, giving a thumbs up sideways. I felt jittery, like I had minimal control over my thoughts and reactions. Bringing my right hand down and curling the broken wrist up against my body, I hissed at the pain the movement brought.

Tears stung my eyes, trailing down my cheek, softly at first then like a waterfall. I wiped them away with my left hand while willing my body to cease the waterworks. My eyes rebelled and produced more.

My head swam becoming light and my vision blurred. My body felt heavy like a fifty-pound sack of flour sat in my lap and on my chest. I leaned forward in my seat. Evander reached out, setting a hand on my back for a brief second before needing his hand back. He slowed marginally, turning on a blinker. His concerned face stared into mine for a second then concentrated on the road ahead.

"I'm taking you to a friend of mine. We need to get your hand and throat fixed."

"Tha-nk you," I whispered.

Evander nodded, concentrating on taking corners. His eyes darted every so often to the mirrors, checking for tails. I stared out the side mirror constantly watching for anything suspicious. My skin prickled at the unknown expectations.

The car pulled up to a gas station. Evander hopped out, swiping a card inside the payment deal then slammed the gasoline nozzle into the side. His meticulous green gaze absorbed all around him.

Evander slammed the nozzle back inside the deal and hopped in the car. I looked in the rearview. The silver-turquoise beam of light went higher into the sky, but appeared to dull.

I glanced tentatively at Evander, opening my mouth.

"I don't think we're safe yet," he said. "Once we get to my friend's place, we will be. Then we can come up with a plan."

I nodded, whispering softly, "Sounds good."

"I'm sorry," he blurted. Gripping the steering wheel tight, he sped off down the road. "I didn't get to tell you this earlier, but I'm sorry."

I put my left hand on his forearm, understanding what he was sorry for.

"You were right. I can't hold you responsible for something you did not commit. And I tried to keep all the emotions straight in my head," he shook his head and drifted around a corner to the right.

I perked a brow, not understanding what he was talking about. I stared straight out the window, still listening, but allowing Evander to get his thoughts together without me staring and silently demanding an answer.

"I like you, Zuri," he breathed out, seeming relieved he said it. "I like you and it bothers me that I like you and knowing what your parents did to me and my pack," he growled. "Part of me... part of me wanted to dislike you on principle, but I can't."

I nodded, shrugging my shoulders. I didn't care for the people who sired me either, but it was something none of us could help. We were similar - both losing and missing out on a true loving family. The only beauty I saw in this devastation was we could create our own loving family. We didn't have to be trapped by the haunting past we didn't create nor escape from.

I kept my left hand on his forearm, giving it a squeeze. He stared at me, beautiful emerald eyes full of promised security and confusion. We were in this together, and from what I could tell, there was a silent understanding about it between us. And something had altered between us. I felt it. I was nervous about it yet thankful.

Evander moved his arm around, hesitantly lacing his fingers in with mine. "Zuri," he began with a sigh.

I glanced over at him. His head tilted to the side, his mop of slicked-over brown hair slowly becoming disheveled while his gray button down came out of his nice suit pants. Somewhere along the lines of running, getting into the car and stopping for gas, he ditched his suit jacket. Letting go of the steering wheel briefly, he rubbed his jaw. He moved his hand out from under mine.

Taking my hand back, I put it in my lap. "It's ok," I rasped.

"Zuri," he said despondently.

I swallowed the scratchiness in my throat. "It's ok," I repeated. "You need an alpha mate, not a human."

Evander took an exit to the left, going in a tight circle and merging on a two-lane highway south toward Maluhia.

He nodded. A tense silence filled the car. Evander white knuckle gripped the steering wheel as the road, straight and narrow, stretched out before us. All the main roads leading somewhere else were small and narrow, not wanting to harm the landscape and the creatures who reside in Quivleren.

I stared out the window, watching shooting stars blaze across the night sky and leave a purple trail in their wake. We were finally far enough away from the city to not see Diomedes and his chaos.

"I like you," Evander admitted again.

I turned, pointing to myself then at him and put up two fingers and crossed them with a perked brow, hinting at a relationship. He smiled softly; a slight upward tick on the right side of his mouth. He raked his fingers through his hair, sighed and slammed both hands on the steering wheel.

The tension that filled this little car remained and only relaxed marginally. There was a lot I wanted to say and couldn't due to my throat hurting so badly. I wanted to tell him, I had feelings for him. Even though I swore off were-wolves when Lazaro had two timed me, Evander was someone I was willing to make an exception on. Throughout our entire ordeal with each other from him finding me at my house, to his rescue of me, protecting me, and saving Luell, he not once made me feel like Lazaro had - a worthless person, like I had to try super hard to gain a modicum of approval. Evander had yelled at me, wished me dead, and called me a stupid human. Even with all of that, it wasn't the manipulative mental anguish Lazaro put me through.

I swallowed hard, my throat still hurting, but not as terribly. Glancing over to my left, I studied him out of the corner of my eye. The soft, moonlit glow cast a handsome shadow on his face, bringing out more of the shaved stubble lining his jaw; and the tick when he clenched his teeth. I leaned forward in my seat to see his face. His steady observant green eyes whirled with emotions and unsaid words.

"Yes?" he asked, not taking his eyes from the road.

I unbuckled my seatbelt, moving closer to him still cradling my right wrist. Evander stared at me, expression slack. I kissed him on the cheek.

"Thank you," I softly whispered. "You could have left me and didn't."

Evander smirked. "I couldn't leave you and let you show me up. Doing what you did was brave and really moronic. I had to make sure you lived to be moronic again."

Grinning broadly, I buckled back up. "It needed to be done. We have to defeat Diomedes."

"I agree," Evander nodded. "Together."

My heart thundered, swelling with rushing liquid warmth. "Together."

CHAPTER THIRTY-FIVE

ZURI

Some hours before dawn we arrived at a backwoods shack where if we weren't murdered, we would need a tetanus shot. Old, red rusted metal farming tools littered the front yard like tombstones. Long wheat grass grew up in between the metal fixtures set side by side in neat rows.

A small dark wooden cabin lit by a lonely light was tucked back far in the pine trees. Evander drove up the gravel drive with a strip of grass growing in the middle. Large, old logging trucks scattered amongst newer, and probably broken down, vehicles acted as spectators as we passed by. Their empty windshield eyes seemed to follow us.

I swallowed, feeling my eyes practically bulge out of my head.

"Chill," Evander smirked. "My friend is cool. He is from another wolf pack - Ylva - your mother and father tried and failed to eradicate."

I made a face suggesting he was an idiot for bringing me here and he laughed.

"It's gonna be fine. *Your* parents will pay for their crimes. Not you," he promised, shutting the headlights off.

I nodded vigorously, readily agreeing. My mother and father meant nothing to me. Uncle Syrus was more of a father figure to me anyway. I licked my lips as Evander put the car in park. I stayed inside even as Evander made his way to the front of the car, displaying an amazing amount of restraint. I was too hurt to run or defend myself and the car provided cover in case something went wrong and I was less welcomed than Evander thought I would be.

Movement caught my eye. Coming out of the house was a man who immediately shifted into a pure white wolf and a female with a hand resting on her belly. The backlight from the house made it difficult to see her face, and I swore I could feel the air chill as these people stared me down.

"It's me, Evander, from Bardou!" Evander hollered.

The man growled, shaking his body as he shifted back into his human self and stood upright in a fluid mystifying motion. The man's cream-colored skin shone in the moonlight. Dark shoulder length hair swished with his movements.

"Evander?" the man called, his baritone voice thundering in my bones.

"Yeah Orlin! Who else did you think would brave the truck and farm graveyard to see you?" Evander teased like a teenage boy. "Hey Resi! You still serving that prison sentence with this lout? Sucks to be you!"

The woman at the door laughed with a light, sweet, honey-like melody. "It's not *overly* terrible."

"Good to see you, Resi," Evander greeted, his voice changing from teasing to friendly. Turning to shake Orlin's proffered hand, Evander leaned in close and whispered something, as the two exchanged the strange man-hug popular among guy friends.

The man's former excited and friendly expression immediately changed as his eyes locked on mine through the windshield. I swallowed.

And this is where I die.

Orlin walked over to my side of the car, yanking the door open. His muscles bulged and I regretted not locking the door as soon as Evander walked out. The door creaked so violently I thought it was going to come off the hinges. I unbuckled rapidly, so I wouldn't get stuck if I was yanked out of the car. Holding my right arm tight against my chest, I hesitated a moment, waiting for him to pull me out. When that didn't happen, I breathed deep and I stepped out, waiting for a strike or something to render me lifeless.

Orlin towered over me. His intense blue gaze bearing down on me and scanning every inch of me like I was a threat to him and his. Orlin's shoulder length copper hair tousled in the light breeze. He bent down to my level, staring me dead in the eyes, unblinking and unwavering. He put his massive giant's size hand on my head... and grinned. I felt myself releasing a gush of warm liquid.

I swallowed, staring back and too terrified to look away. Orlin straightened up, throwing his arms around me and lifted me off the ground. I gasped in pain as my broken wrist became squished along with the rest of my body.

"For saving Evander, you're one of us," his baritone voice reverberated in my ears.

"Perfect," I gasped from being hugged to pieces. "Can I get a change of clothes?"

"Well sure," he said chipperly, setting me down on the ground. I stumbled when he loosened his grip. I did manage to keep the gasp and grimace of pain on the inside though.

Evander walked over chuckling, "What's wrong with those?"

My face heated. "I just peed myself."

Orlin threw his head back laughing uproariously. Evander, taking a more polite manner, turned around so his laughter wasn't overtly in my face, his shoulders rising and falling with his chuckles. Evander cleared his throat, walking toward the car and retrieving the guns and backpack.

Resi came off the porch, sighing with her laborious movements. "Orlin!" she complained.

Her voice, even rising with a tinge of a commanding force, was still sweet and melodic. I made my way toward her, and the security of the home. I paused halfway, turning to watch Evander throw the guns over his shoulder.

"Expecting a war?" Orlin asked.

"Something... I'll explain inside," Evander replied, walking toward the house.

I closed in the distance toward Resi, coming within a

yard of her. Resi gazed at me with large lavender eyes. Even though her expression was open and welcoming, her eyes were terrifying. She didn't just look at me, it was *through* me. A long silky blonde braid swept over her shoulder and down to her waist.

"Come inside, Zuri," she said.

Again, I swallowed. Syrus once told me not to trust someone who knew my name before I spoke it. Seeing as how Evander trusted these people and I was welcome by a wolf my parents had done wrong, I figured why the fuck not. Honestly, nothing else worse could happen tonight. Well, maybe it could, but I refused to go there.

Resi's dark plum gown hugged her frame, accentuating her long lithe figure, olive skin tone and baby bump. She went inside, leaving the sliding glass door open. I stepped up to the threshold of the door and hesitated. A hand on the small of my back made me jump.

"Relax," Evander whispered in my ear, his breath causing me to shiver, "You're safe now."

I nodded, stepping inside the house through the sliding glass door. A small alcove to the right was the living room where several chocolate fluffy microsuede couches lined two full walls and a small third half-wall. A cut-out in the half-wall made it look like a window to peer down the long, dark hallway in front of me.

Resi went into the small kitchen to the left of where I stood, setting a kettle on the burner. The kitchen had this wrap around part where the counters wrapped around to divide the kitchen from the small dining room table to my immediate left. A table with four chairs and a bench seat were to my left from where I was standing by the sliding glass door.

Resi went toward the back of the house, opening one of the doors off the hallway. I timidly went to the left of the sliding glass door, going to the kitchen table and sitting in a chair that was already pulled out from the table. Evander entered, heading into the living room across from me. Orlin came in behind Evander, shutting the sliding door and locking it. To the right of the sliding glass door, Orlin picked up a large metal flat bar for window securities like I had back at my apartment and never used, adding another layer of security.

Resi came back, handing me a long dress, with a bra and underwear folded inside, and directed me to the guest bedroom down the hallway to change. I did so, going down the narrow hallway to the bedroom and shucked my clothes. Resi followed, helping me get out of Evander's shirt and get the bra on. With assurance I was fine, she left me to finish changing. My body hurt, but I wanted a moment to myself. I inspected the clothes and was relieved to see I hadn't tinkled as much as I thought I had, but the change in clothes was definitely a relief.

The gown she gave me was soft, comfortable, and form fitting. The long-sleeved dress, dark blue in color, went down to the floor. I bundled up the soiled clothes and came back out to the kitchen table.

Orlin pulled the long purple velvet curtains over the sliding glass door closed. Evander let out a long, relieved breath to be somewhere safe, propping up the four rifles in the corner and setting the backpack against it.

I set my clothes next to the backpack and took my previous seat at the table.

"What happened?" Orlin asked, taking a seat across from me at the kitchen table and crossing his arms.

The kettle bubbled, not yet piercing the air with its screech.

"Wait for tea, dear," Resi commanded with a perked brow.

Orlin rolled his eyes. Evander took up a chair to my right, running his fingers through his gelled hair. Resi hummed from the kitchen.

"Who broke your hand?" Orlin asked.

"Diomedes," I replied.

Cups clattered on a tray. "Come again," Resi demanded.

"Royan Pright unleashed Diomedes," Evander confirmed, staring Resi dead in the eyes.

"We'll fix you up after a tea leaf reading, dear," Resi assured. "Just hold on."

Resi pressed her plump lips together, taking the tray of tea over to the table. The silverware clattered softly on the table. I offered a wan smile, not understanding fully how tasseography fully worked. I tended to avoid divination like the plague. I didn't want to ever know the future or what it held.

Having a less than loving past, the future was something I imagined being bright and cheerful. I knew I'd have some rough patches. That was life. But I hoped for a happily ever after. Not knowing forced me to adapt and make do, make my own happily ever after. Knowing what the future held would only make me an anxious wreck.

Evander and Orlin spoke in quiet tones to each other. I didn't care what they were saying; my eyes were glued to the water stain on the polished oak table top, refusing to meet Resi's eyes.

Divination is a bad idea.

Resi sat with a sigh, scooting her chair out to allow for her growing belly. She smiled fondly at Orlin. Returning her attention to me, Resi reached out a hand.

"Take my hand," Resi said firmly.

Evander and Orlin stopped chatting. Tentatively I took her hand. My body quivered. I extended my broken hand to Evander. He took it gently, supporting more of my wrist with his warm, calloused fingers. Pain jolted up my arm for a moment.

"I will heal you after," Resi smiled warmly. "I'll be quick, I promise."

I nodded, my throat thickened, too terrified to utter words.

"My brethren. My family. White witches and warlocks," Resi began, "bless this tea and provide us with good fortune."

A foggy white mist evaporated out of each cup swirling together and then dissipating into the air, whether from magic or steam, I didn't know. Resi slid a cup and saucer to each of us. Closing her lavender eyes, the tea pot levitated and poured each of us a drink of the green tea.

I stared at it. The green liquid sent chills down my spine as the warmth hit my face. Resi let go of my left hand. I left my hand to linger in Evander's taking comfort from him.

"Drink, Zuri," Resi commanded.

I downed the tea in three gulps, setting the cup back in the saucer. Afraid of what I might see, I closed my eyes, pushing it over to Resi. My left hand covered my eyes and face because I cared not to see what the hell the cup might hold.

"So terrified of the future," Resi's honeyed voice purred. "Truly, there is nothing to fear, your life is far from over, dear."

I removed my hand, staring at her fully with a perked brow. "I like uncertainty."

"Why?"

"I can adapt. Knowing something only creates fear."

Resi nodded her blonde head. "Wise. She is a good match for you, Evander."

I didn't have to glance at Evander to know he was glowering. The smug, smiling Resi and the quick covered up smirk of Orlin, spoke volumes of Evander's reaction. Not to mention the heat level in the room rose at least twenty degrees. I could *feel* his glare. For a moment, it stung my heart. Like a quick wasp sting in another form of a rejection. I brushed it away. I wouldn't let it really hurt me. I knew his opinion of me. Since day one, he'd been abundantly clear as to what he thought of me, even if he'd kissed me silly. The subsequent rejection afterward just confirmed he'd been toying with me.

"Zuri," Resi's calm voice brought my attention back from my impossible desires. Her face had smoothed out, all signs of amusement gone. She was all business now. She peered into my cup, nodding and grimacing intermittently.

"There are six symbols in this cup. A rat, symbolizing losses through enemies. I see a pear along with a mountain. These two symbolize wealth, social status and a powerful friend," Resi stated, moving the cup in her hand. She gasped. "Snakes - a bad tragedy will happen however the ax means you shall overcome it. Lastly there is a tree representing contentment. Overall, not a terrible read. Four out of six symbols are good."

Resi took a deep breath, extending her hand to take mine. I gently placed my left in hers. She turned my palm over in her hand, staring at it smiling, eventually meeting my gaze and grinning reassuringly.

"There will be trials headed your way. But death is the only thing to really fear," she smiled, patting my hand and letting go.

She leaned back, making a motion for Evander's cup. He handed it over with a smug smile. Resi rolled her eyes, staring into the cup. Resi put her ear over the cup like it could speak words and smiled cunningly.

"One variation from Zuri's," Resi stated, a twinkle in her purple eyes. "Zuri had a pine tree of contentment. You have a swan - a happy love life," she finished grinning.

Evander's eyes narrowed on her. Laughing, Resi rose from the table, collecting the tea, cups, and saucers, putting it all on a tray. I stood with her trying to hide my flaming cheeks; carrying my cup and saucer to the kitchen. I set the cup and saucer on the counter beside the sink. Resi rinsed the soiled dishes and I put them in the washer one handed.

My eyes darted to Evander, watching his expression

change from serious to amusement and emotions in between as he spoke to Orlin softly.

"So, tell us," Orlin said, turning to me, his blue eyes hardening a touch, "what happened?"

"Which part?" I asked.

Evander took a deep breath, raking his fingers through his hair. "Well," he began.

I shrugged. "It really began with him stalking me," I quipped.

"Of course, it did," Resi teased. "Gimme her hand."

Resi smirked coyly, taking my broken hand, and turning it over. I looked away, not desiring to watch my bones snap back into place. Resi closed her eyes, humming low in her throat and speaking unintelligible words.

Evander snorted at my comment. "Hardly."

I gasped, looking down. Resi's white witch magic whirled over my hand, pulling my wrist out and squeezing it. I yelped at the pressure and the quick popping of my bones. It stung like a hornet sting, sending jolting tingles up my arm; making my nose tingle and eyes water. The white magic pulled my fingers out and straight. The dark bruising and swelling of my hand disappeared. The magic misted away like it was nothing more than a light fog. Resi moved my wrist, bending it and stretching the fingers. She opened her eyes and smiled at me.

"Better?" she asked.

"Thank you, it feels so much better," I said, flexing my hand. I peeked over at Evander and scoffed. "Hardly? Really? You stalked me for a week, being everywhere I was - thankfully saving my ass at my house."

"Geez bud!" Orlin said, grinning.

I smirked at the silent Evander. "But since you know about my parent's trying to terminate the paranormal, allow me to summarize - Evander's vendetta included me. My long-lost mother got back in touch, decided to kill me, and I escaped. I unknowingly had the key to the under-world. Evander came after me, taking me to Southside. Royan Pright took Elohi's key and opened the portal to the underworld. Now we gotta close it."

Orlin ran a hand over his face. "Shit…"

"I was thinking more like fuck, but that works."

Orlin chuckled. "Whatever happens, my pack will help you both."

"Thank you, my friend," Evander stated, shaking Orlin's hand. "We're leaving in the morning."

I nodded. I looked at Evander, hoping his quiet confidence and security would quell the rambling shivers in my body. His emerald eyes locked on mine, silently vowing protection and triumph. I smiled wanly at him, admiring his tenacity.

"And we will win," he added, staring directly at me.

CHAPTER THIRTY-SIX

EVANDER

Zuri nodded, grabbing her right arm with her left. The dark indigo dress complimented her in a manner I couldn't rightly express; hugging her in all the perfect places. Her honey brown eyes met mine with fear, courage and determination. Her tenacious manner appealed to me. Zuri wasn't afraid to do what was right, even if it killed her - even when I tried to kill her.

Zuri tilted her head to the side, smiling brightly at me. I felt my lips slightly quirk upward. She was alluring to me. So fearful, yet adamant to do the right thing and do it well. She was more than she gave herself credit for. My eyes locked on hers, staying riveted on her gorgeous face.

"Together," she stated firmly.

"Together," I agreed.

Rising from the chair, I put a hand on Orlin's shoulder. "We will be out of your hair in a few hours."

Orlin rose, shaking my hand. "Stay here as long as you need, my friend. Leave tomorrow instead since morning is shortly upon us and from the looks of you, you both could use some sleep and food," he said with a grin that never seemed to leave his face. Bending his head down slightly, Orlin's hair slid in front of his face, casting his blue eyes in an ominous manner. "By the way, I'm a little upset you haven't asked me about our upcoming child."

Zuri came forward, standing to the side of me, but a touch ahead. *Just like an alpha protecting her pack,* I smirked. Zuri turned her head to gaze at me and Orlin winked, grinning broadly at the show of dominant protection.

"We're terribly sorry," she said diplomatically. "Do you have any names picked out yet?"

"Not yet," Resi stated, waddling over to the living room. She sat down with a contented sigh on the chocolate brown sectional, propping her feet up on the matching ottoman. "We have some time. Three weeks to decide. Orlin dislikes *everything* I find. I want what we are having to be a surprise and Orlin says we'll name it when we see it," she said, giving him a teasing mad look.

Zuri chuckled, following Resi into the living room and taking a seat a few feet down from her. "Ugh men," she grinned.

Orlin clapped me on the shoulder, bringing me back to the present. "She's cute," he said loud enough for me to hear.

I nodded. Everything from the past few days was finally catching up to me. Between wanting her dead and now feeling absolutely at peace with her absolution, it was difficult to muddle through all the emotions battling in my head. I liked her. *Really*, liked her. Yet, I still wanted distance from her. She was human. Although by now it honestly shouldn't matter. It mostly didn't matter. It was just a last little hang up emotion and I wasn't sure how to get around that pesky feeling.

It wasn't because of her connection to her family. At least not now. Prior to knowing her, it was a valid reason. She was as different as the moon to the stars. She resorted to critical thinking then acting on her decision without faltering.

I tilted my head to the side, watching her speak with Resi like they had always been friends and not the acquaintances they were. I caught myself smiling; I loved how her lips moved and eyes lit up, how she tilted her head back slightly to laugh.

"She is cute," I added.

Orlin shrugged. "To each his own."

"What is that supposed to mean?"

"Not sure, my wife uses it a lot... I thought it fit."

I snorted. "Resi is too good for you."

"I know," Orlin beamed proudly. "I'm lucky she loves me."

Tearing my eyes away from Zuri, I picked up the guns and backpack, taking it down the hall to the guest bedroom.

"I'll burn those," Orlin said, motioning to Zuri's tinkled clothes when Orlin hugged her. "So, anyone tracking her won't catch her scent."

"Thank you."

"You need clothes too?"

I nodded. "I could use a pair."

"I'll get those for you then burn everything."

"Thank you, Orlin."

The mountain of a man raised his hand and grinned, "You would do the same for me."

"In a heartbeat."

Orlin walked away with Zuri's clothes. I followed him down the hall toward the guest bedroom. Turning to the immediate left where Zuri changed earlier, I strode inside, propping the guns up by the door.

I pulled Elohi's key from the inside pant suit pocket and plopped it on the bed. I threw the suit pants on the floor by the door and quickly added my button-down shirt into the mix.

"Here," Orlin said, handing me dark blue jeans, a belt, a black v-neck and a pair of hiking boots and socks.

"Thank you."

"Don't mention it. I just expect a *big* baby gift in return," Orlin finished with a wink and walked away.

I rolled my eyes and grinned. Since we were kids, Orlin had always been the kindest person I knew; always ready to help anyone with a smile, kind words with maybe a pinch of sarcasm, and a place to stay. I grinned, reminiscent of all the fond memories of the giant man.

Shucking the rest of my clothes, I quickly stepped into what was provided. Laughter filtered in; the light, melodic, laugh of Resi was drowned out by the snorting laugh of Zuri. Soon as the ladies' ruckus settled, Orlin's thundering laugh reverberated in the tiny house, followed by Zuri's belly laugh.

My brows furrowed, curious about what was causing

all the laughter. I paled, as many embarrassing memories from my childhood and teen years flitted across my memory and I wondered if it was a good idea to head out into the living room.

"Evander!" Orlin called.

"NO!" I yelled back with more force than necessary. "Damn it all to hell," I mumbled under my breath.

"Remember the goat?"

I crossed my arms, refusing to answer and staying inside the room. I remembered the goat. I remembered the prank. What I didn't want to remember was how the prank tasted. I shuddered. Orlin and my two other friends, Kyler and Rowan, the three idiots as I affectionately call them, decided it would be funny to tell me I had giant chocolate chips in my oatmeal.

Still can't eat oatmeal, I glowered.

Zuri stopped laughing. Orlin's laughter died down.

"Orlin," Resi admonished.

"What?" Orlin cried boisterously. "It's funny. Proves Evander isn't such a stubborn goat because he got us back too. Remember the lizard?" he snorted, crackling with laughter again.

I walked out into the living room and sat on the far side of the couch. I glanced over at Zuri. The faint glow of the tv illuminated her crimson cheeks, bringing out the softness of her creamy skin. Her dark indigo dress complimented her in a way that had me riveted, and forgetful of the joke that just transpired.

"I still can't eat oatmeal," I blurted, feeling my cheeks heat.

Orlin heaved with laughter, doubling over with it and falling off the couch. Tears tracked down his face as he sucked in a breath. "That was the best prank ever!"

Resi rolled her eyes, resting her hands on her belly. "Evander has been trying to prank Orlin ever since," she chimed.

Zuri chuckled. "Sounds like some planning is in order."

Orlin stood with a frown. "Nope... No, that's against the rules. No outside forces helping to plan a prank."

I smirked, leaning back casually on the couch and slinging an arm over the side, my fingertips lightly brushing against Zuri's soft blonde hair. "Scared of a human's help? Come now Orlin, I thought you the bravest wolfie of them all."

Orlin's eyes got dark. "I'm not scared of a human."

"You must be," Zuri chimed in, "I mean why else would you protest so quickly?"

Orlin gaped and looked at his wife.

Resi held up her hands grinning, "Don't look at me. I'm pregnant and not helping."

"Evander," Zuri said, rising, "shall we head to bed and plot Orlin's pranking demise?"

"I think we shall," I replied, rising with her and offering her my elbow.

She gleefully took it, resting her hand gently on my arm with a wide smile. I grinned down at her. The warmth of her hand seeping through my skin, leaving a tattoo of her softness. I put my hand over hers, keeping my eyes forward and not on the face that grinned back at me.

She turned around on her heel forcing me to stop.

"Thank you for the clothes, conversation, and safety. I cannot thank you enough," Zuri said.

"Our pleasure. Pleasant sleep," Resi called, rising to her feet.

Orlin turned in his seat and winked at us, cocooning his wife in his arms. "Have fun... planning," Orlin snorted. "I mean good luck trying to prank me back."

"Don't need luck," Zuri replied.

I guided us to the guest bedroom and opened the door. The key still lay on the bed where I left it. Zuri unhooked from me, going around to the other side of the bed. She grabbed the key, clutching it in her newly healed right hand and lay on top of the green down feather comforter since the house was warm. She pulled her dress down low over her legs, curling herself up into a tiny ball.

I stepped to my side of the bed, taking my shirt off and folding it. I felt Zuri's eyes on me, watching me closely. I kept my eyes focused on what I was doing, not wanting to see the mixed emotions swirl in her steadfast gaze and admit I felt the same.

"Yeah?" I asked

The comforter ruffled. Glancing over my shoulder, Zuri snuggled her head into the pillow and toward the edge of it, gazing at me.

"We should put blue paint in his underwear," she finally said.

I snorted at the randomness. "It would be funny."

"Remember the tv show with the tiny blue people?"

"Yeah?" I said, pulling the sheets back.

"We could joke and say he has tiny blue Smurf balls."

I laughed aloud, thinking of the shock on Orlin's face. "It's a good one," I agreed.

Orlin's muffled voice came through the walls, "No helping, Zuri!"

She smiled and rolled her eyes. Her face slowly sobered. She had a contemplative look on her and before I could ask what was on her mind, she said, "I think we should check the Vidis Forest for Elohi."

I perked a brow and clambered into the bed under the comforter. "Why is that? And why this topic? We should be concerned with surviving Diomedes and his desire for the key you possess."

Zuri's soft eyes hardened. "Elohi needs this key. It's not safe until it's returned," she paused, glancing down at the end of the bed. "Or until we figure out how to close the portal ourselves if Elohi can't be found."

I nodded, turning on my side. "I see your point, but we need to amass the rest of the Vilkas and ready ourselves to fight kludde and whatever else Diomedes throws our way."

"I understand that," she retorted, her voice becoming harder and a touch condescending. "I'm not saying you have to come with me."

"You said *we*," I smirked. "*We* can head to Toan Castle because there is no way in hell you're doing this alone. I know a few wolves there who could help us rally. This may turn into a war, Zuri, and we need to be prepared for whatever outcome we may face."

Zuri opened her mouth and snapped it shut. "Ok... My mother needs to be stopped too. There are so many moving parts, it's hard to decide what to tackle first."

"*I* will handle your mother," I replied, feeling the fur on my arms stand on end.

Zuri put a gentle hand on my arm. "I'm sorry for what my family did to yours, and-"

Her soft hand slid up my arm and I felt my body rumble in response.

"So, you've said," I replied, cutting her off.

Zuri rolled over, deflating. "Night."

This is gonna be a long, sleepless night lying next to her.

CHAPTER THIRTY-SEVEN

ZURI

I curled up on my side, facing away from Evander. My stomach swirled with nerves at being snapped at by Evander, and something else, though I couldn't quite place why. We were safe here with Orlin and Resi. We had a place to rest and get our bearings for our next big move whether it was to find Elohi, go after my mother, rally the wolves, or find a way to destroy this cursed key.

I turned the key over in my hands, wondering where to even begin. Legend says Elohi was in the Harrell Mountains, which is why I planned to search the Vidis Forest - the whole opposite side of the world since, if the legend was about me, I'd be as far away from what the legend said. I just wasn't sure if it was the first move we should make.

Legends are like limp dicks - pretty, I know they're there, but pointless, I mused, finding my joke hilarious. *And since they are such, it makes my task suck... Let's see,* I closed my eyes, racking my brain for the old musings of an idiot long past. *Legend says - the lowest point with twisting pines, the forest spirit is forever mine.* I worked my jaw back and forth and grumbled. *Fucking legends...* I knew it was a clue of some kind. Opening my eyes, I focused on the popcorn ceiling flecked with silver glitter hoping it provided some answers.

I couldn't sleep. My mind wouldn't shut off. Outside, the birds began chirping. Small cracks of light filtered in from the partially closed, floor length chocolate brown black-out curtains.

I carefully scooted closer to Evander out of wanting comfort, laying on my back. Turning the key over in my hands, I wondered more on what to do and where to go. Would Evander come with me to Vidis Forest, where I could swear on my soul, Elohi would be? Would he ever want to be with me?

Glancing over, I stared at his sun-kissed upper chest, admiring the defined muscles on his body. I felt the drool slip out of the side of my mouth from staring at him.

Evander snored, his hand dropping to his side. He inhaled sharply, turning toward me and looping an arm around me catching me by surprise. Evander's warm arm seared into my cool skin. I relished the heat and security he provided and I allowed myself to snuggle into his comfort. For a moment, my eyes became heavy; I felt like I could finally drift to sleep.

He snorted awake, glancing at me with wide eyes. "Sorry," he hastily said, turning away from me.

I grimaced. *Or go our separate ways...* He made it clear he wanted to get vengeance on my mother and that I was a human he had no real interest in. I wouldn't thwart his plans. She was evil and needed to be destroyed. If he wanted, I'd help him. As for my being a human being a barrier: That, I was sure, was more of an excuse than a reason.

"Go to sleep," Evander grumbled.

I crossed my arms petulantly. "I can't sleep."

He blew his lips, sitting up and running a hand over his face. Dark brown stubble lined his jaw creating an attractive shadow on his face. His emerald eyes peered into mine, narrowing a bit but reflecting some confusion and concern. He laid back down, turning completely toward me.

"What's the matter?" he asked.

I sat up and held out the key. "This... It needs to be destroyed. We-" I caught myself and stopped.

He wouldn't follow me across Quivleren to complete this. He has his own agenda. His green orbs met mine. I felt my heart drop and quicken, become alive then die over and over again... I leaned forward to kiss him, taking the initiative then stopped. My heart strings tightened as he casually leaned his head away. Faking it as moving hairs off my face, I wriggled my head.

"We, what?" he asked, fully awake and squared up with me.

"Never mind. I-I just don't want you to feel obligated to come with me."

"I'm not. I want to of my own free will. The key needs to be destroyed as you said. And the portal needs to be closed. Is this what is keeping you up?"

"Kinda," I lied.

I wasn't concerned with Evander not wanting to take on the mission. I was more concerned with Evander not wanting to go with me. Because it was me. A human. A species much weaker than him and one that he'd already expressed a great dislike for. I wish I didn't depend on him. I wanted to be independent, but I couldn't imagine doing this without him anymore.

"Well," Evander said, yawning. "I *am* coming with you. No worries there."

I paused for a minute thinking, then, "Does me being a human truly bother you?"

I didn't intend to blurt out what I desperately wanted to know. Having dated wolves before, they never seemed to mind that I was a human. Then again, they'd apparently never been very serious about me either. Maybe being human was a big deal after all. But here is Evander, telling me that who sired me was no longer an issue, but me being a human in general was. I found it odd, but I wasn't about to verbalize and demean someone for their feelings.

Evander smirked at me. His upper lip twitching between a half ass smile and his tight faced mask. My heart thundered in my chest, seconds away from heart failure. Since Evander agreed I wasn't going to do this alone, I wanted to know once and for all where I stood. My heart and head needed to know whether I needed to step back and protect myself or allow myself to hope. Desiring something that may never happen wasn't going to help either of us.

"No," he said with a sigh. "No. Your being human

doesn't really bother me. But it does worry me. You being a human worries me more than anything else actually."

I frowned. "Why?"

"Makes you easier to kill."

"Not necessarily. I survived fae and wolf packs."

"Because I was there to aid you," he sighed, throwing the covers off and getting out of bed. "I really like you."

Grinning, I said, "I like you too. And yes. I survived because of you. But I also survived a few days without you too. I survived Diomedes when no one else could get to me. So don't think I'm *that* fragile. I'll be ok. Especially with you there."

I watched him pull his shirt over his head, and over his scrumptious muscles. He smirked at me and shook his head.

"I like my view."

"I can tell," he replied.

Maneuvering out of bed, I stretched, making my way toward the door. I slipped the key inside the open slitted side in my bra that allowed those stupid pads to be taken in and out. Evander perked a brow, but said nothing. I watched Evander pull on his boots and I shook out the wrinkles in my dress.

"Next door, left side," Evander said, tying his last boot.

"Thanks. I want to head out. I don't want to put Orlin and Resi in danger."

He nodded. "Agreed." Standing, he came up behind me, holding the door open. "You can tell me about your idea in the car on the way to the next wolf pack."

I smiled, heading to the bathroom. Even doing my business, I had a smile on my face. Knowing Evander liked me too put my heart in a happy spot despite the state of the world. Even with all we have to do, having his affection made this impending journey just a little brighter.

After doing my business, I walked out into the kitchen finding two bags packed and sitting by the sliding glass door. I glanced at Evander who was digging through his wallet. The guns and pack full of ammo slung over his shoulder. He set out a few hundred-dollar bills on the counter.

"We gotta go," Evander stated in a forced whisper.

I headed to the sliding glass door, grabbing the hiking boots left for me. I yanked them on without socks. I cringed at the feeling of my free toes uncovered. I wanted to question the urgency in his voice.

Evander pulled the curtain back slightly on the door and glared outside. The light that hardly came in through the window danced with shadows. I felt my blood freeze.

"Kludde?" I whispered.

Evander nodded. "And goblins."

"What are we gonna do?"

"Run."

"Orlin and Resi," I whispered, "they have to know too."

Evander put a hand on my arm. "Relax. They know. Resi found out a few moments before we woke up and told me while you were handling your business. Using her witchy powers, she and Orlin have escaped and are headed to rally the other pack members. We are headed the opposite way. We have to go."

I gathered all the fabric of my dress in front of me. I

pulled it backward through my legs and took a handful of the dress in each hand. I wrapped the fabric around the front of my waist and made a knot.

"That's interesting," he remarked.

"Makes it so I can run."

Shrugging, Evander handed me a rifle with a shoulder strap loaded with bullets. I set it down, leaning it against the corner of the sliding glass door. Hefting on the backpack, I adjusted it on my shoulders. I slung the rifle over next, checking the chamber for ammunition.

Shivers overcame me. My body quaked. I wanted nothing more than to be home with Luell and living my life like none of this happened. Except Evander. I'd still want to know him.

The ground shook. Eyes wide, I glanced at Evander. He stepped away from the door and nodded at me to follow. Carefully, we made our way to the very back of the house.

Unnatural yowling pierced the quietness of the house, sending goosebumps over my skin. My shoulders tightened, preparing to be attacked from behind. My hands closed tight around the rifle.

Glass broke from behind us. I swiveled around, taking aim at a green bulbous mass. Orange eyes that looked frosty like winter glass peered through the darkness. It sucked in a deep breath before a pealing, boisterous call blared through the house. Large long arms swung back and forth, thumping on the ground. It's body lifted, moving forward. It's short, stumpy legs hardly held up the top-heavy creature. I wanted to run.

"No," Evander whispered, catching me wanting to make a break for it. "It can't *see* us. They smell and hear us."

He pointed toward the back of the house. My body refused to move. The rifle shook in my hands and Evander put his hand quickly over mine; a finger to his lips. I nodded, feeling tears sting behind my eyes.

The goblin scraped through the house, screeching once in a while. Booming thunder echoed through the house of creatures landing on the roof. Evander scowled at the roof, moving quietly.

Another goblin, less of a monstrosity than the last, broke through the other side of the sliding glass door, giggling and clacking it's under-bitten pointed teeth. Kludde stomped above us, screeching back and forth. We reached the back door, opening it quietly. Evander shut the door, leaning against it.

"Trapped," he whispered.

"What do we do?"

He reached for me, pulling me against him. Evander kissed the side of my head, wrapping his arms around me close. I leaned my head against his chest, feeling the tears fall freely down my face.

"I don't know," he replied.

"We need to leave," I sniffled.

Evander pulled away, checking the door again. Peering outside, he motioned with his head for me to follow. The sting of the cold air hitting my wet tears felt nice against my hot face.

The outside was bright with the sun trying to poke through the darkness of the purple-blue swirling clouds overhead. Despite the sunshine, all around us was beginning to be engulfed in darkness. Goblins walked on their hands, some on their stumpy legs, sniffing the air and moving around the property. Kludde's booming steps on the roof resounded in the stillness of the day.

I glanced up at the sun trying to gauge what time of day it happened to be, as I forgot to look at the oven clock in the kitchen. I couldn't see where the sun was shining or where it happened to be.

Evander walked ahead, leading me off the deck and toward the forest behind the house. A shrieking wail pierced the air. The forced rushing air of wings taking to the sky sounded behind me. I froze.

Evander glanced behind me, pointing his rifle up. His face said a thousand things, but the only thing I heard was, "Run!"

ACKNOWLEDGMENTS

Brittany G., my friend and editor, I appreciate and admire you more than words can say. You are a true friend and wonderful mentor. I'm beyond grateful to have a friend like you in my life and to have met you and know you. Brittany, you are such a wonderful person and mother. The world definitely needs more people like you. Thank you so much for everything! Thank you for being my friend.

Tiffany P., thank you for helping me along this crazy journey and all your wonderful comments and remarks regarding the craziness of the characters in this book. I'm so happy we met.

Thank you, Amir L. for formatting this book for me and every other book I have thrown your way. You are such a patient, kind, and wonderful person. I couldn't have done it without you. You are the bestest, bestest ever! I'm so happy to know you.

And a special shout out to Michelle F., thank you so, so much for all your help, encouragement, and kindness. Thank you for always being my biggest advocate and ally. I'm so grateful to know such a tender, golden-hearted person. Love you sweet lady!

ABOUT THE AUTHOR

E.A. (Ericka Ashlee) Shanniak is the author of the successful fantasy romance series – A Castre World Novel. She is hobbit-sized, barely reaching over five feet tall on a good day. When she wears her Ariat boots not only does she gain an inch, she is then able to reach the kitchen cabinets. Ericka loves to write at her desk that her daughter's cat lovingly destroyed. Fortunately for everyone, she can see over it.

Ericka resides in a small town of Coldwater, Kansas with her husband, two kids, two dogs and cat. The cat was her daughter's idea.

If you care to follow:
AMAZON
FACEBOOK
INSTAGRAM

or at her Facebook group – Shanniak Shenanigans –

Made in the USA
Columbia, SC
13 April 2022

58704045R00213